Lost Souls

By
Jacey K Dew

Content Information

Please visit the link below for a specific content information guide, leading to page numbers and brief nondescript summarizations should you decide to skip those pages.
https://jaceykdew.ca/books/content-warnings

Published by Crimson Notebook Publishing
crimsonnotebook.ca

This is a work of fiction. Names, characters, places, and incidents either are the product of the author's imagination or are used fictiously.

Hardback ISBN: 978-1-7387710-3-5
Paperback ISBN: 978-1-7387710-2-8
eBook ISBN: 978-1-7387710-4-2
Audio ISBN: 978-1-998486-04-5

To my beautiful children; Emily and Jeremy.

I send you all my best wishes.

I will always love you.

The Story So Far...

Alexa Brenner

Finds out her boyfriend (Darius) is a vampire when he kidnaps her niece (Rayleen) and takes Alexa to a farm (base of operations). He plans on leveraging Rayleen (even threatening her) to control Alexa (making her his vampire queen).

Sandra shows Alexa that supernaturals have been hidden since the 6th century, and many want to stop (extremists put into action a world takeover). Some have gathered forces to take control of the world, including two of the Council members; Seth (vampire – Nocturnal Council Leader) and Aalayah (fire elemental – Elemental Council Leader).

Former friends (now enemies of Darius) come to kidnap Alexa and turn her against Darius (to hurt him and destabilize his region) by showing her that he's on the wrong side (causing war, death, and destruction to take over the world). Miles (accidentally) gets captured and Darius forcing Alexa to hurt him ensures that process.

Rayleen is rescued, but Alexa goes back and forth (rescued, Darius gets her back, but throws her downstairs to be eaten by hobgoblins because he finds her traitorous at the moment, then rescued again).

They make it to James' house (Magic Council Leader) and start collecting people and land for a rebellion. Making friends with the dwarves in the Rocky Mountains (by tree nymph travelling) to get weapons and armour made.

The army finds them at James' and takes them to a school, but sort out supernaturals to kill, so they get away from there and go back to the dwarves to collect the swords and armour.

They go check out a city nearby that seems to be doing well in the aftermath, but tensions blow up soon after they arrive. They collect the stuff and the dwarves and end up at the mall with a large base of people (allies – Nikki's group).

Darius attacks the mall to kidnap Rayleen and Alexa again, but Sandra has other plans. She kidnaps Nikki, suspecting she's from a long line of Dreamers (visions of the future in dreams).

This theory is why James says they have to go rescue her (no one wants the bad guys to have someone who can see the future in their ranks). They go to the farm and try to rescue Nikki. But, Rayleen is kidnapped instead. Sandra and Darius ride away with Rayleen and Nikki on the back of a dragon.

Alexa is a mess. They leave the farmhouse once they recover and collect themselves. They run into Jaiden and her group, then travel to an old couple's house on their way south.

They stop in Fort MacLeod and are welcomed into the old-time village while James follows a lead by himself. Backstories and dynamics are explored until Alexa realizes she missed Rayleen's birthday.

Alexa finds a gift for Rayleen, a light blue raw celestite stone necklace. She's to wear it until she finds Rayleen, then give it to her.

They relax, play games, and bully Jaiden. James comes back; he's found a new lead. Jaiden comforts Alexa and talks her down from running off without anyone else, and tells her to wait until morning.

The go to a jail, then Jaiden says they have to go to Banff. They make it to Banff by night and stay at a hotel on the edge of town.

The go rescue Rayleen and Nikki, and make it through the torture forest to a hotel for the night. Darius visits Alexa to invite her to join him, He'll be back tomorrow for her.

They go to town and try to find supplies. Attacked by a dragon, then goes to Nikki's Uncle's house. Jaiden interrupts Darius coming to get Alexa.

Alexa finds out Jaiden told people, so she escapes to the castle hotel to find Darius with Rayleen. Sandra says he hasn't come back and puts them in a room.

Eventually, Darius returns and tells Alexa that he will date both her and Sandra. Alexa refuses and is thrown in with other prisoners along with Rayleen.

They are let go and rush down the hall. But, someone shoots at them, it's Nikki. Alexa manages to get Rayleen out and down the mountain. They end up at the Uncle's house, as Jaiden is getting fixed up.

Taylor is shot and they go into hiding.

Daniel accepts Alexa's apology and moves them houses. Rayleen sings a song about Christmas.

A bear is in the backyard. There is a meeting of people and Alexa follows a boy to a shop for supernaturals and helps bring supplies back to them. She and Rayleen make it back to their house unnoticed.

During the blizzard, a Cerberus is outside, and people go out to kill it. The boy, Cam, defends the Cerberus with magic and is kicked out of the house.

They get a note for a human-only meeting the next day.

Nikki Marshall

Skipping work to go to the mall with friends (at the insistence of Shawn - an elf who would have prior knowledge of something coming) on the exact wrong day (supernatural uprising) ends with them stuck inside a dollar store (having dodged doomsdayers on the road and supernaturals inside the mall, and collecting some people from the army store upstairs).

They scout out and secure the mall while finding people (including Tyler) and host a party at the end of the world. The atmosphere tenses eventually when rescue doesn't come and they can't agree on how to proceed.

Nikki and her friends go out to find their families but are found dead or missing. Finding no point in staying out, they go back to the safety of the mall.

Some want to continue partying under Tyler's lead, while others turn towards long-term survival. Nikki's friends group is split at the reveal that Shawn is an elf.

Nikki's group relocates to the theatre when Tyler's group ransacks the mall. Then Nikki rescues some people from the hotel.

Kelly and Miles come. It's put to a vote to go or stay. The majority votes to stay at the mall. But, they agree to be allies.

Tyler's group attacks Nikki's and some are killed on both sides. They agree to split the mall and not enter each other's territory.

Kelly returns quickly as James' house was attacked and Nikki prepares for refuge and takes in a trickle of people from James' house.

Once James arrives, James plans for an eventual attack on the farm. Nikki saves Rayleen from Daniel (Alexa's new human boyfriend) after he violently rages toward her age-appropriate temper tantrum.

Darius attacks the mall, and Nikki is kidnapped on the back of a dragon. She's quickly rescued, and then kidnapped again, but this time Rayleen is kidnapped as well.

They land at a jail and are taken inside. Nikki is separated from Rayleen and tortured until she agrees to help them by telling them visions of the future (that she's going to have to make up).

Nikki attacks a guard before being led away with Rayleen. Shale tells Darius that he'll watch them to keep them safe from the others.

Nikki sees a doctor, with minimal tools for treatment. Diagnosed with a bruised rib. Darius and Sandra question her, asking for visions and trying to catch her lying. They let it slip that they have an informant. She goes back to the room with Shale and starts thinking up visions to tell them.

Sandra and Darius move Rayleen and Nikki via dragon because they found out rescue was on the way. They get winter gear on the way to Banff.

At the castle-like hotel, Darius wants to know if he and Alexa get back together. Sandra is angered by this, and when told to escort Nikki back to her room.

Another meeting with Sandra and Darius. This one ends with them fighting. Nikki runs back to Rayleen, then takes her out to the torture forest. Narrowly avoiding traps, ends with them captured and Nikki knocked out.

Jaiden and the group rescue Nikki and Rayleen, and they go to a hotel for the night.

Nikki goes off with Jaiden to talk and catch up. Then everyone goes down to town to collect supplies. Nikki and Jaiden go to her uncle's house and find a note about where they went. They get attacked by a dragon, and everyone goes to Nikki's uncles.

Nikki shows Jaiden her Uncle's train room.

James leaves. Nikki takes the opportunity to go up the mountain and find her Uncle. She brings him back, and many of Banff return.

They figure out Taylor is the spy and put her up in a room by herself so she won't hear anything else.

Jaiden and Nikki spend some time hanging out.

They plan to attack the castle hotel with Banff residents. Jaiden objects, but goes along with it. They go to attack, get inside the hotel, and Nikki accidentally shoots at prisoners. Jaiden stops her in time, and Nikki is taken down the mountain by others.

Taylor is killed by a guy in a mob, and Nikki helps defuse the situation.

Nikki goes to a meeting with Bruce and Banff residents. Bruce and Nikki disagree about Taylor and Jaiden.

They prepare for a blizzard. After being shut inside for so long. They think that they should use the generator for a movie night. Something to look forward to like holidays.

Jaiden Kensington

Gets a vacation from her regular life when the world is attacked and spends a week alone and relaxing.

This ends when people break into her home. She decides to go to her (biological father's wife's mom's house) grandma's house because of a joke about everyone going there if the world ended and because she's also having visions of her sister (biological father's stepdaughter).

Gets to grandma's to find out a separate group is there and no family to be found. They have a set of werewolves captured and show her as proof of a demon takeover.

Jaiden separates from them on a walkabout and finds her sister's ex-boyfriend, who brings her to his family farm (loads of his family/friends – pack of werewolves).

They rescue the werewolves and Jaiden finds out that the group had killed her whole family (assumes Dominique is alive from visions and not seeing her in the pile of bodies). Jaiden decides to go back home and figure out the next steps.

Calli (succubi) takes her to a grocery store with a bunch of people. They are sent on a mission to the hospital and are attacked. Ostracized from the grocery store, they (along with Lucas) go south.

Calli brings them to Jerry's (bar/hotel/delivery service for supernaturals). They work for their worth. Jaiden saves some and herself from dying in an attack that she had a vision of.

Calli wakes Jaiden saying they have to leave (another attack). While running from an ogre, they run into Alexa's group. They take refuge at a house.

Jaiden finds out the group is trying to rescue Nikki (who is also Dominique).
Jaiden spends time at Fort MacLeod trying to learn what she can

about old-timey solutions. She finds out Sara gave her a phone hooked up to a different internet, so she can keep in touch and research things. She avoids the group as much as possible, due to persistent bullying.

James comes back with a new lead. Jaiden comforts Alexa and convinces her to wait until morning to get Rayleen.

They go back north, to a jail. Jaiden sneaks off and hears a guard say they went to Banff. She tells everyone, Kelly confirms, and they go to Banff.

James leads them to the castle hotel, but Jaiden leads them through the torture forest. They save Nikki and Rayleen, and make it the rest of the way through and to another hotel for the night.

Jaiden and Nikki go off to talk and catch up. Jaiden lies, saying she didn't find the rest of the family.

They go to town to find supplies, then to Nikki's uncle's house, then back to the main street. They are attacked by a dragon, then go back to the uncle's house.

Jaiden catches Darius in Alexa's window, and he leaves. She tells James. He leaves. Alexa leaves with Rayleen.

Jaiden follows Nikki up the mountain to find her uncle. They return with many people from Banff.

They figure out Taylor is the spy and put her up in a room by herself so she won't hear anything else.

Jaiden and Nikki spend some time hanging out.

Jaiden has a vision of Nikki killing innocent people, so she objects when they plan to attack the hotel. She goes along and stops the vision from happening, and sends Nikki down the mountain.

She finds Shale, who tells her the hotel is about to blow up. She gets out through a window, then helps rescue others. She calls a truce, and DeAngelo takes her to the Uncle's house because of a gash in her leg.

Taylor is shot, and they go into hiding.

Jaiden is stuck at the house because of her leg, but ends up leaving to go to the ruins to help, and is side tracked by a Cerberus.

Back at the house, Christmas comes and goes. Jaiden is asked to go to a meeting with the supernaturals of the hotel to advocate for them. She talks to Bruce about them after asking for things for them, like blood.

They prepare for a blizzard, and now have a generator (from Bruce who was hoarding them for the humans, on the condition it would be for his house).

X   Chad's
Apartments

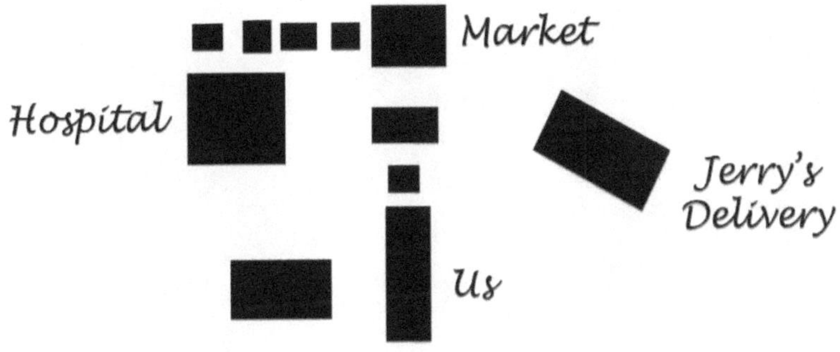

Chapter 1

Doodled in thick elongated sharpie on poster board, is a black boxed-in pentagram with a few extra lines drawn through it.

Its oddity makes me pause and stare.

Everything all around this piece of paper is a charred mess. The poster board is a pristine white; obviously placed there after the fire tore through the city undeterred.

The sheet of paper lies against the broken remains of the building's concrete foundation. The wooden walls, mostly having burned to ash, coal and small splinters, had made up much of the upper portion of the building. A small section of the collapsed roof can be seen about twenty feet in front of me. This building looks much worse than the rest of those around me.

I wonder if the fire may have started here. Or, maybe, this building was just made of incredibly flammable materials; more so than this building's neighbours.

Rubble sits on the road where it had settled; untouched. Destruction from the revolution has all but levelled this town.

I can only imagine what caused all of this. A fire burned, this I know for sure. Unchecked, it spread everywhere in the immediate area.

But, was it an accident caused by someone who was trying to keep warm? Or, it may have been a dragon used to terrorize the people who once frequented these stores. Maybe lightning caused it.

"Jaiden?" Alexa's voice shouts out to locate me.

"Here." My voice comes out just loud enough to wonder if she might hear me or not. Fixated on the image, I can only hear the soft scrapings of her shoes against the rubble. A rock tip-taps as it bounces behind me and passes me.

Alexa stops beside me. I can see her at the edge of my peripheral vision. To her, I must look strange out of any sort of context. She turns to locate what I am looking at as she says, "What are you doing?"

"That paper is out of place. What do you think it means?" I inquire.

The woman glances back at me for a moment. "What?" She steps closer to get a better look at the paper and its emblem. Her grown red hair reaches her chin. Wisps of the remaining black dyed hair form a semi-circle around the base touching her shoulders. "I think I've seen that before."

"Where?" The word rushes out in my eager search for answers.

"Hm. I don't know. I don't remember." She says thoughtfully. "I'll probably remember something later."

Laughter tingles in my ears, but it grates them. I turn around. Behind me yields no one to be the source. How strange.

I look back to an empty field. Exhaustion and heat pull down on me. But, I know I have to keep going.

Twisting my arm back, I grasp my water bottle. Letting the warm water wet my mouth and throat. Grimacing, at the plastic taste of it.

It's relief that's only temporary and teasing. There isn't much left of the liquid inside, and I need to ration it to last until I reach my destination or find another clean water source; whenever that might be.

After so long in the company of strangers, it will be nice to see someone I know.

What was that symbol?

The bed is empty, so I don't have to sneak out of it. I utilize a moment of early wakefulness to stretch out in bed. Not many mornings start off like this; I'll savour this feeling of joy for just a moment. Before I have to get up and join the horde of people for the rest of the day.

I go over the dreams to cement them in my memory. My visions are of no use to me when I forget them like one does a common dream. The more I think about it and play over the vision in my head, the more memories and connections I make to create a solid and long-lasting memory. Each and every detail might be important, so I go over all of it a few times.

Alexa's hair may create a rough timeline. Assuming she doesn't dye her hair again, the events of the first vision should occur in approximately a year; maybe a year and a half. That should give her natural hair enough time to grow to that length; half an inch a month on average.

Next spring or early summer, maybe. There was no snow and the temperature wasn't hot or cold.

The buildings were ordinary. I can't place a location through them. Only, that we weren't in Banff. They lacked the stylized look set on this town. There were no mountains.

Furthermore, I didn't recognize the area. It may not be anywhere I've been to in the past. Or, it could very well just look different after being burned down.

The second vision was a summer vision, but one that could happen any year. There wasn't any time cues. Nothing I can think of that would let me know when this is supposed to happen.

Trees, therefore a forest or large wooded park were all around me. There was a field.

I was worried about rationing my supplies. So maybe I didn't start with a lot of supplies. Maybe I had been travelling for a while and used up what I had packed.

I didn't mention where I was going, only that I would be seeing familiar people again. I had been around strangers, but I was alone in the vison. Possibly, alone for a long while.

That laugh, however, was a little weird and ominous. Might belong to either vision. It might be its own thing. Or, it could be nothing; just a laugh my head pulled in from somewhere.

With the likelihood of someone interrupting me at any time, I jump out of bed. Walking to the door, I open it enough to figure out no one is in the little hall room. Closing the door behind me, I feel safe enough to retrieve my treasure of information.

Hidden out the window, charging in the sun, I find my phone exactly where I had placed it early this morning. I'm thankful that the weather stayed sunny, and I'm not discovering a wet, frozen and useless phone; I don't want to take the chance that it may not be water proof.

Heat emanates from the black rectangular prism. The side button turns the phone on. I hide it up my hoodie sleeve until I am safely hidden in the locked bathroom.

I open up a drawing app and draw the symbol before I forget it.

In the search bar, I type 'boxed pentagram symbol' into the search engine with the hopes that it will be a sufficient explanation.

The image tab reveals pages and pages of just pentagrams inside a box. Nothing like what I saw pops up.

The symbol has a pentagram in it. There is balance in pentagrams. One point up is usually representative of good, while two points up usually take a more evil tone.

On another note, other questions are needing answering. Why was I travelling alone in an open field?

There's no research that can be done for that part of my dream, besides upping my survival skills and athleticism. I assume I do well enough since I was assumedly near the end of my trip, but it could help with the water problem; help me survive more comfortably.

I click into Sara's SuperData account on habit. Perusing the social site provides insight into the world's workings through a very tight and closed circle of friends. The werewolves keep in close contact with packs near and far. It's the closest thing I have to a running news site.

Sara has posted a few new pictures of her and John, and a couple of others in the pack. They are working on preparing another section of the garden for planting.

The usual hum drum postings work on the same basics as the social medias I'm used to; with a supernatural twist to many of them. People post pictures of highly staged selfies, provide status updates of their thoughts and activities, and send news quality highlights.

Some posts would make one think the revolution never happened. People are living relatively normal lives; minimally effected by the end of the world. Others have somewhat rebuilt, like us, and have daily struggles.

Then, there are more who live everyday life out in the world. They are coming across people who are trying to kill them; extremists from both sides of the spectrum or survivors acting before taking any chances. These people are using social media to tell their stories as in the field news stories.

One post catches my eye with an air of warning.

Reed Andrews

Just got pulled over by a vamp asking for ID or proof

of lycanhood. Had to go wolf to show. Watch out for

human companions. Stay out of town.

I click on the replies. A succession of exclamations of disbelief and similar stories trail down from thirteen people I recognize as from around the Alberta Beach area; close packs to the Kadiza's.

This could be problematic.

Clicking back to the search engine I look up 'supernatural identification' and press search.

Perusing the summaries doesn't provide anything I think will help; should I actually click on them. I add 'and the revolution' to the search to help.

The first link takes me to a post on a web page which looks promising.

Dilution of blood and human-smelling supernaturals has caused a problem in our sorting. Smell or power display requests alone cannot reveal the status of a being's species.

Fear not! We have a solution rolling out to the streets now that phase one is complete.

We will be reissuing physical supernatural identifications to all for assured sorting. Each being will be required to carry their ID with them and present it to officials by phase two completion.

Acquire your official identification <u>here</u>.

Humans have been shown our wrath. They are conquered and we now enter phase two. We are one step closer to complete supernatural rule.

An old memory of a vision comes to mind. The official who asked for my identification and either killed me or knocked me out.

This is going to be a huge problem in the future. It's starting out small now, but it'll get worse.

I'll need supernatural identification. Can't go wolf like Reed. I have no proof of anything, and my only link could get me in huge trouble.

I click on the link and it puts me onto a form page on the Council's web address. It's a basic form asking for name, height, birth date, and other identifiers. There doesn't look to be any checks and balances; no upload your birth certificate here.

The information comes out easily until they ask for my species. What kind of supernatural being can I portray? It makes me hesitate. Knowing I can't tell the truth about what I actually am or it can be used against me.

Data bases can only spell trouble with corrupted individuals. It wouldn't do me any good if Sandra, or another, could search and figure out what I am.

I also can't place an obvious lie which I can't prove when confronted. It wouldn't do me any good if I were to put in werewolf, then get stuck when confronted and cannot prove it by turning into a wolf form. Most of the supernatural beings I can think of either have a physical attribute or special power that I couldn't fake on the spot with no preparation; I suck at acting.

Calli once told me to tell people that I am an empath. This is what I fill into the box. I can only hope an empath classification is supernatural enough to gain the identification and pass through check stops.

I had once checked into what an empath is, and it seems very much like me already. It also seemed like an empath could be the closest supernatural being there is to being a human.

I can only hope that an empath is supernatural enough to get me the identification, and therefore a free pass through check stops. However, many supernaturals don't think too highly of empaths.

Pressing the Next button pulls up the camera mode. It's too dark to take a picture in here. I sleeve the phone and leave the bathroom back to my room.

Removing the ponytail and adjusting my hair, I manage to find a good angle to take the appropriate picture. I confirm my choice of an awkward selfie and it processes to a thinking screen.

Putting the phone on the bed, I put my hair back up in a ponytail while the phone moves to the next page. A picture of my identification is on the screen. I screen shot the ID so I have a copy. Then, I realize there is a download button. Downloading the ID places the picture in my photo album. Now, I can just never lose this phone.

That base is covered so I put the phone back in my pocket. Now I can pass through any check points. I can pass through that stop in my vision if I can't avoid the forgotten phone kerfuffle.

The ease of obtaining the identification is a risk to the whole system. One loophole they had not been thinking about when it was created. There was no authorization, no check to see if I am who I claim to be; what I claim to be.

Anyone with a phone could receive the identification. That poses a huge problem. Though, the human would have to get their hands on a supernatural phone, or one connected to their internet. It would have to be on them at all times. They would have to know about it in the first place.

Waving off the thoughts, I figure I should start my day. The sun looks high in the sky, and I'm sure it's late morning. I'm too lazy to pull out my phone to check on the real time. The whole time I had it open, I didn't once register what the time was.

Changing into a clean shirt and sweater from my drawer, brushing my hair and teeth, and putting on my shoes to leave the room. Stepping back, I move to grasp my jacket and then think twice about it. It should be warm enough out to leave that here. I could always come back if I get too cold.

Down the stairs, I enter into a mostly empty kitchen. Dominique turns around in the doorway. Once she looks back she notices me.

"Well good morning, or should I say good afternoon." Dominique chides. She holds a decorative makeup bag in her hands and appears to have been on her way out the door. Her hair is tied up in a bun and she's well put together between her makeup and clothing. Somehow, finding a way to be fashionable in the apocalypse.

"Sorry, I had insomnia last night. I was up until, well, some early risers were starting their day." I walk over to the fridge, pour myself a cup of cold tea, and take a sip of it. Dominique scowls in disgust. I return it with a smile. As soon as the weather turned I switched the hot tea out for cold. My preference makes the rest turn their noses at the bitter brew.

"Oh, why did you have insomnia?" She's shocked. There is an irony to the prophet who has visions in her sleep, also being susceptible to acute insomnia.

"I think it was, I was, um." I stumble over my words in a delay method. Twisting my closed mouth to the side, I decide to go with the half-honest route; exclaiming a what but not the why. "I was exhausted but didn't go to sleep when I got tired, and then when I went to bed I couldn't fall asleep because of an overtired energy boost then that turned into anxiety-induced insomnia. Basically, my body and my head decided they hate me and they like to pull things like this to keep me on my toes." My stress of late, with the rising tensions and terrible visions, is the likely culprit.

Dominique sucks in a quick breath through her teeth. "That sucks."

"Yeah, sucks more when you have to get up for a specific time. Like school, that sucked, when I had insomnia and would be up till five and have to be at school for eight. You get to a point where you debate even trying to go to sleep because you know if you even manage to get an hour that you'll wake up super groggy; if your body even lets you wake up at the alarm. But, you also know that you'll crash sooner if you don't. But either way, you are basically useless in a hazy zombie mode for the whole day. But no one recognizes insomnia as a disorder to get you out of school or work without repercussions so you have to push through it. But, this was nice, because I got to make up for the lost sleep." I bite my lips to stop talking. I'm saying too much.

"So, what? Like, do you do stuff when you have insomnia? Like, do you lie in bed or get up and do things?" Her further questions sooth my social anxiety slightly. She wouldn't ask more questions if she thought I'm a bumbling idiot, nor if she wasn't interested in what I was saying.

"It depends on how much I really need to be sleeping. Last night I got up after two hours of lying in bed. Then I worked out and showered. Then, tried again for another hour. So I got up again and read a bit. And, then I tried again and after an hour I finally fell asleep. But, I've literally lain in bed for eight hours trying to go to sleep before and it didn't work. I watched the clock and said to myself that I really needed to sleep because I have to be up in whatever hours, and to finally give up when my alarm goes off."

"That really sucks." Dominique commiserates.

"Tell me about it." The conversation is finished with my agreement. I look for something else to say. Panicking to keep the conversation going.

"Well, I was bringing this outside. A bunch of us are painting our nails. Wanna join?" Dominique saves me from my failed conversational skills with an offer of more social interaction.

"Sure. What else would there be to do?" I agree in an awkward obligation. We head to go out the door to the back yard.

"Well, you slept through all the morning chores, so nothing." She elbows me lightly.

My cheeks turn red with embarrassment. "Sorry."

"Whatever, it's not like you don't do more than your fair share of work around here." Despite her words, I will make up for missing out on the morning chores. My anxiety can't handle what people might think about me for not contributing enough.

We walk to the next door's back yard and greet a group of girls. Dominique holds out the bag. It is snatched from her grasp as the girls get quick to work pairing off and painting each other's nails. These dynamics were likely discussed when the nail painting party was thought up, or while Dominique has been gone.

Dominique picks her own colour and then Abby starts to decorate her nails.

Sipping on my tea. Quickly counting, I recognize that I am the odd one out.

Never matter, I will do my own. The bag has been raided of most of the colours. There is a choice between a blood red and a metallic green. Between the two I choose the red.

I hold the red nail polish in my hands and sit down in an empty chair. Déjà vu flashes in my head. The memory of my vision playing quickly right before the reality as I let it happen exactly as the vision foretold. I open the polish and start to paint my nails.

The wet paint goes on easily. The deep bright red stands out against my pale skin. I steady my hand and stroke the brush again. Just a simple French tip is how I like my nail polish. It's a fairly easy thing to do with little practice.

Something I've perfected a long time ago after I figured out I didn't like getting my nails done at solons for events.

I glance up at the girls around me. They are all doing each other's nails. It's bonding and apparently so much easier. With the odd number I was to wait, but I decided to do my own.

They gush about how nice their nails are turning out, but I don't see anything special about them. It's just painted nails.

The warm spring breeze brushes against me.

"How do you get your lines so straight? I can't even do that on someone else let alone myself with my good hand." Dominique awes at my nails.

"It's not that hard. You just need a steady hand. It helps if you think about holding the nail polish brush with your bad hand still, and move your good hand to get the nail polish on the nail." I demonstrate.

"I'll have to try that. If not, I think I just found my new French manicurist." She goes back to painting the other girl's nails.

Twisting the cap on, I then set the nail polish aside. Spreading my hands out in front of me, I examine the workmanship. They appear perfect and ignite a spark of joy in my chest.

Maybe I can understand, a little, why the other girls gush over getting their nails done. Though, I know by my track record, that I will have a chip or scratch ruining the look by supper. I crush my joy spark.

To prevent damage while they dry, I weave my fingers together; holding hands with myself. Each finger sits in the indentation of my knuckle. Laying my hands in my lap for comfort's sake.

I tilt my head up and open my ears to the conversations going on around me. While I was in my head, the jibber jabber missed wouldn't have been too important. No one in this grouping talks about anything of any interest to me. This clique tends to be more trained on the stereotypical girl talk; vanity, boys, and gossip.

One of the girls caught a couple of guys skinny dipping in the frigid lake. She suspects they are involved with one another, which is scandalous because the one guy has a girlfriend. And, should she tell the girlfriend?

The girl she's talking to, Sharon, says "no because you can't out a person from the closet and that takes priority over informing someone of their partner's cheating. But, you shouldn't really tell anyone about their partner cheating because it's none of your business, and you don't know the relationship dynamic. So you should leave it alone."

The original girl, I don't remember her name, says she completely agrees with Sharon. I, however, do not. Cheating is cheating. You always need to speak with the person being cheated on and inform them of their partner's infidelity. I have outed my father to a few of his girlfriends once I've figured out he's been cheating. Most of them left immediately, and only one stayed until six months later when she caught him red-handed; apologizing to me for not believing me.

It's better to give the person a choice than to sit back and wait for years to pass by the time they figure it out.

Outing a person from the closet isn't advised, but would only make a need for the situation to be handled a little more delicately. You could leave it gender-neutral by saying something like—I think your significant other is cheating on you. I caught him skinny-dipping with someone. Maybe you should talk to him about it.

I shake my head a little to let go of that conversation and move onto another.

Frankie is talking to Amara about Jamie, and how he's mega hot. She wonders if he's into her. Amara cheers her on and tells her that she should ask him out. If he says no, then there must be something wrong with him.

Or he might like my sister and not Frankie. Their relationship isn't known to many; mainly just myself and the two involved. Though my knowledge of their relationship is unknown to them.

Despite their private relationship, I wouldn't label either of them as available. So, I doubt he will say yes, and I doubt he will tell her the real reason why.

Frankie and Amara will be left to discuss what might be wrong with Jamie when he rejects Frankie. They will come to some wild conclusion about the skeletons in his closet. Anything that will make Frankie feel better about herself.

I listen in on the next couple.

"The blue matches my eyes perfectly. If I hold my finger on my lip, it'll draw his attention down to my mouth." A curly red-haired girl says. I cut off whatever else she was going to say with my mind.

Uhg. No. Moving on.

"I'm loving this weather." Dominique starts up a simple conversation topic with Abby. This topic sounds much safer, though I doubt it will be too interesting.

Most of the snow has disappeared, and grass peeks out of what is left. We could almost say that spring is here, yet from living in this province I know better. We are never in the clear until May long weekend has passed, and it's only the beginning of May. I would guess we are likely in for one more dump of snow. The temperature, however, should teeter-totter between above zero, and minus five; increasingly steady higher numbers the later we get in the season.

"Yeah, me too. It reminds me of slush fights with my friends. And, to think, that summer is right around the corner." Abby lights up at the possibilities. Dominique starts painting her nails. She holds the brush awkwardly because her paint isn't dry yet. A flower is painted on her thumb nail, but not her pointer finger's nail. I will never understand why people paint their nails differently. I think it looks awkward, but apparently it's fashion.

"Barbeques, swimming pools, sun tanning. The beach! Bush parties." Dominique lists off. Her summer time fun is exactly what I'd think she'd have enjoyed growing up and in her recent years.

They are vastly different than my own summers, and for a moment I am envious. My childhood summers were not a vacation. I had tutoring whenever I wasn't in school. Then, I worked with dad for free during the summers. When he fired me, not so coincidentally around the time my brother was born and a paternity test confirmed, I got a job at the dollar store and worked full-time through last summer.

"You know, my family escaped every summer for a trip right here in Banff. We'd go camping and do tourist crap. I used to hate that trip. Sharing a tent with my brother; God, he stunk up the tent. Now, I would give up everything to go on just one more of those trips." Jess adds to the conversation in a darkened tone.

I untangle my fingers. Lightly, I press against the nail polish to test hardness. The polish stays in place and doesn't acquire any finger prints. Only a few minutes have passed by, and I'm confident the top layer is dry. I'll still be careful with my nails, but I don't have to worry as much.

I lower my hands open palmed onto my thighs to rest for a few more minutes.

"I know what you mean. I miss my whole family." Dominque empathizes. "I'd give anything to see them again. Or, to at least know what happened to them."

My eyes widen before I can get them under control again. No one notices as no one is looking my way.

I forgot to tell her about all her family being dead.

Whoops.

My heart pounds, causing an ache in my chest. Is it too late to tell her now? I think it's too late to tell her now. It's been five, six months since they were killed at grandma's farm. Their bodies left in a pile next to the burning house her grandparents had built.

There is a possibility that the werewolves found the bodies when they attended to putting out the flames; not that anyone had mentioned it to me. Or, they may have found them later on. The bodies may have been buried properly. Or, they could all be decomposing in the winter's thaw. The sight it was back when I had found it would be nothing to the wretched sight it would be now with the added stench and decomposition.

It would be tragic for Dominique to have to view such a thing.

"I miss my mom, and even my sister." The whole group echoes the depressing thought with one each of their own. Each has their own story of the family and friends that they miss; some just missing and some confirmed dead.

I feel inhuman, because I don't share these same thoughts with these people. I don't miss my family, and I don't miss my friends; if you could even call any of them that.

"We should go back to find our families. The snow is melting and the roads should be pretty clear." Dominique's suggestion places me in a difficult spot. Do I let her search for her family while I know they are dead?

Eventually, she's going to have the same thought I had. If not, she might just decide to go looking for her grandparents. She'll get there and find the burnt-down house. John's pack, patrolling the area, will certainly tell him we're there. He'll come running and give his condolences after likely finding the bodies by now. She'll ask him what he means, and that truth will come out. Then I'll either have to tell the truth or lie.

She's going to find out sooner or later. It'll be better for me if it's before we spend months searching. It'll be better if I don't have to lie.

If I'm going to tell her, she needs to know before we leave.

"Yes! Let's go! I have a few personal items I really want to get from my house in Wetaskiwin." Another one agrees with her, but for a house in Devon.

"We can start searching for people we know," Abby adds.

"Or, bury the bodies," Jess says under her breath. I don't think she's too keen on the idea.

"You don't have to come with me. There are more than enough vehicles that we can all go off in our own directions." Abby sneers at Jess.

This seems like a horrible idea. A truly horrible idea. Why would they want to put themselves through that? What do they want to do; go back to their homes, their relatives and friends' homes, and see if they can find any sign of their friends and family? Even if they don't find them dead, what will they do? Spread pictures of them around on posters?

There are too many variables, but only one of which leads their family to actually be home. The other ten thousand variables say that they will never see their family again, even if they are alive. It happens all the time in war. Families and friends are torn away from each other and never find each other again. Or, they find each other but it's fifty years later.

If they are alive, the best chances would be to bring the internet up again and go on a social network and hope to find people there. Post pictures of our loved ones and ask people to look at the pictures and advise if they saw them. Even then, you'd have to ensure access for mostly everyone.

Dominique turns around and directs at me. "We should go to your house, then my house and then to grandma's house."

"We can." My voice sounds a little less convincing than it should have. I know she noticed when the smile fades from her face. "But, why grandma's? It was burnt down."

"To say goodbye. Maybe see John. Maybe see if anyone showed up afterwards."

"Sure, of course, we can." I smile to try to convince her this time.

"Come on, Jaiden."

"Yes, okay? Let's go. We'll make a list of everything we need, gather it up, and head out." I affirm. Already, I'm thinking of ways to delay the trip.

She's pushing the matter, and I'm going to have to tell her about their deaths before we go, or never.

I'll do it later, when she's alone. Maybe get a couple drinks into her first. She's always a happy drunk.

Maybe not, as that might back fire, and provide the onslaught of an emotional drunk. It's a fine line.

Either way. She is going to be furious with me.

She's going to kill me.

Chapter 2

With bated breath, I watch as Rayleen stares into the flame of the candle. Ever so slightly, the flame bends then completely dissipates. It flickers out like when a breath is blown. There was a slight bending of the fire but not in the direction where Rayleen would have blown it out. One moment it was there eating away at the wick, and the next it was gone. The charred wick letting off the only evidence a flame was just lit.

"Good, you're starting to learn to control the flame." He rises from his seat; where he was bored and barely paying attention. Cam takes up his sweater and puts it on. "I want you to do that faster and faster until you can do it in an instant. Then, we'll move on to touching the fire, and then carrying the flame."

A time reminder pulls attention to the ache in my elbows. My wrists require twisting to bring them back to life. I have been propping my head up with them for too long.

The lanky teen rubs his hand on the top of Rayleen's head, effectively messing her hair up a little. I grimace at the thought of having to, once again, redo the pigtail French braids. I swear she won't get to choose her hairstyle tomorrow. Rayleen can have a ponytail. At least when a ponytail gets messed up, it only takes a minute to get it put nicely back together.

"Thank you. We really appreciate you teaching her to help control her magic." I say to him. He doesn't have to take the time to teach Rayleen how to do magic. He's a young teenager and I can't imagine he particularly enjoys having to spend time with a six year old. For some reason, he continues to do so and I am grateful he can do what I can't. When I found out James had left, I had thought it would be the end of her magic lessons. She really does enjoy it, but it also makes her stronger. "We'll see you tomorrow?"

"Yeah. You know it's no problem at all. I told you, these are very simple skills all kids learn. She should know them too." He waves me off. "See you tomorrow, kiddo."

"Bye." Rayleen answers back, still engrossed in the candle. The smoke rises in a long strand into the air before it breaks off into a cloud, then into nothing I can see. The whole room smells like the aftermath of a blown out birthday cake.

Maybe we should have practiced this outside. I can already see Jaiden scrunching her nose in disgust, and complaining about her smoke induced migraine.

"Rayleen, say your thanks." I remind her.

"Thank you for teaching me, Cam." She says without looking up at him. Part of me wants to reprimand her for the disrespectful thanks, and another part of me wants to let it go as a good enough effort. Cam doesn't mind or doesn't notice, so I choose the latter.

"You're welcome. Have a great day." He runs out the back door to go home.

A new voice surprises me enough to make me jump. "He's not welcome here. And, if you are going to do that, you can't do it in my home." Bruce's outburst, however, is no surprise. He's shown his displeasure for everything and everyone supernatural.

We moved out of his current lodgings a few weeks after the blizzard. The discourse was too much for us. Having Rayleen there, had her magic been found out then, would have been dangerous.

In the months since, the invisible line between demons and humans has become more tangible. They've had time to stew on their hatred. Now that people are straying from their homes, there have been a few tense stand offs, and one fist fight.

People blame the demons for family and friends being killed, and can't stand to have them as neighbours. The feelings go deep for some, others turn a blind eye; very few have defended them.

If we're not careful there is going to be a race riot breaking out soon. That might be a little much, I don't think it'll get that far, but the feeling is the same.

Many people have legitimate reasons to hate these particular supernaturals, and haven't had any sort of justice for the crimes done against them; Nikki made sure of that.

"It's fine. They aren't doing any harm." I counter.

"Not in my house. And if you value your daughter at all, you will stop this nonsense. She can still be just a normal little girl. You have time to train her and raise her right. Forget about all that danger you put her in." I open my mouth to refute this, but he continues to chastise me. "You're letting them turn her into a monster."

My mouth drops open, while I am taken aback. "She's not a monster, and she will never be a monster. She's a sweet little girl, and that's not going to change because she learns a little magic. That's ridiculous. You become a monster because of experience and what you do, not because of what you are."

"It's all the same when you're a demon." He spits out.

"You need to leave!" My heart flutters as Daniel comes to my rescue. If there is ever a knight in shining armour moment, it is this one. He's even dressed in a grey hoodie to help my imagination picture the fantasy.

"This is my house," Bruce exclaims.

"And, you aren't welcome here." Daniel tries to tell him confusingly; we are the guests. Bruce is, in fact, the owner. I think he may have forgotten that.

"It's my house. Get out!" Bruce screams in his deep tone. He throws his arms up to gesture out the back door.

"You don't even live here anymore!" Daniel counters.

"It's fine, we'll leave." I place myself in between the two and the increasingly heated fight. My hand goes up to touch Daniel's chest and gain his attention. The light touch manages that and his smouldering angered eyes soften when they catch mine.

Rayleen stares at us with a blank stare. I'm worried about what consequences a full out fight might have on her; more than I am worried about the consequences of magic.

"I have to go grab gloves, then we'll leave." Daniel leaves through the dining room.

I walk over to the table. Blowing the candle out, I collect Rayleen and walk her out the door.

Bruce storms by us moments later and ducks into the garage. His movements spike an electric fear of uncertainty, but it fizzles out into nothing.

Why would he tell us to leave, if he was just going to leave immediately himself?

A light female voice registers in the back of my ears, but I don't hear the exact words. It takes me a moment to realize she is speaking to me.

"What?" I question as I turn around to look at the unfamiliar face. "Are you talking to me?"

"Could you go to the river and grab a pail of water?" She has a tin bucket in her held out hand.

"Why?"

"Because I asked." She says it like it's obvious. She assumes that will be enough to convince me to do what she's asking. "It'll be worth your while, I promise." This girl is way too cheery.

It's intriguing enough to say yes to such a simple request, if to just get her to go away. "Uh sure, I guess so." I take the pale as it's shoved at me. "Rayleen-"

She interrupts my asking Rayleen to come along with me. "I'll watch her. You should go. It wouldn't be safe for such a small girl. She could easily get swept away by the water."

"Uhm. No." She may have a small point, but the fact is that I don't know her at all. It would be reckless to leave Rayleen with a complete stranger. "I'll leave her with someone she knows."

"Good plan. Well, you should get someone so you can go get that water right away." She practically shoos me away.

Daniel emerges from the house.

He acknowledges the girl in our company and places himself beside Rayleen.

"Alexa said she's going down to the river to grab a pail of river water for me. Would you watch the little girl while she does that?" She asks, more tells, Daniel.

Daniel looks questioningly at me. I shrug in response. "Yeah sure."

"Good, I'll be around." She walks off toward the front of the house. If she's going that way anyway, why does she need me?

"Well, she was weird," Daniel exclaims.

"Yeah. But, I guess I should go get that water."

"Do you want us to come with you?" He asks.

"No, that's okay." I say. This won't take long. "Go find Nikki. Let her know her Uncle's on a tirade again."

"Okay." His look alone draws me in. I'm tempted to kiss Daniel and act on it by leaning up and pursing my lips. He indulges me by gathering me into his arms. He leans down and his lips cross mine. A brief kiss warms my chest. I feel safe right here.

The kiss aftermath draws up the corners of my mouth in a stupid grin I couldn't wipe off if I wanted to. This man makes my heart flutter and scream with joy.

I couldn't be happier at this moment with my two loves.

One deep breath in, I let this moment of ecstasy sink in and immortalize it in my memory.

A kiss on Rayleen's forehead says my good bye for me. Instead, I say, "I'll be right back."

Walking away, I look back at the two of them. Rayleen is safe with Daniel. He makes her laugh at something before I'm out of sight. Daniel is going to make a great father one day.

The path is smooth now that most of the snow is gone. White frozen water had made treks slow or impossible. Cabin fever never had as much of a meaning to me as it has in recent months.

The smooth running water makes little noise in comparison to the ticks from my boots on the sidewalk.

As quiet as the slight wind whispers around me, a person appears to my right. The sudden appearance incites my defences. At the same time I am lifted up into his arms, the bucket knocks him in the head.

If it hurt, he doesn't show that it affected him.

Darius whisks me off. His appearance has reverted to that I knew as the football player I dated. The sharper, deadly look has softened. His eyes are their typical light blue.

Doesn't explain what he is doing and where he is taking me. "Put me down." He doesn't acknowledge me. "Put me down, Darius!" I say firmer.

Darius still continues on his way. I bash his head with the bucket once more.

His attention on me is earned. Darius slows to a stop and unceremoniously drops his arms as payback to me hitting him with the bucket; no doubt.

One foot hits the ground. I lock my knee and manage to stumble backwards until I balance up straight. Immediately, placing myself on the defensive while knowing there is nowhere I could escape. I'm not fast enough to escape him; not strong enough to fight.

"Take me back." The voice out of my mouth is deeper than I've ever heard it. It's unrecognizable. All the rage and frustration and hatred for him darkens my voice.

"I know, I know. You need to go back and get Rayleen." He rolls his eyes to display his annoyance.

"Yes! No! Leave me alone. I don't want you here. I don't want to go with you. You can leave now." He doesn't budge. Not one word leaves his lips. "Then, I will."

Before I manage one step, Darius crosses five to stand in front of me. Close enough that I bump into his chest. He lays both his hands on my arms to keep me in place despite lacking any actual grip.

"You're mad. I hurt you when I abandoned you. I'm sorry for that." His blue eyes stare deep into my own. It's a haunting, unblinking stare. "I couldn't protect you. I'm sorry."

I don't want to hear any apology. Pangs of pain knock on my heart. Breaking the connection doesn't help alleviate this. "Leave me alone."

"Sandra tricked me into believing all of us together would be the only way things could work. Then, she tricked me into leaving with her on the day of the attack; I didn't know. She stopped and brought down the building while I had to watch and I thought you died; so I left. But then I found out you survived, and I was so happy. So, now I'm back for you." His sweet words sound sincere, but I don't know what to believe.

Tears flood into my eyes. The words Darius says are exactly the ones that I've been waiting to hear for the last few months. It's an explanation for his actions. They hurt my heart as they draw up old feelings I worked hard to tamper down. "I moved on." I choke.

"It's not that easy." He calls my bluff.

"It is. I hate you." I reiterate. Part of me does hate him. Blinking my eyes to clear them of the tears, I muster the clearest confident voice I can. "Now I'm going to go back to be with Rayleen, and I am going to go back to living my life; happy without you."

Darius snarls. "I don't think so." He snickers at his own private joke. "You know, you always do things like this." He mulls something over in his head. Eyebrows twitch up starting a similar action with each side of his mouth. "I have a present for you."

That throws me for a loop. "What?"

"Go back to the farm house. I left you a present." His wicked smirk is back. The confidence beams as white as his teeth.

As stubborn as I can be, I say, "I don't want anything from you."

Darius frowns and snarls. "I wasn't asking. You will go to the farm and find what I left you." His voice drops and warns dangerously of what refusal could mean.

"We burnt the house down." My voice is small and timid.

"It's not in that house. Just go and you will see."

In a quick decision, I decide to defy him. "No."

"Do I really need to threaten Rayleen's life again?" His unspoken threat becomes known. It's his usual play, but it's not to be taken lightly. He's caused enough terror and destruction. Darius obviously has no problem with killing people. "You will go back to the farmhouse and you will see what I left for you."

"Why did you get me a present?" I ask, draining my suspicion into one question.

"It'll convince you to come back to me," Darius answers simply and cryptically.

"What is it?"

He shakes his head. "That's not how it works. Go to the farm, come back here, and by then you will be convinced to join me."

Going one way will be hard enough, but to have to travel there and back will be too much. It'll take days to prepare, more to travel, and supplies that I don't have. The travel will be dangerous.

"How am I supposed to get there and back?" I ask.

"Figure it out. I'll be back for you." His lips touch mine hard and fast in a display of dominance. I have no choice in both the kiss and the trip. The display clearly writes the message for me. Rock solid pressure releases from my mouth. Darius smirks. "Oh, and I'd leave today; if I were you."

His eyes hold mine as he steps to the side to let me by. The stare, as unnerving as ever, flips a switch. Running by him, I sprint as fast as I can. Panic is fueled by adrenaline.

In the few seconds he ran, he managed to run me all the way down the block. It takes me about three times the time to make it back to the same area.

Looking back to the area he occupied only draws up the hairs on the back of my neck. He's gone, and that means he could be anywhere. A momentary stop panics me. I have to get back to Rayleen, and I won't leave her alone again.

He won't take her away from me again.

I don't know exactly where they are, so I go to the last place I saw them; they're not here. The next place to look is on my last request to them; find Nikki.

I go out to the back alley and start jogging left. They are bound to be over on this side. Likely they would have found her outside. Nikki has been practically sunbathing since the winter broke. We've all been trying to soak up as much sun as possible on warmer days; except for the vampires.

Next door is a group of girls, with Jaiden sitting on the outskirts. But Nikki, Daniel and Rayleen are nowhere in sight.

The next yard, and no sign.

Next yard, and no sign.

Next yard; no sign.

I walk all the way to the main street. They are likely inside one of the houses, or possibly branched out further than the block. This is the furthest I've been since the day I helped Cam give supplies to the vampires. I mentally give my head a shake.

I double back.

The girls in the yard may know where she's gone. At the least, Jaiden should know. The two of them are almost always together.

I enter the yard and gain the attention in a throat clearing. "Hey, does anyone know where Nikki is?"

"She left a little while ago, but I don't know where exactly she went. You could just wait here for her. She should be back soon." Jess announces.

I huff a breath of air out. There isn't much of an option. It's either wait for her to come back here, or go door to door and try to find them. I opt to sit down next to Jaiden. She looks at me and then looks away.

"Do you know where she went?" I ask her. They're normally together. Jaiden follows Nikki around like a dog.

Jaiden shakes her head. "Just that Daniel came with Rayleen saying Bruce freaked out. What happened?"

"Bruce went wild about Rayleen using magic." She nods and looks away. "So, you're resourceful. Do you know where I can get things to take a road trip back to Leduc, and then back here?"

Jaiden turns back and looks confused. "Why?"

I can't tell her the actual reason. Why would I go back there when otherwise I would have no reason to return? It's safe here and we should stay. I double back. With recent events, it may not be as safe as I thought. "Because I want to get some family mementos and Crystal for Rayleen."

"You're in luck. We were just talking about a trip out that way. Quite a few people want to try looking for their family and collect sentimental items."

That's not going to work. I don't want to travel all around looking for other people's things. This place is safe. I want to go there and back; a day trip if possible. "I just want to go there and back. Not a long trip. Can you make sure we can work it so Rayleen, Daniel and I don't have to be there long?"

"Okay, umm, I could see what I can do." She looks up. Her fingers come up and wiggle as she's deep in thought. "You're going to need a vehicle with a full tank of gas, and some jerry cans full of gas; enough to get you back. Syphoning equipment just in case you run out. Supplies enough for at least two days, just in case, and three people?"

That sounds about right. "Yes. Thank you." I say.

She gets up quickly and practically runs away. It's like she was looking for an excuse to leave. In her abrupt exit, Jaiden didn't even say good bye. No time to ask her where she's going, but I guess she's going to scrounge up what I need.

I don't follow the group's conversation and they barely give me a second glance.

I look around in the two possible directions Nikki could arrive from. Each false person who dares to pass by in their place brings my hopes up only to dash them quickly.

Every noise alerts me. Darius is likely still there; watching me.

I think about getting up, itching to go search for them instead of sitting here and doing nothing. But, by the time I actually stand up all three of them come walking around the corner.

"Where'd Jaiden go?" Nikki asks.

There are a few "I don't know" answers from the other girls. No one was listening to our conversation then. A few look at where she had been; these people didn't notice she had left in the first place.

Being the only useful source I tell Nikki, "she went to look for a car for me."

"Why do you need a car?" Daniel asks, immediately concerned.

"I want to go back to Leduc for a couple days. Check on the people we left at the farm, grab some mementos from my old house, and grab Crystal." The idea is spun as gleefully as I can make it. Rayleen shrieks in joy.

"Actually, we were just talking about that. I was planning on going back too. I want to go see if my family made it to my grandparents' house. So we might need a few cars. We can travel together until we get to Leduc." Nikki says.

"Umm, sure. Okay. I want to leave today though." It wasn't part of my plan to have a convoy, but I can't argue that more people wouldn't make it safer for the bulk of the trip there.

"No, wait. Why would we go back? It's stupid to leave here. It's safe here. We can survive and live here." Daniel argues.

"It's about hope. You can't stop your girlfriend from holding onto whatever hope she has. You can either go with her, or stay here, but you can't stop her from going." Nikki is a little ballsy taking my side against Daniel like this.

I feel like I should tell her to back off, but she is helping me get my way.

I step in to lightly convince him to come with me. "We'll be fine. I just want to take a day trip out there. We go back, we grab what we need, you can go check on your house too, and then we come back."

"You make it sound just a little too simple." He says.

"It will be that simple. I promise." The blatant lie adds guilt to my mixed-up feelings. He can't know the real reason we are going. It'll break his heart enough when Darius comes to retrieve me willingly against my will.

Nothing and no one can stop Darius from getting what he wants. His return has reminded me of that. He's always going to come back for me. He's never going to let me go.

"Okay. So I guess we should go pack some bags to go." Daniel relents. I withhold a kiss, just in case Darius is watching.

"Thank you." I switch from speaking to him to addressing Nikki. "Jaiden said she'd find us a vehicle and all the fixings."

Nikki smiles. "Great, let's find Jaiden and tell her the change of plans."

God, I miss phones. They made things like this so much easier.

Chapter 3

"Jaiden!" The blonde jumps at my abrupt shout. I cringe and hiss when her head connects with the door jamb of the car she's leaning into. "Sorry. Are you okay?"

"Yeah." Jaiden sits down in the driver's seat and rubs her head. "Ow." She pulls her hand away to look at it before dropping it onto her lap. She closes her eyes and holds herself still. "Hi."

"How's your head?" I ask.

She looks up at me, squinting through the sun shining from over my head. "Not bleeding. I suppose that's a good sign."

"So, I hear you're helping Alexa get to Leduc," I ask accusing her of something; her hesitation earlier.

She looks around me to the three trailing behind. "I know what you're going to say. I went ahead and retrieved two vehicles and enough supplies and gas to split between the two."

"Great! We might need more."

Her eyebrows turn together and the smile drops. "How much more?"

Before I get the chance to answer her, Daniel jumps in. "Nikki wants to talk with everyone in town to see if they want to leave." He's condescending in his tone. I shoot a quick glare back at him. Daniel's still not too keen on the idea of this.

Jaiden looks back and forth between the two of us before she settles on me. "Okay. I get talking to them to let them know the option is there, but everyone else can figure out their own supplies and getaway vehicle."

"We should help them. It'll help us too. What if one of our vehicles breaks down? We could use the extra help. More so, if we're attacked." I try to make my point even though I know I'm going to lose this one.

Hearing it out loud from Jaiden makes me hear the outrageous ambition it would take to accomplish what I had set out to do.

"But, not everyone's going to the same place. Like ten of us, maybe if they want to go, would go back to Edmonton and area. The rest either flew here from far away or lived here." Jaiden's logic persists to break down my idea. "How is Amani supposed to get back to Sudan? And, that's even if they want to leave."

She's right.

It's not enough to just call a town meeting, and have everyone stop what they are doing to talk about it. This isn't like the mall where we were talking about gathering fifty rowdy teenagers and twenty-somethings together from the four corners of a large mall. They won't be goofing around, getting drunk and playing dress up. This would be pulling a whole town together. It would take a lot more time than I would be willing to spare.

Especially, if I want to get to grandma's by nightfall.

My hands go up in defence. "Okay, okay I get it." I won't fight her and the others on this anymore. It would be useless, and they have a good point. But, I would like to ask everyone who had come with us, or rather had come with Jaiden to rescue Rayleen and me. They all had come from that way, so they might want to go back. "So, can you help get together enough stuff for about ten people?"

"Yeah, I can. No problem." She affirms.

"Thank you." Turning around I delegate instructions to Daniel and Alexa. "You guys stay here and help Jaiden with everything she needs to get us going in the next hour."

"They can go get their things. I'll be fine. We're just going to need one more vehicle and a few other things. By the time they get back, I'll be done." Jaiden disagrees from behind me. She stands up and sticks her upper half back into the car to busy herself with whatever she had been doing when I interrupted her. "I won't need long to pack my own things."

If she thinks she can do it all herself in a manageable time, then that's completely fine with me. "Great. I'm going to go talk to people."

"Wait. Uh, can we talk alone before we go?"

"Yeah, later. We have lots to do in little time." I brush her off as I walk away. My head already running a million miles a minute thinking of everything that needs to happen before we go.

There is the question of how to do this.

Do I walk around and ask everyone I see if they have somewhere they'd like to go?

Probably not.

Jaiden talked about the ten people who came here with her. I should just ask them, and let everyone else make their own decisions after finding out our plan.

When they hear we've left, it'll show them that it's an option. If Jaiden can gather together a vehicle and supplies, then anyone else should be able to. There isn't a lack of unowned vehicles.

Is Jaiden breaking into houses and stealing keys? Where else would she be getting keys? I don't remember seeing any car dealerships. Is she hot wiring cars?

Whatever she's doing, she's confident that she can retrieve another easily.

I should talk to Uncle Bruce about us leaving, but our next conversation isn't going to be a pretty one.

My blood boils from the thought. If I talk to him right now, there isn't going to be much talking. I'm going to end up yelling and screaming things at him that are just going to make him tell me we're not welcome to come back.

I can't do that to all of them. Alexa made it clear they were going to come back. She has nowhere else to be and this, despite Uncle Bruce, is a safe place for Rayleen.

Leah, Miles and Kelly are first on my list. The vampires have been kept inside after running out of their special sunscreen. Their house is close and I can almost guarantee at least two of them will be there.

I walk in through the front and announce my arrival. "Knock. Knock."

"Living room!" The short answer is yelled above explosions. They must be watching a movie.

I feel bad that none of them can go outside while it's warm out. It still gets below zero at night.

They pause the movie as I walk into the room. "Hey." Each greets me in their own way, or not. "So, we need to talk."

"Are you breaking up with us?" Greg asks in a lame attempt at some humour.

They really need to get out of this house and visit other people; socialize some more.

"Shut up! What the hell'd Bruce do now?" Leah groans.

She definitely needs to leave this house. How irritating it has to be to get stuck with the same random people day and night; not having an escape.

"Nothing." That I'm going to speak about right now, but he has done plenty I could bitch about. "A few of us are leaving town out to the area in and around Edmonton. A couple days' trip to collect sentimentals, and we are extending offers out to anyone who wants to go out that way. Any takers?"

Many disagree right away, but I wasn't really talking to them anyway. I'm glad when none of the others wish to join us.

"No thanks. We're good with staying here." Kelly answers for both her and Miles. He looks slightly disappointed, then more so annoyed that she answered for him. I'm not jumping between that mess. Their relationship is my gossip, but none of my business.

"No sunblock or I'd go part way with you." Leah resigns herself.

Finally, a problem I can easily solve; maybe. "I could talk with Jaiden. We can find a way to get you out there with us."

"Thanks, but I'm not hiding under a blanket the whole way." She turns back to stare at the screen as it's stuck on a building exploding and falling down.

"We'll find a different way. I promise. Just go pack enough things to last you a few days. Be ready by the time I get back." I won't take no for an answer from someone who wants to go.

Leaving the room before she can get a chance to dispute me, I check the next few yards for the remaining people on my list.

I go inside our house next. No one is on the main level, but I hear a bit of noise upstairs and so I go up that way.

Knocking on the door, I walk inside without waiting for an answer. Two people in the midst of intense kissing part at my intrusion. The guilty parties launch to opposite sides of the bed; denial and defense of their activities ready on their tongues.

"What the fuck are you doing!?" I shout in surprise.

"Kissing." Shawn replies. He knows that's not what I meant.

"Smart ass. You know I meant with each other." Taking my chances at the weakest link, I look to Steph. "Are you broken up with Brad yet?"

"Sort of." Steph's face is a bright shade of red. She looks down guiltily.

She means no.

"If you can't answer yes, then you're cheating on him. Really guys? Steph break up with Brad; officially. He was our friend longer than you were dating him, and despite being an asshole recently, he deserves more respect than that." I scold them.

"Are you going to tell him?" Steph asks quietly.

For a moment I think that maybe I should; as any responsible friend should do. But, I think better of it. "No, because then he'll find a way to spin this as a demon seducing his girlfriend, and someone's going to end up dead. You have to tell him before he finds out about this." I can't do this conversation anymore. I can't do this situation right now. "Anyway, a few of us are going back home for a few days to see if we can find family. Do you want to come with us?"

"Yes, anything to get out of town for a while." Steph gasps in relief.

"Trying to avoid someone?" The words come out a little more

bitterly than I meant.

The tone goes above her head, or maybe she ignores it. "A change of scenery would help. Besides, we can't leave you alone out there." She says excitedly.

"Thanks for the concern. Pack some things, and meet up on Main Street. Jaiden's out there packing up some vehicles. Help her with anything she needs." I leave as fast as I can manage. In the flurry of what I just witnessed I turn the corner to run into someone. "Sorry." It's Jaiden. "What are you doing here? Did you finish getting everything ready?"

"Almost. I'm just packing up my things, then I'll finish up." She advises.

"Can you pack my things for me?" I ask though I know she'll say yes. I take a step to run by her, but I stop because I remember there was another thing I need to tell her. "Oh, and we need a way to transport vampires; for Leah. Shawn and Steph are the only other yeses right now."

"Sure, no problem. I already thought of that. But, can I talk to you alone now?" She asks fluidly.

It doesn't seem like it's important and we have lots to do, so I blow her off in a bid to get everything done. "Later?"

"Okay, but it's kind of imperative. We need to talk."

"Yes, and we'll talk about it later. I've got a bunch of things to do." I leave her to go down the stairs.

How could Stephanie do that to Brad? I know Brad's been an ass, and I would have dumped him a long time ago, but she should at least break up with him before hooking up with his ex-best friend.

I shake my head to get rid of that train of thought.

I'll go next door next. Jamie should be home, or I can leave a message with his parents. Maybe, he might come with us.

There is noise in the living room. Something drops on the ground, and I hear a hushed 'dammit.' I pop my head in. Calli is looking through the books. One fell on the floor, and she is picking it up.

"Hey." I say.

"Hi." She turns her head and looks at me quickly before going back to selecting something to read.

"A few of us are going back to Edmonton area for a few days. Do you want to join us?" I ask her. "Jaiden's going."

"No thanks. I'm gonna stay. There's nothing there for me. Why would I leave?" Her answer stirs up a memory about her saying she travelled a lot and didn't really have a steady home.

"Right. No problem. But, if you change your mind we are packing vehicles on Main Street. We'll be leaving in about an hour. A road trip is always fun." I try to tempt her to change her answer.

"Have fun on your very dangerous road trip. Hope whatever it is is worth it." Calli returns to looking through the books she's read a hundred times this winter. I make my exit while pondering what she said.

Jamie's easy enough to find the moment I leave Bruce's house through the back. Jamie is easily visible through the fence. He is taking axe to wood.

I round the fence. Leaning against the garage, right next to the wood pile I watch as he swings the axe straight through the tree trunk.

Greedily soaking up the view, I settle to just watch him until he notices or it starts to get creepy.

I tug on my jacket to sweep some air underneath as I warm up.

Jamie sets one half of the trunk on the stump to cut again. Strong muscles work to pull the axe above his head. They ripple as he swings down to cut the wood in half once more.

After a few moments, I decide any longer and it'll start being creepy. "I swear you didn't wear a shirt on purpose."

He turns around and smiles in chagrin. "Well, you always seem to show up at the right time to notice."

Looking around for any spectators, I go up to him and kiss him sweetly on the lips; only once I am sure no one is around.

He whispers against my lips, "My parents aren't home."

I pull away so I can see his eyes. Though tempted to take up the offer, I have to decline. "Unfortunately, I have a lot of things to do.

Though, I'd love to take you up on that offer." I realize my voice sounds off. I clear my throat to clear the heaviness. Sweat drips down the curve of his face and lands on his chest. "I came here to talk to you. I'm leaving for a few days. Did you want to come with me to visit my grandparents' farm?"

"Mom and dad would kill me if I left. Besides, you need me watching those two more now than ever." Jamie looks around to ensure no one is around to listen.

He's talking about Brad and Uncle Bruce. Allowing those two together has been a horrible idea. They feed and boost each other's hatred for supernaturals.

 I frown. "Is something happening?"

"Not yet, but they've started calling secret meetings amongst the most loyal allies. You know that can only mean bad news."

It'll be bad news for everyone if they're allowed to continue this. It's like Tyler and the mall all over again. The next thing I know they'll be attacking in the middle of the night and try to kill all of the supernaturals; which they would include me as one. "Looks like I need to talk-"

Jamie interrupts me. "Not yet. Wait until the meeting has happened. I was invited to this next one. I'll tell you all about it, and then you can go screaming at them." I give him a pass on the insult. He makes it sound like that's what I always do.

"Is it safe for you to go?" I ask.

"Dad invited me, so maybe." Jamie's words don't incite any confidence in me. His dad wouldn't let him go if it was too dangerous for him; right?

I pull him in closer and squeeze him a bit with my hug. "Okay, try to be safe. I should only be a few days; at most."

"Don't worry about me. There's more danger out there than there is from those two crank pots." He leans down and softly caresses my lips with his. "Be careful. I'll see you when you get back."

"Bye." I peck his lips and say my good byes.

Back on my way again, I know where Brad should be; about as far away down the block as he could be. He got his own house to hang out in and be, as he put it, 'as far away from the demons and their invasive hearing' as he could get.

I knock on the door of the last house on the block.

Lucas peaks through blinds before shutting them closed. What is he doing here? He's not supposed to be here. I have to tell Jaiden her friend might be a closet demon hater.

They make me wait. Impatiently, I knock again to get attention. They wouldn't just ignore me; would they?

At my last in a trio of knocks, the door finally budges. "What do you want?" Brad glares with all the hatred his face can express. None of the friendship we shared twinkles in his eyes.

I meet him with a smile and speak cheerfully. "Hi, how are you? I'm well, thanks for asking. I was coming to see if you wanted to take a road trip home."

"Why the Hell would I go anywhere with you?" He snarls.

"Because it's a chance to go home, and see if friends and family are alive." I defend abrasively.

"If I wanted to do that I'd choose better company." Brad moves to shut me out of the doorway.

"What the Hell is your problem? We've been friends since we were kids." Picking a fight with him works to keep the door open, and it helps me feel better to get my say in.

"One of us was the friend; the others lied about what they were." His point has no bearing, but he doesn't know that.

"It doesn't change who I am." Because I'm not actually a prophet, but the principal of the situation is worth defending.

Shawn is still Shawn, even though he had lied about being a human when he was actually an elf. He didn't even change in looks. His slightly pointed ear birth defect just became a regular trait of his kind.

"I don't know who you are anymore, but I do know you're a monster." He fully believes in what he is saying. Brad is too far gone to turn back.

There is nothing redeemable in what we once had. I don't recognize the person before me. "I can say the same about you."

"Get the fuck out of here! I never want to see you again." Brad slams the door in my face. Had I been two inches closer, the door would have hit me.

I'm glad Steph and Shawn are cheating on him; though I'd hardly call it cheating now. Their relationship is over, and I'd be willing to bet he knows it too.

It frustrates me to tears over the man he's become. What would his parents think of him now? I doubt they would be proud.

Work. I have work to do.

Air fills my lungs and I rush it out. Wiping away the stray tears from under my eyes, I get back on my way; back to Main Street.

Leah, Stephanie, and Shawn are the only extra passengers. That means we could get away with four people in two vehicles.

Jaiden has lined up three vehicles side by side; two SUVs and one car. Daniel's back is facing me as he talks to someone inside the back of one SUV. Steph and Shawn are tying a rope to the top of the second SUV. If the first SUV is any indication, they will be putting gas cans on the roof.

I walk up to Jaiden as she rustles around some items in the trunk of the car. She's talking to herself; mumbling a shopping list of items she's collected.

"Who's going where?" I ask to get her attention.

"Alexa, Daniel, and Rayleen are in that one." Jaiden points to the first SUV. "You, me, Leah, Stephanie, and Shawn are in that one." Next, the second SUV. "I covered most of the windows in blackout blinds. Leah should be safe in the back seat." Then, she pats the trunk lid. "This one is empty so far."

"You stuffed everyone into the two SUVs?"

"I worked with the people you were sending back to me, besides I figured if Brad and Lucas came they'd want breathing room in the third one." So, she knows about Lucas.

"Fair enough."

"Who else is coming?" She asks.

"No one else."

"Oh, ah, then we have room to move around some people." She sounds more like she's talking to herself, than to me.

"Put Shawn and Steph in the car. Then, we'd be ready to go?" For some reason I'm very anxious to get going. Excitement and terror to find my family all bundled into one.

"Pretty much. If we leave soon and don't stop much, then we should get to the farm Alexa wants to go to around supper."

Wait. "I thought we'd split. They go to the farm, and we head off to Spruce then grandma's farm."

"We figured we should use that farm as home base. A safe spot to meet up, maybe sleep, before heading out or back. We could be able to fill up on supplies there too." Jaiden, with or without the help of the other passengers, has made a bit of a plan change.

I do a quick take; the pit stop shouldn't add too much time to the trip, and it might be better if we split up to have a meeting spot. We can make this work.

"Great, I'm going to get Leah. Park in front of her house when you're done and we'll come out." I start walking away.

"Can we have that talk now?" Her words turn me around, but I walk backwards away from her.

I don't have time for whatever lesson plan or concern she wants to teach me today. So unless she had a vision… "Is anyone in immediate danger if we don't have this conversation?"

"No."

"Then it can wait." I tell her.

"But-"

"We need to leave as soon as possible or we won't make it by night fall. We'll talk later. I promise." I turn around and then practically run back to Leah's place. Jaiden's added extra time onto this trip and I wanted to at least be at my house before nightfall.

I walk right into the house. Leah isn't in the living room, with all the others watching another movie, so I walk down the hall to her bedroom.

She's leaning over her bed unpacking her bag; a mess of her

possessions cover the bed and her floor.

"What are you doing?" I ask.

"Everyone's given me the last of their sunblock so I can try to find more. It's for just in case I have to go out during the day. But, now I have like ten bottles that I have to somehow fit into this back pack." Leah sounds stressed and anxious.

The mostly empty bottles are on the bed. They vary in sizes, but would take up her entire bag. Could she mix them all into one, or would that be disastrous? There are a few different brands.

"They have to have some sort of plastic bag or other bag around here that you can throw those into without having to sacrifice your clothes and make up." I suggest.

"Nothing."

"Did you look?" I voice the obvious question.

"No."

"I'll go look. You put your clothes back in your bag." Leaving her to huff about her bag contents, I venture to the kitchen.

I'm looking for grocery bags, or garbage bags; any bag really. I search the most likely places they would have stored bags.

The pantry doesn't have any.

Under the sink I find garbage bags. They will work well enough.

I go back to Leah and help her pack up the sunscreen bottles. A few I pick up don't feel like they have anything inside them.

Leah still seems a little irritated, but she's calmed down enough that I don't think it'll be a problem. I bite my tongue not to ask about the blood situation; it's a taboo subject.

"Jaiden's here!" A female voice yells from down the hallway.

Leah tosses her bag over her shoulder and takes up the garbage bag in the other hand.

I pull up the light blanket off the bed and hold it out to her. "Blanket?"

"I said no blankets." She growls out.

"It's just until you get to the SUV. Jaiden blacked out the windows." I explain.

Leah glares as I throw the blanket over her head. I leave her face in the open. She has trouble grabbing the edges with her hands full. Taking the garbage bag from her helps, and she is able to balance the other bag on her shoulder.

We walk to the door to greet Jaiden.

Leah pulls the hood further so her face will be better shaded. We walk out the door as she runs fast to the SUV. She jumps over the gate, but her blanket gets caught and pulls off. Leaving it behind, she runs the five feet to the vehicle.

The door is open for her. She leaps inside, and Shawn closes the door behind her. He goes up to the car and gets in.

She didn't burst into flame. The SUV isn't on fire. No alarming shouts are coming from inside, so I think Leah's going to be okay.

"Can I drive?" I ask Jaiden. I can control the speed and buy back some of the time. Something tells me Jaiden would be that person who obeys a speed limit even in the apocalypse and with no police to catch her.

"Sure. Keys are in the ignition." She walks to the front passenger side.

I settle into the driver's seat. Looking back I check on the people inside.

Leah is shrouded in slight darkness, but there is enough of a light through the front window that I can see a hint of red to parts of her face. She got a little burnt in the sun, maybe even through the blanket. The blanket was a little light, and enough sunlight might have been able to get in through the tiny holes. I should have looked for a thicker blanket.

"Hey. We've got Leah. Are you ready to go?" Jaiden says loudly next to me. Who is she talking to?

When I look directly at her I find her talking into a walkie talkie.

Static comes over the other end. "Yeah. We're good. Let's go."

The car in front of us starts and pulls out from the curb. I turn on the

SUV and follow after the red vehicle. They have until we get out of town to start speeding, or I'm going to take the lead.

Chapter 4

I glance out the window to the trees and fields speeding by. Bits of snow here and there are still melting.

Snow remains where the wind had pushed it into larger piles. The same effect happened before the revolution, however was highly more likely to be sprinkled with the piles left behind by people shoveling their sidewalks.

Cows graze in an expansive field. How did they survive the winter? A large tin shed on the property may be part of the answer.

Of course, their owners could still be alive to take care of them.

Keeping cows could be an excellent way to survive. Theoretically, the animals can largely take care of themselves.

If you help them survive the winter, avoid disease, and keep away carnivorous predators then you have milk from the mothers and meat from the others.

It would do exceptionally well in the winter when the plants die.

I'll just continue to take my chances with hunting.

I've always hated milk, slightly lactose intolerant, and I wouldn't have any idea about what to do if one of the animals got sick.

Quarantine, kill it, and burn the body; I suppose would make the most sense to me. However, I am sure a farmer might know enough to be able to keep it alive. Maybe it would be fine to eat still.

It all speeds by so fast. I swear she's sped up some more. Looking over at the dashboard gauges I watch the speed.

The speedometer waves between one hundred fifty and one hundred sixty kilometers an hour. Dominique's speeding unnecessarily fast, but at least she's been hovering around the same spot for the last while.

Stories about Dominique going from Red Deer to Spruce Grove in half the time it would normally take someone going the speed limit, and putting her foot up on the dash while she's driving had been joked around by her family. They joked about the reckless behaviour, even boasted about it, with only a slight reprimanding from her mom.

I had taken it as a joke with only a kernel of truth. Maybe one time she made a joke about putting her foot on the dash while driving. Maybe she speeds ten over the speed limit regularly on the long highway.

Not that she would speed forty to fifty over the limit. I haven't seen her foot on the dash yet, but it makes me wonder how much of that part of the joke was the truth.

I wonder if she sped like this normally, or if it's because there aren't any laws now?

If I had pulled any of that sort of thing, I would have been harshly punished. There would have been a large lecture about car safety, responsibility, and acting like a fool.

There would have been a presidential grade cover up should anyone have seen me; more than once a doppelgänger had been hired to excuse my failures.

Everything my father had ever given me would have been taken away permanently.

If I had paid for the car myself, it would have mysteriously disappeared one morning, and he would have a tailored excuse, such as he accidentally drove into it so he graciously took it to the repair shop for me.

Only after I nicely ask him for six months on the status of the repair, and done something to make up for it a hundred times over, would I get my car back.

But, he's gone now, and I'll never have to see him again. The thought curves a small smile. I'm happy he's completely gone from my life.

Does that make me a horrible person?

I rid my head of the thoughts because there is no use in dwelling now. All of that is over and gone. There are better and more immediate things to be worrying about.

To think, rather, on what is to come is better worth my time.

Visions have come to me in numbers like never before. Many a nightmare has plagued me; many a hum drum dream bored me, many an insightful scene played out in my head. Some, have been obvious just dreams, while others I hope were just nightmares.

Visions can be hard to distinguish. A dream can seem just as real, sometimes, as a vision.

While I can handle what I have seen, I however cannot handle what I have not.

Many unanswered questions churn my anxiety into overdrive.

For a proposed trip expanding from Banff, to a farm near Leduc, to Spruce Grove, to grandma's farm, then back to Banff; I don't remember any dreams which could be helpful.

The generalized road trip of it all is out, as no visions of travelling in vehicles have been had. We may be attacked, and lose the SUV, or we might have a perfectly boring trip. Neither of which I have seen the exact moment of.

I don't know what the one farm looks like, so I don't know if one of the houses I've had visions about is that one. I'll be able to recognize décor, and possibly exterior, but not until we have arrived; if we do arrive.

There's that one house we were at that someone shoots at us. The house with the twins is definitely one to avoid. That burning house we escape from.

I haven't seen anything about going to grandma's farm, haven't seen John and the werewolves, nor their houses.

No mountains. We probably don't get back to Banff. Or we do and we don't stay long.

Then, there is the matter on the 'we' portion.

Some visions contain people I recognize, some contain people I've never seen in my life, and some contain any variations on a mixture of the two.

I was alone in that field one this morning. I was making my way to familiar people. Perhaps right before that is the events when I see those strangers.

Dominique has appeared in many of my visions, so I know she is a part of my future.

I can't say the same about the rest of our present company, or those in the other vehicle.

Sorting by people, I've had a couple visions of Alexa and Rayleen. One vision included Leah.

None between the rest of them; Shawn, Stephanie, or Daniel.

Come to think about it, most of those we left behind in Banff have never made an appearance in a vision outside those I've already had come true.

But I have seen a few of them, familiar faces in our expanded circle of friends, so I know we make it back to Banff and therefore them. Which brings me back to the lack of mountains in my visions, so then we won't stay there long but we will get back there.

I want to scream. It's all very cryptic and confusing when there is no timeline, and I get only seconds to minutes to work with.

The last vision I changed, was the Dominique shooting humans one back at the hotel. I changed quite a bit around that same time period. There's been no need to change anything after that.

All visions before that point have a less likelihood to happen. I changed the course of events, which may or may not have changed what was originally going to happen.

All visions I've had since my last change are one hundred percent going to happen. Unless, I interfere one way or another.

Although, there is always the chance that a dream was just a dream, or that I've changed something subconsciously.

"Jaiden?" Dominique pauses for a moment. "Did you want to go anywhere specific?"

The mention of my name brings me back from inside my head. "No thanks."

"No? No family? No friends? You don't want to go home?" She continues pressing on.

"No, I'm good." I just want to get back to my thought processing.

"There has to be someone you'd want to go find; something you want to grab? We can go check your old house." Dominique insists.

"Nikki, her family's dead." Leah interjects. My mind screams at her to stop helping.

"Oh, I'm so sorry. You didn't say anything about anyone dying." Dominique's concern draws up remorse in my heart. "I'd a thought you would have partied with your dad dead; God awful man. Sorry, if that offends you."

"It's fine. And, he didn't die; not that I know of. Haven't seen him since before everything happened." I smile, and turn my head to look away before she can notice any guilt.

"He wasn't one of the people who died at your grandma's farm?" My lungs drop into my stomach, and I cannot breathe as soon as Leah gets out the words. I forgot I told them that back at Fort Macleod.

Exactly five seconds pass as my heart palpitates in my ears.

My hands throw themselves out for bracing the moment my body feels the intense thrust of a speeding car stopping as fast as is allowed. Feet push against the floor in an attempt to keep me against the back of my seat.

She's going to kill us because of me.

The SUV stops. I chance opening my eyes. The SUV is indeed stopped on the road. She managed not to swerve us.

"Jaiden?" I can't bear to look at her, but I know she's pieced the truth together. This wasn't how I wanted to do this.

"I tried to tell you a bunch of times." I stop my line of thought. That's not what she needs to hear right now. "I'm sorry; I didn't tell you the truth."

The words barely leave my mouth when her fist knocks into the left side of my face. My glasses fly off from the impact of the fist to my face right before my head bounces off the window. I steal a glance at her blurred face.

Both sides of my head are pounding in pain.

"Jaiden, tell me what happened." Dominique searches for the answer in my eyes. I didn't want to do this this way. "I want the truth!"

My mouth opens trying to spill the secret. Nothing comes out. I gape. Breathe in. Short breath out. "I told you I went to your grandma's farm about a week after the revolution started. There were people there; bad people. They said no one was there when they took over the farm.

They were lying.

After the battle, I was running back to the getaway van when I came upon a pile of bodies. They were your family. They had all been shot. They would have died quickly. A lot of head shots; minimal pain."

"Who did you see? Who was there?" Her voice is dangerously quiet compare to her shouts for the truth.

"I couldn't see most of their faces. I was running for my life. I can't guarantee everyone was there; who was there." I try to soften it for her. Make an excuse and reason for not telling her who was there. I don't want to hurt her any more than I already have.

"Jaiden! Who did you see?" I chance a look at her. Even through the slight blur, I can see the glistening tracks from already wept tears.

"Your grandparents, some aunts and uncles." I hesitate. Her face cannot portray any further heartbreak she's feeling. Somehow, I believe I will be proven wrong as I reveal two others. "Your mom and dad. I think I saw most of the family there."

A sharp sting knocks at my cheek as the resounding clap echoes in my right ear. She grabs the front of my shirt and winds up for another slap. I close my eyes.

"Nikki stop!" Leah yells out.

Another hit stings my cheek. My neck wrenches uncomfortably, and then snaps back. Despite the pain, I hold down my arms rather than defend myself. I deserve anything she's going to inflict unto me. I don't blame her for this.

Punches and slaps and the physical pain I feel, are nothing compared to how much I've just hurt her. I owe her this much.

"Nikki! That's enough!" Leah's voice shouts out threateningly. Fabric and pounding come closer. Skin on skin slap is heard, but nothing connects with my face. I dare to look. Leah's arm holds Dominique's inches from connecting with my face again. "Get out and cool down!"

Dominique pulls her arm away from Leah, and turns off the SUV. She escapes out of the vehicle quickly, with Shawn and Stephanie following after her. Both the other vehicles are stopped a ways up the road.

Leah quickly returns to her safe spot.

She hates me. It's probably better that way; safer that way.

"That was cold." Leah announces blatantly as she examines damage to her arm. Burnt flesh fills my nose.

"I know." I feel like I owe her an explanation in exchange for her stepping in on my deserved slapping. "I honestly forgot that I didn't tell her until today when she mentioned that she wanted to leave to find them.

I tried to talk to her but she said she was too busy to talk with me alone; a few times. Then there was no time, and I thought we would have time once we got to the farm and were getting ready for people to break off.

Or, after.

I don't know."

"Thought it was your family that died. So, was it your family? And, if your family is her family, what does that make you?" Leah pries.

"Nothing. I had crappy parents, and a mystery dad. One of the many possible men was Dominique's step dad. I met them last summer, and her whole family was really nice to me, and about the situation. Adopted me as family regardless of whether I actually am or not. Didn't get around to getting a paternity test done."

There is a thick long pause. She knows. I can feel her putting together the pieces. "Can you open a window?" Leah practically chokes the words out, as if the very air itself is stifling her.

"Are you okay?" I say as I reach over to the ignition and turn the key a little. I roll down my window.

My glasses had to of fallen down to my feet. Bending over, I pat around on the floor until I find them; part of them. A lens broke out of it holding place. The plastic string bit broke on impact. I hope the lens itself isn't broken.

"Yes." Her answer is practiced and quick. She means no.

I put the glasses on my head. "You sound like you aren't. Are you sure nothing's wrong?" Am I bleeding? I bend down again. This time I can see with my right eye, and spot the unbroken lens.

"If you have to know, I'm a hungry, injured, adrenaline pumping vampire travelling in a vehicle full of my food source." The words are ripe with frustration.

"When was the last time you had anything?" I ask.

Leah thinks as she points up finger. At three she shakes her head, then answers. "Few days ago."

"But, vampires are supposed to drink around eight ounces of human blood every day, or it could get dangerous, but I don't need to lecture you on that. I'm sure you know, probably better than I do. Why haven't you been drinking? Did you run out of supplements? Why hasn't anyone said anything?"

"Are you volunteering? Because, there was a great lack of volunteers in Banff. Supplements are being greatly rationed. Part of why I'm here." She's moody, grouchy from the lack of nutrition.

Without it the virus attacks the host's body. It will make it like she's sick and starving. One description compared the sensation to that of going through withdrawals from drugs. At some point an insane hunger starts, and will take over any rational thought of the being so as to alleviate the thirst. They call it a rage. Too little or too much blood intake is bad for a vampire.

Too little blood being a greater problem quicker than too much blood. Like how starving to the point of death occurs faster than gluttonous eating to the point your heart gives out or the mountain of problems obesity brings.

"Yeah, if you need blood. Of course, you can have some." I remove my glasses because it's disorientating to see perfectly with one eye and have blurred vision in the other. The cup holder is a safe enough holder for now. There should be super glue in the first aid kit. It'll take a long time to dry. "Do you mind if I fix my glasses first?"

"By all means."

I pop the trunk then leave the vehicle. When I grab the big red bag, I pull it to the front seat. The first aid kit has the little tubes inside a plastic container. The scissors from a side pouch help me open the mouth of one tube.

This procedure is simple. I've done this a few times in the past with other glasses; they never last long. I line the glue thinly all around the outer edge of the lens. Inserting the lens properly in the space and placing the plastic string in place; where it should be.

I hold it there for a couple moments, until the glue holds by itself. Carefully placing it down on the dash, I'm satisfied when the lens doesn't shift or fall out. I put the glasses back on my face.

My fingers stick with the excess glue I unavoidably got on them. Holding my fingers out, I blow until they are dry.

The smell is bothering my nose. I can only imagine what it is doing to Leah's superior smelling. Though it may have an upside by helping to curb her cravings.

Once everything is away and back in the trunk, I climb into the back seat with Leah.

Her arm is red, charred, and blistered. She hadn't said anything. My blood will help with her healing too.

Awkwardly I offer up my arm. It's the best option given the situation. She doesn't want to kill me, but she'd want to have a good flow of blood.

Leah grasps my hand and forearm. Bringing her teeth to my arm, I can see her nostrils flare. She smells out the vein for proper positioning. It's nice to know she's taking care to do this properly so she doesn't damage anything.

Teeth bear. Canines grow from their retracted state. Something not as drastic as in the movies, and barely noticeable if I hadn't been looking for it.

They sink into my arm with only a feeling like that of a needle digging too deep. As the teeth move, it creates a sharp pain around the tip of her teeth, while the parts around the tooth have an odd sensation from never having been touched before while not hurting. Her other teeth dig in, not deep enough to cut, but scrap. It feels like a notable skin tear akin to a paper cut.

The back and forth, and in and out movements of her teeth aggravate the wound to keep it bleeding. Movements which also cause my fingers to twitch.

It pinches but doesn't feel too bad after the initial entry; apart from the constant grinding. I dig my other hand's nails into my palm to distract from the feeling.

I lean back and relax. This is going to take a little while, but not too long. Fifteen minutes to drain a body of all the blood through the carotid artery. A human tends to faint after a third of their body is drained at approximately five minutes.

This is in direct dispute to the movies which tend to portray that a vampire drains a body in a matter of seconds. Furthermore, that a person passes out almost immediately after they start feeding.

It would take a vampire ripping through the throat with intentions of killing the human, for those things to happen faster; or, maybe biting a fainter. Ripping a throat would be a waste of the blood they would supposedly want to be drinking.

I don't know how comparable it would all be for an arm feeding, but five minutes or until I feel light headed is probably a good stopping point.

Since she hasn't fed in a few days, and I'd be willing to bet she hasn't fed properly in the last month, she's going to be like a dehydrated human. Leah will greedily drink up the blood, and be hard pressed to stop until she's satisfied.

Human blood kicks the virus into overdrive and allows for faster healing; especially at first or while consuming. Something small like a first degree sunburn will easily heal in half a day for an average vampire, for what would take a day for a human.

Thinking in terms of the double/half explanation I had read on the one website, their normal healing rate would be double of what it was before they were turned; taking half the time to heal. The virus accelerates with excessive blood consumption. This gives everything an extra boost when feeding or excessive feeding.

Grimacing at the increasing pain.

When I figure about five minutes have passed, I say, "Leah, are you almost done?" No answer. She continues like she didn't hear me. "Leah, have you had enough?" Not one move out of place. My head feels like cotton. "Leah, it you don't stop I'm going to pass out from blood loss."

The words finally register, and she pulls away. She grips the two bit marks with a cloth piece to put pressure on them. "O negative; my favourite." She tries to joke. "Thank you."

"No problem. Do you feel better?" She appears better to me. Her eyes have darkened a little. Skin has regained its natural shade and a plumpness I didn't realize had been missing. She doesn't look sickly anymore.

"Yes. You'll need to keep pressure on this for a little bit." We transfer holding the bite marks over to me.

I hear a car pulling up beside us. It's the SUV Daniel was driving in. Leaving our SUV, I jump out. My head feels light from my blood donation, but I think I'll be fine as long as I can get some sugar and fluids in me soon.

Daniel rolls down his window. "What happened? Is everyone okay?" He sounds a bit panicked.

"Yes and no. Long story short, I upset Dominique, so we're having a pit stop until she decides to come back." I link the two sentences together quickly so I don't worry him more, and he doesn't have a chance to interrupt before I finish telling him what happened.

Daniel immediately looks relieved. "Good job. Is that what happened to your face?" He points up to my head. I haven't dared look yet.

"Yeah." I clear my throat. "Did you guys want to go ahead, and we'll catch up? Meet you at the farm, and make sure everything's okay."

"Nah, we'll stick with you guys. As long as you stop driving like maniacs and leave us behind again." He presses. "Rayleen's getting antsy back there, so we'll jump out for a bit and let her run around." This starts movement inside the SUV like a gun going off to announce the start of a race. Both doors fling open on the opposite side of the vehicle, and two girls emerge.

"Great, I'm going to grab water." I pop the trunk with the key still hanging in the ignition.

My arm still bleeds a little and requires a bandage to be wrapped around it. Wiping the excess blood away with an alcohol swab while also taking care not to aggravate the wound further, I then place gauze and tape it to me. It looks awful. I know it's going to scar.

I dive into our food and water stash. Downing a water bottle worth of water, and snatching a bag of cookies immediately helps me feel better.

Out of the corner of my eye I see Daniel. I give him my attention. "So, I want to hear what you did to Nikki. It has to be a good story if she punched you."

Well isn't he nosy. Air fills my lungs and I let it out in a huff. "Okay, so remember how I told everyone that I went to my grandparents' farm, and found a bunch of thugs there who turned out to have killed everyone. Well, that wasn't my family, it was Dominique's family. So her parents, aunts, uncles, cousins, grandparents are all dead. But, when we found Dominique I had initially lied to her and told her that I didn't see anyone there, because of everything that was going on at the time, and she was recently rescued. I thought I was protecting her by lying to her.

So then today she wanted to make this big trip to find her family and I tried talking to her alone a few times to tell her what really happened. But we never got the chance, and then I gave up and figured we'd just go there and she would either discover the bodies and I could say I didn't see them, or she wouldn't and she could still hope that they were out there.

But none of that happened, Leah had told the lie I told everyone else. Dominique put it together. My lies collided and exploded."

He mulls over the information in his head. "Ouch, dick move Miss Perfect."

"I know." There isn't anything else to say. I know that I didn't do the right thing by Dominique, and I'd take it back if I could.

"You deserved to get punched in the face." His statement rings true. I don't blame Dominique for punching me, because I did deserve it. "You should have told her months ago."

I point up at one of the bruises I know is forming on my left cheek. "I know."

"I get why you would lie initially. She's never going to forgive you until she figures out that you were doing it to protect her. Give her some time. She'll come around once the shock has worn off." Daniel's words are surprisingly comforting.

"Thanks." I utter.

He walks away and goes up to Alexa for a behind the back hug. It's awkward to stand here and watch them cuddle, so I go back inside the back of the SUV to give Leah some company.

"How are you feeling?" She asks me to start a conversation in place of the silence. She might not like uncomfortable silences.

"Better, want a cookie?" I open up the small bag of mini cookies and hold the bag for her. She takes a couple out, then shoves to bag and my hand back towards me.

"You should eat the rest, and you can have my cookie ration too." Leah offers. The sugar in the cookies would help with the blood loss, and she must know that. She's very compassionate under the confident and tough exterior.

"No, it's okay. Thanks though." Her offer isn't necessary, not that we had specific rations like that anyway.

"I'm not asking. I took too much blood. I saw you waiver when you left. You need to sit, you need rest, and you need to eat your cookies. Doctor's orders."

"Oh yeah? Are you a doctor?" I ask. Leah hasn't really spoken about her past beyond a childhood in a small country village located in China, and getting captured by the military to be imprisoned at that school; a wide amount of years missing in-between those points.

It's always possible that she's been a doctor, or equivalent, in a past profession. I've gotten the impression that she's at least fifty years old in years passed.

"I actually come from a long line of herbalists on my father's side. Just don't trust me to do surgery on you." She reveals.

"Good to know." I answer with a small jesting tone. "And cookies count as medicine?"

"Sometimes." Leah says brazenly.

"Sounds good enough to me." We both smile wickedly.

Chapter 5

"I think it's this one." I speak up as Daniel drives by the first driveway split in the trees. The thick trees hide away the buildings behind them, despite the general lack of leaves.

This all looks a bit familiar, yet nothing looks the same.

"No, I think it's the second farm in. Third farm in was," he pauses before continuing, "the other one." He avoids speaking about the other farm in detail. He may think it's for the best with Rayleen in the vehicle.

Although, I don't think that she'd have much for nightmares about the farm; unlike me. She had mostly happy times at that farm. She might have more of a problem with the farm we're going to now, seeing as it's the one she was taken from.

When I see the next driveway, I can't help but think that maybe he was right about the order. It looks familiar.

Daniel turns and drives down the rocky road. The white house appears softly at first as glimpses between the trees. As the tree opens up the house pulls into full view. He was right.

As Daniel slowly rolls to a stop beside and behind a couple vehicles already parked, I undo my seatbelt and get ready to hop out. My hand stays on the handle; itching to pull it and exit.

"Maybe Rayleen should stay in the vehicle." Jaiden's voice deadlines in monotone.

"Why?" I ask, instantly irritated.

Our fun road trip turned sour as soon as she decided to ride with us; Daniel just had to offer. She ruined the mood. Why'd she have to go piss off Nikki?

"Isn't it odd that there's no one outside?" She asks.

Rolling my eyes. "Should it be?"

"Prime working time, even if people are having supper, there should be someone outside. Signs of life; at least. Smoke from the cooking fire. Windows open to cool the house. Some sort of life or movement. Something." Jaiden explains everything that she's noticed in half sentences; list like.

My irritation fades a bit as she talks and her words encourage me to notice these things too. There's lots of vehicles, so where are the people?

"Maybe she's right." Daniel states as he's forced to notice these details too.

"Maybe they just abandoned the farm." I offer.

"Maybe, or..." Daniel trails off. "Alexa, stay here with Rayleen. I'll go check it out."

"No, we'll go out too. We'll walk around here, and you can go check the house. Rayleen needs to stretch her legs. My butt's falling asleep." I reason. I need to get out of this SUV. I need to get to the other farm, and I won't be able to do that if we leave immediately because those people abandoned this farm months ago.

Daniel looks like he wants to say no, so I smile big and toothy to charm him. "Okay, but stay close. We might not have to be here long."

Jaiden opens the SUV door and hurries along to the front door by herself. I have to make my move fast. "Let's go for a walk." I tell Rayleen.

Hopping out, I help Rayleen leave the SUV. Daniel and I cross paths as he makes no rush to catch up after Jaiden; who has disappeared inside the darkened space where the door was.

Ushering Rayleen into the woods I ask, "Want to find Crystal?"

She answers with exuberance. "Yes!"

I feel a twinge of guilt tricking her, but it's as good of an excuse as any. Crystal would have gone with the people, but she doesn't know that.

We follow the same path I took to get there that horrible night. Winding through the trees, stepping over overgrowth, and avoiding any plant that looks like it has spikes; takes time. I pick Rayleen up to help her avoid thorn bushes, only to put her down when the trees break.

No farm house remains. An ashen pit in the ground surrounded by concrete is all that remains. I waiver between getting close enough to see if there is a present left in the pit, and keeping Rayleen far enough away that she wouldn't be in danger or see what Darius left me.

Ash that had been wet and dried together, then heated and cracked in the sun sits at the bottom. Barely a scrap of wood remains, a feat with a log house I'd imagine. Odd puddles of dried molten metal catch the sun light. But there is nothing in there resembling a present; though I really doubt that he left me a pretty purple gift wrapped box with a bow on the top.

If it's not in the house, maybe he left it at the toy shed. "Let's go this way." I take Rayleen by the hand and lead her to the far shed near the driveway entry.

Rayleen picks up a couple rocks along the way. When we arrive, I tell her, "Stay right here. I'm going inside to look around, but it's a little dangerous in there so you need to stay out here."

"But, why-" Last time I was in here Darius was torturing Miles. Who knows who else may have faced his wrath after that, and what might have been left behind?

I interrupt her. "Because I said so. It's dangerous in there. How about you try to find the prettiest rock you can to show me when I get out?"

"Okay." I pat her head.

The large metal man door takes a lot of effort to pull open. The inside is completely dark. Any windows there was are sealed up so the light doesn't enter.

A coffee canister size cylinder of concrete tucked around the inside wall beside the door is the right size and weight to keep the door from closing. The house's owners likely made this, or repurposed it for the exact purpose I use it for.

With light from the empty door way shining in and lighting up a rectangular area, I follow the path of light with my eyes first. Dirt bikes and other farm machines line the edge walls. Down at the end is a work bench. A wooden ladder leads up to a dark space above. Wood rafters have boxes laid across them as storage.

Everything thing I do to advert my eyes from the spot I cut Miles doesn't stop the shame I feel.

My eyes flit briefly by in a scan across the room. I don't see anything resembling a present. This search is becoming a pain. I wish he'd just told me where to look. Telling me what I'm looking for would have been too easy apparently.

Next location to cross off the list is the griffin barn; it's the last place on the list where I'd assume he'd put the present. It checks off of the list of places I visited while I was here.

Turning around, I leave the building; not bothering to close the door behind me.

"Let's go to the griffin barn. Maybe Crystal went back to see her mom." I suggest.

"Let's go. Let's go. Let's go!" Rayleen cheers in a chant. She releases the hem of her shirt, and all the rocks she collected fall to the ground; now forgotten in her excitement. The little girl takes off in her eagerness.

I jog to catch up, but let her stay a reasonable distance away.

Garden land is ready to be tilled. The mostly black dirt is easily distinguishable enclosed in grass. Rare tufts of grass have leached inside the rectangle as the start of an eventual reclaiming of the space.

We cross the road dividing the house from the yard. Grass is already overgrown here; thick and folding over by its own weight.

Rayleen stops at the top of the hill. When she goes no further, I think something may be wrong.

Picking up my speed I find out why she's stopped when I reach her. The barn doors have been blown off the hinges. Something, most likely a griffin, had burst out of the barn in a fury.

"Stay here." I touch her arm and pass her by.

Descending the hill to the base, I can see most of the barn; enough to know there shouldn't be anything hiding inside. At least I know I won't be eaten alive by a hungry griffin.

Other holes, small holes, pepper the walls. The griffins must've tried really hard to escape. Hinges on all but one, bent in half hanging on the wall and door, are busted off the wall. Stress from the pounding crackle in the wood panels.

I doubt the structure is safe, so I opt to stay outside and peer inside. There is nothing in here but the remains of the hay nests, and stalls.

No present here. I huff. This is frustrating.

Returning to Rayleen, I finally break it to her, "she's not here. We should go back."

"But, what about Crystal?" Her smile drops and tears well in her eyes. "I want Crystal."

I know nothing I say will make her feel better. The most I can do is soften the blow. "Sweetie, we've looked for her, and she's not here. Crystal probably took off with her mom. There's no way to find her. But she'll be happy with her family. I know it's going to hurt not being able to have her with you, but there's nothing we can do if she isn't here."

The emotions are too much for the little girl to take. Her first sobs fill the empty air. My heart breaks for her. Another loss for her is more devastating than that for another person.

Picking Rayleen up, she clings to me. Her arms wrap around my neck and her legs around waist. There is nothing that could pry her away.

The hard trek down the hill starts a very long trek back through the trees to the other farm house.

Trepidation builds the whole journey back. It makes a pit in my stomach that I won't be able to rid myself of for a while. I didn't find the present from Darius, and he'll be pissed.

Unless, this was pay back and he sent me on a wild goose chase.

Rayleen finally peels herself off me as we near the exit. Through the tree gaps some of our travel companions are pacing near the vehicles.

Something's wrong.

Nikki gains Daniel's attention as soon as she spots us emerge from the forest. His head whips around to see me, and then he runs up to hug me. He pushes away to hold me at arm's length "Where the Hell did you go?"

"We thought we'd check the forest for Crystal." I say quietly. "What happened?"

"Rayleen go to the tree house. You'll see Jaiden down there. She has Crystal." Daniel informs her. Rayleen takes off like a rocket in her excitement. Daniel waits until she's out of earshot to inform me. "They're all dead. Maybe a day or two."

"What? That's awful." My thoughts immediately turn to Darius. Did he have something to do with this? "How?"

He answers with a shrug.

Rayleen bounds up the slight incline up from the tree house area. Crystal uncomfortably held in her arms looks like a soaked rat; an extremely large rat. Just a few months ago she was the size of a cat, now Rayleen can barely hold onto her at the size of a medium dog.

Jaiden follows after, soaked. "You know you were supposed to wash the griffin not yourself?" Daniel teases her.

Jaiden's glare slaps Daniel in the face. "She didn't want to cooperate." Her face loses the glare as she gazes across to everyone else. "We should gather some supplies before we leave."

"No, we're not going in there and stealing supplies from the dead!" The look of death Nikki gives Jaiden is one of pure hatred and disgust, and far outdoes the one Jaiden gave to Daniel. "We're leaving. I don't care what the rest of you are doing but we're carrying on with the original plan." I'm willing to bet the 'we' doesn't include Jaiden.

Nikki, Steph, and Shawn tidy up the couple food and water items they had brought out in their wait for me to return. The half hour or so I was gone had to of been spent mostly waiting for me to return. It wouldn't take long to discover a house full of dead people.

The three of them walk off to the car.

"And, what do you guys have planned?" Jaiden asks to us.

"We're going to our houses, and then back to Banff. Did you want to visit your house?" Daniel explains. She should have listened while we were driving. We discussed it on our way here.

"No, that's okay. I'm not going with you." Her decline is my relief and confusion.

Leah pops out of the house to my surprise. The deck roof protects her from the sun. "You're going with Leah?" I confirm.

"Yeah. We're just going to make a couple stops then head back to Banff. That way, no one has to wait around here. People can do their own thing on their own schedule. Obviously, there's no point coming back here." Jaiden explains.

It's one less thing we have to worry about. Excitement returns to my chest when I realize that means it'll just be the three of us again.

I tap Daniel on the shoulder. "Great, then we're gonna go now." Looking at Jaiden I reject her supplies gathering on many levels. "We'll pass on the morbid supplies gathering. We should get Rayleen out of here before she does anymore exploring."

"Sure." She says quickly.

"Hey Princess, are you going to help or are you going to play outside until I'm done?" Leah shouts to Jaiden.

"I'll be there in a minute." Jaiden's voice remains at the same speaking level as how she was speaking to us. Leah nods.

It's still a wonder to me that vampires can hear so well. I still forget. I would have yelled right back at Leah.

"Do you know how to hook up a trailer?" Jaiden glides easily from one to another.

We shake our heads. Daniel answers, "No."

"I guess we'll figure it out later."

I want to hurry things along, so we can get on the road. There is no longer any reason to be here. My search ended without discovering Darius' present. "I'll see you later then?"

Jaiden's confusion only trips her up for a moment. "Ok, yeah, see you later."

"Bye." Daniel says.

"Bye." I echo.

Simultaneously, all four of us walk off in our needed directions. Jaiden walks off to the house, while we walk towards the SUV.

Daniel grasps backwards, so I place my hand in his. The warmth of his hand tickles up my arm.

"I thought we'd go to your house first, and then we can go to my house. We'll stay the night there and then drive back to Banff in the morning." Daniel suggests.

"Yeah, that sounds good to me." I agree.

He guides me to the passenger side of the vehicle before he lets go of my hand with a squeeze. He kisses as a peck to my lips, a quick reminder of our love, before Daniel returns to the driver's side.

Checking on Rayleen, I make sure her seatbelt is buckled properly before closing her door.

The vehicle hums to life and mobility once I'm inside. Daniel wastes no time in driving us out of here.

Panicked squawking quickly alerts me. Rayleen squeaks in surprise, right before I hear a couple thumps. Twisting around in the seat I spot Crystal starting to knock at the window with her beak.

A small crack appears then crawls. Each strand breaking further with the consecutive pecking. I need to do something before she breaks through and breaks free. "Rayleen, pull her away from the window before she breaks it."

Rayleen scrambles to pull her away. Pulling on a lioness body that doesn't budge from the weaker girl's strength.

Pushing up, I hunch over, and steady myself.

"Do we need to stop?" Daniel asks.

"No, I've got it." I say. The vehicle lurches a little. My hands reach out so as not to fall, but it doesn't stop me from falling knee first into a seat.

Back up to a semi standing formation, I get back to where Crystal is breaking the window open.

I hug around her torso and yank hard. We fall back into the back seat. She struggles against me, so I hug harder.

"Shhh. Rayleen, help me calm her. Shhh. It's okay."

Rayleen hushes Crystal. She runs her fingers through the feathers on Crystal's head.

Like an off switch is flicked, Crystal stops struggling and her body loses tension. She roars contently and lies down on my lap. I heave a sigh of relief, and relax against the back of the seat.

Absentmindedly, I pet the lion body. She vibrates against my hand and legs. Crystal coos her contentment.

We focus on helping Crystal keep calm.

I didn't think she would react this way to being inside a moving vehicle, but I guess many animals hate car rides.

Daniel stops outside my old house. The large picture window is broken. The rest looks untouched from out here. I can't help but wonder if someone broke in or if someone broke out.

There is only one thing I want, but Rayleen may want more.

"Rayleen, stay in the car. Alexa, stay here until I come back." Daniel orders.

"I'll come with you."

"Someone needs to stay with Rayleen." Daniel reasons.

"She can come with us." I say.

"It's too dangerous." His reasoning is getting a little old movie cliché. It's dangerous no matter what I do.

"It's too dangerous to go in there alone." I throw back in his face.

"I'll be fine. You two won't be." Daniel throws his door open, and sprints to the house. The door opens and he rushes inside.

Surprised, I can do nothing more than stare for the first few moments. I won't take no for an answer. "Come on. Let's go inside. Was there anything you wanted to grab while you're here?"

"No." Rayleen answers simply.

"Okay." I say quietly.

Nothing comes to mind for me to remember for her to take. She has nothing from her parents left. No singular toy or trinket that holds any sentimental value to her. The three of us leave the SUV.

Hesitantly, we file into the house. "Daniel!" I call out, so he doesn't get frightened at someone in the house.

"I told you to stay in the car!" His muffled yell comes from somewhere down the hallway.

"Is something wrong?" The living room is trashed. Someone tore through here. Dust is settled on most of the room. The areas closer to the window are more dirty then the rest. Leaves trickled on the floor and couch.

"Not yet." He says.

Rayleen moves to take off her shoes. "Leave them on. We won't be here long. You won't get in trouble." I reassure her. She puts her shoe back on fully.

Daniel comes out from the hall. "You should go back to the car."

"I just need one thing from my room, and then we can go. You go with Rayleen to the car and I'll go grab my photos." Walking towards him I move to pass. Before he disputes it I tell him, "I'll bring a knife from the kitchen. Go." I say.

A tiny push to his shoulder in Rayleen's direction distracts him enough for me to pull the same move he did earlier. I sprint into the kitchen and down the stairs.

The dark, creepy basement is decidedly less creepy now.

There is no pounding on the stairs after me, so I think Daniel listened to me. The photo album is exactly where I left it. A wave of calm and security settles over me.

Returning upstairs, two stares await my return.

"Got it." I wave the book in front of me to draw more attention. "Let's go."

When I approach Daniel, he draws me in to kiss my forehead. I look up at him sheepishly.

"Let's go." His hand flows down to grasp mine and he leads me out the door. The sky has turned darker in the short time we've been in the house. Rayleen skips ahead of us to the SUV.

His house isn't too far. In days past, it would have been better worth to walk down the alley for a couple minutes than to drive all the way around and to the other side.

The house appears untouched from the outside. Maybe his was spared from looters. Daniel forgoes any discussion before racing to his house.

Watching the animal underfoot in a scurry to get out, I open the door and she chases after Daniel. It must be locked. He's bent over and searching under the door mat for the hidden key.

Stepping down and out of the SUV I turn around and reach out to help Rayleen. She hops out on her own and chases Crystal to the now open and empty doorway.

I close the SUV door. As the last one in the house, I close the front door behind me and lock it.

In the two point five seconds she has been inside this house, she has managed to curl herself up on the couch with Crystal at her center. Her eyes struggle to keep open.

"Okay, bedtime." Crystal growls as I adjust Rayleen into my arms. "Hush."

The left is the kitchen, and the right is a squared open room with three doors; one is open and leads to a small bathroom. I take the chance that this way leads to the bedrooms.

The first door on the left leads to a room with only a bed, a closet and a pile of boxes in the corner; must be a guest room. It's good enough. Drawing the covers back with my foot is difficult, but manageable. Putting her down, I tuck her in.

Crystal nuzzles her way under the blankets to lie against Rayleen's side while completely covered. I kiss Rayleen on the forehead. She doesn't show that she notices it; already deep in dreamland.

I back out of the room only leaving the door open a crack.

Tracking Daniel down by the shuffling and crinkle noises in the kitchen, I let him know, "Rayleen is asleep."

"House is clear. No sign of my family." He goes into the dining room and set down the chips. "Wanna play a board game?" A box stares at me ominously.

Chapter 6

The first cigarette after months of absence burned just like new, like when I first started smoking at the bar; a group activity starting with one cigarillo from the guy whose name I never knew.

Drink, dance, cigarillo, repeat.

Countless sticks later, the smooth smoke goes down easy and they work to calm my nerves. I catch a glimpse of my eyes in the mirror and regret looking. They're completely red and bloodshot.

The odd tear remaining works to clump my eye lashes together.

I look back out the window. One long breath of smoke burns the rest of the stick. Flicking the butt out the window, I contemplate starting up another immediately.

Intense itching to grab another smoke has me hesitating. I had quit. I was doing well without them. But that was before I found out…

Don't think about it.

Invisible tears burn my eyes. I've done enough crying for now. I feel all cried out. It's like my eyes don't want to leak anymore.

I need another smoke to calm my nerves. Rummaging into the pack, I take one while counting the remaining sticks; there are only six left. The lighter I left tucked into the door lights up with a practiced flick.

It's all too easy after that. The cigarette burns and the air pulls the smoke with it into my lungs.

My shoulders lower as the tension releases again.

A sigh expels the smoke out the window.

The smell tingles my nose, but only a little. I'll have to get used to the smell of it again; at least for the next little while.

The stress of all that is going on has allowed the addiction to dig claws into me again. It lures me as a crutch for my pain, and I willfully fall. Anything to stop the searing pain in my heart.

"Whoa!" Stephanie exclaims for the twelfth time this ride.

"Guess we're not going in there." Shawn's remark catches my attention. It's not in his usual selection of sentences. Those extended to explanations and telling her she shouldn't look.

Looking over at Shawn, then around him, I understand Stephanie's whoa and his comment. The puzzle pieces snap together easily.

The Fantasyland Hotel is gone; levelled by a fire. A large pile of building materials and ash remain, along with one wall against the rest of the mall. Scorch marks wrap around concrete openings, and up the walls.

The glass roof of the water park has collapsed inside.

Shawn suddenly flips a U-y. The destruction is on my side in clear view.

"We need to go back." I object. Whipping my head around to look at him.

"We're not going in there." Shawn says.

"Our stuff is in there." I argue.

"Our stuff is burnt to a crisp. That building could come down any minute on top of us. I'm not letting you go inside." Shawn speeds up the car like he thinks I'd jump out if he didn't. "Everything in there is replaceable, but you aren't. We're not going in there when we can go to our houses and take something else."

"You're wrong." Steph's voice is heavy and pained. "My scrap book was in there. Nothing can replace those pictures."

Stephanie's right. Pictures are irreplaceable.

But, Shawn is also right; they likely burned up in the fire that destroyed the building.

Her statement drops us all into an uncomfortable silence again. It takes all I am to keep myself from crying again.

My cigarette has burned itself to a useless butt. I drop it out the window.

Shawn drives out of this city and to the next one. The destruction of what little bits of city I see has only continued over the time gone by since our excursion out of the mall.

The city has never had a huge issue with potholes gone unchecked in the areas I frequented most. But, with no maintenance and spring fill in, I now see exactly how much a hole can grow after the winter.

Shawn drives around a couple car swallowing holes in the neighbourhood. Last year, I'd swear they were just minor cracks or divots.

He drives by his place without stopping.

"Where are you going?" I ask a bit confused.

"Steph's house." He answers.

"No. No! I don't want to go there. I don't want to go home." Steph outbursts.

"Why not?" Shawn asks, but I already figure out a reason. Or, part of a reason. Her dad could still be dead on the bed. The rotten stench of death would have filled the entire house by now. Steph had a major freak out the last time we were there. I can see why she wouldn't go back.

And, why Shawn wouldn't want to go back to his house. He found his parents dead in his house too.

"I told you, nothing could replace that scrapbook. I don't want anything else from there. And, since we're apparently not going to your place either, I guess we're going straight to Nikki's." Her voice turns bitter.

If I was feeling more like myself I'd say something to comfort her.

Both my friends have decided to pass on their house visits.

Did we really come all this way just to go to my house? There's no way we're going to grandma's now; not after…

Do I want to go back home?

Do I get a choice at this point? We couldn't have come all this way to just turn around before getting to any destination.

The farm was terrible.

We're not going to Shawn's or Steph's.

We're not going to grandma's.

This trip would be a total waste, if we don't go to my house.

I briefly question whether I want to visit my own home or not, then put it out of my mind. I need to go back home. I need to get some things to remind me of my parents.

My heartrate rises, breath quickens, and a couple tears manage to fall before I can contain them. I barely manage to stifle a whimper. Shawn reaches over to squeeze my arm.

I hold it together, enough, until we arrive. At this point, holding it together means not sobbing.

Clear trails from the frequently cascading tears drip down to the bottom of my chin, then soak the front of my sweater.

"We don't have to go inside." Shawn offers.

"Yes, we do." My words give me the extra boost I need to open the car door. Determination fuels me. I need to do this.

Maybe it'll bring me some closure.

Besides, it's dark out already. We need to stay the night somewhere, and it might as well be at home for one last time.

Shawn parks in the back of the house; right outside our garage. I jump out as soon as we stop. Not waiting until he has the car in park or the engine turned off.

Rounding the back of the vehicle I wait until Shawn turns it off then finally pops the trunk. I pull open the door and grab my bag that She had packed.

We walk to the house with me in the lead.

The gate sticks while trying to open; it always has.

Dad always meant to fix the post he claimed was the issue. Something about the post moved from its original position and the leaning caused the gate to not align with the clasp.

I huff a laugh.

He was always procrastinating house projects. It's a bigger job that we realize; he'd say. Not something to do with a spare hour or two. It would take a whole day or two; not something he usually had to spare.

The house is just as I left it.

A chunk of my heart rips open at more proof that they're dead. If they had been alive, they would have come back here to start the search for me. They would have seen my note. They would have gone to the mall to find it burnt, but they wouldn't have given up the search.

If She could find me, then so could they. How many times had I told myself that over the winter?

I remove the note. It does no good to anyone by existing. Ripping it to shreds gives me some sliver of empty satisfaction.

Mom and Dad never got the chance to read it, they never will get the chance to read it, and so there is no point to keeping it there.

It repeats like a broken record in my head.

Mom and Dad never got the chance to read it, they never will get the chance to read it, and so there is no point to keeping it there.

The dam breaks in a sob. I remove my shoes in habit. In sadness and anger I pound my way upstairs, and to the left. My parents' bedroom is now a time capsule of the last time they were there. Everything is exactly where they left it that morning.

I know exactly what I want to take with me to remind myself of them.

First stop through my haze of tears is mom's dresser. In an assortment of rings and necklaces, I pick out the ones and wear the ones that carry the most memories; a pink stoned mother's day gift, a diamond studded band from dad on their anniversary three years ago, a simple black band that had belonged to my bio dad, and the red ruby necklace she wore at her wedding.

On a half thought, I shove her opal ring into my pocket. It was one of her favourite rings and an heirloom passed through the family.

Mom was excited when She came along; another October child. Our family was lacking an October baby from my generation to pass the ring onto.

She always told me to never wear the ring, or let the opal touch my skin in any way. Bad luck, like I'd never had before, would follow me; curse me.

A weird superstition passed down through the family; or so I had thought. Now, I wonder if it is likely more. All the rocks and crystals, and their meanings, mean more now that I know about the supernaturals and magic.

It should be fine in my pocket; I hope.

Next stop is to raid dad's closet. His black nerd hoodie was his favourite. Hanger by hanger I draw all of them with a squeak until I happen upon the one I search for. The yellow words are still bright while the black fabric has faded with time and wash.

I set it on the bed as I switch out the sweater I am wearing for the hoodie. Once it's on, I smell the sleeves and hug myself. All the wailing cries I had restrained myself from letting go since I first found out come out with a vengeance.

Standing like that until my eyes are raw, my throat is scratchy, and my heart has been cried out.

The room has darkened to the night without the lights to keep everything bright.

My oxygen slowly returns to normal levels as I take in air at a steady pace.

I should see if She packed me anything useful. I don't feel like leaving this room and possibly running into Steph or Shawn.

The crying has exhausted me. I just want to brush my teeth and hair, and go to sleep.

The duffle bag opens with a loud zip against the silence. Drawing back the flap I see something that churns my insides sitting on the very top of the clothes and supplies.

Anger flairs at the sight of my yellow silk notebook.

It's from Her.

It's a tribute to finding my lost parents, who I had hoped were well and fine. Most of the pages are filled with thoughts, feeling, poems, and letters to my lost parents. It's forever going to be a reminder that they've been dead this whole time; that She lied to me.

Grabbing my mom's matches, for burning her candles, I strike it against the box. It lights up in a whoosh. Grasping the notebook in one hand and the lit match in the other, I meet the two together until the paper lights a flame.

Blowing out the match, I set it on a candle so I don't accidentally burn the house down.

I hadn't thought about what to do with the notebook once it was on fire. Seeing this through is important however, so putting the fire out isn't an option.

I open up the window, and pull out the screen clumsily with my only available hand. Down below is concrete, and it won't catch on fire. Dropping the notebook, I watch in hope that the drop doesn't put out the fire. The cover page bursts into flame, then the notebook as a whole as it burns in a little pile.

The cool air dries all the tear liquid on my face. The salt makes my skin feel tight.

Flame burns the book to something unrecognizable from its original form. Flame turns to cinders, turns to ash, and dies out. When I feel like the fire is completely out and the house is no longer in danger of burning down, I close the window.

The fire has awoken me from my exhaustion. It won't last long. It's been a long day.

Despite dropping my bag on the bed, it has retained a perfectly tucked in appearance.

Mom was always weird about making her bed. I'd make jokes about her secret military life. She would deny it, and claim she likes a properly made bed to dive into at the end of the day; make her feel like she's staying in a hotel.

Pulling the sheet and comforter out from underneath the mattress to slide under and sit against the pillows and back board. Itching to write, I find no more a poetic way to say my words than to write them in dad's notebook.

From the bedside table drawer I pick up dad's notebook and pen. Starting where he left off, I begin to write on fresh pages.

Dear Mom,

Words cannot express how much I miss you. I always thought you'd be there.

Graduation; once I finally figured out what I wanted to do with my life. My engagement. My wedding. My kids' births. Birthdays, Christmases, and holidays. Or those nights that I just need to talk.

God, I just wish I could talk to you again.

I keep thinking about how scared you must've been. Terrified, knowing that you were going to die with the rest of the family as those people killed everyone around you; as they killed you.

I'm deeply sorry that you had to endure that. That that was the last thing you saw. I hope it was as painless as possible. I hope you didn't suffer.

She told me everyone died of a bullet to the brain. I hope that's true, because that would mean you didn't die in pain. You died not knowing if I had shared a similar experience in death, and that must have been terrifying.

I'm alive. I mean, I know it's pointless to tell you, as I'm sure you know. I know you're watching me from heaven, and that brings me some comfort.

You're my guardian angel now. Please, if you can, give me some sign that you are okay.

I miss you so much. It feels like a part of me is missing. The pain is unbearable and I don't know how I'll ever feel okay again. I can't do this without you. I was always going to go out into the world, but you were supposed to be just a phone call away.

It's hell out there and you're gone. In some ways that might be a blessing. To know that you won't have to suffer daily. But, I selfishly would wish the pain on you, just to have you around again.

I'll love you forever and ever. XoXoOO

Dear Dad,

I couldn't have asked for a better dad. There is barely a time that I don't remember having you fill my life with joy. You taught me how to ride a two wheeled bike, and how to defend myself against the boys in my class. You gave me the confidence I've needed to survive.

I wish you could be here to give me advice; though I'm sure I'd know exactly what you'd say to me. Your answers have been drilled into my head all of these years. You'd tell me to talk to her. That I need to find out the whole story. You'd say that she's family, and you always forgive family.

I don't want to forgive. I don't see how I could forgive her.

You're gone and you're never coming back and she knew. She knew and didn't tell me for months.

We had gotten so close. We were like sisters and she betrayed me. She lied to me.

She reminds me of you. She's so grounded and brilliant. I catch her reading every day. She even does a lot of the same little ticks you did, like moving her hair back by swiping it over the top of her head. She'd rather spend her time on the side lines watching, than in the thick of it.

But she's so damn calm. She's the calmest person I've ever known. It's wild how calm she can be; more than even you.

Jaiden is definitely your daughter.

So, for you, I'll try to make things work with her; after I'm done healing. But, I'm not promising anything until then. Boiko grudges run deep and I hate her right now. But, for you, I'll make sure it doesn't last ten years.

I miss having you in my life.

I'll love you forever and ever. XpXpOO

My letters complete with smears of fallen tears where I was unable to contain them.

Needing connection, I flip through the pages previously written. His cursive is neat and well-practiced. I learned my own cursive from him.

Pulling out of the parking lot, I look for traffic where there is none. Driving forward and pulling to the left. WEM parking lot. Back side of the mall—second in from the light to turn down the road home. Blind spot with a car racing. I don't see it until too late. The car crashes into us. Nikki is in the passenger side—likely dead from impact. I break my left arm. Car flips.

I remember this. Not this exactly. We were pulling out of the place he described, but he waited and waited; I told him he could drive. A car zoomed by and would have hit us. He describes the same thing, from his view, below.

He was a prophet.

Pages turn revealing prophecy after prophecy. Under written from time to time is a separately written note of another version; what actually happened. Conversations, accidents, ridiculously mundane things, and life changing moments; at first. Later pages reveal nightmares. Supernatural attacks and nightmares of this world. Visions where we were together; and I died. And, I died. Mom dies and I die. Dad dies. We all die. Horrific visions of horrible things done to each of us.

None of these things happened.

We were supposed to be together through all of this. He knew it was going to happen, but he stopped it; he changed it.

Why would he choose for me to be away from them? If he could see all of these things, then why wouldn't he just stop it all? He could have made sure we stayed together and stayed alive. We were supposed to be together.

But he died; they died. How couldn't he save them? He had visions of all these deaths, so how couldn't he keep them alive?

Why did he choose for me to be alone in this?

"What are you?" The voice surprises me. I don't recognize that deep male voice. A skin on skin smack has me jumping out of bed; notebook dropping to the floor.

"Please, I'm human! Please don't shoot me! Shawn!" Steph cries in agony. My heart thunders.

Running to the door, I pull it open, and sprint down to the bottom of the stairs.

With my eyes adjusted to the darkness, I can see three more bodies than there should be in the living room.

"SHAWN!" Stephanie's voice screams just a moment before six gunshots deafen the room. A body falls to the ground.

I cover my mouth with my hand to stop from screaming.

There is a struggle in the kitchen. The moonlight lights up enough to see Shawn fighting with two people.

Stephanie was shot.

Oh God.

Jumping onto the back of one of the men attacking Shawn frees him up. The man shouts his surprise. "What the fuck! There's another one!"

"Run!" Shawn yells.

Loosening myself from the man's back, I punch him away. Grabbing a pan from above as my weapon, I bash him on the head, and swing at the one fighting Shawn.

"You run!" I tell Shawn. He takes the chance and makes his way out the door. I try to run after him, but my sweater is pulled and I am thrust back into a chest. Drawing the pan up and over my head, I hear a ping when it connects with a head. The pan jolts out of my grasp from the impact.

More come in from the door. It's too crowded in the kitchen to get out.

Kicking then pushing back on the one I hit on the head into the other thugs; I create a little space around me. I quickly but carefully jump my way down the stairs two steps at a time. Sprinting across the room I climb up onto a display case.

As I open the window and pull my way out, I hear the tell-tale grunts and thumps of people falling down the stairs. I never figured those annoyingly slippery stairs would save my life.

Shawn runs over to me from the gate. He offers his hand but it's too late to help me up. "We should go back for Steph." I say.

"She's dead."

No, she can't be. We didn't see anything. "But she might be-"

"She's dead. We need to go." He tugs on my hand and leads me away from the open window. Six gunshots, she wouldn't have been able to survive all that.

A couple gunshots sound from the basement. I duck and run, but I really have no idea where they are shooting. I just know that no pain emits from my body, so I'm not shot.

The door opens just as we open the gate. Shawn opens the doors for the car. The lights are bright in the dark and give us away. "This way!" Someone shouts.

Shawn and I quickly get into the car. He starts the engine and we lurch forward. I'm pulled back into my seat forcefully. We speed out of the back alley.

Shawn drives us out of town through the back. I lose direction on where he's taking us as soon as we exit the city limits. Not that I care too much where we go right now.

After I heard my family was dead there was anger, betrayal, and grief. Steph dying pushed my heart over the edge into a pit of numbness.

Who else is going to die? Who's next?

Bring it on, because no one else could die that would make me feel anything anymore.

Shawn pulls over onto a side road. The vehicle slows to a stop, and he puts the car into park.

His hand grasps my knee and squeezes. It's meant to be comforting for me and for him. Looking upon his face I finally see the tears he cries. The sorrow he feels at the loss of his girlfriend; the loss of his best friend.

I reach over for a hug. The console between the seats jabs into my side and makes me arch uncomfortably.

A bubble of pain rises up as I'm flooded with the emotion lost to me just a moment before. I stifle a cry, and then I hear him do the same. His torso shakes from his grief.

We use each other for the comfort we need to survive this. A physical touch to know we are not alone despite how we feel inside.

Shawn loosens his grip first and I take that as a cue to let go. I retreat back into my seat.

Shawn wipes his tears with his hands. He wipes his nose on his sleeve. Shifting the car into gear, we start moving forward at a crawling pace.

"Where do we go now?" He asks.

My mind blanks. "I don't know."

Chapter 7

Bodies, what's left of them, are strewn about. Red brown blood, some dry and some sticky and wet, is spread everywhere. The flashlight shines highlights in what's still wet.

Long ago, I stopped caring where I stepped as the blood was unavoidable to my human capabilities and limitations. Something, that may have only been avoided by levitation or flying.

My boots and pant legs have been sacrificed to the cause. The sleeves of my shirt pulled up to my elbows in an attempt to save my sweater from the inevitable shared fate of the garbage.

I scratch my palm to rid an itch from the dried liquid. The dried bits peel away with each rub, while the wet spreads further.

I can't wait to shower. The germophobe in me has long since passed out from disgust.

Desensitized to all the blood, skin, and unimaginable horror, I enter the house for the hundredth time for one last look around and collection.

A generator provided enough electricity to continue to run the fridge and a freezer in the basement. To our surprise and delight there was homemade ice cream in the freezer, flavoured with chocolate chips and mint extract. The mint breaks through fresh, but overpowering; they added too much to the mix. The chocolate chips are too large to melt in an instant on our tongues.

Despite all of this, the ice cream is a welcome treat I look forward to devouring on the ride back.

It was discovered quickly that the lights worked. We figured out through the deafening hum of an old tuned out noise.

The true horror of the massacre more picturesque and detailed in the light, but not as creepy.

I miss the expansive light as I navigate by flashlight.

All the food and gas were obvious easy picks from their designated areas. The generator attached surprisingly easy to the back of a commandeered truck. A thread of doubt lingers that maybe it was too easy because we missed something. It would be horrible to lose the generator after going over a bump, because we missed a pin or something to hook it up.

Tricky and nauseating at first, was scavenging for everything else. Weapons had to be unbelted from the dead bodies; none of them safe from the fluids of their owners. Some pockets held treasures like pocket knives and lighters. Other pockets held rocks, tissues, and personal knickknacks.

Pilfering drawers as bodies lay in their beds; oblivious to their danger as they slept, and then died.

Whatever happened, it happened fast. Bodies lay where they died scattered throughout the house. No one had a chance to group and fight.

Not one person hiding in a closet hoping to not be noticed. Not one person made it outside, or close enough to the back door to unlock it.

The people who did this acted in monstrosity. The goal was clear, to kill everyone here; no doubt in that. A horde of supernaturals descended on these people.

Necks are torn open in what Leah expressed as the type of bite a vampire leaves when they aim to kill quickly; messy and wasteful.

Scratches and punctures of all sizes and numbers got most of the rest.

A few still have a blade left inside them where it struck. I yanked out what I could. A couple blades stuck inside, stuck on bone and impossible for me to pull out without seesawing and disturbing the body's internal organs. The couple blades were not worth the effort and body desecration; Leah didn't think the same.

I walk through to the bedrooms. Like a scanner, I start from one side and work my way to the opposite side of the room, and carry this process on through the house.

If we had been thinking, we would have done the final sweep before we removed the generator.

The ice cream could have been moved to the upstairs fridge, but neither was thought of until too late. We were too worried about the amount of time the generator would take to hook up and the diminishing day light.

The two bedrooms were picked clean personally: clothes, weapons, and some children's books. Leah had gotten the bathroom: soaps, toiletries, and linen.

Linen closet provided more linen. The living room was turned into another bedroom; movies and looted items from the bodies.

The image of Crystal pecking and slurping up the soft eyeball of the victim lying on the ground pops up as I see him again. An opportune meal from the man who had his face slashed open to the bone and further.

On and on I check list the upstairs, only obtaining a screwdriver I suppose could be useful. Right off from the kitchen, I walk downstairs.

The basement area is both finished and unfinished; half and half. I want to finish with the ice cream, so I walk through to the far side.

A stuffed owl watches from its mount on the corner to a little hall; a grey great horned owl if I remember correctly. The eyes appear to follow me. The realistic bird is a sign of great taxidermy. I can't help but feel it could jump out and attack me at any time.

To the left is a teen's bedroom decorated in boyband posters and pink. Leah went through the rooms down this way, so I go through with extra diligence. This room is untouched from a carnage aspect. It's a nice break, but it feels wrong to trudge through; like I'm desecrating a tomb.

Supplies from the previous people scatter through the room. Leah likely tossed the sleeping bags to their current crumpled positions. Drawers left open from her inspection.

Small shirts and pants will never fit me, but her closet holds shoes in my size. Most are heels, and therefore completely useless to me. A few are gaudy in size and colours. Flower patterned flats that look uncomfortable, and blister inducing; not to mention hideous.

There is a pair of black All Star shoes. They look like Converse but without the ankle edges coming up so high. I think these look better and more comfortable. I nab them as replacements for what I have on, and two pairs of socks. If the shoes fit, the socks should too. They're black too. The colour is safe as safe can be from stains; namely blood stains.

The room is done. I won't find anything else in here.

A closed and locked room is next. It has a hole in the center of the nob. The dismantled pen from the desk easily lets me in. I burst in for an element of surprise, but I don't need it. No one is in the bathroom.

Maybe someone locked the door to keep people out of the contents. Leah wouldn't have done that.

The bathroom is decorated like a beach. Seashells hang in picture frames on each side of the mirror. A seashell acts as the soap bar holder. Sandy walls and blue floors; I've never seen a blue tub and toilet before now.

On a whole, the bathroom is very neat and tidy. There is no cue that this room has been opened in the last few months; not counting a lack of dust.

Many of the drawers lack anything inside. It is behind three rolls of toilet paper that I find black bottles with reminiscent labelling of a popular sun blocks for vampires.

The bottles have some weight to them. The one feels full, while two others may be half empty. Both will be vital to the vampires back home and to Leah. This could open us up to being able to search during the day.

Summer is coming and with it the shortest night of the year. Imagine only being able to leave your house for six hours over a period of a few months. As a private person and a homebody I likely could, but the opposite spectrum of personalities may have issues with it.

Many of the vampires are already getting cabin fever. These will help them get outside a bit more.

My arms are nearly full after the bottles and toilet paper, so I cut my last sweep short. Finishing up requires the acquisition of the ice cream.

Straight ahead into the unfinished multiuse kids play room and storage, I grab the ice cream and balance it on top.

I trek back to the upstairs. Leah isn't here, and is likely outside still. She's probably waiting for me to get going; impatiently as she would be.

On the way out the house, above the door, is the message in blood. I pause to view it one last time. A reminder of the violence and purpose of the events that had taken place here.

A brutal message, as any would be written in blood, by the hands of someone looking for attention in the worst way possible. Creepier in the lack of proper lighting.

FOR YOU

- DARIUS

A note in once dripping blood, no one but the two of us saw, depicting this heinous act was planned.

A warning and love intentioned act from Darius to the only person we could imagine the message to be for; Alexa.

Why else would he write a message?

Why else would he sign it?

The end game is unclear to us, but the possibilities are numbered. They could be meeting in secret again. Darius could be seeking to destroy Alexa, kill everyone who's had contact with her and scare her to bits until she can't take it anymore. This could be some twisted form of affection meant to woo her.

Whatever it is, it's a secret we shall keep until time deems it worthy to spill; lest we wish to have a Taylor incident repeat. Until then, a careful watch over Alexa and her actions will take the two of us.

The woods turn creepy with the night. Trees create a barrier between us and the rest of the world. Anything could be hiding with in them and we would never know. The light doesn't reach that far back.

Eyes could be watching our every move, waiting for us to separate so they can pounce.

My thinking sends a chill down my spine. If not for the light in the truck showing me Leah moving around in the cab, I may have started a panicked fast walk to the truck.

"Found something you might like." I say after opening the driver's door.

"It better be the ice cream." If she'd only look back at me, she would see I am holding more than just that delicious prize.

"Well, I have that too, but I was talking about two and a half bottles of sun block." Depositing all the objects onto the seat so she can grab what she wants.

"Seriously?" Leah turns swiftly and clumsily. She gathers up the precious bottles, and after a quick examination hugs both of them close to her body. "Where did you find them?"

"Locked bathroom in the basement." I tell her expecting some abashed reaction since she chose not to check that room herself.

"Oh, yeah, I didn't go in there because it was locked." She frowns as looks at me accusingly. "Exactly who were you before all of this?"

I scrunch my eyebrows with confusion. "What do you mean?"

"You have a secret life of crime, we don't know about?"

A moment of pause as I process the question within her statement, then the slight shock that she doesn't know the piece of assumed common knowledge of that particular lock. "I didn't have to pick the lock, not like a usual lock. It's just, the hole in the center. You stick something in there and it unlocks it. It's like a child lock. I don't know how to pick an actual lock. Well, I know how to in theory, and then there was that time my AP English class broke into our class room with a credit card."

"You rebel, you." Leah looks at me proud, and curious for a story.

I hate to disappoint her, but the story isn't so exciting. "Not so rebel-ish when you hear it wasn't to do anything more than sit in class and wait for the teacher; who was late."

Leah turns aghast. "Who does that?"

"Smart kids; dumb teenagers." Placing it succinctly in an adage form.

"Very dumb. I would have skipped class. Teacher doesn't show up by ten minutes past the time, and then you have a free period." And, that speaks to the type of person Leah was in school.

"That's not a real rule. Even if the teacher comes to class with ten minutes left, you have to be there or face a zero for participation in that class." I explain, I don't know when the last time she went to high school was, but things likely have changed since the last time. "Not that it matters much anymore."

"You were a teacher's pet!" She accuses with the most amused smile and widening grin.

"Not really." I leave it spoken with that. Unspoken, is the smidgen of truth that at one point I was just that. It was required of me to put on that type of public image.

My adolescent rebellion involved stopping asking for extra homework just for fun and dialing back on the cheerful chatter with them on my free time.

Other teenagers drink, party, and sneak out.

I ate my feelings until I was obese, drew into myself, and then I fell into line and accepted my fate.

I look to the pail of ice cream, just a few minutes ago I was so excited to eat the rare treat, but now my thoughts have turned to disgust and a lump in my throat.

"Right."

The objects on the seat get moved to other places. The ice cream goes between the seats; utensils at the ready to eat it.

All the rest I toss to the floor below the back seat. The seat itself is clear.

"Uh, I'll drive to Millet. You can direct me once we get into town."

Moving to jump up into the seat, I think better of it. "I think I should change my pants and shoes."

"Good thinking."

The back truck bed seat holds everything including the clothes. Settling on baggy sweatpants with a string tied waist as it's the best thing we picked up that would actually fit me.

My shoes squish, and my socks stretch. Pants peel off difficultly. The blood leached through the clothing to stain my legs. The butt of the jeans are fairly clean; clean enough to wipe down my legs and feet. Leaving the old articles on the ground, I change into the new pants, socks, and shoes.

I settle into the driver's seat and pull closed the door.

Leah nods, and sits properly into the seat she was kneeling on. "Do you even know how to get there?"

"Back to Leduc and drive south." I say. I dig into the ice cream and shove the spoonful in my mouth. The taste is delectable after the initial shock of mint.

"Just drive south until I tell you to turn right. We'll go through back roads, and avoid towns; less trouble that way." Leah has a fair point.

"Sounds good to me." I start the engine.

Pulling the seat into the foremost place allows me to fit properly in place with back to seat and seatbelt on.

"You don't have to wear that." A glance to her shows me she's pointing to my seatbelt.

My cheeks turn red, and I focus on pulling out of the parking place. She's teasing me because of her previous revelation. "I know, but if we crash at least I won't go flying through the windshield."

"Don't crash and that won't be a problem."

"Yes, because I can control that." I argue. There are so many instances where I wouldn't be able to control if we crashed. Inexperience being the tagline to each of those circumstances.

"You are the one driving." I snap my head to the side and glare. When I can't hold the expression, I return to watching the road. Biting my lip with my eye tooth helps me control the smile on her side.

That was a good one.

I have nothing to say back to that because she's mostly right.

"So, where exactly are we going?" I ask to change the subject.

"To see my family." Leah's offered answer is different from the locational information I was looking for.

"Oh. And, you think they'll help?" I reach for another mouthful of ice cream. The pit in the dessert is getting deeper and deeper from our digging.

Her head tilts side to side. "Yeah. My brother owes me. You remember that Hell hole the military took me too? The school place, right. Well, I had been with my brother when they captured me. He stole my supplies and abandoned me with them. If no one else will help, at least he owes me; he'll honour that much."

"So, we go find your family." I confirm. "What about a store? Did you know of any around here?"

Small supernatural family owned boutiques had supernatural products in the back. A being would walk in and ask the clerk for a certain product by name. The clerk would use their discretion to identify if the person was a human or not; on the chance that a human asked for a potentially dangerous product.

"No. It was easier to get it by mail when the postal system was stream lined." She pauses. Her tone grave. "I should have prepared more."

Sooner than I had imagined, we pass into the small town. "Turn right." I do as she says. On my left we drive by a red barn. The stark colour difference stands out against all the other buildings around even in the darkness. It's odd, but I'm sure it was a fairly effective gimmick for the burger company who once owned the building. "Left."

"Here?" The road is quickly coming up. I slam on the breaks to slow quickly.

"Yes." With confirmation I roll the steering wheel. We drive straight after the turn. "Stop here."

Turning on my right signal, I pull in behind a white car.

The house is old. Shingles are peeling back on the roof. Both the shingles and the paneled siding are discoloured. A wooden board covers up the window that had once been in the door.

This house looks old and abandoned, yet twenty or so vehicles are congregated around this one house.

I undo my seatbelt. "So?" I trail off. Are we going inside?

"My family, they're..." She trails off. "The whole house is filled with vampires. The only humans that might be in there will be dead soon. You can't do anything about it. Don't try.

Don't give any weird looks.

Don't draw attention to yourself.

Only talk if you are spoken to.

Don't do anything stupid."

"Should I stay here?" I ask with new concern for my wellbeing. This isn't the normal warning about the family one receives. This sounds like breathe and they'll kill you.

"No, that might be worse." Leah doesn't sound certain. "You might disappear while I'm gone. Stick close. They shouldn't bother you too much."

Her words do nothing to inspire confidence. "Sure."

The air is crisp. My lungs tighten as the cold air chills them in a sudden attack replacing the heated air from the truck. It takes a moment to get used to.

Leah leads us up to the door. "Let us in."

Sliding metal scrapes, then pops. The door pulls into the house to reveal an elderly man. White hair and wrinkles was the last aging group I thought I'd see in a house filled with vampires.

Though it seems ridiculous to be ageist against vampires when I give it a moment's thought. Humans can get changed at any age, and then the virus slows aging; not completely stopping aging.

So why not a vampire that was changed at eighty years?

Or, one that has lived long enough to age to an appearance of an eighty year old human?

Not as sexy as Hollywood tends to portray them as, or as confusing and unrealistic once the real facts are brought to light.

I can never take back the hours Dominique's sat me down to catch up on, apparently, required viewage. Although, commentary from the real vampires may have made it worth the watch any way; I learnt a lot.

Leah takes my hand to lead me inside the dark house. Her eyes better suited for the dark. A door opens up from nowhere and with it a dim light; easier on the eyes. She lets go of my hand now that I can see.

An entire compound lay in the basement beyond the four corners of the house upstairs.

From the hungry looks I am getting, I keep in mind to stick close to Leah.

We don't go far. Three people appear from down a hallway; stiff and commanding of attention. They've certainly got Leah's attention.

A couple, likely her parents, and a grandmother stop walking and require us to step closer to them. I stop when Leah does.

The father and Leah speak in another language. I cannot begin to understand anything of what they are saying, but it sounds reprimanding, passive aggressive, and tense.

Leah's voice, while the undertones are similar, sounds different than the voice she uses to speak English. It didn't occur to me until this point that she might speak another language; I suppose it should have. She did say she had a childhood in China. Mandarin or Cantonese, I don't know which this is, would likely be her first language; not English.

It's weird to hear someone suddenly speak another language fluently after you've known them for a long while, and they've never given any indication of the knowledge. I admire her more; it is a difficult thing to be able to speak two languages, let alone fluently in both.

One man comes over from the other side of the room to the ire of the parents. He hands her a bottle of sunblock and another bottle, then hugs her. Leah returns with a poke to the chest and a few words. They both break out into smiles and chuckles. Maybe he is her brother; they appear close in age and have a jovial sibling temperament.

His lips move, but he speaks in high tone. I hear the pitch but not the words.

"You keep human companions now? What is she: a seeker, a blood bag?" He purposely speaks in human range English so I can hear. I don't miss the intention nor the look.

"A friend." Leah interrupts him to snarl a warning in her two words.

"We don't make friends with our food." He chides. "You were taught better than that."

Leah puts herself inches closer to me, putting herself further between her brother and I. "This human's a good friend. She's a good person."

"None of them are good for anything further than a meal or to turn. So what's it going to be?" A girl puts her input in.

Like a noose, the circle of vampires around us tightens. It takes strength and logical reasoning to ignore my first instincts to run, second instincts to lie that Leah promised to turn me later, and my third instincts to pretend I know how to fight and win against all of these much stronger and faster people.

Is this a good time to blurt out that I'm a dreamer? Would that save me or imprison me?

Did I change something to make this happen? Was this supposed to happen and everything will be fine? I don't remember anything like this. I don't remember anything that would give me away as turned into a vampire.

"She's saved me multiple times. I wouldn't be here if she hadn't." Leah tells them to help convince them; despite not being true.

"Humans can't be trusted." Another person chimes in. Mob mentality is taking over, I've seen it before.

The situation got very dangerous, very fast. Previously absent claustrophobia sets in on me; choking me.

"She can be." Leah tries to defend me.

"She'll bring others and try to hunt us." Leah's brother says to convince his sister.

I have to step in. Try to defuse the situation in any way I can. "I wouldn't bring people here to hunt you. I'm not like that.

Everyone deserves to live, and it was awful for you to have to hide for so long. It's awful that the Council dealt out execution at any threat to reveal your existence.

It shouldn't have taken a revolution for humans to know you exist. But, we can't change the past. We can't go back and undo the Evanesce Treaty. There's other ways we can work this all out."

"Have you been telling her all our secrets?" Leah's father accuses in deep tone.

I raise my eyebrow. "What secrets? It's common knowledge learned by speaking with two dozen supernatural beings that I've been cohabitating with for six months."

"A blood slut and what else, I wonder?" He retorts.

"She's a human." Her mother reiterates for the father. "You either eat her or turn her. That's how we keep safe. Or, you can leave here without the sunblock and we'll kill you if we ever see you again." Her mother's ice cold voice cuts through the room. It stops the father and everyone else; giving Leah and I a chance of escape.

Leah pops the lid on the tube. "Then I guess this is goodbye." In a string the lotion pours out until her brother is able to wrestle the tube away.

Leah uses the moment of shock, to grab my hand and lead me out in a hurry. Pushing through the people in our way. She uses her speed to quicken the process. My legs barely keep up; running faster than I ever have.

We slow on the stairs. It helps me ascend without tripping up them.

Leah opens the door to the dark house. Dragging me through the room. I collide into her when we approach the entrance door.

Once we are outside and half way to the truck, she lets go of my hand. I look back to see if anyone is following us. No one is trailing us. No one is looking out the door we left open. "I'm sorry. That wouldn't have happened if I stayed inside the car."

"They would have got you and killed you before I got back. Or maybe dragged you to the basement to use as a bargaining chip. Trust me when I say they'd never let you live." Leah knows her family best. Speaking from direct experience or presumptions derived from past experience; either way she would know best.

"But, you might be welcome back with your family." The point doesn't even sound convincing to me. It's a ridiculous notion.

"It doesn't matter. We never saw eye to eye on the human matter. Felt good to squeeze out the Sunblock. Wish I would have kept hold of the supplements though. Oh well. Guess I put you in danger for nothing." She crosses in front of me using her boosted speed. "You need to sleep. I'll drive. I'll wake you up in a few hours, and then I'll disappear into the back to sleep."

"Okay." There is no point to arguing this. I do need the sleep. It has to be near midnight, and sunrise has to be less than eight hours away; no one is getting a full night's sleep tonight.

The door opens and some clothes fall out on to the ground. The back seat is half filled with things we scavenged. With no patience to move everything into the truck bed, I push whatever I can to the foot space on each side while still being able to open and close the passenger side door. Grabbing the clothes off the ground and tossing them to the other side's floor space.

Crawling into the back, I lay down. I can almost stretch out fully, but I curl my legs in for comfort.

Gasoline stings my nostrils. I scrunch my nose like it might help. It doesn't.

"Stand back." Someone says. Two steps back for safe keeping.

One small spark ignites one thousand fold into a fire ball around the heap. Most dissipating upwards yet leaving little flames behind. It's brighter in the night, than it would be during the day.

A yelp alerts me, but it quickly turns to boisterous laughter. "You still got your eyebrows. Don't worry."

The most flammable pieces catch on fire first; clothing and hair.

A couple branches thrown in on top cinder then catch fire. The heat grows with the flame. I step back one step as the heat grows unbearable.

Bodies catch on fire as the temperature rises. Flame slowly eating them away.

The wind shifts; smoke, retched burning hair, and charred meat. I choke. The wind shifts again quickly. I don't have to move, but I wish I never had to smell it in the first place.

Yellow, orange and red rise higher and higher. A barrier of heat expands out from the pile as a noticeable dark stain on the grass.

Hair burns away first. The skin burns away to expose each layer beneath. Bones take surprisingly long to catch. Sizzling is an unexpected noise itching in my ears. Blood leaches out from the bottom of the pile.

"There's blood! Someone's alive!" A woman rushes towards the pit. Just as she's about to throw herself in, in her grief delusional state, someone is able to pull her back by her arm. Two others jump in on her. She screams. "They'll die if we don't help them! LET GO!"

I search the pile for signs of movement. Breathing or twitching. The flame dances and could trick the eye.

If anyone was alive, they couldn't be now. They would have asphyxiated by now; amongst other things. No one I dragged in there was alive; I'm certain of that.

"Dead bodies can still bleed. Blood pools, and when wounds open gravity will let the blood out. No one is alive in there." I explain to no one listening.

Well that's gruesome. I vaguely recognized the faces, but I can't pin them on anyone specific. I don't have a location. Not that I really had my eye on anything but the burning bodies. It was all encompassing.

Hopefully there will be some way to save all those people instead. It won't be likely, unless I have another vision of the events prior to the burning.

Leah's attention is on driving. She hasn't noticed my waking. Deep and even breaths are the key.

Pulling my phone out now seems safe. I pull it out of the pocket it's hidden in. Shielding behind the seat in front of me, I turn it on. She'd have to turn completely around in order to see anything.

It's a quarter after two.

No new messages. Opening up the message folder goes straight into my last conversation; one sided conversation.

Dominique and I separated near Leduc. She's mad at me, and may be heading your way. I'm going back to Banff.

Did anyone bury her family's bodies or are they still in the pile behind the house?

Let me know if you see her.

Again not sure if she'll go there, or head back to Banff like the original plan.

I reread my messages to John. He hasn't responded and it's been hours; since the afternoon. Putting the phone away gives me dread.

My head spins as I look up just in time to see the welcome sign into town.

Slinking up into the passenger seat signals to Leah my waking.

"We're here." She informs me.

"Yeah. I saw the sign." My voice scratches, so I clear my throat. "You could have woken me. I would have driven part way back."

"Relax; I'll sleep when the sun's up. You need more night sleep than I do."

Just before the bridge, we turn left; almost home.

The truck jolts up. Leah screeches us to a stop.

"What was that?" I ask. The answer is met with silence. Looking ahead into the little view the headlights reveal four figures laying on the ground. Shadowed bumps in the road lay beyond.

All are dead bodies on the ground.

Oh.

Thanks for the advanced warning visions. Super helpful. I dread what's coming. What happened while we were gone?

Tap. Tap. Tap. I jump and scream as the noise reaches my right ear.

DeAngelo's face is in the window, and he waves at me. A click of the released handle alerts me to his trying to open the locked door. Rolling down the window I squeak out a, "hi."

"What happened!?" Leah shouts from behind me. Her voice a mixture of anger and shock.

"Humans attacked us because they said one of us attacked them. Then Darius returned with a bunch of people. Bastard probably sent one of his guys to attack a human, and then watched the fight unfold. Some went with Darius, but everyone else... Anyone who didn't run and hide well enough is dead."

"What the Hell?! Jaiden?!" Leah and I lock eyes.

"I know." I answer her unsaid question.

"What?" DeAngelo asks.

"Everyone at the farmhouse we went to was dead too." I tell him just enough to leave question. He can make his own assumptions on who was at fault.

"Damn." He gazes over to the back seat, then back to us. "Didn't you leave with more people?"

"They're alive. We separated at the farm. Alexa, Daniel and Rayleen were going back to their places for sentimentals, and were coming back after morning. Dominique, Shawn and Stephanie were going to see about finding their families. I don't know how fast they were planning on returning; if at all." I explain to him.

"Is it safe to be out here?" Leah asks.

"So far." DeAngelo answers, evidentially unsure of it himself. "We've been taking shifts patrolling around. No sign that anyone's returned. Go back to the vamp house. Everyone left has set up camp there. I'm going to finish my round. I'll see you back at the house."

"See you." He turns around. I roll up the window.

When he's out of hearing range Leah hits the steering wheel. "First we go to the farm and everyone is dead; fresh dead. And, a nice little love note from Darius. Now, Darius attacks Banff just in a small window of time, while we are conveniently gone." She speaks all the words she had meant to while DeAngelo was here. I'm glad she held her tongue.

Darius certainly could have had time to kill them and return to Banff before we did. "Alexa-"

Leah interrupts me. "She has to be talking to him again. He knew Alexa planned to go to the farm and back here, so he could attack here while she was safe. Is this retaliation for rejection, or for dating Daniel? He could still be here."

"He's probably close. He'll wait for Alexa to return and find this." He'd want to see her reaction, at the very least.

Leah continues in a panicky tirade. "Whatever the next move is, whatever we do next has to be the opposite of whatever Alexa wants."

"We stick to our plan. The both of us watch her." I hope to calm her.

"We should tell the others now."

"If you want Alexa to get killed the moment she comes back; sure." Reason might work.

"She'd deserve it." Leah says bluntly. "Look at how many people died because of her."

Being the voice of reason, I point to the errors in her statement. "I see where you're coming from, but we don't know the whole story. And, Darius is ultimately to blame. He's the one who physically did this."

"Jaiden."

"Leah." I copy her inflection. "We don't have all the facts. She may or may not be a willing participant in this. It was an abusive relationship. Until we find that out, we shouldn't set up a man hunt for her."

"Fine. Did you need to get anything from your house?" She asks.

"No, everything I have is in my bag." My heart starts with a panic. I look to the back seat. "Which is still in the SUV." We forgot to grab my bag from the SUV. I should have done it one of the couple times I had thought about it; reminding myself not to forget it. At least it wasn't anything extremely personal.

"That sucks." She pulls the truck forward. The body rolls under the back wheels, but miss the trailer. We pull up to her house.

Inside we are met with solemn people. Beaten down and grieving for the loss of their loved ones. Exhausted from a hard battle.

It's awkward. I had no real attachment to anyone here; to any who passed. It sucks that they died, but no tears will be shed on my part. Especially since I don't know exactly who all is dead; unless they were human.

I make busy pulling supplies into the house while Leah takes stock with those in the living room.

Pulling a box from the trunk, I jump as Joe speaks low in my ear. "You know you're the only human around here now. You're a delicacy." For each step I try to place between us, he steps in closer; threateningly close.

"Back off." Leah forces herself between him and me. "She's mine." She growls her words. A high pitched ringing signals a conversation happening above my hearing range. I wish people would stop purposely talking in ways so that I can't understand the words.

He moves forward. Leah is faster. Her arm reaches out to grasp his and wrap it around his back in a hold. She grasps his neck with her free hand.

"Okay." He chokes out. Leah releases him to sputter and run off. The few others watching go back into the house. "It was a joke. Relax."

It didn't feel like a joke.

"Thank you." I whisper.

"Looks like you need a body guard, or blood guard; same thing really." Leah half jokes.

"I guess we need to work on a blood supply before this becomes an issue." I whisper.

"It's already an issue. I'd suggest you run away, but you'll run into this wherever you go." Leah honestly answers. "We should wait for the others to get back then we leave. Do you think Dominique will show up?"

"Maybe. They still think this is the safest place to be." No matter her opinion of me.

"It'll be safer once all the remaining humans are back; slightly safer for you at least. In the meantime, you need to stick close to me and your non-vampire acquaintances." She goes to the back of the truck and pulls herself up to stand on the tire.

Leah reaches in and shifts some objects around. She pulls up a short sword and waves it to show it off. "Maybe get yourself a sharp pointy stick."

Chapter 8

"We really should get back." His persistently nagging voice negates my own selfish thoughts.

Opening one eye stubbornly retains the sleepy peacefulness I cling to. I could easily just nod off again.

The sun soaks my skin, warming me. Rayleen's twinkling laugher is off in the distance. Crystal's variety of growls and chirps break up the laughter now and then.

"I don't want to." While true, much of what I mean is left unsaid. The guilt of the lies and the trepidation of returning without the gift, leave me wishing to never return.

I close my eye and resume sun bathing on the lounge chair.

Some time passes. I expect him to speak again, but he doesn't.

I open both of my eyes. They adjust to the light slowly. Rayleen and Crystal are still playing in the grass. Daniel is nowhere to be seen.

I leave to go find him. Rayleen should be safe enough in the yard for the couple minutes it should take to find Daniel.

Inside the house, my eyes adjust to the darker insides. I quickly locate Daniel when there is a dull banging noise and a grunt of exertion at the front door.

Two duffle bags are on the ground, and one more slung over his shoulder. He's has to be moving them out to the SUV. The back door is open. "What are you doing?"

"Packing up." He says.

"Do we have to?" An added playful whine and pout complete the words, but it is lost on him when he doesn't look at my face

"Yes. It's safer in Banff. Go get Rayleen. We'll be ready to leave right away." Daniel starts to leave the house, trying to end the conversation.

I don't know about that. With Darius lurking around it might be safer to stay away from Banff.

On a second thought, it may be more dangerous to avoid going back. Darius is the type who would search the ends of the earth for me; a trait I once found endearing is now a frightening sign of how far he'd go to keep me.

"We could stick around here for a little while longer." I think out loud while following him as far as the front step.

It might not hurt to spend a few more hours here. It's peaceful, quiet, and a pleasant touch of privacy.

He turns around. "We've already wasted half the day. They're going to get worried that something happened to us.

What if they decide to send a search party after us?

Would you be happy knowing that someone might get injured because we decided to laze about all afternoon too?"

"Fine." Resigning to his determination to leave, I huff then turn around to get Rayleen.

Footsteps run heavy behind me. Arms scoop me in and lift me up. I panic and kick to get loose.

"Leaving without a kiss?" Daniel asks.

"How can I kiss you like this?" I return.

All panic has left me. Arms I thought to be Darius, are not. They belong to my boyfriend. He lets my feet touch the ground.

Spinning around, I greet his eager lips with my own for a brief encounter; perhaps all the panic hasn't left me.

I itch to break free and check on Rayleen.

Pushing back on him, we part ways as I break the grasp he has on me.

I leave him and go through the house to the patio doors.

Following her laughter brings me to her exact position; right about where I had left her.

Rayleen and Crystal chase and roughhouse with each other. Crystal pounces on Rayleen; pushing her to the ground by her back. The little girl rolls over, knocking the griffin off. Rayleen tackle hugs Crystal to the ground.

I watch in adoration.

An arm curls up around my shoulder.

"Time to go." Daniel announces to all present.

Rayleen and Crystal continue wrestling; likely not hearing him talk.

"Rayleen, we're leaving now!" He shouts at her.

Rayleen immediately stops. Crystal rolls over her, not ready for the sudden stop. Rayleen pops herself up.

"Come on, Crystal." She says, patting her leg for the animal's attention.

Daniel releases my shoulders to take my hand. Rayleen crosses by us to race to the SUV with Crystal. It's a straight path through the house to get to the front door.

Forlornly, I burn this house and its memories into my mind.

We were happy; played board games, children's games, loved, and laughed.

We were like a carefree little family.

But, with a crashing realization it is over, and we have to return. There will be a new start when we arrive. Darius will be waiting, and I will have to go with him.

I can only hope to delay this along the way.

A thought comes to me. "I'll drive."

If I drive, I can get us lost. Not enough to prevent us from getting there at all, just more like taking a scenic route to get back.

"Are you sure?" He asks in courtesy as he holds out the keys for me to take.

I take hold of the keys, and then kiss him gently. "Yeah, I feel like driving."

We arrive at the SUV. A moment of forgetfulness has me opening the passenger door. I duck around the front when I realize what I did.

Act like I did it on purpose to save face on the embarrassment.

Inside the vehicle, I start it up.

Checking on everyone's status, I find all are inside and the doors are shut; seatbelts are on all the people.

It's good enough for me.

Putting the SUV into drive, I set us off. Drive out of the neighbourhood, and out towards the city exit.

At the last set of lights, a convoy of vehicles blocks off the exit.

They weren't there yesterday.

This is the way we came back into the city, and none of these vehicles were here. I stop with a little confusion. Now, I guess we find another way out of town.

Two burly men with high powered guns come out from one of the cars.

"Drive. Drive! Drive! Drive! DRIVE!" His voice gets louder and quicker; more urgent.

Hurling the steering wheel to one side and stomping on the gas screeches the tires.

It's not until I look back in the rear view mirror that I see why Daniel continues to freak out in the seat next to me. A couple of the vehicles blocking the way out are now following us.

There's more than one way to get out of this town. Just a little past the high school I turn to the right. The straightaway allows my speed to shoot up fast.

The vehicles are still tailing us. I know this road ends, but to get out of town means following the same highway that leads us towards the farm, and the opposite way of Banff.

This wasn't how I wanted to delay things, but I'll take it as long as no one is injured in any way.

From time to time I look back. The people are catching up. Driving faster and faster, until they are practically on my bumper.

The indoor pool passes on my right. I need to slow down to make the upcoming turn, but I can't let these people catch us.

Who knows their intentions? They set up a road block at one of the main ways out of town, and started chasing us.

Next, I expect gun fire and vehicle ramming; like what you see in the movies.

At the last moment, I slam the breaks and turn.

Crunching metal and a jolt from the back side throw off my aim a little. The SUV hops up onto the curb, narrowly missing the light post.

I hit the gas until all wheels are up on the side of the road. Veering back to the road, we take off fast.

Once control on the SUV is in hand, I look up to the mirror. People from the second vehicle are rushing out to the first.

Terrifying and exhilarating as the whole chase was, I am glad they stopped following us.

Adrenaline keeps my fingers and legs twitching. My speed remains naturally high with my foot like lead.

The familiar road is the same one we would take to get back to the farms.

"Turn right, down that road." His words bring me back to reality.

"What?" I ask dumbly.

"Turn right. Down that road." Daniel instructs. He points down the road he means.

I slow down and take the turn he wants me to.

Shoulder checking on Rayleen in the back seat I see her pulled up into a ball, clutching onto Crystal. "Are you okay?" I don't expect an answer back. "It's okay. They stopped following us. I know it was a bit scary, but we're fine now."

"What was that? Who the Hell were they? Do we have to worry about thugs now? They had to be human. They looked human."

"I don't know." I answer for all of his questions and statements.

"Should we have tried to talk to them?" Daniel asks.

"I don't know, but probably not. They didn't have to chase us but they did. They might have robbed us, or worse." I offer. They wouldn't have good intentions with actions like those.

"Right." He answers. We drive in silence a ways before he gives instructions again. "Turn right up there. It'll connect to the QE2."

We fall silent again.

I pass glances to each of my travel companions through the journey.

Rayleen eventually slowly uncurls and falls asleep. Crystal weaved through her legs. Daniel stares out the window to only pipe up to tell me where to go. His instructions create a barrier between my plan and putting it to reality; stopping me from losing our way and delaying our arrival.

The bright day turns to a red dusk as we drive into Banff.

We are met with the oddest of sights as we near the big field not far into the city. Mounds of black are sprinkled in the field. One bonfire burns near the center.

"What are they burning?" I ask out loud mostly to myself.

"Pull over." Daniel quietly says. I just stop the vehicle instead. "Are they our people?"

The thought hasn't occurred to me that we might not know them. What if Darius sent them?

The question is nixed just a moment later. Long golden blonde hair atop a shorter girl's head, held within a ponytail, is undeniable in her identity. "There's Jaiden."

With Rayleen still asleep, I leave the vehicle.

Left and right, I don't see a way to get through the fence, so I must go over. Putting my hands on the metal pole at the top and a foot into the chain link fence, I kick up. The fence piece wobbles unnervingly. Carefully and quickly, I hoist myself up enough to kick my leg over.

"Why are you climbing the fence?" Daniel asks. I expect him to be on the side I had come from, and yet he's on the side I'm headed to.

"To get into the field." I say.

"There's an open gate right there." He points down about ten feet. Now that I am on this side, I can see the opened gate clearly.

"Well, I didn't see that." I admit. Pulling my other leg over, Daniel grabs ahold of my waist. He supports my weight so I let go and let him bring me to the ground. "Thanks." I peck his lips to reiterate the sentiment.

"Silly girl." He endears. "You always have to do things the hard way, don't you?"

I brush off the tease to walk towards the events. Looking over to where Jaiden was, I call her name, "Jaiden," loud enough for her to hear.

She turns around and looks. When she spots us by the fence she walks to a person nearby. Taller than her, with black hair up in a bun, it must be Leah. When she turns around to look over at us, I confirm suspicions.

At least, two people made it back from our trip. I don't see the other three yet.

Jaiden walks over. She has a neutral look as opposed to her natural smile.

"Hi. Uh." She looks over at the fire.

"What's going on?" I ask, impatient for the answer.

Jaiden looks back at me and bites her lip in the corner with an eye tooth. "They were attacked while we were gone. Brad and his group of extremists started the attack because they said a supernatural being attacked them.

Turns out that Darius initiated an attack while we were gone.

Every human here died with no exceptions. They killed some of the supernatural beings here too; those who didn't want to join them again. And, whoever hid well enough or weren't here, got to live."

My heart is struck and my body quakes. "Who?" Only the one word makes it through my lips. Who died? Who is still alive? Why did Darius attack them? Is this a punishment for me?

Who is still alive?

"Kelly and Miles are alive." It brings me some relief to hear those two names, but when she stops there it does nothing to relieve my discomfort. "I don't know who else you would want to know about."

"What about anyone else from our original group?" Daniel asks.

Jaiden shakes her head. "No one else that stayed behind is alive. Nikki, Shawn and Stephanie haven't returned yet."

"Lucas and Calli are?" Daniel trails off in is question. He already has an answer from her previous statement, but he double checks anyway.

"Dead." She says.

"I'm sorry." Daniel says. Those were her friends.

"Thanks." There is an awkward pause. "I'm sorry too. Everyone has lost a lot of people they cared about." My eyes do all they can to advert her gaze. "Where's Rayleen?"

"Sleeping in the SUV." Daniel answers when I can't.

"Cam?" My voice squeaks. Jaiden scrunches her eyebrows. She may not have known him. I clear my throat in a swallow. "The boy who was teaching Rayleen magic?" I clarify in hopes she knows.

"No, sorry. I haven't seen him. He's either dead or went with Darius."

It takes all I can muster to not break down. My breathing quickens and I feel the beginnings of a panic attack.

Rayleen is going to be devastated.

Daniel notices, and pulls me into a hug. The up and down movement of his hand rubbing my back doesn't do anything to calm me down.

Darius did this. All these people are dead because

Darius killed them.

He told me to leave.

He got me to leave so he could attack them all.

He said I'd be convinced to join him when I...

The words return to me. He said that I had to go to the farm and see what he left me. That when I returned, I would be convinced to join him.

He did it. The gift was death; at the farm and here. Darius killed all of these people to get me back.

He's gone insane.

How could he possibly think I would like that, and be okay with it? He's trying to scare me into submission, and part of me thinks it's working.

Darius killed everyone around me to convince me to return to him. It's a deafening message.

"I need a drink." I say.

"I'll go get you water." Daniel releases me from his chest, and starts off towards the SUV.

"Alcohol. I mean a drink of alcohol." I clarify. Water just won't clench this thirst of a different variety. I need to drown the explosion of feelings.

"Oh. I'll go find you some." He offers.

"No thanks. I can find it myself. That Irish Pub is right over there." I remember.

"I'll come with you." Jaiden offers. "I could use a drink after the day I've had. Daniel, someone should watch Rayleen. She shouldn't be alone for so long. We can walk to the pub just fine."

He hesitates, while crossing looks with Jaiden. "Sure. I'll watch her." Daniel says. He kisses my forehead.

Jaiden and I walk in silence to the pub. I guide us by walking just slightly ahead of her.

She pulls open the door to hold it for me. I walk through it first.

Jaiden goes straight to behind the counter and into the back room. Moments later she comes back with a bottle of Cherry Whiskey.

"Did I cause this?" I ask.

"Cause what?" She asks in confusion.

"Did I cause all those people to die?" I swipe my hand out towards the field.

"No." Her answer is too quick and insincere.

"Jaiden, please. I need you to tell me the truth. You, of all people, can tell me the truth." I need her to tell me the truth before my feelings crush me. The truth from someone else will set me free from my mind.

"You didn't stick a sword in them or rip out their throats, but yes, in a way all of this is partially your fault." Ask and you shall receive. Jaiden doesn't hold back on the punches. "Did you know he was going to attack?"

"Of course not!"

"So your wanting to leave real quick from here didn't have anything to do with Darius warning you?" Jaiden accuses me.

"No, I mean…" I should have seen it coming. In hindsight, I should have told someone he was there. I should have told them what happened; the exchange between us. It could have made all the difference. "He came to me. I didn't see him since the hotel. He didn't tell me he was going to attack. He told me to go to the farm because he left me a gift there. We left soon after."

"That gift was the massacre you never saw. I'm guessing, because you were off looking for a gift, not Crystal like you said." I nod to her assumption. "He left you a bloody note inside the house. Said it was for you. Darius killed everyone there for you, then came here to get you to go see that, then while you were gone and safe, he killed everyone here. Once again a clear message that it was done just for you."

"I didn't know!" I yell as if that would convince her that I'm telling the truth.

"I'm not saying otherwise. But, you didn't exactly tell anyone that Darius was here either. That he was purposely and suspiciously making you leave here suddenly." Jaiden holds up both her hands. One hand is palm out and the other one clutches the bottle. "You don't need to be defensive and you don't need to blame yourself. You didn't know what he was going to do; fine. I didn't know either.

I was just stating the events. Darius is after you and he's proving that he will kill everyone you know in order to get to you." She pauses to reflect and take a gulp of the alcohol. "He's coming back for you, isn't he?"

I swallow a lump. "Yes. He said he would."

Quick as a flash she throws another question at me. "Do you still want to be with him?"

Her question was once a hard one to answer. A couple days ago, my answer might have been a little different. But, now I can confidently answer, "No."

"Then you're our best chance at killing him."

Jaiden's leap in the conversation throws me off. "What?"

"If you don't want him to keep killing everyone you know, including Rayleen, then he needs to die. Darius is clearly obsessed with you. He's not going to think logically. You can get close enough to him to end it all."

"I can't stake him. I'm not strong enough to drive in a wooden stake." I say the first excuse to come to mind. It's one thing to not be in love with him anymore, and another to kill him; it's not something I think I could do.

"It doesn't have to be a wooden stake."

I roll my eyes. "So I've heard."

"It doesn't have to be as hard as going through the sternum to the heart either. You could go for the throat. Nice and soft with a sharp pointy knife."

Jaiden doesn't get it. "I don't think I could kill him."

"Or, distract him. I'll kill him so you don't have to." She offers a plan B.

"How?" I want details. How am I supposed to distract him enough for Jaiden to kill him? How will she kill him?

"I'll figure that out depending on the events that happen. Can't plan for something when you don't know what'll happen."

Distracting Darius requires me to be close to him; dangerously close to him. "You'll protect Rayleen, right? If something happens to me."

"Yes."

"Thank you."

She takes another swig. "Oh, and don't tell anyone about you meeting Darius. We don't need another Taylor incident." Jaiden warns. "The vampires are already looking to feed on us. Humans are a scarcity around here. Don't give anyone a reason why they should just hand you over as food."

"But everyone knows about the farm and about what happened here. They'll piece it together." If she can piece it together than someone else is likely to come to the same conclusion.

"As far as they're concerned, anyone could have killed the farm people. Leah and I are the only ones who saw the note, and she's keeping her mouth shut about it. No one's expressly said this was your fault. As far as they know, Darius came back for revenge. We'll try to keep it that way."

"Okay, thank you." Not fussy about the type of alcohol at this point, I grab the first bottle I see. It's a bottle of vodka, from a company I've never heard. I'm more concerned about getting the alcohol pumping through my system as fast as possible.

This wasn't the type of conversation I was hoping for when I initially asked my question. I was looking for niceties. The optimistic version of the truth. Someone to hold my hand and tell me everything is going to be okay because I had nothing to do with anything.

I should have expected Jaiden wouldn't do that.

Jaiden has fed me the undeniable truth, like I should have expected her to after asking for it. She tried to play nice, and I went and asked for the truth.

Ultimately, it wasn't what I was looking for. It didn't make me feel better about everything; it created a numb space where the turmoil cancelled out.

Her with her cherry whiskey and I with my vodka return to the SUV.

Daniel has turned on the inside lights in the front of the vehicle.

"I'm going to go back and see Leah." She points over to the fire. I just let her go without a word.

The door opens easily. Daniel jumps a little at my entrance. "Better?" I hop inside and close the color behind me.

"Much." I open the cap and take a couple swigs. It burns. The flavour like nail polish; bottom shelf vodka. "Would you like some?"

"Nah." He looks behind me. "Where'd Jaiden go?"

"Back to Leah." I say. "Back to the fire."

"Hmm, most of them left."

"What?" I look over to the fire and the dark piles. There aren't as many people left as there was when we had first arrived.

"Most of them left. I guess they were done. A few stuck behind to watch over the last of the fire, but I guess the rest left to go back to the houses. I guess we'll head back too." He starts up the vehicle and drives us forward.

"I don't want to sleep. Don't think I could." Another couple gulps of the vodka go down smooth.

"We don't have to go to sleep. There's plenty we could do after we put Rayleen to bed."

Years of experience tell me otherwise. She's a light sleeper, and once she's up, she's up for a while. "You know she's hard to move after she falls asleep. By this point, she'll wake up when we move her, and I don't think she'd fall back to sleep. You know that means she'll be super cranky tomorrow."

"So we leave her in the SUV." He states a solution too simply.

"We can't just leave her in the SUV all night." I argue.

"I didn't mean that. I meant we could stick close by while we're up, then either take our chances, or one of us could lean back a front seat to take a nap."

Now the idea makes sense. "Oh, okay, yeah."

We drive down the roads to pull in through the alleyway. There's a campfire in the back of the vampires' house. We're waved down before we can go further by a familiar face alit by the headlights.

Miles gestures for us to pull over. Our SUV stops near him.

Daniel rolls down the window. "What?"

Miles walks up to his window and rests his hands where the window once was. "Hey. Glad you're okay."

"From the sounds of it, we should be saying that to you." Daniel commiserates.

"It was chaotic and tragic." Miles stops at that.

We don't need specific details to know that what did happen was completely horrible. He might not want to talk about it.

"So, were you just waiting to get ran over, or...?" Daniel jests to lighten the mood.

"Everyone's sleeping at this house. No dead bodies or remnants of anyone in there. Can't guarantee the same about any of the other houses." Miles informs us of the change.

I look to the house. The vamp house may not be the safest place right now. Darius may have relations with any of the demons. He could have left them behind to watch me.

Jaiden already warned me about the vampires wanting us for our blood; I know they can't be trusted. Why are we sleeping in a house full of them?

"Good to know. I guess we'll stop here then. We weren't looking to sleep though. Alexa's got alcohol and no one's tired. Except Rayleen, but she's already sleeping in the back and we don't want to disturb her."

"Kelly's two trucks up." Miles looks over to where he means.

"We'll pull up there so we can keep an eye on Rayleen." Daniel waits until Miles takes just one step back before taking his foot off the break. He lets the SUV coast forward until we parallel the truck. There isn't much room on either side of our SUV.

We park, and exit; me with one last glance at the sleeping girl in the back. Rayleen looks peaceful. Crystal coos in a sort of acknowledgment in our departure.

"How'd you beat us back?" Daniel yells, astonished. I hold back a shout to keep it down. When I see him directing the question to Jaiden the same question runs through my mind.

"It's only a block and a half and Leah helped me run back." She answers.

Handing my bottle to Daniel, for safe keeping, I climb up into the back of the truck where three of them are awaiting us.

Kelly, Leah, and Jaiden are seated on pillows. Jaiden is wrapped almost entirely in a blanket, while Leah has one covering her legs. I pull an unused blanket around me like a towel, and then sit down.

The nights are still cold, but not enough to worry about frost.

Daniel hands me the bottle of vodka after he's up inside the truck; forgotten in my bid to settle down. Twisting the cap, I take a couple gulps.

Kelly recounts the story of how she and Miles escaped Darius and the others. She tells the story as an epic telling, but it could have easily been summed up as a tale of running, killing three people, and hiding in a basement for a few hours.

Done her story and her drink, Miles gets up to go to the corner of the open tail gate with the box of coolers. He takes the whole box.

One bottle is handed out to each person. I take mine and open up the top with my palm. Taking a drink of the liquid inside. It's sweeter than my vodka; too sweet with the contrast but that will ebb. It's a strawberry daiquiri; of course it's sweet. This drink does taste better.

"Is she sleeping?" The words bring my attention to the person speaking them; Miles. For just a moment I wonder if they are talking about Rayleen.

Jaiden is leaned back and hunched over. Her head has fallen over to the side at an uncomfortable looking angle.

Leah says, "She hasn't slept much."

"Should we wake her to go inside?" I ask.

"Let her sleep. She's not bothering anyone and I don't feel like having to go inside yet." Leah counters.

Why would she have to go inside? The question has no chance of being asked by me; Daniel beats me to it. "She's a big girl. She's can go to bed by herself."

Suddenly, it dawns on me; the vampires. The same reason I worry about sleeping in that house.

Jaiden was the very person who warned me about it.

"Oh yeah, one of only three humans in a town full of vampires, who haven't fed properly in months, will be completely fine in a house of vampires all by herself." Leah's sarcasm is palpable.

"We can take bets on how long before one decides to take a bite out of her. Oh wait, Leah already has." Kelly takes a jab at her.

"I was about to rage, and she offered to take the edge off." Tension builds between Kelly and Leah. The violent image that I had created morphs to one more like the memory of what happened in the bathroom at the school.

"What do we do now?" I ask, hoping to cut the tension, and eventual fight.

"Drink and party until we fall asleep." Kelly switches gears so quickly I'm not certain she is serious.

I roll my eyes. "I meant later," after the partying and sleeping off the hangover.

"We leave. We can't stay here. Darius has made it obvious that he's going to keep coming back here." I'm relieved Daniel is on the same page. We need to leave. Run far away from here. Somewhere Darius can't find us.

"Where? Is any place really safe?" Kelly questions. "I've got the answer for you. Nowhere is safe."

"What if we crossed the border?" Miles suggests.

"What the Hell would that do?" Daniel outbursts from his confusion and frustration.

"Darius won't chase us. He has responsibility here. His territory is in Alberta. He'd be killed if he crossed territories without permission or warning to the other leader." Miles explains.

Knowing Darius as I do, I don't think something so simple will stop him. He doesn't like following rules when they don't suit him.

If he wants to get to me, Darius isn't going to let an imaginary line tell him he can't.

"Yeah, okay, until he gets permission. Then what?" Daniel asks.

"It'll buy us some time. And, he might not get permission. It's not like he's well liked among the other leaders." Miles says.

"So we're banking on Julius not giving him permission? And, what if he decides that he doesn't care what Julius says? Darius will come straight after us." Kelly's line of thinking aligns with my own.

"Or, he could come back here and kill us tonight, maybe tomorrow." Miles reminds me of the urgency in leaving. Darius said he'd be back. He might already be here; waiting for me. "We can't just sit here and wait for him to kill us. I say we go to B.C. now; tonight. As soon as we can get ready."

"Why do we have to go to B.C.? Can't we just go somewhere else, that's not over the mountains? Darius is bad, but he's more of an annoyance. Julius is just cruel." Leah joins in.

"Nothing says that we'll even run into this Julius guy. It's a big province; a big territory. Right now, we are trying to get away from the guy who seems to just love hacking up our friends." Daniel pushes. He's on board with the idea now.

"He's targeting us for a reason." Kelly glares straight at me. I look away, red in the cheeks, and hope no one else notices.

Daniel puts a hand on my knee in support. "We should just do it. We've got everyone here."

"Not everyone. Nikki, Shawn, and Stephanie aren't back yet." Leah reminds us.

"We can't wait for them for forever. We don't even know if they're coming back." Daniel argues. "Jaiden pissed off Nikki, so I wouldn't doubt if they decide to stay away."

"Can we just give them some time to get back here first?" Leah asks. "What would you have done if we decided to pack up the minute we returned?"

"We'll give them till morning, but we have to leave." Daniel decides for everyone.

"Jaiden's not going to like that." Leah says.

"Jaiden's sleeping. She doesn't get a vote. What would she do anyway, Leah? Stay here by herself; hoping for her friend's return? A friend, mind you, that hates her guts right now." Daniel persists in pushing us to leave as soon as possible.

He is right, they might not return. Those three are all they had; if you take Jaiden out of the equation.

Are we to risk our lives because of a small possibility that they might make it back here before Darius does?

"It's better for everyone if we leave immediately." I echo.

"That open to everyone?" The new voice surprises me. DeAngelo makes himself known along with five other people.

"Of course. Everyone is welcome to join." Miles says.

"Good, because we were just discussing the same thing. No one wants to stay here. There's no point anymore." DeAngelo speaks for his small group.

"Then I guess you should go get ready. Everyone should. When we're packed up, we leave." Daniel tells everyone as a collective.

"You said we'd wait until morning." Leah jumps on his words quickly.

"Use your senses; I know you've got them. I'm sure even the humans have noticed by now." Kelly must notice my look of confusion. "They're back. Discussion's over."

I look around, but don't see them. I'll take her word on it.

Most people leave to pack up by the time the two of them make their way over to us. Daniel, Jaiden, and I remain behind as the others gather.

Our belongings and supplies are still in the SUV from our journey. We don't need anything else.

"What took you so long?" Daniel goads.

"Gas problems. Got a flat tire. Everything that could go wrong with our vehicle, went wrong." Shawn answers with an amused smile.

"Where's Stephanie?" I ask when I notice she's missing.

She watches Jaiden sleep with a drop dead glare. "Dead." Nikki seethes. My stomach drops.

"I'm so sorry." I say, knowing it won't make a difference in what she's feeling.

"What happened?" I lightly elbow him and his lack of tact. Now isn't the right time to question them on it. For all we know they were attacked on the way into town, and she died just minutes ago.

"We were attacked last night. She was shot." Shawn explains. My mind make an assumption in one word; humans. If she was shot, the perpetrators were likely human; right?

"I'm sorry." I apologize both for their loss and for Daniel bringing up the painful memories.

"It's fine." Nikki dismisses my condolences sharply. It obviously isn't fine. "What was this I heard about B.C.?"

"We're going to B.C. to try to get away from Darius. He attacked everyone while we were gone." I explain it all. I don't know how much they know.

"Or we could stay and fight." Nikki finally looks over to us from Jaiden. "Nothing good comes from leaving."

"Nothing good is going to happen if we stay. Darius is just going to come back and attack again." Daniel argues.

"So we fight and kill the bastard." The anger snarls her voice. With all the loss she's experienced in the last day I'm amazed she hasn't broken down to a shell by this point. She, out of the rest of us, had made many good friends from the vast majority of the people here.

A few of them I will miss.

"General consensus says to leave. We'll leave with or without you." Daniel shrugs.

"What did Jaiden say?" She asks.

"She doesn't get a vote. She's sleeping." Daniel reiterates from earlier.

"So wake her up." She scoffs. "Everyone's just going to go?"

"Yeah. So are you coming with us or not?" Daniel forces her to make a decision.

"Doesn't look like I get much of a choice. No point in staying if I'm the only one." Nikki spots the remaining bottles in the box of coolers.

Taking one for herself she pops the top and chugs down the entire bottle. She removes two more bottles from the box, and then walks the couple steps back over to Shawn.

"You're driving." She holds up the keys to their car for Shawn.

When he takes them, she walks off to where she had come from.

Chapter 9

God!

What else is going to go wrong today?

First, we run out of gas. The taste of gasoline and throw up still lingers in the back of my throat despite my best efforts to drown it out.

Now, I stare at the flimsy donut Shawn is replacing the deflated tire with; the culprit being a nail sticking out the side.

He groans from the effort of turning the X thing. "Tighten these up in a star pattern; one, two three, four, five. Pull out the jack, and you're done."

"Great." I try to sound interested in his tutorial, but I'm not.

"I don't know how you have a vehicle and don't know how to change a tire." He admonishes.

"I have AMA." I remind him, forgetting for that exact moment that the company no longer exists.

We share a knowing smile when we both realize what I said. "Well, why didn't you say so? We should've called them."

"Shut up. You know because your dad taught you. No one ever taught me, so how am I supposed to know how to change a tire when no one ever showed me.

My mom swore off doing anything mechanical after she put windshield washer fluid in the oil, and dad bought me the AMA; for obvious reasons." He releases the jack and the car falls back into its proper place. "And it's not just me. It took five of us once to figure out how to put air in a tire."

"Five? Really?" His voice sounds of disbelief from behind the car. He puts the jack back in place. I wonder if we should move our things back to the trunk area and out of the back seats. "That's disturbing."

I shrug even though he can't see me. "None of us had done it before. Barely knew it was a thing that people have to do with their tires now and then."

"It's still disturbing." Shawn shuts the door.

"Shut up. At least, I know how to check my oil level." After I got yelled at by the mechanic for destroying my engine; letting the oil run out and continuing to run it. An expensive and embarrassing mistake, which he made sure I would never repeat.

"Good for you." He doesn't sound sincere.

"Shut up. Can we go yet?" He looks done.

The tools are back in their place, so we should be able to go.

He holds up his grease and dirt ridden hands. "Just need to clean these up."

"Well, we should hurry; it's getting dark." The sun is setting and creating a red hue on all it casts its light on.

"Right," he says as he quickly gives up the search to wipe his hands on something disposable. Streaked handprints paint up from above his knees to fade near his thighs. Shawn climbs inside through the driver's door. I get inside through the passenger door. "Are we even heading in the right direction?"

If I had something soft in reach I would throw it at him. I lose my chance when he starts driving before I find something not quite solid; cheese puffs.

My mom's voice screams at me to not mess with the driver.

"Shut up!" I speak with a grin. It's not my fault I had my directions backwards; I always screw them up. He listened to me. He could have asked if right actually meant right, or if I meant the other right. "I told you to take the main highway down, but no, you wanted to take a scenic route. A way there neither of us have been before. It'll be fun;

he said."

"It is fun. Hasn't this been fun?"

I huff and laugh in one shot.

Almost a full day has gone by since we started our trip back, and yet the whole journey should have taken us only four or five hours; and we're still not back yet.

Damn car trouble.

Damn getting lost.

I'm- I don't know; a bit apprehensive about our return.

Life is suspended in this vehicle.

Reality waits for us in Banff. It's an inevitable rut in the road. At some point, we'll have to stop and talk about it all.

I'll have to bear witness to a constant reminder of my losses. Every day she'll be right there. Every time I see her, I'll be reminded of her lies.

The seat below me is lined with rocks; or at least, it feels that way. My butt and lower back seem to have a decreasing tolerance for sitting here doing nothing.

My fingers dance on my knee as we eventually turn off the highway.

The style of building looks familiar, but the buildings themselves are strange to me. We have to be getting close to Banff now, or maybe we're in Jasper. I think they have the same look, and I'm not confident I read the map right. "Where are we?"

"Banff."

"What? Really?" The moment he turns down the next street, reveals all the familiar buildings. They look different in the dark, but the buildings are still them. Coming in a different way, and the evening shade, tricked my head.

Shawn parks us outside Uncle's house. We exit and I walk straight for the backyard. Someone should be out and about in the back yard. Likely, they've got a fire going. I'm hoping some real food might be left over from supper.

"Should we bring our bags inside?" Shawn asks loud enough for me to hear.

I turn around to face him. "No, I'm exhausted. I just, wanna eat and go to bed." I shout back to him.

He jogs to catch up with me. "Right. We can do it in the morning."

"Did you lock the car?" I ask; a bit paranoid from being out and about.

"No." The keys fumble from his fingers and to the ground. I pick them up faster than he can. Listening for the two honks once I've hit the lock button twice; a nice telltale sign the signal reached its destination.

"WAIT!" A faint scream sounds immediately after the beeps. Abby pops in from around the back corner of the house. She looks out of breath from running. She carries a hiking bag and her acoustic guitar. "You don't want to go in there!" Abby alerts us with her sudden shout. "You already have your things, right? And your car, is there much gas in there?"

"I mean we packed up most of our things before we left. Maybe half a tank, why?" I answer her question. Quickly, I realize I have questions of my own that have gone unanswered; starting with why she stopped us. "Why shouldn't we go in the house?"

"We're packing up and going to B.C. Darius attacked while you were gone. Killed almost everyone." Something gets her attention out of view. "I've got to go. Drive the car to front. Don't go in this house; just the vampire house."

Abby leaves us with bated breaths. Darius attacked. My heart can't take anymore. It breaks into nothing.

Without a word we rush to the vehicle. I race us to the house and screech to a stop out front. I lock the car as I hurry to the door.

Going inside the house is nothing more than a flurry of people and directions. We're greeted by looks of relief, pity, and concern.

All along the way, I search for faces to tick off my list of important people; it's not a very large list. Not one person I care about has passed me by but it doesn't mean they're dead.

The light from the house has taken away my night vision.

"This way." Shawn says.

He leads, and I follow to a line of vehicles. The presence of the truck and trailer from the farm tell me that Jaiden and Leah made it back; hopefully the both of them made it back.

"What took you so long?" Daniel's joke annoys me. I hold my tongue so the brutal honesty doesn't fly out.

Jaiden sits in the back against the side. Her head is tilted down and her eyes are closed. I look for the rising and falling of her chest to tell me that she's alive and well. Not that I doubt they'd keep her dead body next to them.

Is she actually sleeping or is she just pretending so to avoid me? How can she sleep so peacefully? I wish her insomnia would keep her up as a small inkling of karmic payback.

"Gas problems. Got a flat tire. Everything that could go wrong with our vehicle, went wrong." Shawn answers in my stead.

"Where's Steph?" Alexa asks.

Her question breaks the seal on my lips. "Dead." The voice that comes out is not mine.

It's Jaiden's fault; all of it.

"I'm so sorry." Alexa responds softly.

My fist clenches as I resist the urge to throttle her.

My chest hurts. Tears burn at my eyes. My throat closes around a lump.

"What happened?" Daniel asks.

"We were attacked last night. She was shot." Shawn explains.

"I'm sorry." Alexa apologizes again; like it would help.

"It's fine." The two words replace the string of curse words I actually want to scream at her. We need to end this conversation immediately. "What was this I heard about B.C.?" And about the attack; can't forget about that.

"We're going to B.C. to try to get away from Darius. He attacked everyone while we were gone." She says.

So, they're just going to run.

No. I'm done running.

Every time we go somewhere, someone dies. "Or we could stay and fight." I look over at the two of them. "Nothing good comes from leaving."

"Nothing good is going to happen if we stay. Darius is just going to come back." Daniel counters.

"So we fight and kill the bastard." All I need is to get close enough with a knife, and I know I could kill him.

"General consensus says to leave. We'll leave with or without you." If absolutely everyone is leaving, it forces a change in options. Darius is never alone. If he brought an army before, he will bring one again.

Angry or not, I wouldn't survive long enough to break through everyone to get to him.

I won't survive being kidnapped again.

"What did Jaiden say?" I ask.

"She doesn't get a vote. She's sleeping." My eyebrow pops up as Daniel tells me this.

If I were in her place, I would be beyond pissed.

Fuck her. I'm mad at her.

I'm not going to be the one to wake her up.

"So wake her up." I scoff in displeasure. "Everyone's just going to go?"

"Yeah. So are you coming with us or not?" He makes it sound like a have a choice. I do, but not much of one. Stay here completely alone, or go with everyone else.

"Doesn't look like I get much of a choice. No point in staying if I'm the only one." The near empty bottles of alcohol they sport have me thirsty like a man in a desert. I eye the box at the end of the truck bed.

The cap twists off easy. Too easy, the alcohol goes down to my stomach. It'll work its magic soon; with the help of two others I take.

The keys burn a hole in my pocket. I can't get rid of her voice telling me not to drink and drive.

"You're driving." I tell Shawn as I hand him the keys.

An accidental glance at Jaiden has me averting my eyes. I can't be near her. Everything is packed up so I have nothing to do.

Walking back to the car, I intend on sitting in there and drinking my two friends. But, the plan is nixed when the vehicle is locked; I forgot about that.

One more bottle downs like the first. The third becomes a sipping drink when the liquid has to be choked down. My throat has tired from all the liquid and wishes to reject my drinking so much of it.

Only one person, Abby, spots me and comes out to check on me; concerned by what she sees. "Hey. Are you alright?"

My unasked question was never answered.

"Who died?" She gapes like a fish out of water. "Who died in the attack?" I restate.

"It's almost easier to say who lived." She grins sadly. Why does everyone have to make a joke out of death? The smile disappears to a frown. She wipes away falling tears. "I'm sorry. This is pretty much it." She motions back to the house. "None of the humans survived."

Jamie. Brad. Uncle.

"What happened; exactly?" The words choke out.

"Brad started it; we thought he did. Conspiracy theories have since been; sorry." Abby stops herself from rambling. "Umm, restart.

Darius sent someone to attack one of the human haters. Brad organized the haters together to attack supernaturals and anyone that tried to stop them. Brad stabbed first.

We didn't get very far into that when Darius showed up. He gave supernaturals the option of joining his side and said he'd kill everyone else. They attacked then.

I know a few shouted that they'd join him and were spared. Others ran and hid; that's most of who you see alive. Some stayed and fought. But, he came with a large army. They didn't have a chance.

We hid until the fight was over and they left. Then, gathered the bodies and parts to give them a fire burial."

"Stop. Just stop. I can't hear any more." My eye lids shut off the world. "Please leave. I just; I need to be alone." Jamie's dead. Brad is dead. My uncle is dead. Numerous people are dead.

"I'm sorry." I hear her footsteps as she walks away.

Everyone's sorry, but it doesn't help. It-just-it's not going to bring them back. It's senseless. I down the rest of the alcohol.

Sadness fades to numb, turns to a pit, and grows into frustration. Frustration fuels anger. A volcano of emotions erupts.

My eyes flash open. Fury flares. The empty bottle smashes against the ground. Glass bounces to hit my leg.

Some fleeting moment of satisfaction taken from the broken bottle feels good. I crave to hold onto the feeling. Again. I smash the last bottle against the ground.

Glass lays about my feet. Destroyed and broken like me.

How is this my life? How did this happen?

My hands twist and twitch. They itch to break something else. I restrain my rage well enough when I promise to find a pillow to beat up.

My anger settles to a roar, but doesn't rid my hands of the itch. Weaving my fingers together, I hold my hands tightly together. Bringing them to my mouth to nuzzle the rings against my mouth and nose.

Having no other outlet, the fire inside spills out into tears.

Before the deluge can really start, the dull click of the locks unlocking, and the lights brighten on either side of me. It shocks me out of my dwelling.

Wiping the wet away with my sleeves, I clean up just as Shawn comes out of the house with a case of water.

"Hey, I've grabbed a few extra things." He comes in closer. "Are you alright?" Shawn pauses for just a moment. Not long enough for me to answer. "Of course you aren't. Stupid question."

He sets down the case to hug and comfort me. I let him hug me, as much for me as it is for him. The both of us share a moment of mutual misery.

I pull myself away when I can cry no longer. "When are we leaving?" I ask.

"Soon. As soon as everyone is packed up."

"Fine." There is a finality and resignation in the one word.

"We could stay." He offers.

"No, we can't." Jaiden's name crosses my mind for a split second before I shake it loose. It would be suicide to stay here alone.

"No, we can't." He echoes. "It doesn't make sense to and you know that. And, I know you hate Jaiden right now, but she's the only family you've got left. You need to go with her."

"Fuck you." I won't admit it to him that he's right.

That the first reason I had thought to leave was because of Jaiden. His apparent mind read puts me on the defensive, however. Why would he think she would be my sole reason for going? I want to distance myself from any obligation to her in other's eyes. Give a reason so I can drop her if she's toxic and have no one tell me I have to take her back.

If only out of spite, I argue with him. "Family doesn't betray each other like that."

"She wasn't raised with your family. For all you know, betrayal was a regular occurrence at the dinner table. You told me you think her father is shit. That you think she was abused growing up-"

"I don't care."

"Yes, you do. I know you." He pronounces hard. "You care with a passion. If you lose her now, you're going to regret it later, because you're you. As your last best friend, I can't let you lose any more people; when you can help it. Besides, it's not like you're going to get a choice. As your last best friend you have to come with me wherever I go."

I play to his attempt to lighten the mood. "Why can't you follow me?"

"I'm more stubborn."

Half snorting an escaped burst of air. "Yeah right." Laughter explodes from my chest. I stop and turn serious immediately. "Why are you defending her so much?"

"If you didn't hurt so much right now, you'd be fiercely defending her. Whether she was right or wrong, whether you knew the whole story or not, because she's your sister." I look to the house to make sure no one is outside and in hearing range.

"Like your sister." He fixes himself once he realizes the slip. "It's who you are. It's why we're back here instead of anywhere else. It's why we're going to B.C.

At the end of the day, she's like your sister. You're family to me, so that makes her family too. When you can't be there for her, I will be.

You hate her now, but eventually you won't. And, I don't feel like tracking her down five years from now when you get over your grudge."

I almost regret confiding in him our secret, but he's right. "Five years?" How did he come up with that number?

"Have you met your family and their infamous grudges?" Shawn explains.

My aunt didn't talk to my mom for twenty years because she kissed a boy my aunt had a crush on in junior high; apparently ruining her life. "I might recall something like that. But, I think this offense might require fifty years. I have a family reputation to uphold."

Tears overcome me at the reminder. My family is no longer alive. Stephanie is dead. Jamie was killed. Brad is gone. Dozens of others, at the farm and in Banff, were slaughtered. Too many people are now gone.

Maybe alcohol was a bad idea.

Shawn places his hand on my arm in a form of comfort. My head clears just enough like a damper switch nudged up.

"Better?"

"A little." I clear my throat of the thickness weighted inside. "Do you need anything else?"

"No." He picks up the water.

"Here." I help him by opening up the back door for him.

Moving into the passenger seat, I wait for him to get inside. Shawn starts the engine, and drives us around to the back of the vehicle line up.

"I'm going to check in. Did you want to come with me?"

"No, I think I want to stay here." And wallow in my sadness alone.

Two seconds alone, and I realize that the numbness has returned. I feel completely sober again despite the alcohol I know is still running through my system.

To wallow in sadness I must be able to feel sad. Taking back my earlier thought, I think alcohol is exactly what I need right now.

Exiting the car, I walk back to the truck. Jaiden remains where I left her, but Alexa and Daniel have returned to their SUV beside her.

The box at the end only contains one last bottle. I snatch it up in declaration that it is now mine.

A low moan escapes from Jaiden as I walk by her. Examining her expression I figure she must be having a nightmare. Her frown and creased eyebrows betray her. Her head twitches.

Should I wake her? Save her from her dreams.

Out of spite, I continue walking by. She deserves whatever bad karma is coming her way.

Shawn fills the gas tank up with a jerry can. Hiding the bottle behind my back before he notices, I then ask him, "were we out?"

"Not really, but we might have a long trip. Would rather put the gas in now, than have everyone wait on us to fill her up."

A crowd of twenty, or so, people descend on the vehicles.

I hop inside ours. Chugging the liquid down, I get rid of the evidence by rolling the empty bottle under my seat.

Shawn gets in and all too fast the convoy rolls out.

Back tracking out of town, we drive until a sign is named for Castle Junction. The lead vehicle turns down the road.

"What are they doing?" Shawn mutters under his breath.

"What?" I ask.

"Come on. Where are they going? We should drive the main highway all the way there. Some idiot's decides to take a scenic route." Shawn mutters mostly to himself.

"It could be fun." I remind him. I don't see what the big deal is, as long as it gets us there. He sends a playful glare to me.

Trees and rock interchange as we drove along.

We slow, then stop rather quickly. Rolling down my window, I stick my head out to see around the truck in front of us. Headlights reveal why we had to stop.

When I spot the rocks blocking the way I say, "We should turn back. It's not meant to be. The universe is against us going to B.C."

"I think you can explain that one to them." Shawn gets out.

Leaving on my side of the car, I walk to the grouping already gathering.

"Grab what you can carry. It's not far from here." The discussion already had and the choice already made for us.

Jaiden looks on from her spot.

"You alright?" Leah asks her.

"I feel a little kidnapped." She reveals.

"You were sleeping. We didn't think you needed to be woken."

Uninterested in the rest of their conversation, I go back to the car.

Grabbing what I can carry; a couple bags do the trick. One for each hand to balance me out. The one has personal items, and the other is mostly a mystery except for the first aid kit. A crinkle leads me to believe food is packed away in here.

Shawn grabs the remaining hiker's bag; it's Jaiden's. I had stolen it yesterday; thinking she might have other secrets hidden away. If I was being a little less petty I would have taken that bag for ease of carrying.

"I can take that. It's my stuff anyway." Her voice surprises me with how close it is. I half expected Jaiden to still be in the back of the truck talking with Leah. Shawn gives her the bag.

Shawn comes up to me. "Here." He takes the bag closest to him. It sends me off kilter, but I regain my balance almost immediately.

As we pass the generator, I think about what a shame it is that we have to leave it behind. Electricity is hard to come by now.

One by one, people step up onto the rocks and dirt burying the road. I step in previous steps; they seem to be the sturdiest places.

Few rocks fall as people make their way over the twenty feet long rock slide. Now and then someone trips over and crashes to their hands and knees.

At the end, I jump down the five feet rather than climb down. I land hard with the extra weight of the bag.

Something wet lands on my face. If not for the drop coming away on my finger, I would have thought it to be imaginary when another fails to fall.

When all have passed, we all trek onwards. The road is clear and should lead us straight to Radium Hot Springs according to a sign.

"It's raining." Shawn says softly.

It takes a moment of concentration and sticking my hand out to discover that it is; barely. I dread what this will do to my hair. It's up in a bun, but the shorter hairs that will stick up and out won't be once they dry.

The further we walk, the more water falls from the sky. I wipe the liquid off my face and away from my eyes. Grey skies cover the rising sun.

We should have stayed with the vehicles. There had to of been other ways to cross over into B.C.; such a long border wouldn't have only one crossing. Shawn was mad about the route, so he must've known another way.

I should have argued; we should have turned around and gone another route.

The front of the pack takes off in a dash. I look around for any danger I might have missed, but I don't find any. They veer off onto a side road.

Quickly, more follow at a run. Picking up my speed, I hope there is a point to this; a building at the end of this road.

Not disappointed at the sight, when a house is revealed. The door opens as soon as the first person gets to it. Each person goes inside the house.

The break from the rain is great, but nothing as magnificent as this house; a mansion in the middle of the mountains.

Many don't stop to dry in the entry way. They start exploring as soon as their shoes are off; if they even took them off. I find it a pity to track mud and water through such an obviously expensive house, and carpeting.

I dump my bag on the growing pile and drain what water I can from my clothes.

Jaiden is the last to join us inside. "We should keep going. It's just a little rain."

"It's not your decision." My voice is cold and dead.

I walk off and go up wooden stairs. In my jacket, I pull out a flashlight to help guide through the darkness.

A house like this should have a bathroom upstairs, and a nice linen closet to go with it. Up the stairs and immediately to the right, I find a small children's bathroom.

Two towels hang on the rack inside. I help myself to both. Wrapping one towel around my body and using the other to wipe and dry off everything exposed. Soaking up water from my hair. Curious to the people who lived here, I can't help but explore.

All the doors are closed, but there are five; not including the bathroom. In a line of order, I pick the first room.

The walls are blue. A child's room. Superheroes, spaceships, and dinosaurs. A very stereotypical boy's dream bedroom.

Next room holds the complete opposite; a pink princess room. At one point, this would have been my dream bedroom. Pink walls and white furniture. The bed even has a white veil around it. A display case holds and showcases a hundred dolls. I bet the closet holds pretty, frilly princess dresses.

I shut the doors to respectfully move on. A linen closet hides behind the next door; right across from the bathroom. I exchange my soaking towels for two new ones.

A simple room with a bed and no other furniture is next. Maybe a guest room. It seems too plain and simple compared to the last two rooms, yet the bed is unmade.

The last room is the master bedroom. A four post bed and two night stands. Two open doors inside hold a bathroom and a walk in closet. Three quarters hold the woman's clothes and the last quarter holds the man's.

Her expensive taste in dresses, bags, and shoes is displayed out in the open, while equally expensive are his suits. In the few drawers she does have, I find and pull out pajamas to change into. The baby blue pajama suit will be warmer than the wet clothes I have on now.

My clothes stick to me as I change. I towel off the remaining wetness and put the new clothes on. I take out my pocket items to put in the pajama shirt pocket. I hang my clothes to dry in the bathroom.

It's so cold up here. I go back down the stairs. The entry way is clear. There is noise coming from throughout the house.

I admire the granite tile and hardwood moldings as I explore and wander.

Loud laughter runs down the hallway adjacent to me. Rayleen runs into me.

"Whoa, where are you going in such a hurry?" I ask her.

"I'm playing tag with Abby and Abe." She runs off in the direction she had been headed.

I know an Abby, but not an Abe. That name doesn't belong to anyone here. Did we pick up someone new? Is it a nickname?

I walk into the kitchen; where I hear the most noise. "Who's Abe?" I ask.

"I don't know. Why?" Shawn responds. His eye brows furrow together in confusion.

"Rayleen said she was playing tag with him." Abby is in here too. But, she doesn't appear to be playing with Rayleen at all. "She ran into me saying she was playing with Abe and Abby."

Abby enlightens us all. "They're her new imaginary friends. She was telling me about them because I heard her saying my name, but she wasn't talking to me. Um. They're twins; a boy and a girl."

"When did she get imaginary friends?" I ask. I see her every day, and I've never seen her playing with imaginary friends.

"A few minutes ago. That's the first I had hear of them, at least. Maybe ask Alexa. Rayleen might have had these friends for a while. Not many kids around to play with." Abby explains.

"Did she say what they looked like?" Jaiden asks.

"No, she didn't." She replies. "Why would that matter?"

"No reason. I was just curious." Jaiden eyes me up. I feel like she is conveying a message, but I ignore her and look away. She doesn't get to do that.

Flicking my eyes back to her after a moment, I find her staring off into space. She looks especially on edge now. Jaiden leaves suddenly.

Something pulls me after her. I don't know whether it's to yell at her, or because I'm concerned for her, but I'll keep my distance until I figure it out or see where she's going.

A child's scream next to me chills my heart. Rayleen flies through the air face first. Before I have time to react, Jaiden's running and catching the child. The momentum throws Jaiden to the ground.

"Are you okay?" I ask as I come up to them. Picking Rayleen off Jaiden gently and carefully, I place her on the ground right beside Jaiden. I pat Rayleen's limbs, but she doesn't yell in pain. She didn't look like she would have any major injuries. Jaiden caught her in time to ensure that.

"I think so." She looks beyond me and up the stairs. When I follow her gaze I don't see anything. "I don't want to play anymore."

"Are you telling the twins you don't want to play with them anymore?" Jaiden inquires in what I think is an odd question. Rayleen cowers to then nods. "Did they push you down the stairs?"

"He pushed me." The small girl cowers.

Jaiden looks to the stairs. "Abe and Abby, I'm only going to say this once. You need to leave Rayleen and the rest of us unharmed. We'll be gone soon, and we won't bother you anymore. We just need somewhere to stay while it storms outside. We don't mean to be any bother." Her voice is firm and demanding, yet also has a soft edge. I'd think she's gone crazy, but who knows.

"I don't think they liked that." Rayleen's features are cast in horror.

"You're fine, right. Go find Alexa and stay with her. Don't leave her side. If anything else happens you need to run outside as quick as possible." Rayleen starts to get up, so I help her. She runs off as soon as she's upright.

Jaiden slowly stands up. She winces in pain a couple times. Once up, she looks back to me. "We need to leave immediately. They didn't like being told to leave us alone." She whispers so quietly, I have to lean in and partially read her lips to figure out what she's saying.

"It's raining." I tell her. Copying her hushed level.

"It's just water. What's in here, is worse than what's out there."

"Oh? And what's in here." Annoyed with her talk.

"Ghosts, I think; poltergeists. Spirits." Jaiden speaks so low that I have to lean in to hear her. I watch her lips move to help figure out what she's saying. "The twins Rayleen was playing with haunt this house. They pushed her down the stairs, and they'll do much worse if we stay."

I can't help but laugh at how serious she's taking this. She sounds absurdly ridiculous. I speak to her in a normal level. "Rayleen has an overactive imagination. She's embarrassed and made an excuse for why she fell down the stairs. Let it go because we're not leaving."

I walk away without giving her another chance to speak. I ignore he call of my name.

Maybe there are ghosts here. I always felt like ghosts were real, and certainly if demons are real then ghosts could be too. But, I wouldn't think two little child ghosts would be dangerous.

What would be the chances that not only do we find a haunted house, but also one haunted by poltergeists. And, poltergeists with enough power to hurt us. And, would want to hurt us.

"What happened?" Shawn asks when I get back into the kitchen.

"Rayleen fell down the stairs." At their quickly concerned looks, I add quickly. "She's fine. Jaiden caught her."

"Oh, ah, that's good." People go back to their own things. Chattering to one another, as they explore and relax. "I thought you were going to talk with Jaiden." Shawn says.

"No, not really."

Chapter 10

Dusk clears to night; so late that it's technically morning.

The rain is gone.

I don't have much time left to convince them to change their minds. I just don't know how to without revealing my visions to everyone.

We should leave.

There is no reason we should be staying. Most rested up during the day, the rain has stopped, and the vampires can travel without using up sunblock at night.

Then, there are always the poltergeists that are ready to attack us at any time.

Leaving my spot at the window, I get up and locate the self-proclaimed leaders in the kitchen.

"Hey. Sorry, excuse me. The rain has stopped and it's getting dark. Should we start getting ready to go?" I ask delicately.

"Nah, we're gonna stay here another day; maybe more." Jess answers for everyone. It makes it harder to convince them to leave if they've already made a decision. I should have tried talking to them earlier today.

"Oh. I was just thinking that we're really close to the border, and we should go into the interior of the province before Darius decides to risk a plea of ignorance of where the border actually is." I explain my thinking while I leave out the paranormal activity that is sure to meet us while we're here.

It's urgent we leave.

"Chill girl. Relax. Darius isn't going to get us here. We're tired. It's been a few rough days. So calm down before you get hysterical and have a panic attack.

Go to sleep. You humans always feel better once you wake up. Okay? Bye." She waves me off.

I walk away as my brain can't think of anything more to say than a simple 'wow'. There is so much wrong with what she said and how she said it, that my brain can't comprehend a reasonable response.

Ignoring that Darius is likely ignorant of where the border is, she attacked me unprovoked as a human. Like my humanity discredits my point of view and opinions; everything that I have to say.

How rude.

I hope the twins haunt you first.

I take back the mean thought. I probably took what she said the wrong way, and jumped to conclusions. She might have been teasing me as a person and my personality.

Though, I don't know which would be a harder pill to swallow.

Relaxing does seem nice, but I want to avoid a repeat of my vision, so I'll avoid the bedroom and reading.

I go to the window seat and lay down.

Within an hour, I know sleep will elude me tonight. The deep pit of anxiety will keep me up.

Sleep just isn't going to happen at all tonight. I don't want to just lie here for hours until I possibly fall asleep, or until the twins start their party.

Momentarily, I think it would be better if I could run some energy or something off, but it wouldn't help anyways. I think it's my mind that will keep me up tonight, and the likely impending doom.

We haven't been here a long time, but this house has already taken its toll on me. I can feel the start of a migraine at the start of my eyebrow.

As a second thought, relaxing doesn't seem to be in my future. I can't just let everyone be killed by the twins, not when I might be able to help it.

I should have researched ghosts and poltergeists in depth a long time ago. With the many supernatural being species around, I had taken them to be a priority when it had come to my research.

My vision is my only clue. I was reading a book, and the twins wanted to play tag. We ran to the basement, where there was a room they said I wasn't allowed to go into; rather they weren't allowed into.

What is in that room?

A little exploring is in order. Going into my bag, I take out my flashlight. There are no lights but mine as I creep down the stairs. If anyone went down here, there is no sign of them.

I get to the bottom, and choose the door closest to me. Grasping the door knob proves electrifying in a spiritual sense. The air around me turns colder as I enter the room.

It's a sewing room. Sweeping the light around, I don't discover anything nefarious. Closing the door behind me is a natural movement.

Three sewing mannequins rest lined up against the one wall. Pictures of the people they represented are pinned to the necks; Abby, Abe, and the husband. Complete outfits adorn all of them, but only the purple princess dress for Abby looks homemade.

A shiver runs through my soul. Something isn't right.

The room is in an organized chaos that comes from being in the midst of a project. Stencils and flower patterned cloth lay on the table with a marker and scissors. A pumpkin pin cushion holds unused pins. Fabric rolls or many colours and patterns lay on the floor or against the walls in piles.

The circle of light brightens the room. I set the light down on the table. I can't help but to think that the placement of the table is odd. People normally want to maximize their space by putting a desk against the wall, but this table is on an angle slightly off from the middle of the mostly square room. On the left side of the table, the one corner nearly hits a wall that juts out a few feet in.

A window lets in a little moonlight and peers out. The back yard lights up from the large moon.

The exact view one would have standing up from the chair in front of the sewing machine is of the swing set. Likely the reason for the weird table placement; a mom's way of keeping an eye on her playing children.

The seats of the swings are not empty however, and I have to do a double take; too small to be children, and too big to be a trick of the eye. What are those?

One sweeping glance around the sewing room, and I don't see anything out of the ordinary. Perhaps this was just a room the children were constantly told to stay out of, and that has carried over to their death.

I head out of the room and upstairs to check out the swing set, as my mind is in a flurry with curiosity. Half way up the stair case I remember the flashlight I left on the table. I'll have to go back and grab that in a bit.

There is the rest of the dream to consider. I went upstairs to chaos. A guy was crushed up against the ceiling; I know him now as Jeff. I had screamed for Lucas and Calli. Then, I ran outside.

Lucas and Calli were supposed to be alive. What happened? What changed? I didn't change anything; I don't think I changed anything that would have mattered.

It could be the small things; subconscious changes in my behaviour due to a vision.

But, then again, maybe I did. I obviously did something to make it change.

Maybe Lucas and Calli were supposed to go to the farm with us. That would have meant they wouldn't have been killed when Darius attacked Banff.

What changed? Why didn't they come?

Dominique handled asking them to return. I didn't do anything directly to change anything there. Lucas was with Brad, and Calli said no.

Lucas was with Brad because they had become closer, after I spoke with Lucas about my worries with Brad, because of a vision I had. I may not have spoken to him about Brad had I not had the vision. I might have previously had my worries, but didn't voice them. Check one.

Calli, I started drawing away from her once I had that vision of her aggressively asking me about visions of her. She threatened to out me if I didn't tell her. Called me selfish, among other names, for deciding to keep my visions to myself. The dream scared me and changed my feelings about her. My pulling away likely affected our friendship. She might have originally come along because of our friendship. Or, maybe I asked instead of Dominique. Check two.

I'm the reason they're dead.

I changed things and they're dead because of it.

Their deaths changed the future of the vision I had of this house, and the twins in a small way; possibly a huge way. I yelled for Lucas and Calli on the way out. I had been thinking of going back inside for them.

That's no longer an issue.

What is an issue are the other people I now wish to keep from a horrible fate. And, an impossible to answer question about why I hadn't worried about them in the vision. Maybe they weren't there, or I didn't have a good friendship with them.

Walking out the back door, I shake my head to rid myself of the line of thought. There is no use dwelling on it right now.

As I step outside, I suddenly I feel better. Like a weight lifted off my chest. The air is much better out here. It's only now that I leave there, that I realize I was slowly suffocating. My lungs take in the much needed air.

It's peaceful out here. Not a sound out of place; silence to help me think and clear my mind.

The swings draw me closer. I stop a respectable distance away, hoping my assumptions are wrong; knowing they are not.

Each seat carries a beloved toy of each of the twins. A soaked plush princess doll sits on the left and a weathered car on the right. Underneath the swings are rough ovals of equal size; child sized. The ground has been disturbed and roughly filled back in. Grass hasn't had time to fill in the space.

The tokens from each child acts in place of a tomb stone. I look back at the house. Something nefarious happened here. People don't just normally bury their children in the back yard.

Looking back at the graves, I see beyond the toys. Another grave lies from pole to pole at the back of the swing set. This one seems older, like the grave has been there longer. The grass had some time to fill in as patches.

Three people died, that left one behind. A violent life and death trapped the children's souls in the house. Doomed to echo in the halls.

Chilled to the core, I decide to go back inside, but not before I gather the two toys; draining the doll of as much water as I can. The person who left them is no longer in need of them, but maybe the two ghost children would like their toys back.

The back door refuses to open. I shake it, turn the knob harder.

I jump back when a child appears in the window. Abe's coal eyes, paper white skin, and black hair contrast like a black and white film. His eyes are black and empty; I can't take my eyes away.

There is a faint scream from within the house. The walls block most of the noise.

Blood spots his white shirt. A line appears, then two, then three. Blood oozes from the stab wounds, then out of his mouth. White teeth spill out red until they themselves are covered. The edges of this mouth move into a smile.

I draw up the hand with his toy car in it. "Abe, let me in."

His smile drops, and he disappears from my sight. Banging on the door fails to bring him back.

I try the door knob again. It still won't open.

Hands, then torso, collide into the window. I scream in surprise when Jeff crashes into the door. I get out of the way as he grabs for the door knob, but the door doesn't open.

He panics. Banging on the window. He tries to break the glass with his bare fists, but it doesn't budge.

A painted rock on the ground becomes a great projectile to break the glass. Despite throwing it as hard as I can. It doesn't break, not even a crack.

The look of desperation and futility he has as he runs away has me screaming. "No! Don't go that way!"

I know this moment. It's when I was supposed to come up from the basement to outside. I passed him when he was pulled and crushed into the ceiling.

Okay. The door won't open and the glass won't break.

Think.

No one else got out of the house.

Why was I let out of the house? Jeff tried the door before me, and he couldn't leave, so why did the door work for me.

I try again, but the door still doesn't open. The vision changed. The twins are keeping me out, and everyone else in. Why? Was it by chance? Was I nice to them originally, so they spared me?

If they aren't allowed in their mother's sewing room perhaps that window will be free for the breaking.

Picking the rock up from its fallen place, I run to the window facing the swing set. The flashlight I left inside helps greatly in choosing the right one.

I peer inside.

A face gazes back at me from inside. I drop the rock in surprise. Inside, hidden from my view inside, is the mother propped against the wall. She's sitting. Her head is leaned over to the one side. Forevermore unblinking.

Her cheeks are sunken in and bones jut out from her oversized skin. She looks as though she starved to death. If the ghosts have the means to keep everyone inside, maybe they kept her inside as well. Her only sanctuary may have been this room, where she slowly died. Or, perhaps there were other reasons she died this way.

I can't help to think it was recent. Her body doesn't look decayed from this point of view, and I didn't smell anything rotten inside.

Gathering my wits together, I pick up the rock and slam it against the window. I lose my balance when it actually works; I hadn't expected it to. The glass gives away in a stone shaped hole. My fingers bleed from a graze against the sharp edge.

Now that it's broken I kick the rest in. Brushing the rest of the glass away with my shoe. When it looks safe enough, I sit on the ground and stick my legs through. I toss the children's toys inside. Leaning over, I get my upper body inside the window. I jump and fall to the ground.

Throwing the sewing machine to the ground I drag the table to the window. The flashlight falls on the ground. Once the table is in place, I put it back in place as a beacon of light. Other candles and flashlights around the house can light my way.

The body stares at me the whole time. It's unnerving, so I throw a sheet of fabric over her. Other people don't need to see this. Time is of the essence. For all I know, each second wasted is another death.

With Dominique my main target, I exit the room. Immediately, I am blasted with a cold chill unlike the one outside. The screams heighten in volume.

There were people down here. I open the door to another room.

Whatever was happening, it's done here. Bodies splatter the floor. A few are stuck to the walls with kitchen knives. Blood spills onto the floor from fresh kills.

A scream from another room commands my attention. There is no time to check list the deaths. One room over are more screams.

Running to the rescue is stopped by a locked door.

Bang. Bang. Bang.

"HELP!" A desperate scream cries from inside.

"Hello?" I twist at the door knob but it refuses to move. "The door is locked."

"It won't open! Please! Help me!" Each word is sobbed in his desperation.

Banging on the door is useless, I know. "Stand away from the door. I'm going to kick it down." My voice is a whole lot more confident than I am.

Grounding myself, I kick at the door. It doesn't budge. Harder and harder, I kick and kick.

A couple thuds answer my banging from the inside. I call out. "Hello?" There is no answer. I echo the word again, but to no answer.

With no answer, no sign of life from inside, I decide to go elsewhere.

I run up the stairs. From here, I can see the bodies in the kitchen.

Turning, there are a bunch of people at the door. They bang at the door; trying to get it open.

Rayleen sits huddled on the ground covering her eyes.

Crystal stands guard to protect her owner. She squawks at me. I swipe her head with my fingers to calm her.

I grab Rayleen's hands to uncover her eyes, but her eyes are closed too. She jumps, frightened by me. "Rayleen, you need to come with me. I'll get you out."

She opens her eyes. If she sees anything through the tears I would be amazed, but she loops her arms around me. I pull her up.

Locating her cousin, I grab onto Alexa and pull her back towards us. "Come with me. I've got a way out. Help me get their attention."

She goes to Daniel, and gets his attention much the same way I got hers. "Jaiden's got a way out."

Before I can get the attention of the others, they hear this and stop trying to break the door down.

"Grab bags, we'll need the supplies!" I order them. I do my part to grab my hiking bag. All the extra weight pulls me down hard. I power through it with only the adrenaline in my veins.

We aren't far. I walk as fast as I can; it's all I can manage with my cargo. The second I get inside the sewing room, I drop my bag, and then set Rayleen to her feet on the table.

I hop up and grasp her in my arms again. Hoisting her up and through the window. At least this works. She crawls out and pokes her head back through.

"Alexa! Don't leave me." She cries.

"I'm coming right now, Sweetie." Alexa calmly answers back. She puts Crystal down on the table and crawls up to help bolster her words.

"Rayleen, you need to move back so others can get through." I tell her. I jump down from the table. Out of the bunch of people that had tried following me down, only four have made it; Alexa and Daniel, and Miles and Kelly. I think three are missing.

I pick up the forgotten toys from the ground. As I try to get by Miles he grabs my arm. "Where are you going?"

"To go get more people." I try to yank my arm away from him but his grip is too strong. "Let go!"

"I'm not letting you go back there. Did you see what happened to the others?" He insists.

"No, but you need to let me go. I have people to find. You have all your people here. So, you need to get out with them." I explain to him. I don't have time for this.

"Miles!" Alexa pleads.

He lets me go. I know this is stupid, to run back in; I wouldn't do it under normal circumstances. But, I need to get as many people out as possible. Or, rather get those out who deserve to survive; Dominique.

Outside the room, I trip over a body, but manage to stay on my feet with the help of the railing. Brandon's neck is broken and at a weird angle. Nothing I can do there.

Up the stairs. Against the wall, outside the kitchen, are the other missing two. Jess hangs by a knife through the chest. A vampire killed through the gaping holes in her chest. The other, Armen, bleeds green from the chest in his position on the floor. Both have been stabbed in the exact places Abe had been; recreating his death.

How did Abby die? Did she get pushed down the stairs?

People, the last I knew, were spilt mostly between the kitchen, living room, and the bedrooms.

I didn't pay attention to who went where.

Closest to me, from here, is the living room. I hear some banging coming from that direction. Leah holds a chair at her side. Swinging it, then letting go. The chair hits the window and bounces off. It clutters to the floor below the window.

"Leah." I draw her attention. "Downstairs, to the right. A sewing room. You can get out a window there."

"Great! Why aren't you there?" Her question has me feeling like I'm in trouble.

"I'm getting people out." I weakly defend.

"Great, me too." I open my mouth to tell her to just get out, but she interrupts me. "I told you I'd be your body guard. I'm not leaving without you."

"Fine." I say. There's no time to argue. The vast room is empty, except for one more body on the ground; Abby. "Upstairs?"

I don't wait for her. If it was a matter of speed, she would beat me in a second. Leah trails right behind me.

Six rooms to look inside. Leah opens the one almost straight ahead. It's a linen closet. Leah closes the door. Across from it, she opens up to an empty bathroom.

Leah practically runs me over to open a room at the left end of the hall.

Abby sits on someone's chest, with a pillow over their face. The struggling body tries to buck the little girl off to no avail. I recognize Dominique's clothes she had on earlier.

Leah rushes over to grab the pillow off of their face. She manages to raise it very little before the ghost girl's strength overpowers her.

A note for later to research whether ghosts are tangible, or there is only a visual manifestation of them. Leah hasn't moved to touch Abby, so maybe she's only a visual representation.

"Abby, let them go. I'm sorry your mom did those awful things to you and your brother. It wasn't fair." I say firmly. Walking closer to the twisted girl. "Look. I have your doll. I brought your doll back for you. Do you want to play with her? Is she your favourite?"

Abby's complexion returns to that of a living breathing child. Her face sad and ashamed as she looks down at the pillow she's holding.

Disappearing from on top, she appears in front of me. I hold out the doll to give it to her. Pulling it in, she cradles the doll like a baby, and then fades to nothing.

Dominique sits up in the bed. Both she and Leah stare at me.

"What did you just do?" She asks between gasps of air.

"Hopefully gave her a little peace so she could move on. We have to go now. It's a long story and I'll explain later." Without waiting for them, as I know they move faster chasing after me, I move onto the next room.

Someone lies still in Abe's bed. Abby must have gone there first.

Dominique collides with my shoulder in her bid to get by me. "Shawn! SHAWN!"

The body comes to life. Shawn springs up in a fright.

"What?" He panics.

"Oh God." Dominique hugs Shawn in a tight grasp. "I thought you were dead!"

"People are dying. We need to leave before we're next. Now!" Leah's irritated voice shouts from behind me.

I watch as she uses her speed to search the other two rooms and any occupants that had been inside. She comes back with a shake of her head, and then starts for downstairs.

Looking behind me, I see Shawn and Dominique out of bed.

They'll be right after me, so I follow Leah down the stairs.

At the bottom of the stairs, Leah's body is thrown against the same wall Jess still stands stuck against by only a knife blade.

The blade pulls out of Jess' body, and dives into Leah's chest.

"Abe stop this!" The little boy appears. His back is to me, and his hand is on the blade handle.

He let's go of the knife to spin and look at me. I walk calmly to the bottom of the stairs and hold out his car.

"RUN!" Leah sputters up some blood.

My body picks up and slams into the wall beside her. The air rushes out of my lungs faster than I can pull it in.

I drop the car from the impact. My chest refuses to move. I gape and cough, and then finally a little air returns.

Pressure on it feels like something big is pressing against it. My arms and legs are free to move. But kicking and flailing won't help me.

The pieces fit in my head for what happened to Abe. What they are doing echoes their deaths. Abby, suffocated as her mother held a pillow over her face. Abe held against the wall as his mother stabbed him to death.

"Abe, please don't do this. No one else has to die. I brought your car back. I'm sorry for what your mom did to you. It had to of been horrifying. You didn't deserve it. Neither did your sister.

Just please, take your car and move on. She's no longer trapped, and you don't have to be either." Abe bends down to pick up the car from where I dropped it. He closes the engine compartment which had opened when it landed. "Please, let us go."

He blinks. The white returns to his reddened eyes and his complexion normalizes. He reaches his hand out towards me, then disappears. With him, the pressure on my chest leaves too.

I turn to Leah and examine the knife wound. "Should we leave it in there?"

"We're not leaving it in there." She insists.

"Well, I don't know. Are you going to bleed to death before we can get out outside?" You aren't supposed to take out stabbed in items. Leah, determined to get the knife out of her chest grabs the handle herself. "Stop! You might hurt yourself more by taking it out at a different angle. I'll take it out!"

She lets go so I can replace her hand with mine. My other hand uses her shoulder as leverage as I yank the blade from her.

Blood pours out of the wound. It's in the wrong place to hit her heart, but there are so many other things inside a chest that could cause so much bleeding. Dropping the dirty blade to the ground with a clang.

Without a word, I hold my arm to her mouth to drink. She takes the blood, knowing pulling the blade out her was a mistake. Her paled complexion a result of blood loss is a clear sign to me.

I know the blood with hasten her healing, but I don't know how much it will help.

Was the first stab a killing blow?

Will the vampirism heal in time?

Grasping a chunk of her shirt, I put pressure against the wound.

Shawn pulls my hand out of the way. His hand touches her wound. When he pulls away the hole is the same, but the blood flow lessens significantly.

"The door still won't open." Dominique informs us.

"Is it unlocked?" Leah asks with a smug grin.

"Of course. I checked that." Dominique's eyes light with the offense she takes from the question.

"The dad." I think quietly out loud, as a terrible thought hits me.

"Excuse me?" Leah asks as to have me both clarify and to repeat what I had said.

"There are three graves outside. Mom's dead in the sewing room."

"And, you didn't think this was important." Leah grabs my hand to drag me down the stairs.

"I said it was a long story." I counter.

There wasn't a trinket of the fathers. I know if we come across him, I'll be useless in defending us. Something tells me he wouldn't be so easily swayed.

My body loses balance. Pushed from the back with a great enough for to push all my air out, I collide into Leah. Both of us catapult to the ground.

My hands do little to break my fall, but Leah gets the brunt of it all; me landing partially on top of her.

Head cracking against something soft on the ground. Abby's doll cushioned my head. Possibly saving me from worse than a kinked neck or small concussion.

My body lifts up. The ground leaves me quickly. I stop. Suspended above head height, near the ceiling. A soulful tug of war battles for control of my body as I waiver in spot. My scream chokes in my throat and I can't speak. Nearly suffocating from the hold they each have on my body.

Dominique grabs at my waist to pull me down. Her grip is strong, but her strength isn't enough to do anything.

"Room. Now!" I breathe out. The room is just feet away from me. They should be safe in there. Trapped in this hold, I count the moments until I die. I'm going to die.

Shawn yanks Dominique hard enough to move her. He pulls her inside the door and puts himself between her and the outside. She struggles against him to break out.

 Leah stands up off of Sam from where she fell, but she stands and stares at me. Her face is puzzled as she looks around me, and tries to figure out a way to get me down.

I've already resigned to my death. There isn't a way out of this. Changes in the future, changes I made, have turned to horrible consequences. Palpitations course the blood through my veins as fast as fearing death will allow.

My body flies toward the room. A force lifting until I cross the threshold. Shawn half catches me. His arms slow me down for the second they hold me. He loses his grip and I land on my side against the ground.

"Sorry." He says and helps me up. My wrist hurts but nothing feels loose or moves out of the ordinary.

Leah, one step from the door, panics as her body is stopped. It shoots up. The moment her head collides with the top I hear a crunching noise. The body drops to the ground.

Dominique tries to go after her, but Shawn catches her before she can leave the room.

An indent is where her skull caved in; blood pouring out. Vampire or not, without an expert medical team, access to all necessary medical equipment, and a miracle, there is no way she would survive that kind of an injury. The virus will only heal so much, even hyped up on human blood.

I watch as the twins appear holding hands as they face on their father. His black and bruised form morphs into Abby. An exact image of her when her as she looked ghostly. A twisted grin upon her face. Morphing again. He replicates Abe; bleeding holes in his chest.

Slowly growing, the father turns back into an image of himself. Disapproval written in his features when they do nothing.

His eyes flick to us.

Disappearing, to reappear at the door. He presses on the invisible barrier. When he isn't allowed inside, his temper flares and he beats wildly with his fists.

Not knowing if the barrier has a time limit, or only so much energy it can withhold, I take up my bag and go to the table.

Waiting to receive more people, hands reach in to grab the bag I'm lifting out.

My wrists protest as I prop myself up on them to leave the rectangular hole. Hands come to my arms to help me out and onto my feet.

Ushered five feet away, I turn to see Shawn coming through. He doesn't allow himself to be carried away. He reaches back into the house to help Dominique out.

Once I know she's free, I stop paying attention to the on goings around me.

Taking stock of my injuries passes little time. The gash on my arm will scab over. The blood is thickening and blood flow as subsided. My cut fingers have large scabs over them with intermittent reopening. Blood has piled and dried many times.

My wrists move. They hurt to move, but without an x-ray I can't see the damage. Patting down my neck is painful, not in a broken way, but maybe whiplash. My knees ache but I don't feel like checking for scratches or bruising beneath my jeans. My right ankle hurts when I roll it.

I look up when Dominique yelling catches my attention. "THE HELL DO YOU THINK YOU'RE DOING?"

"MICHELLE MIGHT BE ALIVE. I HAVE TO FIND HER!" The women's back is to me as she tries to plow her way through people to get to the window.

"YOU CAN'T GO IN THERE!" Dominique grabs ahold of her arm and pulls her back from the opening.

"I NEED HER." Chantel pleads.

"She needs you to stay alive. There's no one left alive in there. We checked." Dominque shouts at her as Chantel tries again to move around her. "LISTEN TO ME."

Chantel stops to address everyone. Plead for support in others. "We didn't think that anyone else was coming out, but they did. Maybe-"

"She's dead. Okay? Sucked up to the ceiling. Her neck broke. I'm sorry." Dominique says. We never did see Michelle die. But she might be trying to ease Chantel's mind. Prevent her from going back in there.

I scream at them inside my head; what I wish I could say.

Next time I'm insistent at something, you need to listen to me! We could have avoided all of this if you had just listened to me.

Counting the people outside and I know we're down by at least two thirds the people we came with.

A few I can account for; seeing their dead bodies myself. But, others I cannot. I think for a moment that maybe I should go inside again to see if I can collect anyone that might still be alive. The twins might protect me.

Then, I think better of it. It's ridiculous to go back inside.

I won't survive another trip.

Abby was dead in the living room, and two, Jess and Armen, in the hall. Jeff died near the back door. Leah died in the basement beside Brandon. Sam was at the bottom of the stairs.

I can account for seven of the missing people through the majority of the house. There were a number of bodies in the basement.

Leah had checked the two bedrooms and shook her head. Anyone left might have been dead in the two bedrooms; suffocated or whatever before we got there. Or, they hid, and didn't come out when we were stampeding through the house.

Chantel and DeAngelo somehow managed to get out while evading me. While also knowing how to get out.

If they were alive, the father would have gone after them next. They'd likely be dead by now.

Chantel, DeAngelo, Kelly, Miles, Dominique, and Shawn stand near the house. Turning, I see Alexa, Daniel, Rayleen, and Crystal have staked a place over at the swing set.

Everyone else is dead or will be immediately.

I turn and run into a body. "Sorry." I say reflexively.

Arms enclose around me in a hug. It takes just a moment to realize it's Dominique. "You have two minutes before I go back to being pissed off at you. Thank you for saving me. I'm glad you're okay. You are okay, right?"

"Yes. How are you feeling?" I return the hug lightly. I expect her to let go but she isn't done yet.

"I'll have nightmares forever, and I don't think I'll ever be able to use a pillow ever again, but I'll be alright." She says. Abruptly she pulls away from me to hold me at arm's length by the shoulders. "What the Hell were you thinking?"

I say the first thing that comes to mind. "I thought I had two minutes."

Dominique looks at me confused for half a second. "This is different from that. You could have gotten killed. If you knew a way out, then you should have gotten yourself out." Her voice is angered for my lack in concern for my own safety.

"If I did that, I would have been the only one to live. I was already outside when they locked down the house." I tell her.

"We could have found a way out." She tries to argue, but I know that wouldn't be true.

Ignoring that she was a minute away from suffocating to death, and Shawn was in a dead sleep; a next likely victim. And, no one was even in the sewing room looking for a way out there. I'm going to have to go with no. "No one would have gotten out.

I was outside when the ghosts locked down the house. I was exploring the house when I came upon the sewing room and their dead mom. I saw toys on the swing set, so I went outside and found three graves. I grabbed the toys and tried to come back inside but I couldn't.

Jeff and I tried to get the back door open, tried smashing the window, but it didn't work. By luck, I threw a rock at the sewing room window and it broke; when nothing else would.

What other choice did I have? Yell at people from outside the house? We know how well I yell."

"Don't do it again." She warns thickly. I imagine a common confusing threat added to the end; if you die, I'll kill you.

If she's still concerned over my wellbeing then maybe there is hope she'll forgive me. Or, we might just continue this confusing love/hate display until one of us dies.

"Shawn! Come here." She orders him. Swiftly he does as told. "Can you check her? She says she's not hurt, but I know she's lying."

"I'm fine. Some cuts here and there. I'm a little achy, but nothing to be worried about." I defend myself.

"You know she won't shut up about it if you don't let me check." Internally, I sigh. Externally, I hold out my hand. Shawn takes it and concentrates. A few moments pass. "Nothing permanent." He finally says.

I take my hand back. Immediately noticeable are the lack of aching in my wrists. "Did you-"

"Shawn! Dominique! Jaiden! What's your vote?" Miles breaks our interaction with convenient timing for Shawn; right when I was about to accuse him of healing some internal wounds.

We stare at them confused and wait for one of them to explain. When they don't Dominique asks. "For what?"

"Banff or B.C.?" He responds.

"Banff!" Dominque immediately votes.

"B.C." Shawn answers. The two of them exchange a glance.

"Neither; both. I don't know. Not Banff." I stumble over my words when my mouth won't catch up to my thoughts. "B.C. might be terrible too."

"That's another two for B.C., but Banff is still winning." Kelly grins, happy with the way the voting is going.

"Why don't you want Banff?" Dominique asks me.

"It's not safe." I say quietly. Weary of what I say around Shawn and hearing distance of the rest. B.C. might be terrible too, judging by that vision earlier.

"Nowhere is going to be safe." She reminds me needlessly.

"I know that. But, Banff seems to be the least safe option right now. B.C. doesn't seem like a great idea either."

Dominique pauses for a moment; thinking. "Well, where would you want to go then?"

"I don't know. But, I think there should be another option, maybe. Banff seems like a horrible idea. Darius will be back. And we have, what, ten people now. There's no way we could fight him and his army."

"What about B.C.?" She asks.

"I have a bad feeling about B.C. And, how far are we going to be able to get without vehicles? The nearest town could be destroyed. It could be weeks before we get somewhere safe; if at all."

"Okay. So what would you want to do? Where would you want to go? I want an actual place." She sounds a bit ticked off at my round about answers.

"It's a little more complicated than that." Especially without disclosing my visions. "James wanted us to fight. He got our group together so we could help fight when the time was right. He ran off so he could gather more troops, but hasn't returned.

There is strength in numbers, however. So, I think we should find more people to live with and to fight with. And, that's not going to happen isolated in Banff; if that's even safe. Darius will be back with his army."

"Okay. So, if going back to Banff is stupid. Where would you take us?" She annunciates each word.

Something tells me that she won't take another anywhere else answer, so I think to my visions and a logical step. "Red Deer. I have contacts in Red Deer. I would start there. Lots of people I met there, lots of access to more people, and it's a large territory in the relative center of the province.

We might have a place to stay once we get there, food to eat too. If we could control all of Red Deer, it would be a huge loss to Darius."

"Yo! Everyone! We're going to Red Deer." Dominique informs everyone at the top of her normal speaking range.

My eyes go wide. She can't just do that; can she? "What? No." My words go unnoticed.

"Shawn, Jaiden and I are going to Red Deer. Jaiden knows people there. Join us or not; we're going." She reiterates her words and adds to them. She's fully sure of herself that we are going to Red Deer with or without them. Anxiety slams doubt into my decision. I wish she'd just ignore my suggestion. Less pressure.

"We'll want to top up our gas in Banff. That way we can make it to Red Deer without stopping." Miles says.

"Do you think it'll be safer in Red Deer?" Daniel asks me. They've come closer to discuss this with everyone.

"Maybe. Safer than Banff; for sure. It's not really safe anywhere, so I can't guarantee anything." I answer him honestly. Especially if Alexa joins us. It's only a matter of time before Darius comes looking for her again. "I met people while I was there. Ran some deliveries for Jerry to a bunch of supernaturals. It's civilization; sort of. Safety in numbers. If they survived winter."

"You're a horrible salesman." Daniel comments.

That wouldn't be a surprise. I tend to describe salesmen as a personality type. A person who is extremely charismatic, but will say anything to close the deal.

Complete truth, stretched details, or outrageous lie; they don't care. They tend to be people who promise great things, but ultimately can't deliver.

I'm a realist. I like straight facts.

"It's better than our other options." Dominique adds.

"I guess we're in." He says. "I guess we're going with you."

"We'll I'm not going to be the only one going to B.C." DeAngelo concludes.

Chapter 11

"Wait. Should we be stepping on that? I mean, it's a mud slide/rockslide, right? So wouldn't last night's rain exasperate the situation and make it likely to slide again? Or, at least make it unstable to walk on." Jaiden asks as Daniel starts hoisting Rayleen up to the most level surface of the rocks and mud. I lift Crystal up.

"Don't worry so much. It's fine. We have to cross it to get back." Nikki bites back at her. I had thought they reconciled, I saw them hug, but apparently not.

I just want to get out of here as quick as possible. Grabbing gas from Banff is more dangerous than anyone knows. Darius might be waiting for us. Yet a valid argument, in lieu of me explaining everything, cannot be made for bypassing for the next city.

So, we go. And, I will be ready to bolt the first glimpse I think might be Darius or one of his people. I won't let him get me or Rayleen.

"Stay right there, Rayleen. Wait for me to get up there and I will help you." I call up to the little girl. She is eyeing the way across, but I won't have her go alone. Like Jaiden mentioned, it might be dangerous from the rain.

Daniel gets down on one knee and folds his hands together to give me a boost. Putting my boot in his hand, and my hands on his shoulders, I unsteadily raise up. I'm almost head over heels before I think to grab onto the massive rock in front of me.

My body shakes, and my stomach leaps to my throat in fear of falling. Something hard collides with my knee. Placing my other foot on his shoulder, I stand up and practically leap onto the rock.

Tiny rocks slide down to the pavement, but this one is sturdy.

Getting my bearings, with both feet on the ground, I stand up straight. I look back to Daniel and the others down below. Shawn is helping Nikki up; close to where I stand. Most of the others have chosen a couple meters down. Jaiden, missing for just a moment, pokes her head up. She climbs up from a section without aid from anyone. I shake my head.

Rayleen's tiny hand wraps around mine. She tugs a little. I look into her eyes and see fear. "Are you okay?"

"I don't want to be up here." She whimpers.

"Okay." I look down to Daniel. "We're going to get across quick. Rayleen's scared."

"Yeah, it's okay. Go on ahead without me. I'll catch up." He smiles. He looks on to Shawn, and I stop watching just as he moves in that direction. They'll get each other up.

I pick Rayleen up. The scared child clings to me. I walk, sacrificing safety checks for speed; not that I can do much with Rayleen in the way of the view of my feet.

A female's surprised scream throws me off. My foot sticks behind a rock. Momentum keeps me going. I crash to my knees. Gripping Rayleen's body and head with my arms shields her from much of the blow when my torso bends over. Arms and elbows take the brunt of the sharp edges.

I hiss in pain, but it catches in my throat when I don't hear anything from Rayleen. Crystal comes right up to my face to check on us.

Trying to pull my body away to look at her does nothing. Her grip on me is too tight.

"Rayleen, honey, you need to let go. I need to see if you're okay." She shakes her head. "Are you okay?"

"No." My heart pounds.

"Where are you hurt?" I ask.

"No."

I stop when I think of scolding her. She needs to tell me if she's hurt. "Are you physically hurt, or are you just scared?"

"Scared." I sign in relief and frustration.

"I'm sorry, Honey. I didn't mean to trip and fall. But, it's okay. We're all okay. We just need to get up now, but I can't do that if you're holding on to me." I explain to her.

She squeezes one last time before letting go. "Are you guys alright?" Nikki helps me up, and I in turn help Rayleen back up to her cradled position in my arms.

"Thank you. We're fine. I just tripped."

"Here, I'll help you get across." She offers. I nod in thanks.

We proceed forward; me holding Rayleen and Nikki holding onto my arm. Crystal skirts around my feet.

The rocks lower to a foot off the ground, and then drops to the pavement. The vehicles are still here, so that's a good sign.

"Thank you." I tell Nikki. "Rayleen, you can let go now. We're on the road."

I let her down, and then turn back to Nikki. Her body is now missing from her spot. The back view of her is climbing back up onto the rocks, with direction set towards Shawn.

Jaiden jumps down from closer to the mountain. She ignores us to walk on to the truck she had arrived in.

Rayleen's hand clings to mine, as the other pets Crystal.

Daniel and Shawn arrive in a pair, then the rest in a group. Once I see everyone here, and the, now, excessive amount of vehicles to return in. It hits me exactly how many people we lost just a few hours ago.

It all seems like such a waste; a completely unnecessary loss of life. If we had only turned around and taken the next road down, we would be in B.C. now. All of us alive and well. Free from Darius forever.

People scurry to the vehicles. Daniel collects Rayleen, Crystal, and me to return to the SUV we arrived in.

Everything is how we left it. We return our bags to their spot in the back, and take our seats. It's almost as though the day never happened. We resort the previously abandoned supplies to occupied vehicles before we get going.

We each turn to leave with the back now in the lead. Jaiden, with the trailer, takes a hundred point turn trying to turn around. I feel bad for her. No one gets out to help her, not that I would be any help; perhaps why no one else goes to help her.

After a frustratingly long time, she's turned around in the proper direction.

With one or two to each vehicle, excluding us, there are still not enough people to bring back each one. Doubling and grouping up, makes for a four vehicle convoy. Ghosts will forever haunt the ones we leave behind. Maybe they'll be of use to someone at some point.

My thoughts flash back to last night. Invisible forces killing the people around us. Terror at a helpless level. Until, Jaiden saved us.

We barely enter town, but it sets me on edge. Rolling into the gas station, I watch as people get out of their vehicles.

Inch by inch, ground to sky, city to mountains, I search for anything out of place. An eye or clothing. Movement I can't explain away as an animal.

I jump. Realizing that I had been hyperaware of my distant surroundings while ignoring those closest to me. It's just Daniel.

"I'm going to go fill 'er up. You alright to stay here for a bit?"

"Yes, of course." I say. Not like there was anything else I was going to do. I'm not leaving this SUV.

I might need a quick getaway.

Chapter 12

Wordlessly, Shawn and I sit; watching for a sign to leave. Yet, knowing it would also be our decision as the front of the convoy.

People look like they are settled in or returning to their vehicles. I know each of them has finished gassing up; it had been a team effort. Stragglers return from one last raid of shops in the immediate area; having been advised not to venture too far away.

It shouldn't be too long now.

It occurs to me that I hear honking. An SUV shoots forward to rest beside ours. The sudden sight of it makes me jump back in my seat a little.

Daniel mouths the words 'let's go,' as he motions with his hand forward. Both hands come up in a 'what are you doing' motion and he sneers at me. Rude little prick.

Looking back at Shawn I point back at Daniel and ask, "Is that really necessary?"

Shawn shrugs. "He seems to think so."

I turn my head around to look back at Daniel. Waving him on as Shawn starts up our SUV.

"What's the best way out of here? Should we loop back or go out-" He stops himself as Daniel screeches out of the parking lot to go deeper into town. "Never mind."

Behind us three vehicles follow; Jaiden is in one, and the remaining are in the other two.

My vote would have been to loop back, but I'm glad the decision was made for us. As much as I didn't want to be reminded of what happened here, one last look of this town fuels nostalgia; and not negatively like I had thought it would.

"Werewolves." Shawn's voice suddenly exclaims. His voice brings me out of my memories.

"What?" I ask, but I see them immediately as I finish speaking the word. Clothed wolves standing on hind legs. Our caravan speeds up; we speed up. I think the worst. Another attack from Darius has been waiting for us.

Familiarity in the one wolf's morphing face has me hesitating. Once his face becomes clearer and undoubtedly the werewolf becomes John, I scream, "Stop the car!"

Tires screech as Shawn slams the breaks. A chorus joins in behind us. I open the door and jump out. Keeping close to the SUV and leaving the door open; just in case.

"What the Hell are you doing here?" I ask. He better not be working with Darius or I'll-. My anger clears my head when many examples should be coming to mind. It wouldn't be good, and he would regret it.

"I came to see if you were alright!" My ex hollers at me, irritation in his voice and features match my own.

No one ever wants to run into their ex under such circumstances; especially when that person is the one who broke it off. Why the Hell would he be checking up on me, and how the fuck did he find me?

"Go catch up with Daniel, and make him stop to wait for us!" I shout back to Shawn and close the door; a little too forcefully in my anger. He drives off with a last wave of motivation from me.

Walking closer to them, as they walk closer to me; we meet in the middle. I make sure to keep a safe distance between us. We wouldn't want my fist connecting with his face accidentally. "How'd you even know I was here?"

"Hey! We were just getting ready to leave for Red Deer. Do you guys have a car? Do you want to come with us? I have room. We can talk and drive." Jaiden interrupts.

"Get the fuck back in your truck!" I order her. Jaiden takes one step back from the force of my words, but moves no further. I can't deal with both of them right now, so she needs to leave.

She glances to me, spotting my angered glare, before she decides to ignore me.

The girl with John shrieks in joy and attacks Jaiden with a hug. Strange.

"No car. We ran after it blew up." John answers me.

"What?" I ask John, opting to ignore the other two.

"Well, it didn't actually blow up. It broke down, but there was smoke coming out of the engine." He explains. I'm part annoyed that it didn't blow up, and part glad nothing too horrible happened.

"If you don't have a car, then all of you can ride with me; until we catch up. If, you'd like to." Jaiden offers.

"Great! I'm exhausted. Someone didn't want to stop until we got here. He was all worried and stuff." The woman reveals. Her emphasis on the word implies the someone is meant to be John.

"You didn't have to come." John bites back to counter.

"Of course I did." She gestures back to Jaiden in a big sweep of her arm and nearly hits her cheek. "You saw-"

Jaiden puts her hand on the woman's arm and places herself in front of her. "We should go! We can talk about this on the way there; privately." Jaiden glares at the both of them. I wave off Shawn.

She takes lead to her truck, dragging the woman behind her, where we cram into the unsurprisingly cramped cab.

Shoving different things around, I make a clear spot on the back seat and the floor below. I tuck into the seat behind Jaiden, so I don't have to look at her. A petty act at best, but it's the little things that make me feel better.

When she turns on the truck, a country melody fills the air. The surprising noise, though of a music genre I absolutely despise, is music to my ears. We haven't had much more than movie soundtracks and Christmas CDs to listen to.

It's been so long since I've heard popular industrial produced songs, that I take a moment to appreciate it; despite my previous hate. She turns it up a bit.

"So is anyone going to introduce me or do I have to do it myself?" The woman says.

"Dominique this is Sara, Sara this is Dominique, but her friends call her Nikki." John introduces me to the girl.

"Hi, nice to meet you. I've heard so much about you." She extends a hand out, so I shake it.

"Nice to meet you too." I return the polite greeting. I haven't heard anything about you, I add in my head. I try to drive jealousy down when I figure that the two of them might be dating. Why else would she be here?

I forgo my seat belt as Jaiden drives on. I won't be staying here long.

"What do you got for ears around here?" Sara weirdly asks Jaiden. Is she asking about music, like headphones?

"Vampires, elves, a witch and unknown." Jaiden answers. Now I understand the question and why it was asked. The vampires have better hearing than us. Couldn't she've just asked that?

"Unknown?" She fires back.

"I've never asked him what he is." Jaiden answers Sara's question.

"Oh." Sara turns down the music a little. "Why haven't you asked him what he is?"

"It didn't seem important. I didn't really care, and it never came up naturally in conversation." Jaiden offers multiple explanations; a little bit of many reasons. "He's strong and fast, but I've never seen him drink blood and he doesn't need sun block to go outside in the day."

"Well, that limits it to not a vampire; good job. The distance, road noise, will be enough to make sure the vampires and most supernaturals won't hear it.

Loud music is a little redundant. As the music gets louder, you just yell louder so the other person can understand, and it mostly just cancels each other out. Except maybe, makes it a little harder to understand; sometimes." Her reasoning only makes a little sense. I wonder if she's ever been to a loud club and tried to talk to someone. You don't yell as loud as the music; that would be impossible. We just get close and talk into each other's ears.

Jaiden turns the music down a little. "A werewolf in transformation has hearing sixteen times greater than that of a human. A vampire's hearing is better than a humans on a regular blood diet, let alone when overindulging, and they have their high range hearing. Who knows who's around?"

"I see you've been doing your research." Sara sounds impressed. "Nerd."

"It's fine." John steps in. "We didn't smell anyone to be worried about in the area. It was just your group here." It occurs to me that while I now know he's a werewolf, and I'm prepared for him wolfing out, it didn't occur to me that he would have highly increased hearing and smell.

The thought of it has me wondering if I'm breathing too loudly. Do I stink? Of course I stink, I didn't think of putting on deodorant this morning. When was my last shower? Should I open a window? It doesn't look like my stench is affecting them. How self-conscious should I be about this?

"Yeah, what he said. So what the Hell happened?" Sara asks Jaiden and I; looking between us. I don't know what she's talking about.

"Umm, well," Jaiden starts then stalls. "Like I texted, Darius attacked Banff while we were gone."

Texted? "Wait! You have a phone!" My anger increases as I realize she's been keeping more secrets. She's had a phone this whole time and she hasn't told me. "The Hell?"

"You didn't tell her." John asks in a statement.

"Yes, I have a phone." She answer me first, then John. "No, I didn't tell her. She's supposed to be bad at keeping secrets."

"Hey!" Offended, I jump my attention to the front of the seat.

"Well, it's true." John mutters. He looks away sheepishly when my glare shows him I heard his words.

"I didn't tell you about it because a secret only stays a secret as long as only one person knows about it." Jaiden explains. "As soon as you let anyone else know, then it's no longer a secret."

"Are you keeping any other secrets for me?" I ask almost needlessly.

"Of course I am." She answers too fast and unapologetic. Jaiden's keeping more secrets from me. "Everyone has their secrets. Every secret is secret for a reason. You'll find out what you need to find out, when you need to find out."

"Marshalls do like their secrets, don't they? So how strong are your visions?" Sara's eyes bore into her skull as Jaiden remains silent.

"They're there. I see enough of the future to help sometimes." I answer for her. I'm too buried in this lie to give it up now; no matter how I feel about Jaiden now.

"Not you, you wouldn't have any visions." Sara wrinkles her nose up and scrunches her forehead down. "You have a bit of magic in your family, but no visions. I was talking about Jaiden."

Magic?

"I don't-" Jaiden tries.

Sara interrupts her. "Of course you do. Any idiot with a nose can figure that out."

"Maybe not an idiot. You're a Marshall. You smell partly like your father. If you know what the parents' blood line base smells like, then you could figure it out with a good whiff." John explains.

"And, if it skipped a generation?" Jaiden asks.

"Are you really going to play that card?" John questions her.

"Well, it is dangerous to be a prophet." She counters.

"It could be argued it's more dangerous to pretend you're not." Sara's words are surprisingly insightful. "And please, Nikki, you don't do a very good job at faking it."

As they keep pushing, I know it's useless to keep this up. Jaiden's on her own. "I fooled Sandra and Darius. Jaiden and I made a deal that I would continue to pretend to be the prophet. Plausible deniability, she's never told me that she is a prophet.

We tell people that Jaiden and I are not sisters; she's just maybe a

Marshall to those who knew about that before. There are doubts to who her father actually is. But, we told everyone she doesn't get visions."

"That's ridiculous. To protect her? You think that you claiming to be the prophet will protect her? That plan is going to get her killed. They're not going to kill a prophet, they're too valuable if you can find a good one, but they will kill her friends." She explains.

Sara has a point.

"What do you mean a good one?" I ask.

"Human blood dilution or, like you said, skip a generation." She starts over on a different track. "Not all prophets are created equal. There are different types and strengths.

The Marshall visions are of an unusual type; they're dreamers. But, more so unusual because the blood line has stayed consistently strong for so long; they have a bit of a reputation in the supernatural community.

They have their intuitions and empathic abilities during their wakefulness, sure, but the real work is in their dreams. They have uncontrollable visions while they sleep. What makes them completely useless at times, is also their greatest strength. They see everything; every detail they would see when it happens."

"Feel it too." Jaiden pipes up.

Everyone stops for a moment at her admission.

John speaks up first. "Feel it?"

"Yeah. I see things, hear them, smell them, feel them. Everything that happens in the vision is an exact replica of what actually happens; most of the time." She carries on after no one speaks for a few seconds. "On occasion, I've had visions that were more symbolic."

"Like what?" Sara asks.

"Like my mom bashing her head into the rocking chair; blood rushing everywhere out of her skull. That afternoon, she died of a brain aneurism."

"Oh God." My exclamation is the only noise in a deafening silence. It slips out uncontrollably. My heart aches for her.

"I have just normal dreams too, vivid dreams, so it's hard to tell sometimes what's a vision and what is just a dream." Jaiden breezes by her confession like what she said was nothing out of the ordinary.

"I'm sorry. That's heartbreaking." I say to her.

Jaiden doesn't show any sign of hearing me. She just continues. "Sometimes it's obvious, but then again I thought my nightmares were just dreams, but it turned out the monsters in my dreams were real."

"Your mom, did she have visions too." Sara asks her in the thick air.

"No, not that I know of. She didn't say anything before she passed, but dream talk was discouraged growing up. Everything creative and illogical was discouraged.

I think there was mental illness stigma in the family. There was one time, when I was older, I told my father about my visions and he threatened to send me to a mental institution, so I played it off as a joke, and learned that I had to hide them." Every time Jaiden opens up about her childhood makes me hate her parents; hate her father.

"So, no one told you that you had visions?" Sara asks.

"No, I had to figure it out on my own. It was after so many times of my dreams coming true, I finally was like, okay something's going on here.

I thought I might have been going insane at first; that I was just imagining things. That I would see something happen in real life and then convince myself that I had a dream about it prior to the actual event happening. Um-" She trails off. "But, yeah. No one told me about them. I had to figure it out."

"So did the Marshall's explain things to you when they found you?" Sara asks.

My interest is peaked as they turn to talking directly about my family; curious of her answer.

"No, but I think they tried once. The grandparents had asked me about dreams and if I kept a dream journal, but I shut them down fast because of my upbringing and didn't think about the connection until later on. It was never mentioned again, so I think they just thought I didn't get them."

"Well, and how do I put this nicely? Marshall's tended to marry within the family. I mean they don't marry sisters and brothers; not anymore. But, definitely marrying others with the same type of visions. So with your mother being human…" Sara trails off.

"Incest." Jaiden says bluntly. "Incest, in older times was perfectly acceptable and a common practice at times and different places. Keeping it with in the family was huge for some; especially in royal families.

Or, there were those who essentially had no other options but to marry in the family because there simply wasn't anyone around who wasn't related to them.

If you want to look at keeping something hereditary, like visions, then it would be plausible at the time to think that incest would allow the visions to linger in the family a long time down the line; which is also true.

But, they also didn't know that there can be repercussions to continual incest back then. Like the royals who killed their blood lines with hereditary conditions or that family who had blue skin.

It didn't mean something bad always happened but it could. Genetics like diversity.

But, that also means that dominant and recessive traits would have a play on it. With humanity being a recessive trait, the more you introduce it the more likely it'll happen.

It's like blue eyes. You get a dominant recessive against a recessive recessive then have four kids, chances are two end up with brown eyes and two with blue, and everyone can pass on blue eyes to the next generation.

Versus, having dominant recessive against a dominant recessive; you'll have one dominant dominant, two dominant recessives and one recessive recessive. Meaning one of those kids isn't passing on a blue eye gene and one of the kids has blue eyes.

Versus a dominant dominant with a dominant recessive, where no one has blue eyes, but two kids can pass it on to the next generation.-"

"I have no idea what you're saying." Sara interrupts Jaiden's lecture.

I'm glad she did; there's only so many times a person can hear dominant and recessive before it sounds weird.

But, I also remember something like what she's talking about from science class in high school; we paired with a partner and figured out what our children would look like based off dominant and recessive traits.

"Sorry." Jaiden knows she went off on one of her tirades. "Basically, the more often a person with visions reproduces with humans, the more you'll likely lose the visions in the genetics game as the generations pass. Then, there would be percentages of various traits passed as weaker or stronger.

And then there's genetic mutations. Dreamers are a genetic mutation that was developed at some point; maybe from the incest. But, it's all complicated."

"Werewolves did it too; incest I mean. Every werewolf on this planet is related, sometimes in multiple ways. That's why John had to break up with Nikki."

"Sara!" John tries to stop her.

Sara continues without skipping a beat. "He's practically required to marry another wolf because, God forbid, he might have a hybrid baby. His mom was a human, and his brother didn't get the wolf gene as much as John. He can't transform, and barely got any extra senses."

"Sara, shut up!" John yells.

"It's true." She goes back to talking with Jaiden and I. "That's why his parents divorced. Well, the mom thinks his dad cheated on her because of course she wasn't allowed to know about the werewolf thing. John's bound to mate one of his cousins, or whatever, to make sure there are no humans in the pack."

"Can you shut up, please?" John pleads with her.

While I am grateful for the new information, Sara has no right to tell John's business like that.

It does change things though.

"Well, since you said please." She mocks, but stays quite afterwards.

John sighs. He sweeps his hair out from his face.

I feel like he needs a rescue. It seems like a lot of awful from his past was just dug up. Besides, it looks like he might not have broken up with me because he actually wanted to. Which, will need to be a conversation with him later; privately. "My phone didn't work. Did the phones go back up later?"

"Supernaturals in charge, shut down the human networks and kept the supernatural networks up and running. You'd need a preprogrammed phone, or know how to break into our networks." John explains.

"Like the dark web." I try to connect it to something semi familiar.

"Sure." He answers.

"So you guys have like, internet and everything."

"Yup." He says.

"How were you charging the phone?" I ask Jaiden.

"Solar power. Put the phone out in the sun and it charges." Something about that seems impossible with the technology we have out. Maybe supernaturals are more technologically advanced than we are.

"So, and you guys have been texting back and forth this whole time?" I open up to questioning everyone.

"Yeah, when she actually responds." Sara jabs at Jaiden.

"It's not like I could just pull the phone out anytime I wanted. Besides, it was always charging half the day on the roof." Jaiden's excuses sound poor, but many people had done the same before all of this. I, on numerous occasions, would look at a received text and ignore it for hours. If forgotten, I would never respond.

"Speaking of, where is my phone?" Sara asks.

Jaiden tells her, "It's in my pocket."

"And, you haven't felt like answering since yesterday." Sara accuses her. "And, you still haven't answered my question."

"I was a little busy and short on privacy with the spirits attacking us." Jaiden statement is a bit of an understatement.

"What?" Sara asks. Her impatience shows in her raising voice.

"Spirits attacked us at a house we had stopped at. We were on our way to B.C., but had to stop at a house. We lost most of our people, what was left of them, there." Jaiden explains simply. I open my mouth to elaborate about those freaky little twins and their gruesome father but another is faster.

"You pocket dialed me. People were screaming." John tells her.

"Sorry. The screen must be against my leg, and I had left it in your text message screen. The power button must've gotten pushed at some point."

"Sorry? You gave John a heart attack. And, you owe me one because the pack found out about the phone and I was reprimanded for putting the pack in danger." I look to John as she talks, but he avoids my gaze to look out the window. Does his family, pack, know that he's here? Do they approve?

He seems to have restrictions and obligations, so would his people approve of his taking off to find us. They didn't seem too pleased that they are conversing with Jaiden.

Jaiden takes her eyes off the road to stare at Sara and gasp. "I'm so sorry. I didn't mean to get you in trouble." She pays attention to driving again.

"Relax. It was an accident." Sara lets her off the hook easy.

"I'm still sorry." She has been doing a lot of apologizing. I wonder if it even means anything to her.

"I know." Sara confirms.

"Did you guys pass any check stops on the way here?" Jaiden asks.

"No. They sound scary though." Sara's eyes widen in excitement and fear.

"What check stops?" I ask before anyone has the chance to speak. They seem to forget I'm out of their loop.

"People are stopping travellers and asking them what type of being they are." John explains.

"Okay?" I say. "I think I'm going to need a bit more than that." That doesn't sound that scary to me.

"Check stops are being set up to check genetics by people who are representing the Council; the half that decided to riot. Supernaturals get a pass through, but humans are imprisoned or killed. They're allowed to kill if necessary. Some are using that to their advantage to kill every human that passes by." Jaiden paints a different and scarier outlook on the check stops.

"Are you sure?" John breaks the silence.

"Yeah, I'm sure." She says.

John shakes his head. "I haven't heard anything about that. How d'you find out?"

"Visions and Reed's post lead me to do some searching. It's happening all over; more and more as time goes on." Jaiden says. "They'll get uniforms soon, so you'll know who's official and who's not. Not that that matters much."

"What happened in your vision?" Sara asks.

"I was pulled over and the officer asked for my ID, which I hadn't known about and didn't have. He said I was under arrest for theft of supernatural property; a cell phone. Once he confirmed that I wasn't in the database, confirmed that I was human, he knocked me out or maybe he killed me; I'm not sure but everything went black. But the reason I was asking was because I wanted to know if you guys registered with the database, and we need to get Dominique registered." It angers me that Jaiden seems to know all of these things. Which, of course she does, because she's had that cell phone this whole time.

I feel so useless in this conversation.

"We're registered. Alpha Ken had all of us registered at birth. The Council put up DataBase as soon as the technology was there to keep track of all the supernatural beings. Some rejected the practise so it was voluntary. How did you register?" John tells her and half tries to explain things to me.

"There's a form online. I got the ID sent straight to the phone." Jaiden says.

"What did you register as?" Sara asks her. "Dreamer?"

"Empath." Finally, Jaiden says something that is familiar to me.

"That's low on the supernatural scaling." Sara snidely comments.

"It's not like I was going to put seer or dreamer on there." Jaiden counters back. Of course she'd find something else to put on there. Hiding what she is had been important. "I figured that could put a target on my back."

"You should have. Can I see it?" Sara asks.

Jaiden squirms in her seat before producing a phone to pass to Sara. "It's in the photos as a screenshot and a download."

"What last name did you use?" John asks.

"Kensington."

"Do another one as Marshall." He tells her.

"This doesn't look official; ours are purple and gold." Sara passes the phone on to John so he can take a look. After a quick look, he passes it back to Sara. "You really need to learn how to take a better selfie."

"I don't know. The form was on a website. As far as I was able to research, it's a hundred percent official. Aalayah and Seth took over everything. They have all the Council resources, including the website and registration services.

Because of a lack of ability to get cards out to people, they are doing phone IDs. People can also look up names on the database when no card is present. And, registration is now mandatory.

My bet is that's why they got Reed to prove he's a werewolf. If he didn't have his ID, and the person didn't have their tablet, then they would have gotten him to prove it. If you can't prove it, then you're dead." Jaiden ignores the selfie comment. I'm curious to how bad the picture is. Likening it to the awful driver license pictures everyone has. "And, that's the first selfie I've ever taken, so go easy on me."

"You should do another one, directly on DataBase, as a Marshall and put that you are a seer." John repeats to her. "And, you need to get one done too." John pulls his phone out and fiddles with it a moment before handing it to me.

"Yeah sure." I look at the registration form in front of me and fill out what I can. There is one blank left to fill out at the end. "What should I put as the supernatural race?"

"Empath. It's easy to fake and hard to prove otherwise." Jaiden answers. "You're a fortune cookie. It'd be natural for you for figure some line up that'll convince them."

I put down my anger at the question of whether that was meant as a compliment or an insult. Inputting the information and taking the selfie as needed. I pass the phone back to John once I am done. "Do you want me to continue to pretend to be the prophet?"

"No, it's okay." She says after a moment of hesitation. "If it puts you in danger, it's not worth it. Besides, most everyone that knew is dead. Though you might want to think about it, if Darius or Sandra come back around."

"Well, you two seem like you worked things out. What were you fighting about?" Sara's questions drudges up all the pain and anger.

Putting all the hatred I can in to one sentence, I tell her what the fight was about. "She didn't tell me my family was dead."

"Ouch." Sara remarks.

"I forgot to tell her-"

Tired of her excuses I unleash my anger unto her. "How do you forget to tell someone their family is dead? Like, it's just." Breathe. "I asked you if you saw our family and you said no."

"At that exact moment, that you asked me, I didn't think you needed to hear that your family was dead. I didn't think you could take it, so I had planned to tell you later, but I forgot. I didn't think about it until a couple days ago when you wanted to find your family. Then, the morning was so hectic, and I didn't exactly want to tell you and have you break down in front of everyone."

"Oh, don't try to do me any favours." I decide to call her out. "No, you just didn't want to be the cause of a scene. How could you tell other people and think I wouldn't find out?"

"I forgot that I had told them, and I didn't tell them that it was your family. I'm sorry you found out the way you did."

"No you're not!" I shout. "If you were sorry, you wouldn't have done it in the first place."

"That's not how being sorry works, but if that's your logic then fine; I'm not sorry I didn't tell you when I first saw you." My jaw drops at how cold and heartless she is. "I'm not sorry for withholding that information right after rescuing you from imprisonment and certain death when that troll was supposed to break your neck.

I'm not sorry that I thought we were going to be attacked at that hotel, and I still don't understand why they didn't come after us that night. I'm not sorry I didn't tell you after finding out your aunt died.

Then, before you organized a group to attack the hotel, and I was trying to prevent you from going in with a nothing to lose attitude. I was already trying to prevent you from a complete mental break down after you were supposed to kill those people in the hall with your gun.

Then, a building crashed down on me, and rescuing people, and Taylor's mobbing murder, and keeping peace, and staying alive through the winter, and I guess it kind of slipped my mind that I hadn't told you that your family had died. But, I'd do most of it again. Just would have told you after things settled after the hotel. But it doesn't matter because you'd still be mad at me for withholding the information, no matter what my reasons were."

"I was supposed to kill those people." The sinking feeling that devastated me after the bullets left the chamber, returns. It was bad enough for me to think that I almost killed them. Jaiden stopped me from actually killing them; like I was supposed to.

"You thought they were supernatural beings rushing at you and you shot them all. I stuck with you this time to make sure that didn't happen this time. I saw what it did to you, and it completely broke you. I couldn't let that happen." Jaiden says softly.

Anger morphs into another form of the same word. "You should have told me."

"I'm not used to telling people my visions, and I don't know if I even should be. It feels wrong to talk about them. Besides, by telling you a vision I could be preventing it, or making it happen, or making some other horrible thing happen. If I'm the only one that knows, then I can control everything and hopefully ensure a desirable outcome."

"That's bullshit." Sara claims as she chimes in. "Seers have been telling people their visions since the beginning of time."

"Right." Jaiden confirms. "Dominique, you go to psychics all the time. One time they told you you were going to be getting a kitten. Within a week you bought a kitten, and a month later you realized having a cat was not your thing so you gave it away. You wouldn't have gotten the kitten if that woman hadn't told you that you were going to get the kitten. People are suggestable. Especially, when they believe that the psychic has concrete knowledge about the future."

"So?" I ask.

"So, what if I told you that John was going to kill you-"

John interrupts her. "Does that have to be the example?"

"Fine. What would you do if I told you Sara was going to kill you?" Jaiden says.

"Confront her and bring a gun." I say. If she is going to kill me then I would confront her about it and bring a weapon to defend myself.

"Exactly, and one of you would probably die anyway, and people would be wondering why you attacked Sara; blame you for whichever one died. But if I don't tell you then I can watch and maybe have more visions that show me why Sara attacked you. I can try to prevent it from getting to the point that she'd go to kill you, or I saw the moment she killed you, so I can move to prevent that exact moment."

"What if I didn't confront her?" I offer.

"Then knowing she is supposed to kill you would create animosity between you two, and maybe she kills you sooner. And I didn't see that one, so she actually kills you. Or maybe you two fight and she leaves. Or, you leave to prevent it. Or if I don't tell you and I prevent it from ever happening, then you two don't know what was supposed to happen, then maybe you become the best of friends and save each other from dying in other attacks." Jaiden sounds like she's talking in wild circles.

"This was hypothetical right?" Sara laughs nervously.

"Yes. I swear I haven't had any visions of you two killing each other." Jaiden reassures us. "So don't do anything you both wouldn't have done in the first place."

"Good." I say when there is nothing else to say. She's so confusing yet also makes a little sense.

Through the front window I can see the rest of our vehicles stopping on the road. I practically sigh in relief at the sight of them pulling over. The tension in my shoulders release.

"So, you're a control freak." Sara surmises.

"Yes. Very much so." Jaiden confirms.

Sara turns more in her seat to face me comfortably. "I think you need to forgive your sister. If for nothing more, she saved your life at least twice, and she wasn't telling you about that either."

"That's not your decision." I say.

Jaiden's barely stopped behind the SUV when I open the door to escape the uncomfortable situation. I don't need someone I don't know telling me to forgive Jaiden. I'm not ready yet.

Chapter 13

Candle light dances and flickers in the windows, giving off the presence of the people sure to be inside. Where there is controlled fire, there are people.

I hope this is the right place. I'm exhausted.

With the bar in shambles on the ground, detective work began to figure out where Jerry relocated. Driving around Red Deer to various past delivery locations until giving up at number five when they all said they wouldn't tell us or didn't know.

A random happen chance upon Ziam doing deliveries allowed us to follow him back to Jerry's new hotel.

Had we come across it in the day, there would have been no mistaking it. All the hotels ground level signs have been painted over and his name scrawled over the white background.

With no desire to repeat the horrifying experience of trying to turn the truck with the trailer on back, I try my best to wide turn into a far off stall. The trailer and truck stop at curve, and I'm somewhat in the stall lines. The parking job is plenty satisfactory for me; I don't care what anyone else would say.

I turn off the engine and leave the truck. John is out and on his way to meet up with Dominique. Sara's door slams shut and walks around the front, giving me a signal to lock the doors.

The other three vehicles find parking a bit closer and manage perfect parking. I brush off the embarrassment of an extra-long walk since no one else has a trailer.

Ziam waits for only me, once I near him he escorts me inside. I don't bother to wait for anyone else at this point, so only Sara follows directly behind us. The others will straggle in as they are ready.

We walk into the lobby and to the left; through the lounge doors. Jerry looks away from his current customer to us entering the room. He looks back to his customer. At the exact moment of recognition, his head snaps back to look at us.

I wave a little wave as just a sweep of my outward palm.

Jerry finishes serving the customer his drink as we walk up to the bar. Ziam leaves us with a pat to my back. He goes around to behind the bar, and relieves Jerry of his duties.

"I thought you were dead." Jerry says. He comes around the counter to get closer.

"Ziam said the same thing." I smile as if it were some joke.

"Now you can pick up the deliveries you abandoned." His smile creases at his slight eye wrinkles.

"Wasn't I just covering for Ziam in the first place?" I jest again.

"Chad refused to take deliveries from me after you left; we thought you were dead." Not one ounce of my jest chips away at his serious attitude. "Said I should protect my people better than that."

"Sorry." I hadn't thought my leaving would affect him at all. I hadn't thought about Jerry at all. I hadn't been there long.

Jerry looks beyond me to the people entering the bar area. I wave them over to us. When I look back at Jerry, his smile has flat lined. "What did you want?"

"A place to stay; for all of us." I tell him.

"You, yes. Them, no. I don't know any of them." I imagine Calli's conversation went this way at first, but he owed her a favour. I don't have that luxury. If anything, I owe him a favour. I'll need something for bargaining power.

I remind him. "You didn't know me."

"I owed Calli a favour. Where is she? And, that boy?" Jerry looks at the bunch briefly. They hang back a bit to give us space.

"Dead." I tell him. "Our town was attacked while I was on a supply trip. They didn't survive the attack."

"I'm sorry to hear that."

"Thanks."

Jerry doesn't skip a beat. "It doesn't change anything."

"That might not, but you're a business guy. I'm sure we can work something out." I say.

Jerry perks up an eyebrow. "Okay, I'll listen."

I start by listing off what I know he wants from me. "I'll start doing deliveries again. Everyone will work to earn their keep. I'll talk with Chad and get him to buy from you again."

"That's not enough." He says.

Pulling out my biggest ticket item to offer him. "I have a generator outside that could be yours."

"Does it work?" Jerry asks.

"It was running before I hitched it to the truck." I tell him.

He looks over our group as he mulls the offer over. "You got humans with you?"

For a fraction of a second I debate lying to him, but think better of it. "Only two and they're the guardians for the six year old witch."

"Follow." Jerry leads me to the lobby counter. He pulls out a binder from under the desk and opens it to the third page. He pencils in for three rooms. "I need names and species."

"Sara and John Kadiza; Lycans." Sara announces to him.

"First names are fine." He tells her.

"Alexa and Daniel are the humans. Rayleen is the young witch. They have a griffin named Crystal. Dominique is an empath. Shawn and Miles are elves. Chantel and Kelly are vampires. And, I'm not actually sure what DeAngelo is." Between each race, I pause so Jerry can get them written down without rushing or repetition. I look over to DeAngelo for assistance.

"Aziza on my dad's side and wood elf on my mom's." DeAngelo says an unfamiliar type of supernatural being for his father's side. I'll have to remember aziza to look it up later.

"Split it off boy/girl; four and four. The humans and the witchling have their own room." I consider the room placements a win and deal done.

"That's not enough. We've got five girls, not counting Alexa and Rayleen." Sara mentions.

"Jaiden's getting a ground floor room with the other delivery staff." Jerry writes room numbers onto little plastic rectangles. He hands the three key cards to Sara; 23C, 24C and 25C. "I don't care which rooms you give out to who but split it off per my instructions. Off you go now. Get settled for the night. It'll be an early morning." He points to me. "I want to see that generator."

"Should I come with you?" Sara asks me. I don't think she fully trusts Jerry. I don't blame her. I don't fully trust him either.

"I'm fine, thanks. Go help everyone get their things up to the rooms. I'll see you later." I promise her.

Jerry and I walk immediately outside.

"Why is it parked so far away from the other vehicles?" He asks.

"Because I don't know how to park with a trailer." My honesty is the only response I can give. I barely know how to park a car.

A laugh huffs out of him. "You can tell your friend that she doesn't have to growl at me."

Though I wasn't aware Sara had growled at him, I wouldn't put it past her. "She's protective over pack."

"And, she considers you pack?"

"The Alpha made me a honourary pack member after I helped them in an attack by some humans." Not that I am supposed to be telling anyone, but I doubt this will do any harm. Jerry thinks I'm not human. I'm actually not, so they shouldn't be in any trouble.

"You must've impressed him. Wolves don't accept non-wolves into their pack lightly." Jerry says.

"Yeah, I guess so." I pass it off as nothing, because I don't feel like I really did anything special.

We come up to the generator. Jerry takes his time circling the generator. "Alright, it looks like a metal box with solar panels on top. I don't see any damage on it. You said it was working when you unplugged it?"

"Best ice cream I've ever had." I reminisce. "I took it from a farm on that run I was doing."

"I'll, uh, have someone look over it and figure out how to hook it up. I have no idea what we would need to plug it in, but someone around should." His confession isn't ground shaking after calling it a metal box with solar panels on top.

"Didn't you have a generator at your old place?" I ask.

"Professionally installed. I never had to touch the thing. It got destroyed in an attack after you left." Vehicle doors open and shut behind me; distracting me. The others are all grabbing their personal items and supplies. "Did you have things you wanted to bring inside?"

"Yeah, I have a bag and a few things." I unlock the truck. Only personal items right now. I grab out two bags; mine and Leah's.

"I'll help you bring it to your room." He says as he takes the one bag from me.

"Thank you."

We cross paths with the others just inside. I feel like I'm back in high school again when they stop what they're doing to gaze at me and Jerry. Rejecting malicious intent, I think they may be curious of the events and worried about the future. Perhaps, they might be angry for the separation and special treatment I've already been shown and will likely continue to receive.

Jerry takes the slight lead as he shows me to a room; 13A.

The door opens at his touch. "The doors had electronic locks that automatically unlock when the power is down. When you're in your room you can manually lock it, but that's about it."

I wonder why he didn't have the locks redone when he moved in. The ability to lock a door is essential for privacy and security.

I note to keep important and valuable items on my person. "Is theft a huge issue?"

"Honour code. No one steals from you and you don't steal from anyone. Justice is dealt out by the victim of the crime."

Honour code only works if everyone is honourable; otherwise it's a system asking for problems. "And who judges if the culprit is guilty."

"I do." He lowers his voice to the barest whisper, and gets close. "Your humans will have to stay in their room."

"Why?" I question quietly.

"It's for their own safety." Jerry says.

It's concerning for Jerry to warn about the humans' safety. Whereas Calli said Jerry had an issue with humans, he may not be the biggest threat. "If they don't put it out there that they are human, and then who would know? Besides, it's a new world and we should all be making an effort to get along."

"It doesn't work that way."

"It will. It does. Humans and supernaturals living cohesively and peacefully. We had it in Banff, for five months, before we were attacked. It wasn't perfect; I won't lie. But, we made it work." I tire of whispering when there is so much to say. "Is there somewhere we can talk in private that we don't have to whisper?"

"Let's go for a drive." Voice returned to a regular volume, Jerry turns about face and leaves the room. I follow quickly behind him after looking forlornly at my bags. I hope no one steals anything while I'm gone. There's no sense in dragging them out with me again.

Jerry stops in at the bar to grab a set of keys and tells Ziam we will be heading out for a few minutes. Ziam's look of concern has me questioning if this was such a bright idea. Jerry has never seemed like he would hurt me, but I don't know him well enough to say for sure.

I calm my nerves and remind myself that there is a pocket knife in my jacket.

Jerry and I leave into a chilled night. We take the end delivery pickup truck; it's red. He settles into the driver's seat and I into the passenger's.

He pulls out of the parking lot. "Tell me about Banff. That's where you went after abandoning us, right?"

"I didn't mean to abandon you." And, I wish he wouldn't use that word. The kind of speech and exaggeration reminds me of the manipulation Jacob would pull with me. He parks just up the road, and turns off the truck. "Calli woke me up and said we had to get out of there. She made us go through the window. There was an ogre outside that attacked us.

While we were fighting it, James Ellesworn nearly ran me over with his truck. When we were talking with him he said he was getting people together to fight back and they were on their way to rescue a couple people; Rayleen and Dominique. The little witch and the empath. So they invited us along. It was a leave now or we leave you behind type of thing.

Dominique is a family friend, so when I heard she was alive; I had to go help rescue her. So, we ran around for a bit until we found them in Banff. Darius, the rep for this region, had taken them to his outpost in Banff. We fought them and took over the city.

Unfortunately, Darius came to get revenge after the snow melted. He attacked and very few of us survived. And, more were killed the next day when we tried spending the night at a house with some angry spirits. Then, we came here."

"I think we were right. You need to write a soap opera about your life because you just can't stay out of trouble; can you?" He jokes about something said months ago. I relax more.

"Doesn't look like it." I respond in kind.

"Did James pass as well?" Jerry asks.

"No." I elaborate. "He left us in December because he had some other Council things to do; he didn't elaborate. We were hoping to be able to find him again."

"Good luck with that. He and Niklas have targets on their heads, and have gone into hiding. No one's heard from them directly."

"Lovely." Sarcasm cuts the word as deep as my hope plummets with finding the man.

"Does Darius know you survived the attack?" Jerry asks.

"No." I say. I know he knows Alexa was gone, but did he know who else left with her? Did he know others survived in Banff? "As far as he knows, everyone died in Banff."

"Are you bringing trouble with you?" A resounding yes echoes in my head. Darius is likely to attack again, because of Alexa.

His question is a difficult one to answer. There are so many variables. "No. There's no reason to think he'd be after us anymore."

"You can't expect me to let you stay when you have Darius after you." Jerry asserts.

To save our new lodging I twist everything back on him. I may bring trouble with me, but he isn't free of his own trouble. "Yeah, I can. What about you? You have people shooting up and burning down your bar. You have enemies that would love to take you out, so what makes this any different? Darius is an idiot. He's incompetent. He's got a lot more worries than hunting us for the rest of our lives. You, have competition that would love to shut you down permanently, and that's the immediate threat."

"So?"

"So, we could help each other." I offer. "Like I said, I can get Chad to consider being your client again; he owes me a favour for saving his life. That's a lot of vampires that will have a vested interest in keeping you up and running. John is the beta of his pack, and that carries weight with the lycans; maybe more business from the packs in the area."

"I'm supposed to be neutral in this war." He reveals his position to me. He didn't start the revolution, but he certainly isn't going to fight against it. He benefits from the business on both sides. "How can I expect to remain neutral when I house traitors?"

"Because remaining neutral always works out." Sarcasm drips in my words. I could name many examples but I feel like that would defeat the purpose. "The world isn't going to be like this forever; it's not sustainable. You're going to have to pick a side eventually, and I hope you pick ours. We just want life back to normal, but this time with supernaturals out in the open and free."

"This sounds like an awful large risk for little reward." He points out the flaw in my plan; a business tactic.

"Business wise you would have more customers; supernaturals and humans if you expand. That equals more money." I speak to his business side of him. It worked to get him to let us stay, so it may work to get him to let us continue to stay.

"I could sell the humans." A business practice I'm sure he's already contemplated, and possibly already done.

"Logistically, that makes no business sense. Live cargo costs a lot more than alcohol. You'd have to charge more because of storage and up keep. Humans die rather easy. One gets sick, and they all do. Then they die and there goes profit, and all expenses with it. What do you think profit margins could be on selling humans?

Not to mention, if the supernatural being takes care of their human or reproduces them, they could make them last a long time.

How many people are going to be in the market to sell humans? You're going to have to keep competitive prices. Lower profit margins. Higher risk if something happens to your humans.

You're going to have to sell a lot of humans to make it worth it, and is there really that kind of availability anymore? Letting us stay would be better for business."

"You think this would be purely a business decision." Jerry declares.

"It might be one of a few points to your decision, but I think it might be a worth exploring as a key point." I state.

"If this were purely a business decision, what would you propose? What do you bring to the table for a mutually beneficial deal?"

"There's your business and expansion of course. We all work for you, and, in the meantime you house us indefinitely. We'll be delivery people, maids, whatever you need. Labour for our expenses, food, and room. We'll get the word out about your business. More customers for you."

He interrupts me when I take my breath in the middle of my speech. "It's still hard to see what would be in this for me."

"What about recognition? James Ellesworn banded us together. Could mean recognition straight from the Council." I continue after he appears to consider that point. "Short term, extra business, almost free labour, extra protection from your rival troubles. You've got a generator, only if you let us stay, which is extremely beneficial to business. No one likes a warm beer, or cold blood.”

Jerry interrupts me once again. “For the possibility of being executed for treason.” He’s still not completely convinced.

I move tactics to use time against him. “Your enemy could discover where you moved operations to and attack next week. You might die then. Versus a tiny unlikely possibility that you might be killed for treason against one side of the war. The other side would commend you for your services.”

“I still get everything you offered?”

“Yes.” I say.

“Deal.” He announces.

“Deal.” With a seal of words, our contract is drawn. Relief fills me. Giddy at actually being able to make a deal on my own.

“You start deliveries tomorrow. No one does deliveries but you. I’ll give you time to figure out what you’re going to do about Chad, but I recommend you do it in the next couple days. He won’t like it if he hears you’re back from someone else. I’ll find jobs for everyone; there isn’t a lack of things that need to be done. I’ll figure out what your humans can do that won’t put them in contact with anyone.”

“Thank you.” Pushing my luck, I decide to ask for one more favour. “One other thing. Are there any magic folk in the building that might be willing to train a six year old to use and control her magic?”

“I might be able to find someone.” He utters.

“Thank you. James was teaching her before he left, and then she lost her other teacher when Banff was attacked. Before that, she thought she was human. She’s way behind on learning.”

“It’s a shame when they’re raised human. It’s a complete loss of potential.” Jerry Shakes his head.

He’s not wrong, and I can sympathize with the remark. “It’s not right to take that choice away from them. That was the world we lived in though. It happened so often. There are so many people I’ve met that mom or dad was a supernatural and the other human, but they were raised human until their abilities showed up. Either their parents split up after, or it was a big secret. Training was delayed. Or, the kid thought they were insane for a long time. It’s just a shame that it all had to be hidden.”

“Which one was human?”

“Excuse me?” I ask, lost on his question.

“Your family, which one was human?” He clarifies.

“Both. Remember my soap opera story? Well, it was my biological dad, who didn’t know about me until almost a year ago, that was the supernatural. My mom and Jacob were both human, and made me think I was insane. Jacob had me committed for a couple weeks while I convinced the doctors that it was a joke.” I surprise myself when I reveal in was institutionalized. I’ve never actually told anyone that. Usually, I opt to end the story with just the threat of it. Maybe it’ll earn me some sympathy points.

He purses his lips and shakes his head in disgust. “Tragic.”

“I think that’s something that has come out of all of this. The hush hush, secrecy, and for all the laws the Council had, it didn’t stop supernaturals and humans from having kids together. Nor did it stop creation of new supernatural beings; most evident by young vampires still existing. It just made it a secret and something to hide. It’s like the prohibition era. You can make alcohol against the law, but people still find ways to consume alcohol. They’ll make it themselves, or go to their buddy who makes it, or smuggle it in from elsewhere. The law can only catch so many people. Even with an execution order. People will still do what they want when they don’t think the law is right.”

“I see what you did there.” Jerry smiles as he catches me.

“I have no idea what you’re talking about.” Tying in this conversation to our previous one happened by no accident. Jerry will be convinced to support us by the time we get up and running.

Jerry starts up the truck and parks it back where he found it.

“Do you need anything before you go to bed?” He asks as he turns off the engine.

“No. I think I’ll just check on the others, and then go to my room.” I unbuckle my seatbelt and open the door. The warm air leaves in a whoosh, as the cold air quickly replaces it. Goosebumps and a shiver top off the temperature difference. Shutting the door behind me, I almost rush into the hotel, but Jerry dawdles and I wait for him. The cold doesn't seem to bother him.

"Alright, if you need anything I'm in 1A. I'll be checking on Ziam, and then sleeping for the night. So if you need me, make sure it's an emergency." He warns.

"Alright. Have a good sleep." I say.

"You too."

I watch as he ducks into the bar. An expansive winding staircase leads up to the floor above. Like a spiral, I walk the circles up to the third floor.

Candles light up the second floor brightly, but it seems lacking on the third floor. Doubling back, I steal a candle from a seating area next to the stairs to light my way.

Wandering the dark hall, I hold up the candle to the room numbers. It starts with 1C. Walking down the hall and around the corner, I find that the three rooms are practically opposite to the main stairs. Jerry put them as far out of the way as he could have without resorting to the fourth floor.

Murmured voices talk behind the door on the right; room 24C. Listening to the other rooms, I don't hear any noises coming out of them.

24C opens suddenly, and Sara looks at me expectantly. "Are you coming in, or are you going to lurk in the hall a little more?"

"As much as I like the thought of lurking, it doesn't seem like the other rooms have anything going on in them." I get inside the room and Sara closes the door behind me.

"The kid and the two with her went to sleep. The rest of us are in here." She informs me.

"Did she know? Nikki told us she isn't a dreamer." Kelly asks.

The admission surprises me. I hadn't thought she'd tell them, but maybe it's a tactic. "Empath is safer than being a dreamer. Anyway, I convinced Jerry to let us stay in exchange for work. Also, the humans-"

"Aren't you human?" Dominique questions me.

We cross eyes. I try to secretly reflect irritation back at her. "Calli lied about my humanity to get us to stay with Jerry the first time. He thinks I'm an empath." I explain to her, but also for the sake of everyone's knowledge. "Anyway, the humans need to stay inside their rooms, or work jobs away from the supernaturals. There's a lot of people who come through here, and not all of them think of humans favourably."

I address Dominique with a look. "Keep with the empath story. I'm sure you'd rather have the freedom to go wherever you want rather than be stuck with Daniel and Alexa away from all of us."

I redirect to get back on track about the deal I made. "That's another thing. Everyone is going to have to work to earn their keep. Jerry is going to figure out what that means tonight and let you know tomorrow. But, you could be cleaning, serving drinks or food, handyman jobs. Whatever he says, you do it. It's that or you're out of here. I gave him the generator too."

"No. That wasn't yours to give." Dominique argues.

Why would this be a fight? That generator meant nothing to us, but now we'll benefit from its use. "Leah and I picked it up. It's not like it was being used. It was a major part of the deal."

"Anything else you give to him? Our souls maybe? All of our supplies?" She's being difficult to be difficult. The annoyance of a thorn in my side, yet bonded there permanently by family ties.

The arrogance has me pulling up my entire to do list in reference to the deal I made, whether it was an actual part of the deal or my own agenda. Plumping up my speech to make my point, while exaggerating and making up some things along the way to make things seem worse for me. "The rest is on me. I take back my old delivery job. I have to pull a favour with a vampire leader to get his clan back as a client, and ask for protection for Jerry's business. I have to find James, who is practically a ghost at this point because of the target on his head.

Start a revolution based on peace and equality. Negotiate peace talks between supernaturals who think it's their right to rule, and humans are slaves and food. All to take back this entire city and make it a safe zone before branching out to surrounding areas. Figure out a way to stave off attacks during all of this. While keeping Jerry out of the loop so that he has reasonable deniability if we fail and someone, like Darius or Sandra, comes to execute us all for treason. Is that enough for you or should I continue in more detail?" I rather hope she doesn't because I don't think I could really continue. Nothing else comes to mind on what I could say; likely I would just repeat myself babbling on. "I'm sorry you have to do some cleaning or waitressing."

"And, he trusts you to do all of this?" Dominique lashes out.

"He's trusting us. But if you don't want to help then you don't have to." I fully expect to have to do ninety nine percent of this myself. It suits me just fine to do all the work myself.

If half of it even happens at all. A natural progression of the state of things, has somehow turned into me planning a full on revolution; and I'm not entirely sure how it got to that.

"Well, what can we help with?" John offers a helpful question.

"I don't really know; most of it and none of it right now." I answer confusingly. I have no plan for my impromptu revolution, and they can't assist with anything else. "I don't know if you guys will be allowed to leave the hotel right away. Jerry said he didn't want any of you delivering because he doesn't know any of you. It would be helpful if you suss out the patrons and workers. Maybe find out where alliances fall. We're going to need as many people as possible for a revolution and to take back the city. See if allies have any information on where James is."

"We have no idea where James could be, where would we even start? Everything's going to be word of mouth unless one of you has a magical phone you've been hiding that actually works, and we can find him through that." Dominique tries to bait me into revealing my phone. I dare her with a stare to out me.

"My phone died." Chantel starts.

"Same; no charger." DeAngelo commiserates.

"My phone accidentally broke when I smashed it to pieces because I hated my phone." Kelly's answer has me laughing a little on the inside at the image it creates.

Dominique glares at me. I think she's using her anger as an outlet. Why be sad when you can be angry? Maybe she knows that she has all the power in this situation. I was in the wrong, so that gives her the power over me.

"You said he was a ghost right? So, what happens if we can't find James?" Miles questions.

"We do it ourselves. You could do nothing more than just try to survive, or you can fight back with this revolution. James wanted people to fight back against this war. We need to convince people that we can win, and give them something to fight for. We don't need James for that. We do need him eventually, maybe; he's still the Magic Council Representative, but not right now. By the time we find him, or he finds us, then we'll need him." There is a large chance James stays lost when we need him, or he could be long dead before that.

"Do we even need him?" Dominique asks. A hint of her distaste for the man underlines the question.

"At some point, yes. In what capacity, that'll be figured out later." I tell her. He can't be completely ruled out, at this point, just because she hates him.

"I don't think so. Look, you can make all the deals you want. Doesn't mean we have to listen. No one's going to follow you in a revolution. You aren't built for that. You don't have the charisma, and you're a proven liar." Dominique tears into me.

Trying to remain calm on the outside, I talk through my thoughts on it. She should know that I never intend on leading the revolution. I know my capabilities and capacities, and none of those are suited for leading a revolution. "I'm not planning on leading it. You're right; I would make a horrible leader. My anxiety alone with public speaking, would make me bad at it. I couldn't sell anything if I tried, and I suck at socializing. No one would ever follow me. I'm better at being the brain behind the operations." I simplify everything to the core of what the deal means to our group as a whole. "I bought us time to figure out the next step. That's it. You're welcome to forget everything else. I'm going to go to bed. I'm in 13A if anyone needs me." Walking with my head held high is about the only thing I can do at this point.

Leaving under a greater weight than when I came. Heart pounding and cheeks flush in embarrassment. Each moment from when I entered the room goes through my head; again and again and again. I shouldn't have said all of that.

I shouldn't have let Dominique get under my skin like that. I shouldn't have said anything about the revolution. It just popped into my head to make things worse for me, than for them. She was kicking up such a fuss about having to work to stay, that I didn't want to admit that after the Chad situation, my job would be some deliveries each day, and maybe trying to find James.

Talking about James connected the idea. He was trying to start a revolution, and things got away from me from there.

My surroundings get brighter as I near the lobby, and then darker again as I walk down the hall to my room.

A revolution might be a good idea. James would still be working at it, and we can't keep living like this; in constant threat of being killed. Something has to start somewhere for things to change.

But, she is right. There is no denying what I already know. No one's going to follow me. I'm a liar, and a fake. I need someone to be the face of it all. James already has the notoriety, but he's nowhere to be found. I'd need to find someone local and unfortunately my first pick hates me right now. Even with visions on my side, it's hard to say if she'll forgive me and get over it, or when that might happen.

Entering my room, I make sure to lock the door behind me. I survey the room to make sure my bags haven't been touched, and no one is hiding anywhere.

Until then, there's always faceless propaganda. A symbol for people to grab at and cling to. One pops up in my head. The one from my vision.

I don't know what it was for, but a pentagram is a good symbol. Recognizable and easy to reproduce.

It's perfect for what I have in mind.

The image burned in my memory translates onto paper as soon as I get to the desk. Running over it a few times I spell it out to ensure I have all the lines in the right place.

A few tries is all it takes to draw the image well; best starting off with the star and to build the box and extra lines around it.

Not everyone is going to get the symbol as a symbol alone. They would need other verbiage to make the connection at first.

I break out a new page on the notepad. Doodling images and words until I'm satisfied that this could finally be the one.

FIGHT 4 EQUALITY AND

PEACE

The imagery is bold and tells people exactly what we would stand for. The symbol stands in the center with the message all around it. It's clean and I would think my father's marketing department would be proud.

Garbaging all other ideas cleans up the desk. My eyes burn from working by candle light long into the night and after a very long day. Sandpaper rubs with each blink.

I need to go to sleep.

As the covers draw back, I hear four knocks at the door. A moment passes and I think that I could just ignore it, but the knocks rasp against the door again.

I go to the desk to hide my work by flipping it over. Knock. Knock. Knock. Knock.

Eyes roll directed at the person behind the door as if it'll make me feel any better about being interrupted.

My hand touches the lock, but I think to look through the spy hole first. Sara's distorted head does nothing to damper the look of annoyance she has with being kept waiting.

Unlocking the door, and opening it. I open my mouth to greet her, but the numerous knocking has her impatiently asking, "can I come in?"

"Yeah. Sure."

She shoves her phone in my hand before she shuts and locks the door behind her. I can't help but look at the screen. She's on her messages to me and an unsent note is written out.

Text and show. Don't send. Never know who's listening. She makes herself comfortable on the bed.

"Shoes off, please." I tell her. Handing the phone back to her. "I don't want to get mud on the sheets."

Sara smiles. "My shoes are the least of your worries about what's in this bed."

"That's disgusting, and I really don't want to think about all the nastiness that is hotel room beds." Sometimes ignorance is bliss.

I sit down next to her so I can see what she's writing without wait and a back and forth phone exchange. It saves time to read while she's typing out her message. I yawn.

Sorry about Dominique. I know that didn't go how you would have liked it to. She starts.

I take the phone to type back to her; continuing to write where she had left off. *Not your fault. I kind of deserve it.*

The phone is ripped from my hands. *Kind of?* She continues her message with a huffed laugh. *Are you really going to start a revolution?* I nod my answer to her. *And Jerry wants this?*

Sara passes me the phone. *Officially, he wants to be neutral until a side will clearly win. James recruited us for that purpose before he disappeared.* I wait with the phone in my hands to collect my thoughts. *We need to fight back regardless. The sooner we do so, the more lives can be saved. We already sat back for five months, after James left, with not one word about a rebellion, not one word about stopping this war. Someone needs to say something and start something.*

She takes the phone from me.

You? I shake my head. *Why not? You have me pretty convinced, and I haven't heard much.*

You like me, for some reason, but most people don't. I make bad impressions on people. You should have heard the way people would talk about me in Banff; it was bad. Not to mention how people talked to me and treated me beforehand. I was bullied in school. Stopping my rant track, I set us back on to right trail. *Honestly, we need someone like Dominique to be the face of it all. She's confident, brave, headstrong, not afraid to fight back no matter what that means. In a matter of days, she managed to bring together a large group of people to work together; no matter their background and ideals. Lead them, and she took a hold of leadership at Banff. She was able to stop a civil war there. She's a born leader. People follow her.*

But right now she hates you. So she isn't going to listen to you. Sara types.

Exactly. I can't think of much more to say.

Sara takes the phone back. I yawn three times as I wait for her message to finish typing. Getting comfortable in the bed was a bad choice to further my remaining awake. *So we leave her out until she has no choice. We leave most of them out of this. The way they talked about you, after you left, I get an idea about what it was like in Banff. John and I will help you. If we can rally enough here, Alpha Ken will agree to back you up with the pack.*

What do you need from us?

I take the phone back. *I need to know what side the patrons are on. I need to figure out resources. Propaganda. Things to trade with for support from large groups. Not everyone's going to want to join for free. Figure out how to get word out without putting people in danger. We're going to need weapons to fight anyone who comes looking to shut us down.* I search my brain for other examples but come up empty before the phone is removed again.

You know, the last revolution sounded like a good idea at first too. Until, it wasn't and you know what happened. What if no one wants equality? There are a lot of angry supernaturals out there. Even if they didn't agree with attacking the humans, they sure weren't going to stop it from happening.

We need to sell normalcy as equality. Like the old world but living as equals. No one wants to live in apocalypse town forever. Humans didn't know that supernaturals even existed. It was guerilla warfare, and we didn't know we were under attack until it was done. We should have the numbers to make a difference.

Humans are going to be mad too. There are going to be people on all degrees of thought about it. But, we just have to convince enough people to stop fighting, to make peace, and work on it. There's a lot that can and will go wrong. We need so much to go right for us to even have a chance at peace even within the next ten years. But it needs to start somewhere.

Write down a list of things you're advocating for. We'll go over it when you're done. When you're finished we'll make up some posters and deliver them. She types up her orders for my homework of the night.

Like what? I ask her.

Start with peace and equality, then go to how we'll get there and what the world will look like. School assignment. You're running to become King of the World, what promises would you make to the voters?

I'm not sure that's how becoming King works. She elbows me lightly in the ribs, effectively stopping a fledgling yawn.

"Okay, you've yawned about twenty times. I'm going to go to bed. You need to go to bed before you fall asleep on me. I have a feeling we're going to need you well rested." Sara takes the phone back and makes a show of deleting our conversation.

"Okay." I say with another yawn. She'll catch no arguments from me.

"Lock the door behind me." I walk her to the door. "Good night."

"Night."

I sigh when she's gone. Locking the door and crawling into bed. Our conversation makes me feel better about how the conversation upstairs went. It wasn't a complete and horrible disaster.

It all has to start somewhere. Complacency isn't going to change anything.

Another sigh releases from my lungs. There's an overwhelming amount of things to do, and so much unknown.

Sara's right, I need to be well rested. The visions don't come when I'm too exhausted to dream.

Maybe I'll get lucky and a vision might show me exactly what I need to do and exactly what will happen.

I scoff at the thought; with that kind of thinking I'll end up having an absolutely useless vision tonight or none at all.

Chapter 14

Claws dig lightly into my leg. The pin pricks awaken me with a start. I jolt my leg away from her claws. Crystal chirps her anger with the sudden ride.

She's just lucky she didn't get booted to the ground.

The barest of light creates an outline of her figure. Her brown and golden colours are black in the shadows. Standing up on her four paws, she slinks over to Rayleen and lays down on the small child's legs; promptly closing her eyes and falling back to sleep. Rayleen, in a dead sleep, doesn't even notice the extra weight holding her down.

My heart calms slowly from the fright she inflicted on me. Lying back down, I close my eyes. Trying to go back to sleep doesn't work. My body is well rested and refuses more sleep. Irritation of the small creature next to me may have something to do with it as well.

Getting up to the freezing room, I walk over to my bag, and remove the makeup bag from it. At the flashlight we left going on the dresser, I take in hand a match box and candle that sit next to it.

Cargo in hand, I enclose myself into the tiny bathroom. Lighting the candle brightens up the room significantly. I hold my hands around and over the flame to ward off the cold biting them.

Shame the shower doesn't work, but I can relieve myself in a toilet. Each day, more and more, I miss running water. Baby wipes wash my hands and my face, but they lack a certain something.

Leaning into the mirror, I examine myself. Features have softened due to a lack of attention to my natural hair growing in. My natural hair and dye job could pass as ombre in a few months; not that I plan on letting it get that bad. I'll go out and grab dye. Big city is bound to have somewhere with dye. How could I let it get this bad?

With two ponytails I draw my greasy locks into a tight bun; bobby pins hold in strays. A mask of foundation, fierce eyeliner, and grey tones of eye shadow provide a base for whatever I'll wear today.

Walking out of the tiny room into the colder bedroom has me shivering up my spine. I can't wait for the perpetual heat of summer. There is no way I'll last another frigid winter here. If no one else is going to go south with us, I'll drag Rayleen and Daniel with me to go alone; if I have to.

The bag lies where I left it. All I go for is another black t-shirt and grey sweater. The winter jacket hangs in the closet; ready if I need it. I last changed my jeans about a week ago; I still have time before I have to peel them off of me. The condition of them is not bad yet. They don't appear to have any large stains, or dirt patches on the main portions of the pants. The cuffs have darkened from who knows what.

In the midst of changing, a knock hits the door lightly. Shirt pulled down in proper placing, I look to the three on the bed to make sure they haven't awoken. Snagging my sweater, it too goes over my head before going to the door. I open it to see Nikki with a candle lighting her face.

Out into the hall, I close the door to the room. "Hey." I say quietly.

"Morning." She practically yells compared to my whisper. Nikki doesn't seem worried about waking anyone up. I wonder what time it is and look around nervously to each door. "They're going to have to get up anyway. And, they might as well hear what I have to say too." Nikki lets herself into my room. "Knock. Knock. Time to wake up." She says loudly.

"What the fuck?" Daniel greets her.

"Language!" She admonishes him in a gesture showing Rayleen is right beside him. "Get up. You're going to want to listen to what I have to say." Nikki doesn't wait for him to show us he's getting up. She waves and smile big for Rayleen and Crystal, then goes back to indifference for Daniel and I. "Jaiden made a deal with Jerry. They don't like humans around here, so you aren't allowed to leave your room unless he gives you a job away from the demons here. So, your first job is to unplug and turn off everything on the third and fourth floor, and leave all the doors cracked open. She gave Jerry the generator, so he's getting that plugged in, but doesn't want anything unnecessary to drawn power. He also doesn't know how hard or easy it might be to figure out the key card machine, but the locks will engage when the power goes on."

"Why doesn't he just flip the breakers?" Daniel asks from beneath the blankets.

"I don't know." She pauses. "Just do what he says or you'll never get a chance to leave this room."

Daniel rolls over and draws down the covers; sitting up slightly against the headboard. "He can't keep us here."

"No, I suppose he can't. But, the alternative is having a demon figure out you're a human and rip your throat out before you can even think to run." In part, I think she's warning him that she'll tell someone he's a human if he acts up. Might be one way to keep him in line.

"It's fine." I tell him. "We'll just avoid them as much as possible. It'll be good anyway. You never know who Darius could have lurking around. I don't want him to find us again."

"Someone's gonna have to take the lion out to pee." Daniel grimaces.

"I'll do it. It's fine." I tell him.

"Can I go with you?" Rayleen asks.

"Hurry up and get ready." I tell her. She's not technically human, so there shouldn't be any problems with her running around.

Rayleen throws away the covers and runs off the bed. Taking the bag with her, she hides away in the bathroom as she changes. Something hard drops, by she immediately responds to the unasked question. "I'm fine. Just the hair brush."

"A little tip, Daniel. If you're going to go around supernaturals, don't call the griffin a lion. I'm not saving your ass if you get found out." Nikki looks over all of us. "I'm gonna go. I apparently get the pleasure of playing bar maid."

"Could trade you?" I joke.

"I'd rather wait tables." She responds.

"Come on. Let's go. You got to pee? Let's go, Crystal." Rayleen pats her legs. She exited the bathroom without my noticing.

The excitable griffin skirts Rayleen's legs as they exit the room right behind Nikki. Afraid to lose them, I tail behind them without a goodbye to Daniel.

Crystal surges down the hallway with Rayleen chasing after her shouting, "wait for me!"

I have to run to keep up with the both of them. "Careful on the stairs!" I yell when Rayleen runs towards them full tilt.

Catching up to the both of them on the stairs, near the lobby, I take Rayleen's hand to steady her.

Crystal takes off for the doors the moment she spots them. Running through a small group of people talking in the lobby.

"Crystal wait! Wait for me!" Rayleen shouts. Her hand yanks out of mine at she dashes after the little creature. She too, runs through the group. I apologize as I run around them.

Rayleen and Crystal are out the doors moments before me. The bright light of the midmorning sun blinds me for a moment.

Across the street is a little lawn area with some flower beds and decorative trees. Crystal is squatting down to do her business there. I wonder if anyone is going to make us clean that up. I have no plastic bag with me.

The little red head stands near her, and lets her do her thing. "She really had to go." Rayleen tells me.

"Looks like it." I say.

"She won't like being locked up all day. She's going to need walks." Rayleen thinks out loud to me.

"I know. But, while we stay here we have to follow the rules. And, it's not exactly safe around here to just go for walks whenever we'd like." I explain to her the best I can.

"Why are we here? I want to go back to Banff." She confesses.

I settle on telling her only a part of the truth. "Banff wasn't safe anymore." I repeat my earlier non-explanation.

"They were just angry with each other. If they just talked to each other they would be fine." Rayleen's understanding of the events that took place are wrong, and it's my fault. I didn't tell her the truth about why we left, and why we only returned for gas.

"No sweetie. That's not-" Deciding to tell her the truth to shut down this kind of talk, lest it go on for days until she gets used to this new place, is an easy decision made in frustration. "Do you remember Darius? Well, he came back with a lot of his friends, while we were gone to Daniel's house. They fought with each other and a lot of people died. Who we have with us is all who survived the attack. There's no more community in Banff."

Her face scrunches in confusion. Bottom lip sticks out and quivers. "NO!" She screams her pain. "No! No! No! NO!" The air suddenly whips wildly.

"I'm sorry." I tell her with immediate regret, knowing it won't help a thing. Crystal squawks her disapproval, and growls to warn off an invisible assailant attacking her owner.

"Control your child!" A woman shouts from behind me.

"Mind your own fucking business! She just found out a bunch of people she cared about are dead!" I turn around and yell back at the lady, whom I can't locate in the mess of people near the hotel entrance.

Rayleen runs by me with Crystal as her faithful guard, back inside the hotel. I give chase.

"I'm sorry." The woman says as I pass her by. Spitefully, I think that she deserves no response.

Speedy as she is, I catch up with her at the stairs. "Do you want a hug?"

"No." She bites back. Rayleen stomps with each step. I feel the heat of people staring.

"Do you want to talk about it?" I ask.

"No, leave me alone!" Rayleen yells, before picking up her pace.

"Don't talk back to me!" I shout in frustration. "I'm trying to help you.”

“I just want to be alone.” She replies.

“I think we should talk about it.” I say.

“I don’t want to!” She bolts when we reach the top of the stairs. Tired of running, I let her get a head start on me as I take a ten second walking break. There aren’t many places she could go at this point.

I round the corner as she enters into a room near the end. I assume this is our room.

Entering into our room, I find Daniel yelling at the shut bathroom door. “What happened?!” He hugs me upon my entrance. “Thank God, you’re alright. What happened?”

“Is Rayleen in the bathroom?” I ask for confirmation.

“Yes.” He says.

Relieved that she made it back in here safe, I start to tell him what happened. “I told her about what happened in Banff because she was asking why we couldn’t stay there, or go back there. She freaked out and ran back.”

He knocks against the door. “We have work to do. You’re gonna need to calm down, come out and help us.”

“No. Leave me alone!” Her shrill voice screams behind the door. Crystal squawks and roars.

“Rayleen come out here and talk to us.” I say calmer.

“I don’t want to.”

A vein practically throbs on my temple. “Rayleen Marie Brenner! Get your butt out here right now!”

“No!” She sobs.

“Look I know you’re upset, but you need to get out here and deal with it. Talk to me about it. I know that you had a lot of friends there, and you’re upset that they’re gone now. You’re upset we can’t go back to Banff.” Nothing else seems to work, so I try empathy.

“Alexa, let’s just give her some time.” Daniel grabs my shoulder and squeezes. “We have work to do. She can stay here and calm down.”

"She's too young to be by herself." I tell him. She's only six.

"What are you going to do? Yell at her some more? Break down the door and make her come out?" He rationalizes. "She will be fine. We will be upstairs. If she has any problems she can come get us, and you can go check on her whenever you'd like.

People are going to be in and out of the other rooms all day, so she can also ask them for help."

I put my forehead against the door to get as close to her as I can. All I wish for in this moment is to be able to hug her. "Does that work for you? Will you be okay here if we go upstairs?"

"Yes. Go." The little girl's voice is hardened and dead. A sob leaves her throat when she's done talking.

I have qualms about leaving her alone here, but Daniel might be right. "Lock the door behind us, and don't let anyone you don't know inside."

"Okay." She says.

"I'll be down to check on you soon." I can't stop myself from asking the question again to reaffirm to myself that this is the right decision. "Are you sure you'll be alright?"

"Yes." Daniel answers for her. "She just needs a chance to calm down. Sometimes people like to do that by themselves."

He slings his arm over my shoulder and kisses my temple. It does nothing to help me, more so just makes me irritable towards him.

We start upstairs in the first room. Tackling each room one by one. After a few, we get a rhythm and strategy going. He tackles the TV. I unplug the lamps, clock, and check the outlets for extras.

Sometimes, the room is empty and sometimes there are forgotten belongings inside.

We leave each room wide open using the door stops if vacant, and block the door with the trash can if the room has belongings inside.

I want to come back later to shop, maybe after we finish.

Bending over to unplug the lamp, I pull it out of the socket. Bumping into something behind me, I squeak in surprise.

Dread fills me when I realize what is happening.

I'm in no mood for this.

Rising upright as hands grasp my hips to pull me tighter against his front, I tell him, "Not now. We're busy."

"I'm trying to get busy." While normally I'd find the word play charming, I just find it annoying right now.

I pull his wandering fingers away from where they are painfully rubbing. "I said no. I'm not in the mood."

"That's not hard to fix." He pushes me roughly onto the bed, and pounces on top of me.

"Get off of me." Pushing on his chest to no avail. He's stronger and has the advantage.

"Oh come on, how often are we going to get alone time?" Daniel argues. His hands wander, to rub against the spot he thinks will give me pleasure, once again. It's nothing but painful.

"I said no." I try to remove his hand, but it goes back in place immediately. "I'm upset about Rayleen."

"You know what'll make you feel better?" A wet tongue laps lightly at my neck. Excess drool drips to the back of my neck. His actions, meant to incite pleasure, are about the least sexy things to me right now; a complete turn off.

"No, it won't."

"We'll it won't make you feel worse, so let's do it." His reasoning is weak, but somehow makes sense in his head.

"I said no." Part of my own head wonders if I should just give in. Five minutes and he'll be done. It would be over and done with faster and easier than fending him off for the next few hours. Better than dealing with his anger and frustration.

I know how this goes. Yet, I remain resolute.

"But you mean yes." Daniel incites fury inside of me.

"I mean no." I say absolute and firm.

"Not for long." His words call for a change in tactics.

"Okay, fine. Roll over." Daniel smiles and rolls us over. With him on the bottom I can finally rip myself free. "I said no. I'm going to check on Rayleen."

Running from him and out of the room as fast as I can. Two distinct crashing noises hit in the room I leave behind. Whether he's throwing things or hitting things, I don't know; maybe both.

Wiping the saliva residue from my neck and lips with my sleeve, before I pick up my speed again to get some distance from him.

Flashes of an angered Darius, Karl, Walter, and the father of that one foster mother only introduced as grandpa come at me; rocks through my head. I had tried to deny the same thing Daniel tried to coerce out of me just now, but there was no escape from them.

I'll apologize and make it up to him later.

Back to my room, on autopilot, my heart begins to panic anew. The door is opened wide and a bright light lightens the whole room to a daylight quality.

A bright lantern brightens the whole room up. It's difficult to directly look at.

An old woman holds Rayleen to her chest as they sit on the bed. Her short white hair covers her eyes and nose, but I can see her lips moving. Crystal has her head rested faithfully on the little girl's lap. Jerry stands near the two, but his attention is on me as I enter. "What's going on?" I ask.

"Hi, Alexa right?" Jerry confirms my identity. I nod to agree. "I was introducing Margaret to Rayleen to fulfil part of my deal with Jaiden. Margaret has agreed to assess and train Rayleen to use her magic. She is sympathetic to you and your partner's condition."

"Condition?" Margaret's head pops up from whispering in Rayleen's ear. "You make me sound like a saint for being a decent person."

"I meant no disrespect. I was attempting to be discrete." He bows his head. "I'll take my leave now. You can discuss the details." Jerry hightails it out of the room in a comically quick fashion.

"Hello there." She pulls away from Rayleen to greet me. "You may call me Margie. I was never to particularly fond of Margaret."

She reaches out her hand to shake mine. I indulge her. "Alexa."

"Perhaps you could fill me in on particulars. I'm afraid I haven't gotten much out of the young one. She seemed particularly upset when I arrived."

Unsure of what particulars she means, I go with the first thoughts in my head to explain why Rayleen was upset. "Umm, I told her why we were here, and why we can't go back to the city we were staying at. There was an attack, and those we came with are all who survived."

Margie pulls me into a motherly bear hug. "I'm terribly sorry, my dears. That must be so hard. You have been through a terrible ordeal. My deepest condolences."

Between Daniel's actions and her hug, tears falls from my eyes. I turn around and pull out of her arms so Rayleen doesn't see the liquid falling down my cheeks, but they won't stop.

I exit the room while I pull myself together.

Margie follows me out. Her hand rubs my back soothingly. "There's no shame to crying. It's good for young people to see their heroes cry. It's healthy for them and teaches them to understand how to cope with their own feelings. Hiding your sadness doesn't make you weak, and it doesn't make you strong. It's just unfair to you.

Take it from someone who raised two emotionally unavailable children because I followed the wrong standard advice of the time."

"You have children?" I ask to distract myself.

"Had two boys." As soon as the past tense is uttered, I regret asking. "One was shot by a human boy. He was drunk and entitled. Thought he was better than the human in every way. No difference when you're a corpse. His arrogance got him killed.

The other, in retaliation, unleashed what you humans like to call the mothman in West Virginia. You may have heard about that. He was executed by the Council for his actions."

"I'm sorry." I say my condolences to her.

"I'm not." Taken aback from her directness, she notices and explains. "Don't get me wrong. I loved my boys. But if they weren't my boys, I would have hated them.

Besides, they've been gone for decades." She stops. "We should go back inside. Dry your face if you wish, but go hug your girl. I have questions to ask the both of you."

Following her directions, I wipe my tears and go inside. Pulling Rayleen into a tight but brief hug. Settling on the foot of the bed, I allow Margie to take the reins.

"Take a seat darling. It's going to be a bit before we do much more than talk." Rayleen sits a couple feet away from me. "When did you start learning?"

"After the war started." I tell her.

"Not long at all then." Margie leans up against the table. "And, that's when you found out what you were, or did you know beforehand?"

Rayleen shrugs. "James told me."

I continue for Rayleen. "She found out then, about a week after the war started."

"Did you have any idea before? Any accidents that you couldn't explain?" Margie asks.

Rayleen thinks really hard. Her mouth twists to the side, and her eyes look up into her head. "I don't think so."

"What kind of accident?" I ask. Maybe I noticed something and didn't realize it.

"It could be anything. An unexplained event." She looks to Rayleen. "Maybe a fire that lit when you were angry." I look over in hopes that Rayleen might think of something. It seems important that she had done magic when she was younger. "Unexplained things when you were angry or upset?"

Her blue eyes light up. "What about flat pop?"

"Like you made it go flat. Took the bubbles out of it." Margie confirms.

"I think so. Our last foster mom, she would always make me get her pop. When I was angry at her, the pop would be flat when she opened it. But it would still sound, like that whooshing sound, when it opened so it wasn't leaking." Once Rayleen mentions it, I remember her getting so angry at the pop cans. The woman had kicked up a stink with the company, but nothing was ever found to be the cause.

Rayleen caused her hilarious grief, and scored her some free pop.

"It's possible you were moving the carbon dioxide to the top of the can. Is there anything else strange that you couldn't explain before?"

Rayleen thinks hard. "I don't think so."

"You didn't have any Matilda moments, with things flying around the room?" I ask, hoping to jumpstart other ideas.

"No." She shakes her head.

"Alright, and you said foster mom, so you didn't live with your biological parents." Margie pushes.

"They passed away." As she had explained to me, I give her the courteousy of knowing how they passed as well. "There was a plane crash. My parents and her parents, my sister and her husband, didn't survive. Rayleen is my niece.

We've been bounced around and separated a lot since then. She was about two at the time. She gets her magic from her dad's side apparently."

"I'm sorry for your loss." Margie gives her condolences. "So you wouldn't remember if your dad taught you anything.

Do you remember if anything unusual happened with her as a baby?"

Immediately and confidently I can tell her, "no. I had no idea. She seemed like a regular baby. None of the foster parents ever had anything bad to say about her. I guarantee you any foster parent would have kicked up a stink if things started flying around on their own."

Margie strokes her chin and thinks for a few moments. Looking back and forth between Rayleen and me as she figures out what she wants to say. "So, you're behind, but that's no fault of your own.

Magic is like a muscle. The more you use it the stronger it becomes. The less. The weaker.

Magic is hereditary, but there is wiggle room.

Different people are born with different abilities and strengths and weaknesses. Some are exhausted after floating a pencil to draw a line, and others think manipulating paint to create a wall to wall masterpiece with their powers is nothing more than child's play.

Then there are varying abilities. One might be able to float, but not be able to manipulate matter to perhaps turn it into something else.

Not to mention the differing elemental strengths. You mentioned the flat pop, so my bet is you have stronger air elemental abilities. You might only be able to manipulate through air, or you might be able to control any number and combination of the four elements."

As she pauses, I take the chance to interrupt. "James tried to get her to cook a marshmallow, but she couldn't. But then Cam taught her to put out a candle out. So, she might be able to make fire too right?"

"The candle, was it by controlling the fire, or controlling the air?" Margie asks.

When I look to Rayleen, she looks at me guiltily. "The air."

"Didn't Cam want you to manipulate the fire?" I scold her.

"Yes, but it wasn't working." She huffs and crosses her arms. "I was tired of trying to move the fire. I wanted to go back to flying the airplanes."

"Cam had her move some things; some gift bag tissue, a paper airplane." I explain to Margie.

"More air qualities. Have you tried anything with water; like boiling it? Or perhaps using earth by moving dirt?" Margie digs a little further.

"No." Rayleen says.

"Who were her teachers? You've mentioned two names now." Margie questions me.

"James and Cam." I tell her.

Her eyebrow rises. "Yes, but who were they? Old; young. Which elements did they possess?"

"James was James Ellesworn."

"The Council Rep?" She asks incredulously.

I nod my head. "Yes. I don't know what he can do. And Cam was a teen we met in Banff. She had a couple lessons with James, but Cam came over daily for about a month and a half. I don't know what he could do exactly either. Maybe water? I once saw him make a wall out of snow."

"James is old, has centuries of memories from the old reps, and acquired strength through knowledge.

He'd make a horrible teacher for a beginner. That's why he tried to get her to cook a marshmallow. He knows how to manipulate the water to heat, and to cool and compress the air to keep it from expanding. To keep the balance so you don't explode or implode the marshmallow, or turn it to mush. He knows how to create an oven like environment while one effecting the marshmallow. Too many variables."

Only some of what Margie said makes sense to me, but what I do know is what Rayleen was supposed to be doing. "I thought you were trying to roast it like a campfire?"

"I was." She says.

"Like set it on fire? Spontaneous combustion? You'd need to control multiple components to accomplish that. Making fire where there isn't already a flame is difficult for new sorcerers, especially if you can't control the fire element, you need to control multiple elements and/or create the perfect conditions.

Magic, while it is magic, follows some rules in science. To create fire you need to have oxygen, fuel, heat, and a chemical reaction. While this can be accomplished many ways, like using earth element to create friction between two objects like rubbing two sticks together, it's difficult for children to even grasp the concept of combustion; like you'd need for roasting a marshmallow.

Forget what James taught you. If he'd known how to teach a child, he would have had you light a match, then manipulate the fire to perfectly roast the marshmallow rather than burning it, or purely heat up the water, or superheat the air, or even ask you to manipulate the sugar compound.

There are many ways he could have explained it to you, but he didn't." She shakes her head in disapproval. Along the way she worked herself up. "It sounds like air would be the place to start. Cam seemed like he was getting somewhere with that."

Margie changes her tune. "Some class notes before we start.

Interrupt me. If you have a question, either of you, I need you to speak up. It's better for me to stop and explain something in the moment, than for you to wait until the end when you're completely confused. Got it?"

She waits for our heads to nod before she continues. "Magic. Is like a different type of science. It has its own rules, but the two also overlap.

If you want to make something fly, don't try to erase gravity, try to follow the rules of aerodynamics. The rules of aerodynamics are wordy and complicated, but think of your floating object as an airplane rather than an astronaut floating out in space.

I want you to think of magic as manipulation rather than creation. Manipulation is what sorcerers do, and creation is what Elementals do. You are a sorcerer."

"I thought I was a witch." Rayleen speaks out.

"If you prefer to be called a witch, it's fine. There are many names for us, and everyone seems to prefer a different name.

Don't get me started on how many names there are if you include every language out there.

Don't be offended if you are called a witch, magical being, magic folk, sorceress, enchantress, wizard, magician, conjurer; there's more but you get the idea.

There are of course, also the bad names to be called and you can be offended at those.

One that translates well to the human world, and you may know, is a necromancer. Usually, necromancer is used to describe someone who performs what humans call black magic. This includes anything that could be used to harm another being."

"Blood magic?" I ask.

Is blood magic black magic?

"Blood magic is forbidden." Margie snarls and her voice turns hard.

"I'm sorry." I apologize in quick reaction. "I had blood magic used on me to show me a memory. I just thought it might be useful to know."

"We don't like to talk about blood magic as a community. It's forbidden, and you're lucky that's all they did."

"I had a friend who ended up an unwilling spy from it." I tell her. I know blood magic can go bad and do wrong.

"Nothing good comes from blood magic. You must never preform blood magic. It is evil and I will not condone it." Margie warns Rayleen.

"But what is it?" Rayleen asks.

Margie fixes me with a glare. I suppose I am to blame for introducing Rayleen to the idea of blood magic. Something Margie would have hoped she'd never know; if her tone and looks are depicting her thoughts. "Blood magic is using your blood to manipulate another person. Two examples, already given, include hallucinations and linking. It is also used to torture, control, and kill." Her three words unleash a beast of a revelation to what I've exposed.

"Can't those things be done with regular magic?" Rayleen asks.

"Not in the same way." Margie fixes another glare to me. "The soul protects internal and body manipulation. For instance, someone couldn't use water based magic to boil your insides, but they could use blood magic.

Blood magic virtually has no limit on distance once initiated, just a time limit. While, element based magic requires a form of touching in the manipulation process.

Air, you're touching it, you're breathing it. As far as you can breathe, and extend, you can manipulate.

The other elements require more of a direct touch for manipulation. You want to light a piece of paper on fire with the fire element, and then you need to be touching it. You want to heat water in a cup using the water element, and then you need to touch the water. You want to shape clay using the earth element, you need to touch it.

It all gets more complicated from there, but those are the basics."

"What about wands? Does she get a wand?" I ask.

Her one eyebrow pops and she shakes her head in disappointment. "Wands don't serve a purpose like humans have come to know. It's nothing like that.

Wands can serve a purpose, for example, to fire magic as material to burn. That's how the idea of wands came about. Sorcerers carried around sticks to use as burning material. They would light the end and then throw the fire.

Then others caught on. Different materials in wand or brick form were popular at one point. Nowadays, one might return to that out of convenience. But, in modern years, one would have used something less conspicuous.

Gemstone jewelry is popular to magnify and store power.

This is, of course, all moot point. You are starting with basics and will learn from there. I don't need your head spinning from too much all at once. You'll be confused, and I'll need to repeat it a hundred times.

Basics. Air based magic is wind, it's breath, it's gas."

"Farts are magic?" Rayleen interrupts.

In light of the serious talk we're having, the childish question helps break the tension. She giggles, as Margie and I laugh.

Margie explains through her laughter that "they could be. Yes, that's one way to put it. I don't know where I was going; with before." She starts again once the funnies have ended. "You floated tissue paper, flew a paper air plane, and choked out flame. We have paper and candles, and tissues can substitute for gift tissue; though it's heavier.

I want you to show me how you did each exercise, and explain how you are doing it; what you are feeling."

We each set about gathering the items Margie mentioned, and set them out on the desk. Rayleen stands between Margie and I, as she sets about preforming the magic tricks she's learned.

Margie watches and encourages along the way. I fall silent as I let them work it out between them. My role falls more to observing them do their magic.

Boredom sets in once I figure out that Rayleen and Margie won't be doing anything new in the immediate moment. While the tricks had been wonderful and amazing at first, the novelty has waned.

I take to petting Crystal on the bed to keep my hands busy.

Rayleen makes the paper air plane through practiced folds. She's most excited about revisiting floating the plane.

Margie sets the candle a flame with a stricken match against the scratch pad on the match box. "Start where you wish."

To my surprise, Rayleen demonstrates with the candle first. "It's like blowing out birthday candles. I blow and concentrate on bending the air, and pushing it fast through the fire."

"Could you snuff out the flame by depriving it of oxygen?" I ask Margie.

"I don't know. This works good." Rayleen answers instead.

"But you're basically just blowing it out. You might as well just blow it out with your breath." I explain my thinking to her.

Margie places her hand on my shoulder to gain my attention. "Part of teaching magic is understanding that generally there are multiple ways of accomplishing the same task, and each person may have a different way.

You can teach different ways as they grow and develop powers, but instinct works best with beginners. Instinct works best for all. However," she says with a pause to redirect to Rayleen, "she is also correct to a point.

There is such thing as pointlessly using your magic, or wastefully using your magic.

You don't have an unlimited supply of magic, there is an end, and you will become aware of how much you can do at a time.

I would suggest blowing out your birthday candles using your breath, rather than using your magic, if you plan on using a large amount of magic later on.

It's like energy. You only have so much energy in a day. If you plan on running a big race, you don't want to be playing tag with your friends right before it. You'll likely run out of energy in the middle of your big race and you may not be able to finish."

With the candle out, Rayleen moves onto floating the airplane. This time I pay attention to her, rather than the floating paper.

The little girl breathes fast, blowing it. Her hands move in sync with the twisting and turning airplane. Floating lasts for as long as the breath. Wavering near the end and then dropping onto the carpet.

Rayleen looks to Margie for her approval and commentary.

"That's great." Margie encourages her.

Rayleen looks back to the desk and the last item; the tissue lying next to the candle. Her eyebrows scrunch with her nose as she concentrates hard.

The tissue barely moves up, instead skirting around on the top of the desk. Despite her ever quickening puffs of air the tissue doesn't lift off the desk until she tosses it up in frustration.

Rayleen manages to hold the tissue up for a moment. It spins and flops in a small space before it falls back to the desk.

Margie strikes a new match against the strike pad and lights up the candle again. "Balance is hard. It takes effort and concentration, and skill to keep something floating in place. It's harder than floating a moving object like the plane, right?"

"Who are you?" Daniel's voice booms from the door.

"Margie. I'm training Rayleen. Who are you?" Margie introduces herself in a daring fashion.

"Daniel. I'm Alexa's husband; practically Rayleen's step-dad. I didn't say you could be here." I feel slighted as Daniel announces an imaginary status he's never received permission for.

To stop a fight before it happens I jump in and explain to him what I know. "I didn't know about it either. Jaiden put it in the terms for us staying here."

"Then, I guess I'll be having a discussion with Jaiden." As much as I don't care for her, I'll need to try to warn Jaiden about said discussion, so she can avoid Daniel until he cools down. She doesn't deserve to be yelled at for trying to help Rayleen.

"It's her right to learn about her heritage, and learn magic; if she wants to." Margie defends Rayleen, but in doing so also restarts the fight with Daniel.

I decide to stay out of whatever happens next. I agree with Margie but Daniel is my boyfriend; which means I'd automatically have to side with him if this continues. I wouldn't want to betray him against someone I barely know.

"I didn't say that it wasn't." He agrees with her, and I sigh with relief. "I would just like to of been in on the decision."

"Right, well, it's done. And I will be teaching Rayleen, because she wishes for me to." She puts the fight to rest, but the tension doesn't release with it. "Rayleen, this time I would like for you try to blow on the candle again. This time we are looking for control. You are looking to make the fire flicker but not go out."

Rayleen turns from her stare down with Daniel to concentrate on the flame. Daniel walks over to us and puts himself between Rayleen and Margie. Effectively block her view of Rayleen. He places his hand on Rayleen, and breaks her concentration for the moment she looks at who is touching her.

Rayleen works at flickering the flame with her magic.

Nothing happens.

I watch her again to see what she's doing. Her air flows out in quick bursts, and her face is scrunched, but nothing continues to happen. She doesn't seem like she's doing anything different from before.

The only difference is the atmosphere in which she's trying to work. Daniel has inserted himself into the picture and ruined the image. If she truly has to concentrate hard to make the magic work, then maybe Daniel has made her nervous enough to break the concentration.

"I think we're done for the day." Margie announces suddenly. "You did great. We have a lot of work to do, but you have a good basic understanding of your magic. We'll build on that, and explore other elements. Many things for me to do today. Tomorrow, I will come grab you in the morning. Alexa and Crystal are welcome to join along; I know you wouldn't want for Rayleen to go alone with a stranger."

"They aren't going anywhere without me." Daniel bumps out his chest in a broad display, like a father literally putting his foot down.

"No boys allowed." Margie tells him, wagging her finger at him playfully. At this point, I think she likes to egg him on.

"Then they can't go either." He says.

Margie steps closer to him. She looks the boy straight in the eyes. In a no nonsense tone she reminds him, "They are free to go wherever they want, and don't think that you can in anyway control them. If you'd prefer, I can force the issue. I'm certain there are many fun and creative things I can keep you busy with, while I train Rayleen."

Margie turns her attention back to Rayleen. She turns motherly once again. Her features soften and her smile returns. "My room is filled with supplies to help you learn. More than just candle and paper. Get a good night's rest, and come relaxed."

Margie takes up the bright light. She waves good bye to the both of us, but ignores Daniel on the way out.

"I don't like her. You shouldn't let her anywhere near Rayleen." Daniel says loudly as she's still likely in earshot. I half expect the sharp-witted woman to come back through the door to lash out at him again.

"I like her." Rayleen counters quietly.

"Rayleen likes her and she wants to learn magic. Jaiden trusts Jerry and Jerry trusts Margie. I'm sure it'll be fine." I reason with him.

There isn't any reason, I can imagine, for why he's acting so obstinate with Rayleen and the magic; except to spite me. For whatever the reason he's ridiculously moody, but I will not let him get in the way of Rayleen learning how to defend herself.

There wasn't an issue with it back in Banff, so he shouldn't have an issue with it now.

"You're not going with her tomorrow." He tells me stubbornly.

"I'm going because if I'm not, I'll still be letting Rayleen go. I'd rather have her supervised than not." I say.

"Then I'm going." He tells me.

"You're welcome to try." Is all I say.

Margie seems like she could handle herself in a fight with Daniel. Part of me would like to see Margie's threat come to life. In what ways could the old witch make him stay away?

Maybe she can keep him out with a wall of air. Maybe she could teach Rayleen that.

"You've wasted enough time." Daniel berates the both of us. "We have work to do. Rayleen, you need to help too. We're going to go upstairs and finish our job. Get your shoes on, your butts upstairs, and start unplugging everything."

Chapter 15

The moment she walks in, no one but I notice her. Engulfed in their own little worlds, the people dedicate their attention to their own needs and wants; mostly drinking and conversing.

Jaiden looks around the room. She's looking for something; someone.

The wet cloth glides over the table surface. Wiping bits of food into the cloth and onto the floor.

She walks through the middle of the room until she spots who she's looking for. Turning quickly, she makes a straight line for whoever.

The poker table lifts their eyes up for a moment in search of me. Waving me over with an empty bottle in hand in their attempt to let me know that their thirsts need to be quenched.

"What can I do for you?" I ask as polite as possible despite the rage brewing inside from resentment in this task and dealing with drunken idiots. Jerry has to have other jobs I could do that aren't so degrading and demeaning.

"Another round of drinks, beautiful." Curiously, I smile at what he thinks is a charming compliment, unaware that the word makes me want to throttle him.

"20 gold." I tell him. He hands me a coin that looks very much like a toonie. There is an inner circle of gold, and an outer ring of another metal. There are no pictures, just the numbers engraved.

Reading the inscription for the correct numbers, I walk over to the bar and request the four beers while handing him the coin. Each beer is worth five gold; used to be four, but Jerry raised the price with the location change. All the prices went up. Something I've already had to tell a few customers.

I wonder what use there is any use exchanging actual coins for currency anymore. He should be exchanging beer for tooth paste, toilet paper, weapons, water, or literally anything else.

In waiting, I spy Jaiden talking with a mountainous purple fellow sitting at a table near the window. His white tusks are cut off near the base; I've seen the same thing with elephants. They move with each word he speaks to the girl.

What is she up to? A secret meeting in the brightest part of the room isn't exactly smart of her.

Multiple thuds hit the counter when the bartender puts them down. The four beers fit two in each hand and cradled together. I deliver promptly, and split to another table before they can acknowledge me.

By the time I turn around, Jaiden is on her way and hopping behind the bar. What's his name, H—something, lets her grab a bottle and work the till. All three things I haven't been allowed to do at all and I started waitressing a couple hours ago.

Jaiden walks the drink over to the purple customer, before returning to the bar. I pick up bottles and empty dishes while watching her.

Piling my load up on the counter, away from customers, I watch as she comes out of the back with three smaller cases of the blood. Jaiden walks out of the lounge with the blood.

Is she stealing that?

I can't tell if H noticed her or not. But, I don't think he did. H was looking the other way, serving a customer.

Curious and furious, I leap to action on a whim. "Taking a break." I shout to H behind the bar. I need to find out what she's doing now.

Once out of the lounge, I see the tail end of her just outside the entry doors.

Jaiden moves quicker than I'd imagined she could, while still walking, with the boxes in her arms. Trailing behind her is easy with her speed, and by luck she doesn't look behind her. She speeds her way over to a delivery truck.

She puts the boxes into the cab versus the back; which is loaded with bags and boxes. Ducking behind another truck, I ensure she can't see me.

When she shuts the door, I pop my head around the corner. Jaiden opens the driver's door.

Taking my chance, I climb into the back of the truck as she gets into the cab. Moving as gently as I can, so I don't alert her through a bouncing back, I manage to fit myself between a few boxes. Lying down, I hope she doesn't see me until she gets wherever she's going; when it'll be too late for her to just tell me to go back.

Thinking that covering myself in some of the bags as extra cover would be overkill, I stop short of doing so. The bags rustle and the bottles clang as she drives. I dare only to look at the sky, and the tops of close and tall buildings. The traffic lights come and go at first, but then they are no more.

My fingertips ache from the chill I had been ignoring. I breathe into them with a deep hot breath. They warm enough so they no longer bite and sting. Tucking them into my pockets will help keep them warm. The temperature is deceiving. Heat from the sun is warm, but the air is cold.

The truck eventually stops. Popping up, I spot the surroundings. We're in a housing neighbourhood.

"What are you doing here?" Jaiden questions me. She stands at the crossing between cab and truck bed.

"What are you doing here?" Throwing the same question back at her buys me time to get on equal ground as her, as well as getting on the actual ground.

"Deliveries. You need to go back. Jerry didn't want anyone else leaving the hotel." Jaiden spouts a rehearsed line.

"No." I tell her.

"Yes."

Dig my heels in. "No."

"Dominique, you need to-" That name coming out of her mouth brings pain to my chest.

My anger ignites and flares then explodes. "Don't call me Dominique. You lost that right." I seethe.

"Nikki-"

The pain sears again. "You can't call me that either. Only friends can call me that."

"Really?" Hands rise and open to question me. "Then, what am I supposed to call you?"

Nothing comes to mind, but right now I don't want her to call me anything. "Don't."

"Fine, whatever." Her hands drop in defeat, but her eyebrow pops. "I don't even know why your name is a problem right now." I don't know either. I just know it hurts to hear the words come out of her mouth. "You need to go back to the hotel. Jerry said-"

Interrupting her, I insist she tell me the truth. There has to be something else. "I don't care what Jerry said. I want to know what you're doing."

"I'm doing deliveries." Jaiden says again.

"Your alternative motives." I press.

"What alternative motives?" She asks. Irritation finally leaks into her voice.

Breathy laughing once at the joke she makes of herself and the situation. "I don't know. You're the one who's always lying and keeping secrets."

"What else am I keeping secrets about now?" Jaiden's voice raises up one note, but she might as well be screaming at me.

"Maybe you should ask Sara!" Screaming makes me feel all that I can feel. Jaiden pushes her body upper body back. "She told me you were planning on me being the face of a revolution. When were you going to tell me that? Or ask me? Were you just gonna put my face everywhere, and let me figure it out on my own?" I twist the situation around so she thinks I know more than the ten second piece of conversation I overheard between John and Sara. It might be the best way of getting more information, true information, out of her. "You seem to like making me figure it out on my own."

"There's no revolution yet. It's barely in the idea stage."

I remind her. "That's not what you said yesterday."

"Forget what I said yesterday." Her frustration with me widens her eyes and flares her nose. "I shouldn't have said anything at all."

"I can't just forget. It doesn't work like that." Cool air allows me to feel the chilled tracks of tears I wasn't aware of.

"What is your problem? I don't understand what is happening?" Her voice calms back to normal.

"You're my problem!" I scream with all my rage. "How could you not tell me that they were dead?"

The quick change of topic is a revelation hitting her in the face. "I forgot-"

Interrupting her from her stupid explanation again, "I don't want that bullshit."

"Then what do you want from me?" When I stay silent, she fills in the blanks. "Another apology? You're not going to listen to whatever I say anyway. Would you like me to just go away? Die? Would that make you happy?"

"Why aren't you upset?" I ask relatively quiet in sudden exhaustion from all the mental anguish.

Her shoulders drop, and she looks shocked. "Excuse me?"

"I've seen you more upset during this conversation than I've seen you about their deaths." Tears flow freely. I choke back a sob.

"You're upset, because I'm not upset?" Jaiden surmises.

Her admission pours gasoline on a dying fine. My energy renews. "He was your dad too! They were your family too!"

"And I knew him for only a few months. I knew all those people for only a few months. And, not only that, but I only met them a few times; some of them only once. You can't expect me to mourn as much as you would; you can't expect me to act and be upset in however way you want me to be. Look, it sucks that they're dead, and part of me is upset that I won't get the chance to know my birth father better. Cue more dad issues; if you will. You can't expect me to mourn acquaintances like they were family."

"They were your family. You're a cold, heartless bitch!" Resorting to name calling filters all my thoughts of her into tangible words.

Her eyes go wide for a moment, before her whole face falls neutral. "Fine. Okay. I'm upset." Jaiden's voice waivers and tears drain from her eyes. Eyes close and she breathes a deep breath. A couple whimpers escape. Her hard shell dissolves in a flash, and just as quickly as tears start falling, I start to feel like crap. Maybe I had it wrong. "I have feelings, but I bottle them up because I was taught to never show them. To cry is to be weak."

Her voice waivers and squeaks. "Can never be anything but happy. You can have feelings. I can't. It's not how I was raised. If my dad saw me now, he'd be shoulder deep in damage control. I'd be in for a huge lecture the next chance he got me alone.

Of course I'm upset. I balled my eyes out when I found them lying there in a pile; all shot to death. I've cried, in private, a lot. Gone over it a thousand times in my head. The image is burned into my memory and will stay there for an eternity. But, I'm also six months into knowing. The wound is fresh for you, and I'm assuming this is your first major family death. Because, unfortunately, it gets easier the more times you experience it. Need I remind you, that I found my mom dead before all of this mindless, needless death happened. I had that band aid ripped off young."

A scared girl opens up her heart to me; flushing out my anger and frustration. Crying takes off ten years from the age she carries herself as. It's hard to remember that she's still just a child; a very screwed up child.

I wrap my arms around her to bring her some comfort. She stops talking as I do. In turn, in a way, it brings me comfort too. They do say misery loves company; I guess this is what they mean.

In a screwed up way, it makes me happy that she's upset with their deaths.

I break off from the hug first so I can talk to her and reassure her. "I can't let you go by yourself. It's dangerous, and I'm not losing anymore family." Raw truth shakes me. Jaiden's the only family I've got left. As shitty as her actions were, I have to forgive her now. Dad would want me to; if for nothing else.

"I've done this all before. The most dangerous delivery was a grumpy guy at the door. He didn't want to sign the paperwork." The little girl wipes her tears and smiles. All traces of her breakdown are gone in an impressive couple seconds.

"If you take me back, I'll just steal one of Jerry's other trucks to follow you." I warn her. "What do you think he's going to hate more?"

"Can't you just go back peacefully?" She asks in a way, that I know she knows the answer to that already.

"What do you think?" I return a reply in a question form.

"Fine." Jaiden relents.

"So, what are we doing?" I ask her.

"We have a few deliveries. Then I have to go talk to a vampire named Chad; alone." Jaiden emphasizes the last word.

"Why alone?" I ask.

"Because he's the leader of a clan and they won't let you into the apartments alive." First she tells me that this won't be dangerous, and now she brings up a life threatening situation.

"But they'll let you?" I inquire.

"I bring gifts and they know me. I saved Chad's life. They won't kill me." Jaiden must be speaking about the blood she stole.

Not wanting another fight so quickly, I let it go; for now.

Jaiden confirms all the information on her clip board. We retrieve all the proper bags and boxes for the customer, and deliver it to whoever answers the doors. Jaiden gets a signature, and we move on to the next place.

Repeat and repeat. The whole trip goes by in the same way until nothing remains in the truck box.

Jaiden had been correct, that the most dangerous aspect of this job is the grump at the door. More often than not, this job is absolutely boring. Perhaps that is the most dangerous thing about this job; she'll die of boredom.

Or maybe, she'd just get so lost and turned around that she'll never find her way back. She needs a GPS. Jaiden's turned us down the wrong road a few times, but luckily always noticed soon after. We've back tracked a few times.

When she stops in front of apartments, she tells me this is that vampire's place.

"Are you talking to him about the revolution?" I ask her.

"No. When I left to rescue you, Chad abandoned Jerry as a client because Jerry didn't keep me safe. Part of the deal requires me to get Chad back as a client." I wonder briefly how many other things Jaiden gave up in this deal. I don't remember her mentioning this one last night. But, I had drowned her out.

"I'll come with you." I offer.

"They don't like strangers." She reminds me.

"You were a stranger and they like you."

Her head shakes. "I don't think they're going to let you in."

"You could use help carrying the boxes." We could go back and forth on this for a while, but I'd rather try. Better to ask for forgiveness than to ask for permission, or speculate what might happen.

Opening the door, and slipping out. "I'll get them out-" The shutting door cuts her off.

Rounding the truck, I meet her on the other side. Jaiden stacks all three boxes in her arms. Removing two from her with little protest, I walk away to the assumed building.

Half way there, glass shatters behind me. Jaiden dropped her box; I realize. "Are you okay?" I ask as I turn.

Towering over the short girl is a man with a hand on her throat. Her arms lay straight at her sides from the bear hug he has her in. She's completely immobilized.

Sickeningly, the man watches me heatedly as he licks her throat. Jaiden looks equal parts shocked and disgusted.

"Jerry won't like it if you kill us." I spout in an effort to save her. A vampire's most dangerous weapons are inches away from ripping out Jaiden's throat.

"Jerry who?" A voice sounds behind me. I jump at the sudden

voice. Expanding my tunnel view to our surroundings, and the dozen or so people circled around us. Human in looks, I can only assume they may all be vampires until they reveal themselves.

"Chad won't like it if you kill us." Jaiden offers up instead.

"Good thing we don't like Chad." A woman to my right says. "But, that does make it more intriguing. If blood wasn't getting so rare, I'd drain you and leave you as a present."

"What are you going to do?" I ask.

"Keep you to feed on." She says. The woman grabs my arm from behind. "I thought that'd be obvious."

Jaiden moves under the control of the tall man at her neck with no struggle. He takes her back to our truck, and lets her climb into the back. Jaiden's helping these people kidnap her. Jumping up, he uses the tailgate to vault into the back. The man rubs his hands over her clothes in a procedure much like pat downs I've had done in the past.

Refusing to go down as easy as Jaiden, I yank my arm away and thrust my elbow at her chest. Her hand intercepts and pushes my arm away in the opposite direction; throwing my body off balance.

Using the position to my advantage, I kick back at her. Five vampires lurch on to me. Wrenching my body side to side barely moves my capturers.

Not giving up, I thrash through my own pat down. Hands grasp hard and painfully. My pocket knife is taken as new property for another, and with it my killing defense.

"This one's a fighter. Put her in the van." The woman instructs her team. "Wouldn't want her to run."

My legs are forced to move to keep under my body. The five of them pull and push me to the back of a minivan.

Fury renewed, I manage to swing my legs in front to kick the door before they can open it fully. Yanked back, they open the door fully and control my limbs to throw me inside.

My back hits the seat and feet hit the other door. Knocking to the ground on my left side after the initial hits. Wheezing breath back inside. Forcing the air into my lungs while trying to get back up on my feet.

One follows in. My hand, helping me get up, is grabbed and swung around my back. The other joins it quickly, and both are wrapped in a lengthy piece of rope.

"Get her feet too." A man's voice tells the one tying me up.

A foot on my back holds me down, and in my position I can't kick too much to defend myself. Another rope binds my legs together.

A couple people load up into the van and take their seats. The foot never removes itself. The person just gets comfortable in the seat and adds another foot.

Face down to the ground, I can't see much more than shoes. I don't know anything, but I can hope they don't kill me before I can escape. At least Jaiden might be able to get herself free by jumping from the back of the truck.

Chapter 16

Picturesque French bread. Fresh out of the oven and steaming on a white background. Blurs and clarifies, over and over as my eyes focus in and out in my stare. It's dimly lit by the spot lights shining on the feeding area and throughout the store.

The pit in my stomach grows to the size of a bowling ball.

Bile sticks in my throat; rising each time my head goes through the memory. Containing a shudder requires all the strength I can muster. Attached at the vein, I wouldn't want him to know how utterly awful I feel.

Over and over I feel the wet appendage track its way along my neck. The dried saliva is still there.

I'm going to be sick. I want to throw up.

Never have I ever wanted to shower myself in scalding water more than I do now. Sterilize myself. Burn the first layer of my skin off to somehow remove him from me; though I know it will never work.

Ashamed of myself. How could I let it happen? I should have tried to do something; anything would have been better than nothing.

I froze in the moment. Iced veins bound me in place. My entire body unwillingly in the control of someone else. The strength of him frightening on its own. Pure and absolute control via strength; a terrifying reminder of how weak I am.

He easily overpowered me without any effort. I could do nothing to prevent anything he could have decided to do.

Whether on his mind or not, another dire thought hot pokers into my thoughts.

Another scenario, another time, another place.

Rape is a very real possibility in this world; even more so than it used to be. Without the constraints of society, those who ever had an inkling of the thought may no longer hold back. Those who dared to act before this all, wouldn't hesitate now.

After rescue comes, I'll need to find a medical facility. Birth control pills or morning after pills are an essential requirement now. They are the only defence I can offer to the possibility of being raped.

If a lick to my neck feels this horrifying, then there would be nothing more terrifying than to be raped and further more to have to deal with a permanent consequence; if I even manage to survive.

The needle bites at my vein from little movements of the tube connected. Bored, the man fidgets in place. His head moving with the other end of the tube inside his mouth. I wish to tell him to stop, but I don't feel like I don't have that right and I don't want to make things worse for myself.

I gaze at the SuperData page he's scrolling through. Nothing extraordinary pops out at me. However, amusing is that these people are the first I've come across where I've seen cellphone use.

Four people have pulled out phones as regular use behaviour. In a great lacking of cellphones amongst supernaturals I've been around, it's crossed my mind a few times why there aren't more of them that have them.

"Time's up." A tall woman, Alisha I think, calls out. One by one she pulls out IV in a gentle and practiced manner. A tape and cotton ball goes over it to protect it. We're stood up and a thin rope is retied around our wrists; in front this time. It's more comfortable that way.

The man next to me holds the tube up and drains what's left of my blood inside to his mouth.

I don't feel any worse off than usual. Alisha comes back around with a cookie and a juice box, and hands them to the vampire. The man who drank my blood holds the straw to my mouth and I'm to drink; another violation.

As fast as I can, I guzzle the liquid down. He replaces the straw with the cookie shoved into my mouth; no warning. His fingers don't linger, he removes my binds and takes me to the dairy section. It shocks me again to see so much food on the shelves.

A whole dry cookie is a lot of work to chew and swallow in a dry mouth.

The shelves are empty here but the floor is lined with people; humans mostly. One man, a psychic, explained to me that vampires don't just hunt humans. The blood isn't so different between many supernaturals and humans. He had said before he cursed himself for not being stronger and wishing he was born something else.

It makes sense why, if I'm not completely human myself, vampires can drink my blood. If there isn't a distinguishable difference in blood, then it brings even more ridiculousness to a race war.

Vampires can't drink werewolf blood; per the example he had used. It's too different from human blood. It would be like eating something that's turned bad; a stomach ache and evacuation.

It makes sense from what I've read on them.

I look at Dominique—Nikki—Her, hiding my guilt. I know she wants to get back together with John but I also know she wants kids. John is likely sterile from being a hybrid. If not, they'd want him to procreate with another werewolf; or he might only be able to reproduce with one species or the other, but not both.

And, he's Beta. He'd have to refuse his Alpha, and reject his pack. Reject his claim to be Alpha; which I'm betting he barely had from his status.

His pack might not have had a choice; Alpha rule. Ken Kadiza's son would be John's father. His father might have been stripped of his rights as Beta because of marrying John's mom; if he hadn't given them away himself.

If John has a brother that's more human than werewolf then he wouldn't have much claim to the pack position.

For Ken to name a grandson Beta after such an event isn't abnormal, blood is important to werewolf packs. In a lack of choice it might be better to succeed a hybrid, than to give the spot to another bloodline, or merge with his siblings' packs.

It may mean that John's father and John are the only male heirs.

"Are you okay?" She asks.

"Fine." I say with a reassuring grin.

My head spins as I sit down. It's the least of my worries after what's been running through my thoughts.

"No, you're not. Talk to me." When I don't respond immediately, she pushes further. "Jaiden."

Aware of the ears around us, I whisper to near mute. "I feel absolutely sick. Like I'm going to throw up. He licked my throat. It was awful."

"That's what's going on in your head?" She continues speaking at the only slight hushed voice. "He licked your throat. You're fine. Get over it. He didn't really do anything to you. We need to focus on getting out of here." Her light hearted tone doesn't match the words she says.

The words convene her stance and discredits my feelings.

Am I over reacting? She seems to think so. Maybe others will feel the same.

A heat comes over me. Everyone here must think I'm an idiot. She certainly spoke loud enough that everyone knows what happened now. Shame reddens my cheeks. I shouldn't have ever mentioned anything.

Perhaps it's my complete innocence in the matter that is making me feel this way. What may be nothing to her is everything to me.

Just another thing to burry deep inside. I'll deal with it at my next break down. Given my track record, I'm about due for one.

In my previous life, they were coming about once every month or two. Since announcing my lie to her, my headaches have begun anew and my anxiety increased. All I'm missing is the need to exist only within the confines of my room; my depression.

One of the vampires, the woman D- She had smacked earlier, comes to us and picks her up.

"You're never breaking free, so you should probably stop talking about escaping. Although, by all means let all of us know what you're planning." They walk off with the other humans for their turn at blood donation.

She will come back with her own bandage. I should have warned her. Alisha had tried to use a pre-opened IV needle on me. I requested a new one for sanitary reasons. Alisha seemed genuinely nice as she smiled and apologized. She even indulged me with my request. Had the vampire drink less when I mentioned I'd already fed a vampire my blood this week.

Vampires have better hearing than humans do. We should have known better than to talk so loud in a store full of them.

At least, I should have known better.

Phone and pocket knife dig into my hips. She had been good for one thing; if nothing else. In the moment of her distraction, I had been able to hide both.

Sitting down is uncomfortable but I dare not move the objects. Rescue is coming but I don't know when. John may or may not have seen the message written in haste as we came into the parking lot. My single guard got distracted long enough for a quick message.

Superstore vampires

The two words will incite a rescue; hopefully. I hope John takes it as unusual and alerts someone. I should have put 'help' in the message, but a well thought out and detailed send help message is a luxury.

D—I sigh mentally.

I need something to call her, whether it is ever to her face is another question. She told me I can't call her Dominique or Nikki, so I suppose I should have to figure out another nickname.

Dom. Mini. Nique. Nik. Kiki. D. Chantel. Chan.

They mostly sound weird.

I'd prefer to call her by her actual name but, I fear that even if given permission, it will forever forward feel wrong to call her either of the given names; even her middle name.

When she said that I lost the privilege to call her Dominique she suggested that I'm not her family and she seemed to suggest I'm not her friend so I'm not to call her Nikki, it felt like a huge statement.

Her betraying me, in a way, by not allowing me to call her by her names; it's a control thing.

Mustering up the tears and giving her the sob story she seemed to need is the only reason why she seems to tolerate me right now.

I don't want that taken away by calling her by her name; reminding her of her family and friends. We aren't either, apparently.

Running through the names a couple times before I finally settle on Nique. It feels like a combination of the two names.

Nique- it's strange to refer her as such but I'll get used to it; I suppose.

Nique had been trapped in another vehicle with no chance to escape. Perhaps, they thought I wouldn't run strictly because of her.

They were right. I couldn't just abandon her. Especially without knowing where they would take her.

If I could even escape without the vampires chasing after me and capturing me immediately. They'd catch me, and I would be seen as a flight risk.

When her time is up, Nique comes back. The woman practically drops her in my lap.

Nique moves herself from overtop my lap, to her own spot beside me. She looks like she's in great pain.

"Are you okay?" I ask her in kind.

"Woozy." She says.

"They took too much blood." I say more to myself. "Did they stop when Alisha told them to?"

"She took more. Said they'd make it so I couldn't fight." Nique likely echoes what they said to her. In their position, it would be the smartest move.

"They'd rather risk you dying than to chance you fighting back." It says something about these people.

"Mmhmm." She says sleepily.

"If you go to sleep, I don't know if you'll wake up. So you need to stay awake." I do the only thing I can think of when her eyes close. Pinching her skin gives her a fright.

Her eyes snap open.

Eyes practically whirl as her head spins. She's in bad shape.

I take her hand. "Fine. Close your eyes until the dizzies are under control. Squeeze my hand every couple seconds so I know you're conscious. I'll pinch you if you don't."

Nique does as I ask without moving too much. She leans against the wall and my shoulder. Squeezing my hand lightly until her head feels normal. When it does, she sits upright and lets go of me.

Our guards, slowly but steadily one at a time, walk away to where they feed on us. High pitched messages call at them, vampires talking in a frenzy.

Something is happening. Louder noises and talking catches others attention.

Confident in the commotion, I search for my knife. Pulling it out from my pants in careful movements to not attract attention. Pulling it open, I flip it in my hand. Sawing through the rope is easier than I thought. A sudden break through has the knife pressing into my skin. Without looking, I can tell the knife broke through the skin on the side of my arm.

Extending the ropes around my wrists until I could free my hands in a split second. The cut on my arm isn't large and is barely bleeding. It'll close up and clot quickly.

At the end, three human captives jump up and start sneaking off.

Clearly, in my memory, I can see myself jumping up. Running over to the vampire trailing after the three running away. One arm loops around their shoulder. The other shoves the blade tip first into the neck. Removing the steel unleashes a spurt of red. The vampire gargles as the blood fills their throat. They fall to the ground to a puddle of their own blood. Then, her heart broken face as she screams an unintelligible name and pushes me off the dying body.

But, I stay in place and pretend to still be bound even when the opportunity appears. I don't think these people are evil; they're just surviving. They need blood, so they stock pile humans. I can understand why they took us, and fed off our blood.

Now, it seems like it would be an unnecessary kill. The rage that filled me was awful; understandable but awful. That I would be inches away from taking a step that would be no better than someone evil. That I would need to remind myself to not kill innocents.

It was a nightmare when I had that vision. It's going to stay just a nightmare. I won't let my horror turn to that sort of rage if I don't need it to survive. Besides, I don't remember Nique being with me originally.

More victims start running when they figure they can make it. Crashes knock off in the distance. There is a fight. Better to get lost in the horde of fleeing people, than stuck last at the mercy of whoever wins.

Blade at the ready, I stand. "We need to go. It might be John." I tell Nique.

She scoffs and rolls her eyes. I can feel her accusation in my lying again, but I feel it's undeserved. It's not like I could have told her without our captures finding out.

Nique refuses to take my outstretched hand. Unsteady as she is, she stands herself up and walks by me, then runs to freedom with the others.

Running after them, I look at the people around. People hiding in aisles, dead on the ground, in the midst of fighting, or having a standoff with others.

The light is bright when we get outside. Nique waits for me impatiently. A limo waits with a familiar face. With Nique's attention on me, I point to the limo.

"Jaiden?" It's the guard woman from Chad's clan.

"Hi." I greet her. It feels too late to ask her name. Diligently I'll listen for another to say her name, and hope it doesn't create an awkward situation before that.

"Jerry sent us to retrieve you." She tells me.

"Thank you." Nique comes up beside me. When I look her direction I'm reminded of how we got here. "That's Jerry's truck. I'm sure he'd like it back. Someone in there should have the keys still."

"I will let someone know to find the keys and return it to you. Chad would like to speak with you, so they will bring the truck to the apartments." The guard opens the door and motions inside.

She eyes up Nique. "She's with me." I go inside the offered door.

Nique follows me inside as she grabs the conversation. "How did Jerry know we were here?" The other woman takes a seat near the door. She pulls it shut. I hear a high pitch then the limo starts up.

Digging out my phone from under my belt, I show her it. I sit onto a seat. "I sent John a message and told him where we were."

"They let you keep your phone." She's incredulous.

"You distracted them in the middle of my pat down." Noticing she still has her wrists bound. "I can untie your ropes if you'd like."

"How did you get out of your ropes?" Nique puts her hands out so I can cut her ropes at a better angle. I'd thought with her being so close she would have seen what I was doing.

"My knife." I answer simply. The sideways ride is spinning my head something awful. I move myself to the back seat so I can look forward.

"Somehow you managed to hide both a phone and a knife." The guard woman says, sounding almost impressed with me.

"They would have found both immediately, but she decided to fight. It distracted the guy patting me down. I managed to get the knife and phone under my belt, but it didn't matter anyway because he forgot to finish the pat down."

"You got lucky." She settles deeper into her seat. "That wouldn't happen within our clan."

"Extremely lucky." I echo the sentiment.

"So, who are you?" Nique asks.

The woman straightens in her seat, tense now under the scrutiny. "Carol. I'm the head of security. Chad's my brother. Who are you?"

"Nikki. I'm Jaiden's body guard." There's an edge to Nique's voice, but I doubt the warning means anything to Carol but to watch her as a possible nuisance.

"Doesn't look like she's the one who needed a body guard." Carol points out with a sneer.

It's a short drive to the apartments.

The box and the blood seeping from broken bottles have been cleaned up. Barely a trace remains. The sidewalk needs a good scrubbing to get the remaining red stain.

Carol escorts us to the apartment suite Chad inhabits. There is a noticeable lack of people here. They must have sent as many as possible to rescue us.

Carol walks us into his room without knocking. The room is significantly brighter than the last time I was in here. Electricity brightens every bulb in the apartment. It has to be for my sake. A vampire's eyes adjusts and sees in darkness better than a human's does.

Chad is in the living room smoking as he watches out the open balcony doors. Chad turns to greet us. He smiles at Carol, frowns at Nique, and settles with a smirk for me. "Delivery girl."

"Hello." I smile cheerfully in return.

"Still alive, I see." A redundant observation given that I stand in front of him.

"Thanks to you and yours." I make sure to thank him profusely. He's helped so much, and I want to make sure he knows my gratitude before getting to the original reason for the visit. "Thank you for sending people to rescue us."

"I would call us even now."

"Perhaps," I say; using the word to help collect my thoughts. "If you keep score, rather than calling it a mutual respect and understanding."

My temple starts aching. "Would you call it that?"

"Yes."

Chad pauses in contemplation. "I believe you were on the way to speak with us." He turns serious. Chad gives me his full attention.

"Yes." Glad that small talk is over so I can maneuver the difficult part and just get it over with. "Jerry wishes for you to reconsider being a client. I have returned and will handle deliveries personally."

Chad doesn't look shocked at the request. He likely knew where the conversation intent lay. Jerry calling for help may have been a huge hint. "Where did you go?"

"It was urgent," I excuse my disappearance. "I had to go rescue a friend. Had I been a couple minutes later, she would have been dead."

"And where is she?" He asks.

"Here." Nique's voice booms confidently behind me. She steps out beside me.

"Friend, why were you with our delivery girl when Jerry said that only she was taken?"

"My name is Nikki." Her name is powerful and she demands to be called by it. "I followed her because I wanted to protect her. Jerry didn't know because I snuck out. It's too dangerous for her to go out alone."

"And what protection could you offer her; none obviously." Chad takes a dig at her confidence. I can see him testing Nique and playing at her confidence and temperament.

"I'm a seer. I prevented worse from happening. Jaiden was supposed to die and she's alive isn't she." Nique copies the same words I've said to her; it's reassuring to know she processed some of what I said.

Chad's view shifts to me. "It appears that our debt may not be paid after all, if it was your seer who orchestrated events to prevent your death. I will exchange your debt for our loyalty to you. For so long as you are the delivery girl, we will purchase from Jerry. Beyond that, we will work on this mutual respect and understanding you suggest."

"Thank you." I immediately show my gratitude once he stops talking. The language he uses is interesting. It's like he means that he's buying from me and not Jerry.

"Thank me again in a moment. I am willing to turn you into a vampire; personally. It will provide you more protection. You seem to have a penchant for danger." Chad offers.

There is a moment of hesitation, not because I wish to be turned but because I don't know if I can turn it down without offending him. I try to be as sweet as possible. "No, thank you. I have to decline. But, thank you for the offer."

"You would decline more strength and life span. Or does the blood and lifestyle bother you?" Chad's face twitches on his brow and on either side of his nose. He's angry with my rejection.

"It's not that." I try to reassure him. This isn't the first time I've contemplated the vampire turn choice. "It's just not in my future, and while she likes to change things, I like the certainty of what she tells me will happen."

"And, does she become a vampire?" He asks Nique.

We look at each other. I beg her with my eyes to give the same response and nothing more. "Not that I've seen, no."

"The offer stands should you wish for it. You may leave now." Carol walks two steps to collect us and push us out of the room. "But, Jaiden." He calls and Carol stops. "Allegiances lie with the highest bidder in a lack of loyalty; remember that." Chad waves to Carol. "Escort them out."

"Thank you again." I smile and nod.

Carol escorts us out the way we came in. People flit through the halls, exuberance has seeped in. The excitement from their success fuels them.

In our passing, Carol is tossed keys. She holds out the keys behind her for me to take. I take them from her hand and shuffle them in my own until I realize the grating metal is likely grating on her sensitive hearing. I clamp them tightly.

We arrive at the doors. Carol walks through a door and holds it open for us. "Don't get kidnapped on the way home. We can't always risk ourselves to rescue outsiders." Carol warns as she mentally shoves us out the doors. Nique tasks the bait and leaves.

"Thank you, Carol. We won't make a habit of it. Have a great evening." I assure her and walk away from her.

"Jaiden." Carol calls me back. "Chad has enemies. The ones that took you were waiting to ambush anyone in connection to Chad. You so happened to show up while they were here and waiting. There are others who will do the same or just kill you on spot. Make my life easier and scout the area before you stop by.”

“Thank you.” I smile to her. She didn’t have to tell me that; it’s nice of her. “Have a good night.”

The truck is parked right out front. Almost exactly right where we left it earlier today.

We enter in silence. I start up the vehicle and drive off, away from the apartments and towards the hotel.

“What was he talking about?” Nique asks me once the apartment is no longer in sight.

“I don’t know. Maybe it was a warning. But about who or what, I don’t know.” Allegiances lie with the highest bidder in a lack of loyalty. The words echo in his voice within my head.

Theories form about what he could be warning me about; rather who he could be talking about. There is a general sense of life about it, but I don’t think he’d give me any old random piece of advice. At this point it boils down to three thing; Jerry, Chad, and unknowns.

“Do you think Jerry told him about the revolution?”

I almost have to ask her to repeat what she said. In my head I only half hear her words until the full question registers in my head. This again. “No. Jerry wants nothing to do with the revolution directly. He’s neutral and doesn’t know anything that’s to happen. He stays out of it until he no longer has a choice.”

“So, you’ll just start a revolution all by yourself?”

“No,” I defend myself. “It’s what James started. Others are starting. We just need to progress it. It can’t be like this forever.”

“James did nothing. James was useless. He gathered random people, and couldn’t lead any of them. He failed so bad that he abandoned us.”

She’s particularly hard on James; never has seemed to like him. But, I have a feeling that we don’t have the full story. For James to have left before he really had a chance to kill Darius, when that was his whole goal, is a paradox in action. “To be fair, he had to go into hiding because he’s one of the most wanted supernatural beings right now. I don’t know if that was before or after he abandoned us.

But, uh, yeah.

And, he might have been on the right track. The key to Darius is Alexa. Darius took Rayleen and of course Alexa is going to follow. James might have been using her to get close to Darius and kill him.

It's a decent plan. I've got the same idea. Alexa's on board.

But anyway, James could be a great asset to us, and a way to officially end the revolution. His title does still mean something to a lot of people."

"But he's not here."

"And he might be dead." I add to her point. "But, the options are living to just survive this world or do whatever we can to end this war." I slow down. This conversation feels like it is longer than the ride should take.

I hate war; it's unnecessary. I want it over as soon as possible. Unfortunately, it'll likely take years. Wars tend to last years.

"And what about that vampire gang?" I wish to interject. I think they're called a clan. But I refrain. "You convinced a gang of vampires to rescue us from another gang. Then brokered a deal with them?"

Technically, I didn't do half of that directly. "To be fair, I knew them from before. I saved the leader by pure fluke of timing and a little observation. One of his clan was trying to kill him. I think I impressed him. Or he owed me through honour. I don't know."

"So you could convince him to join the revolution." Nique says.

"We're a long ways off from that." I start.

"Sure, but you could right?"

"Maybe?" I have my doubts.

"He said you have their loyalty." She reminds me.

"Sure, but that only goes so far."

"People die for loyalty. They might die for you. You should be the face of the revolution; not me." Nique suggests.

"No way." I can't help but laugh at the idea inside my head. The idea of taking a grenade for someone, for dying for someone, is ludicrous to me. Impossible to think that another might do it for me, and I wouldn't want them to.

"Why not?" The question is more loaded than she knows.

I focus on the portion that won't offend her. "I'm not that person. I'm not a leader. I never want to be the face of anything again. You're a born leader. You have all the charisma and confidence."

"And you're another born leader. You already have a bunch of people willing to risk themselves to rescue you. Two separate groups you've convinced to be allies with you." I have to stop myself from scoffing and rolling my eyes. I'm certainly not a born leader. "Fuck, you have visions and that alone would make you a killer leader. You make friends wherever you go. You have this cute and innocent thing about you, but hide phones and knives in your underwear and break yourself free while captured.

Or, you manage to get a deal with someone to house your followers, or have vampires rescuing you. You have the loyalty of a whole vampire gang. You saved us from ghosts when we should have died. You survived a building falling on you to turn around and call a truce; and everyone listened to you. You rescued me. You don't give yourself enough credit."

"Perhaps, you give me too much credit." The high praise is weird given recent events, but maybe she is actually putting the incident behind her. "Those were either because I had a cheat sheet, or because someone else laid things out and I just had to give a little push.

I'm lucky.

The problem lies in me. I don't garner respect like you do. People look at you and they think you are a leader to follow. Strong and confident.

They look at me and they see cute and innocent; you just said it yourself. Or, the annoying know-it-all. Or, Miss Perfect. Or, stuck up. Or, whatever else everyone calls me."

"Okay, I'll play. You're not a leader, yet. But someone needs to be."

"You." I insist. Unsure if she is aware, I drive us down another road to loop around to the hotel; giving us an extra couple minutes to talk.

"You know more about them than I do. I don't know anything about the people I'd need to convince."

Going for it, I hope she won't get offended. "They're just people. They've been oppressed for two thousand years. They're angry. They're still people, and come in many kinds of experiences and personalities.

They didn't want to be oppressed anymore, so they had a revolution. Speak to that. Empathize with them.

And yeah, I know more, because I've learnt through research. Honestly, with my knowledge and your charisma, I could make you into the best leader around; better than I ever could be.

 You took control at the mall, and you took control of Banff with ease. That should count for something."

"Between the two of us we'd make one great leader, but that would still require you to be a leader."

With her more receptive outlook I decide to head back to the hotel. "I'm more suited for background work, unless I have a vision and am required to change things."

"Did you?" Her words jump quickly out of her mouth.

"Did I what?"

"Did you change things?" Nique asks.

"Yes. Maybe?" I didn't kill that vampire. That certainly changed that particular scene. It might have consequences; good or bad. "I don't really know until it's happening, sometimes it's an immediate change, and sometimes it's down the road when a different vision doesn't happen.

But I've had quite a few visions lately. Maybe just dreams too. I'm still trying to work out how it all works."

"So why wouldn't you want to become a vampire. He offered. Wouldn't it be cool?"

I hesitate to answer. I'm on the unpopular side of this argument. A very small part of me does think that it might be cool to have heightened abilities. I could be stronger and faster. I could hear better and hear higher pitches. But, there are the downsides to vampirism.

"It's a quote; I think. Someone's had to of said it at some point. Only the foolish choose to become immortal. I was born a human because I was meant to be a human. Humans are only meant to live so long, and for good reason.

It's what makes us human; per say. Knowing we only have so long, that we are so fragile." I trail off, just stopping short of telling her the actual truth. "I'd be afraid of who I'd become if was made immortal."

With my life, anxiety, depression, bad luck. Life's been bad to me. Not that there hasn't been good, but the bad far outweighs the good. Why would I want that extended? I'm not for suicide but I sure would hate to have my life extended further than it has to be. I'm exhausted with life already. I don't need to live five hundred years more.

"But, you aren't exactly human; are you? Why would you be afraid?"

I try not to look woeful while searching for a good answer. "Because a lot of who I am is because of what I am, and to change what I am would also change who I am." I smile at the inside joke shared by John. "Usually you sound like the fortune cookie."

"Shut up." Nique smiles and laughs a little at the joke.

As an after though, I add. "I'm afraid about what it might do to my visions. They're so ingrained into me that I'd be afraid of a life without them."

"Like, you think you'd lose your visions if you became a vampire." It's like an epiphany enlightens her.

"It's certainly possible. The virus might attack that part of me and kill it. I don't know enough to say exactly what would happen. It could heighten my visions or decrease them; maybe get rid of them completely." The general rule about vampirism is that it strengthens or weakens traits in humans, so it's possible that either could occur. "It's even possible that the virus could kill me, depending on how it reacts with my supernatural parts."

"He looks pissed." Nique voices. A split second later the words echo in my head from my own eyes. Jerry stands poker straight with his hands in fists at his side. Mouth turned into a frown and eyebrows furrowed together. His glared gaze aimed right for us.

"Maybe we should run away. There's still time."

My joke goes right through her. "He's already seen us."

"That means nothing." It dawns on me to remind her to be nice to him. Make sure she doesn't anger him more by arguing about it. "Seriously though, just apologize profusely. Don't give him a chance to talk first. Maybe just apologize and run inside."

"Apologize for what?" She asks, a little annoyed.

"You abandoned your shift, and broke the never leave the hotel rule. We play by his rules if we want to stay." I remind her.

Once we park, she leaves the truck quickly. I have to hurry to follow after her, while also collecting my paperwork. Nique gets to him first. "Sorry, I left in the middle of my shift and broke your rule about leaving the hotel, but I wasn't going to let Jaiden die when I could prevent it." Nique baffles Jerry with her on point apology and non-apology reasoning. She doesn't let him respond. She runs inside the building.

"Hi. We should talk in private." I suggest.

"Yes." A practical growl darkens and roughens his voice.

Jerry leads me inside the hotel. Instead of going off to some isolated part of the hotel, he leads us into an artificially lit kitchen in the lounge. He opens the freezer and leads me inside. A small hum and colder temperature let me know this room is working too. The generator has been installed and turned on.

I speak first to hopefully stop a meltdown, and possible chopping me up for dinner. "Chad will order from you again, but only as long as I deliver the goods."

"Alright." The vein still throbs on his temple.

I continue on to help my case and ease his anger. "And the vampires from the other clan, a lot are dead. The operation there is over or on hold right now. If you act quickly and send a group over you could take over the superstore. There's a lot of nonperishable food there.

You may get more business since they are no longer drinking blood from the human captives. The humans ran off."

"One minute." He walks out of the kitchen. Jerry is gone for a couple minutes before he returns with a small smile on his face. "Ziam will handle the Superstore. I can't have that girl thinking she can just leave whenever she wants."

"She told me after that she had a vision and I was supposed to die. I'll talk to her and make sure she doesn't run without notifying you with a good reason."

Jerry nods at my reasoning. "Not just an empath. She's a seer?" I nod. "Perhaps, with recent events, you should have a body guard while you're out."

"Not her." My voice beams before I can stop it, then I chastise myself by having to come up with an explanation. "We have a love hate relationship. And the last few days have been more hate than love.

Also, when it came down to it, she really couldn't do anything in the fight. She acts first and doesn't think about things. They flagged her as a threat and treated her as such. They drained her until she was passing out so she wouldn't cause any more issues.

If I hadn't texted John, we'd probably be dead."

"And yet she says she saved your life."

"She created a distraction that allowed me to hide a knife and my phone. If she hadn't then I wouldn't have been able to text John. But, she could have just warned me in the first place, and then everything could have been avoided." I reason.

"Alright. We'll pair you up with another delivery person then?"

Mulling it over, I have to decline. "I wouldn't want to bother them and you'd lose a guy for deliveries. Maybe I'll grab Sara or John, or DeAngelo. They're friends and I know they might actually be able to protect me if we're ambushed again."

"Alright." Jerry looks me over. "And you're okay?"

"Yes, thank you. Though I'd kill for a shower." I admit.

"I might be able to help you. If you can wait until after supper, we can boil you some water. It won't be much, but enough to get you clean in better comfort." His words excite me.

"That would be wonderful. Thank you."

"Come." We leave the freezer to stop in the kitchen. "Jules, make her whatever she wants; no charge." He turns his head back to look at me. "Eat some supper. You look pale." With that, he leaves abruptly.

"He's right, you don't look so good." Jules stands tall and lanky in a chef's apron. Hair shaved shorter on either side of a longer patch in the center, but I get the impression that the point is not to make a mohawk. It's mostly swept to the one side.

I stare for a moment. One moment of panic at a lack of familiarity strikes away the manners I was taught through childhood.

I rely on Carrie's rules instead. Jules has an overall appearance of a word I've only heard once; androgynous. Within a lack of obvious gender I have to consciously make an effort to refer genderlessly until they tell me what they are and would like to be referred as; which may be a genderless pronoun preference either way.

Carrie had explained gender preference back in high school. I'm thankful for her patience with my complete ignorance back then. I send out a mental thank you and wish for her to still be alive.

"I've had my blood drained twice in the last week." What is meant to come out as a joke is an awkward depressing reality.

Their eyes widen. Jules rushes out into the lounge area, but comes back through the door only a moment later. They deposit a chair right next to me. "Sit. If you feel like you're going to faint, make a noise and lay on the floor. Are you allergic to anything? Food preferences?"

I sit on the chair. "No, I'm not allergic to anything. I eat pretty much anything."

"Human meat, brains, eyeballs?" I shake my head to all those suggestions. "I didn't think so. I cook for humans and supernaturals, darling. A little tip, always specify that you are on a fruits, vegetables and animal diet. You don't and you might get served up human meat or something that might be poisonous to you."

"Thank you." My cheeks turn red again from the faux pas.

Jules turns around and searches through the fridge. "So does Jerry know you're human?"

"I'm not." I defend.

They look at me in disbelief then return to pulling out something. "You don't know a basic cultural rule. All supernaturals know how to specify their eating preferences."

"I'm an empath but I was raised human. My birth dad was the supernatural, but I was raised human by my mom and stepdad. My birth dad didn't even know I existed until a year ago. I didn't fully find out what I am until the revolution was happening." Exchange the one word and my defence is the truth.

Jules fires up a pan with a slab of meat in it. They add it to an already full stove top; pushing a pot to the side for its spot. "It's what all the humans involved with supernaturals are posing as. Lie or the truth, I won't tell, but I also don't want to know.

But make sure Jerry doesn't have any reason to question you. He hates humans and barely tolerates the weakest of supernatural kind."

"I've been told that before. Should I be worried about the two humans I brought with me?" I ask. "Jerry knows they're human."

"It's surprising he's even letting them stay."

I explain. "He owed me a favour and I put them into the deal."

"He'll hold to his word. Nothing more and nothing less." Maybe Chad was talking about Jerry. We don't have loyalty; we have a deal. He'd betray us to a better deal. Either, I have to make ourselves indispensable to Jerry and make our loyalty better than any deal, or we risk him selling us out. "Packaged beef gravy?"

"Yes please." I don't know what for but gravy is always good.

Jules plates a meal from buffet warming trays and the cooked meat. They present a large plate packed full of, "steak, mixed canned vegetables, boxed mashed potatoes and packaged beef gravy. But mostly, a lot of what you need to help you get back nutrients you'll have lost to those vampires."

"Thank you. There's so much."

"You'll eat as much as you can without throwing up." Jules orders.

"I'll try. Thank you so much."

"You're welcome. Oh here." Jules goes into the freezer and comes back before the door can stop moving. "Take three juice boxes and a water bottle with you. And come back anytime in the next day or two if you think you need more. Vitamin C is good for you and no one else seems to touch the fruit juices."

I look at my hoard of food and drink, and dread the questions that may go along with walking outside this room. "Do you mind if I stay in here to eat? I just, I've had a long day."

"Don't." Jules lifts a hand and lets me off the hook for an explanation of my anxieties. "I get it Sweetie. Here." They come over and clear off just enough space on the counter beside me. "I don't mind the company. We can get to know one another more. There's a reason I prefer to work in the kitchen rather than out there with Hec. I don't like big crowds. Drains me too."

Tears almost sprout from my eyes from how grateful I am. "Thank you."

"You're welcome. You eat and I'll talk." Jules sets back to work on the food items forgotten for my sake. I set to work eating everything but the steak; saving it for last. "Let's see. I was born in Ontario, but we moved out here for my dad's work when I was five so I barely even remember living there.

I met Hector, my significant other and our hunky bartender, in kindergarten. We've been best friends for, God, thirty two years. We've been friends longer than you've been alive."

"Twice over." My candid comment draws exaggerated ire and a knife shake. I duck my head down to escape. "I'll just eat. You talk."

"Are you sixteen?" They did the math from my comment.

"Fifteen. October 31st." I indulge.

"Oh, a Halloween baby; emphasis on the baby. Where are your parents?" The last sentence almost sounds scolding.

"My step mom and dad are dead, or rather missing. I was at school when things happened, and they never made it home. My mom is dead; died a few years ago. My other dad and step mom are dead." It sounds confusing out loud in their generic positions, but the names would have been more so. "My family's complicated."

"No worries. It would be more unusual if you only had two parents to report on these days. I have two moms and one dad; and plenty of family drama. I won't bore you with ancient history. But my mom split, and then my step mom moved in.

Everyone swears there was no cheating involved, but the adult in me doesn't believe them, and they still won't tell me otherwise.

Any who, I went to school for physiotherapy and got a paid internship to work at council headquarters. Loved it, but hated the politics. Hated being away from Hector.

Once I finished the designated sentence, I declined an offer to work at headquarters and negotiated a deal to work at the satellite office here."

"So how'd the chef thing come about?" I ask curious to their current work station.

"Roommate in London was a culinary apprentice. You learn a lot when they come home and want to test recipes on you like a guinea pig."

"Are you boring her with the torture of having a personal chef cook for you every night?" Hector's voice makes me jump in surprise. My back is to the door and my engrossment in Jules' conversation left me deaf to the door creaking.

"I still have nightmares about hobgoblin tongue." Jules argues.

"I know." Hector says dismissively.

"Delicacy my ass." Jules adds for emphasis.

"That reminds me, where is my food?" A snicker escapes and I dive into my food to hide my response from his joke. "Customers are starting to ask what's taking so long."

"That better not be a commentary on my food." Jules' finger goes up in warning. They turn to collect a tray of prepared food. Jules hands it to Hector in an exchange of practiced ease. Jules kisses Hector on the cheek. He leaves to go distribute the food.

"Hobgoblin tongue?" I ask, knowing there is a story behind it.

Jules makes a gagging noise. "It's so bitter and tough. And, the texture of it. You know how rough a cat's tongue is? Now, imagine having to eat and swallow that but thicker. You feel it scrape all the way down."

"That's disgusting." I cross hobgoblin tongue off an unknown list of things I never want to eat.

"Exactly, but they eat it because, oh, it's a delicacy. I've seen and eaten a lot of delicacies in my days and I'm almost certain delicacy just means disgusting food you aren't supposed to say is disgusting because someone somewhere would be offended."

"No, you're right. There seems to be two definitions of delicacy. You have the kind that mean luxurious and expensive, and maybe difficult to obtain. Or it takes a ridiculous amount of time to make.

And then there seems to be the delicacies where you are just waiting for someone to jump out saying the joke is on you. I've had both. And, both sides have their wonderful and their awful."

"Very true." Another tray packed and in hand, Jules excuses themself to take the food out.

Only the steak remains on my plate, and yet I already feel full. But, I can't stop now. Food shouldn't go to waste untouched, especially now.

Jules picked these specific food items for their nutrition. It's better to over indulge on this meal, than to face a possibility of mild to extreme symptoms including exhaustion and organ failure.

Exhaustion more likely at this point, and just as likely very dangerous in the right circumstance. Never know what tomorrow brings. There are copious amounts of food tonight, but tomorrow could bring a famine.

Jules returns. Rushing to the ovens. In a whirl, they are stirring and checking on the finished quality of what's been cooking. Five bowls are placed on the tray. In quick fashion, each bowl is filled with a chili, and the tray removed by Hector. Another tray filled with pasta baked in the oven. Jules takes that one out.

Am I the only one with a steak? It occurs to me exactly how rare and expensive this meal may have been. Fresh animal meat just may be a delicacy in this world; at least in certain parts.

Finishing what is on my plate, I take the empty dish to the sink.

Not one bit more could fit in my stomach, so I stuff juice and water in my arms, and into my hoodie pocket.

Jules and Hector are busy with a large crowd. Every seat is filled. People stand wherever they can.

Pushing through the crowd, saying "excuse me" every second in a mantra is the only way I get by anyone.

Claustrophobia, not something I normally suffer, closes in on me; likely a side effect from anxiety gone too far. My heart starts pounding, and my ears deafen to tone everyone out. Wishing for nothing more than to push and shove everyone away. I need a buffer space between me and them. Their presence and touch suffocate me and drown me. My pace quickens; frantic to escape.

Something brushes my neck and I swallow a scream. A shudder scrapes each bone from chest up. My lungs starve for breath until, at last, I escape from the lounge into the lobby.

Short quick breaths fuel my lungs. Tunnel vision draws me in to my room, where at last I let go; only after locking the door.

Grasping my chest; it hurts. Familiar chest pain is only comforting in that I know it isn't likely a heart attack.

Aware of the ears around me, I keep everything quiet. The tears, crying, and screaming all comes out mute.

Stumbling to the other side of the room, I put my back into the corner created by the night stand and the wall.

A lump threatens to break my silence. Holding my breath, I wait until the sob is choked down.

The tears splash onto my glasses. A fog creates from the warm tears on the cool lenses. Putting the glasses on the bed, I continue my break down.

The ghastly sight of so much death; twice in so few hours. I touched it. It seeped into my bones like it did my shoes and clothes. Burning bodies burned into my nose.

Death of my best friend; Leah died because of me.

The spirits killed so many because I wasn't convincing enough. I should have tried hard to get everyone out of that place as soon as I figured it out. They'd be alive if I told them about my vision.

Keeping my visions, my abilities a secret is causing death to those around me. Should I tell them that I'm the seer? Should I tell our group about them? John, Sara, and Nique seem to do okay with the information. It might help. But, they might feel entitled to the information like Calli did.

Lost Souls

Calli and Lucas died because I changed things.

The names on the death list grow; faces where names elude me. A list even larger of those who are likely dead, but aren't confirmed. I could have prevented many of them.

Dominique-Nikki–Nique, our relationship will never be the same. I shouldn't have tried to spare her feelings. I should have told the truth from the start. I made a judgement call based on how I thought she'd react. I forgot to tell her. Maybe I chose wrong. The level of trust we had is forever gone. Our level standing ground is gone. Marred by an act of betrayal; my betrayal.

That man licked my neck. I was sexually assaulted. Can I call it that? Or, does it not count because I wasn't raped? I don't know, but I feel gross.

All those people, too many people, touching me in the lounge. I can't handle all those people. I can't handle any people right now.

If Nique won't be our leader without me then that means that I have to find someone else. I can't be that someone else. I'm not strong enough to help her lead.

I don't know who I can trust.

I suppose the short answer is no one. Settings change. The specific people change. Situations change. But overall, the human condition, the people condition, doesn't. If they aren't maliciously backstabbing you then there's a reason; everyone has a price.

No one has loyalty like people have been brainwashed to believe from movies like the ones I had to watch over the summer. People have motives and reasons for everything they do.

Jerry, Chad, Carol, Nique, John, Sara, Shawn, Miles, Kelly, Alexa, Daniel, Rayleen, DeAngelo, Chantel, Ziam, Hector, Jules. None of them can be trusted. I can't even trust myself.

What is wrong with me? I'm such a horrible person.

Ha, I have my own private laugh about it. Of course I'm a horrible person. Look at who my father was. I had a crappy childhood. There is bound to be lifelong repercussions when you have crappy parents. I never had a chance.

This rabbit hole is all too familiar. However, now there is one difference. Now, my father is no longer directly influencing my everyday life.

Knock. Knock. Knock. Knock. My heart jumpstarts. No one can see me like this.

I swallow to clear my throat. One deep breath in. "Who is it?" I sing song. Not even I can detect any hoarse tremble.

"I have your water." The voice sounds like it belongs to Jules.

Wiping my hands over my face clears the tears. I dry them on the bed. I line my eyes with my index fingers then straighten my eye lashes. This is yet another reason why I hate make up and am happy that I never have to wear it anymore.

Picking up my glasses I heat my breath into them and hastily clean the lenses. A tissue box on the nightstand wipes away snot.

Within a short acceptable time, I clear away evidence of my break down. Smile on my face, I go to the door and let Jules in. "Thank you.

They carry one large soup pot to the bathroom and set it in the tub. "Be careful. The water is still boiling hot." Jules shows me the oven mitts as a sort of proof. "Enjoy."

"Thank you." I repeat.

Jules leaves me quickly and for that I'm glad. I drop my fake smile as I click the lock shut. I don't have to pretend to be okay behind closed doors.

Tears cloud my vision again. A good scalding away of the day will make me feel better. In a very small way, it helps me feel slightly better.

Prepping, I get new clothes and a towel for after my cleanse.

My peripheral notices a change, a very small change. A double take has me questioning my desk top. The notepad is different. No, it couldn't be. Yes. Looking underneath the notepad, I know that someone has gone through my things. My flyer page is gone.

I check the rest of the room and all my things. My belongings are here. I rifle though the bag to make sure nothing was touched.

Why would someone come into my room just to take the flyer? Maybe it was Sara.

I can't deal with this right now. There must be a priority. One thing at a time. And right now that thing is cooling in the tub.

Chapter 17

"I told you, you aren't welcome." Margie greets us, rather Daniel, coldly. She switches modes quickly to talk to Rayleen sweetly. "Hi sweetie, why don't you go inside and get settled."

"They aren't going in there without me." Daniel declares as Rayleen goes inside without the both of us. Crystal tails after her.

A hand on my shoulder from the man beside me is all that keeps me from following after my little niece.

Margie's left eyebrow arches up and her chin turns down. "You'd inhibit Rayleen's learning for pride?"

"I won't leave them alone with some demon who could kill them at the first chance they get." He doesn't answer her exact question, but gives a reason for his actions.

I had hoped sleep would help change his mind, but it hadn't. He woke up with the same sour attitude which had plagued him for much of the day before.

"I'm not a demon. I'm a witch. There's a huge difference." Margie clarifies and defends herself.

"Doesn't change the fact that I don't like you or trust you, so you're not going to be alone with my family." He insists.

"And, do you share this belief?" Margie questions me. I panic and freeze, unable to voice my feelings. "If you feel the same way, then we will stop lessons right here; right now.

I'm doing this as a favour, and I won't tolerate being insulted and scrutinized the whole time."

Rayleen needs this. I don't see the harm in trusting her. "Daniel, Rayleen needs training." My voice is quiet. Loud enough for the two of them to hear, and quiet enough that Rayleen shouldn't. "Could you just wait outside the door for us?"

Even though I don't look him in the eye, I know his face has to show some form of the betrayal I enacted in my request. I chance a look up as far as his mouth, where a frown meets my gaze; confirming my fear.

The hand comes off my shoulder. The first two bangs of his stomping away scare me before I can realize what's happening; what's not happening. Daniel storms off in a stomping thunder.

I'll have to apologize profusely later for hurting him and our relationship in such a large way. But for now, I put it behind me and internalize my pain and annoyance.

"Alright. Come in." I hurry inside to the entryway. Margie closes the door behind us and locks the door for good measure. "Woo, that was intense. I can see we can all use some relaxation exercises this morning."

"Sorry about him." I apologize.

"That's alright. I may have antagonized him a little bit. Both of you get comfortable; we're going to meditate." Skepticism has me almost rolling my eyes.

How is sitting on the floor with crossed legs and clearing your mind supposed to help Rayleen with her magic?

Margie commands. "Get comfortable. However, that means to you. Lay down on the bed; boots off. You can sit wherever or however you like. Stand if you wish. However you are most comfortable for a longer period of time."

I remove my boots and jacket; it's unusually warm in here.

Sitting on the bed and against the headboard, I get as comfortable as possible without lying down and falling asleep.

Rayleen lies down on the bed as Margie sits in her arm chair and leans back. Crystal hops up on the bed and lies against Rayleen.

"Close your eyes." Margie's voice takes on a soothing tone. I'm reminded of how a yoga teacher will speak to a class, yet not so exaggerated. "We are going to relax with my meditation method. It's a basic model that you can use, but as you learn and discover, you might find something that works better for you.

What's important is that you meditate and continue to do so to stay connected with yourself. I recommend at least once a day.

You may find you need to reconnect through the day as well. In time, you'll find that you may be more focused and attentive. You'll have a better understanding of your mind and body; and by extension your magic and elements.

Magic or not, overall, there are benefits to meditation. At the very least, you may be better able to understand yourself.

It can lower stress and anxiety, lower your blood pressure, allow you to more deeply relax, higher appreciation of yourself, and other benefits." She pauses. "Eyes closed."

She reprimands Rayleen. My eyes weren't open. "We're going to start. Just going to sit for a couple minutes.

I want you to breathe and count each breath as a one or a two.

Breathe in; one. Breathe out; two.

Breathe in; one. Breathe out; two.

Breathe in; one. Breathe out; two."

I sit and breathe but refuse to count; it sounds silly to me.

About a minute later, she speaks again. "Your mind may wander, and that's okay. Deal with your thoughts as they naturally come forth.

That's step one; to check in with yourself. How are you feeling? What are you feeling? Is there a certain event lingering in your mind? Work it out as it comes.

If it's an emotional feeling, let yourself feel, but we aren't looking to just rehash emotions, rather than find acceptance and understanding. It may help to look at it objectively. Look at it like you are figuring out what's happening to someone else."

I find this to be an utterly ridiculous exercise. There isn't any point at looking inside myself to go over my feelings. I know how I feel. I don't need to go over it again and again. If anything, I need to clear my mind and relax.

My personal meditation takes a detour.

Doing as she said in the beginning, I set to counting my breaths as a way to clear my mind.

Breathe in; one. Breathe out; two.

Breathe in; one. Breathe out; two.

Breathe in; one. Breathe out; two.

My mind clears, so I stop counting.

"Check in with your body. Start with your toes, and slowly move up your body. Are you in pain? Is anything starting to fall asleep? Is your body just existing? You can double this check in by checking in with your environment, or you can check in separately.

Lights, sounds, temperature, energy, wind, dirt, ocean, flame. Your elements and your magic. How your body interacts with your environment, and how does it feel. Feel the air in your lungs as you breathe in and out. How does it taste and smell? How far can you extend?"

I listen to her speak. Just as fast as she says the words, I finish checking in with myself on what she's speaking about. I wait impatiently for her to continue.

Breathe in; one. Breathe out; two.

Breathe in; one. Breathe out; two.

Breathe in; one. Breathe out; two.

The exercise is taking forever. Time slows when there is nothing to do. I open my eyes briefly to take a peek at her. Once I realize her eyes are closed and she can't see me, I open my eyes and look around the room.

It's a hotel room just like ours; decorated just like ours. Margie's paintings just might be exact copies of the same one in our room.

A noticeable difference is the singular bed, and a slight difference in the size of room; accounting for the lack of second bed. Her belongings fill the room.

"Smile." My eyes slam shut in the sudden spoken word. My heart hammers in thinking that I've been caught. "You're done the hard part. Physically smile and hold onto that smile the whole rest of the meditation.

Imagine you are in your favourite place, doing your favourite activity, or with your favourite person. Maybe you're sitting down to family dinner or on a beach soaking in the sun.

Do a full scale imagination; use all your senses and focus on the details. Hold on to the details for an overall picture."

Apple cinnamon tingling my nose. Red, blue and green lights paint the walls in a dim light from the Christmas tree in the corner.

The tree is overfilled with all the decorations collected through the years. Mom and dad's ornaments from grandmas and grandpas, and those collected in the years before kids; angels for mom and bells for dad.

My eclectic ornaments from my different favourite shows growing up. Kathleen's are missing because they would be on her tree despite her coming back to spend Christmas with us every year.

Rayleen and I would get up really early, but let our parents sleep in, so we could snoop on presents and stockings.

In our Christmas themed pyjamas that we got the night before; a Christmas Eve present opening tradition.

With French braids pulling our long and natural hair out of our faces. We'd match our wavy hair, later, for Christmas dinner.

Childish excitement at the prospect of an effortlessly perfect Christmas.

Waiting, not too patiently, for seven to come around so we could wake the parents.

Scarfing down whatever was in the fridge not designated for the evening's festivities.

Maybe we'd sneak a bit of ice cream or whipped cream meant for the pie; maybe a little bit of both. Some of mom's Christmas surprise dip.

Eat our advent calendar chocolates and a few of any cheap

chocolates set up in bowls; old tasting chocolates but it's the sentiment that makes it better.

Rayleen would still believe in Santa because our family believes in letting the kid figure it out on their own, and encourages pretend belief long into adult life.

I'm flashed back to grade six, eleven years old, and the sudden revelation that Santa doesn't exist; thanks to my classmates.

Getting caught up in the back and forth and conclusion answer; I was just pretending to still believe because I didn't know if you knew.

Christmas with my family as it could have been; as it should have been.

"Open your eyes. You should feel more relaxed." Margie tells us. I do as she says, but I can't say I feel relaxed; more like unsettled and upset.

"I do." Rayleen smiles. Laughing when Crystal tries to push her back down. Rayleen gets up. When Crystal figures out she isn't going far, she settles and curls up on the bed.

"Great. Now we'll get into it. I want to test you for the other elements." She goes over to her desk. "Come. Come." Margie beckons us over. The closer vantage point allows me to see two bowls and their contents; water in one and dirt in the other. "We need to figure out if air is the only element you can control. It's obviously your strongest element.

Sit and get comfortable. Stick your hand in the water and we'll see what you can do. No cheating though. You have to shut off all air control."

Rayleen sits down in the offered chair. "What do I do?"

"Your air comes natural. You breathe, you focus, extend; it works. It feels like an extra limb. Water should feel like an extension to your limb."

Margie sticks her finger into the water. Instantly, the water climbs up her hand and coats her hand like a glove. "It feels like water, but the water feels like it's a part of me. A muscle I can move with as much effort as natural as asking fingers to wiggle."

The water glides back into the bowl. Not one drop left on her hand.

"Your turn. Feel it out. If there is a connection, explore it."

Rayleen dips her whole hand into the water. I watch intently at the water and her wrist for any sign of movement. Excitement fills me when the water shifts in ripples, but it's stomped when I realize her hand moving causes it. She pulls it out. "I can't move the water."

"Okay." Margie sweeps Rayleen's hand to collect all the water and place it back into the bowl. "Try the dirt next. Same concept."

Margie takes a hand full of dirt, and squishes it between her palms. A much smaller object appears in its place. A perfect ball is formed. Margie drops it on the table. The balls bounces a little, and clinks against the desk "It's as hard as rock now." Margie picks the ball up and pinches it to break it back down into a pile of dirt. The dirt is placed with the rest and Rayleen is let to try.

Rayleen picks up a handful of dirt and places it between her two palms; mimicking her teacher. Rayleen opens and closes her palms a couple times but nothing has changed in the dirt that isn't from a simple squishing.

She gives up and puts all the grains of dirt back into the bowl. Brushing her hands to get all of it. "I didn't feel anything."

Margie reaches into her pocket and pulls out a match book. She swipes the match against the sand paper, and it lights up in a whoosh. "Take the match." Rayleen does so cautiously; the first time she's been allowed to hold one. "Take your other hand and try to burn the fire hotter, faster."

Unlike the other two, she doesn't show Rayleen how to perform this trick. Margie must have water and earth element magic.

Rayleen squeaks then drops the match when it gets close enough for her to feel the heat. Margie acts quickly to dunk Rayleen's hand into the bowl of water. The match is smoking, but out on the desk. A possible scorch mark burned into the table.

Picking Rayleen's hand out of the water, I examine it and find nothing. I put her hand back into the water just in case she got burned.

"We'll assume you can only control air, so we'll work with that. Air techniques require control over air. Your breathing extensions are your magic. Extend like a limb.

It's all baby steps; literally. You weren't born running. You learned how to roll, then crawl, then stand, then walk, and finally run, but only after stumbling and falling a few times. Don't expect to do too much too soon. We're talking realistic expectations here.

You can extend, like with the airplane, an arm's length away for the length of a fast pushed breath. A light aerodynamic object. Eventually, you can go heavier and maybe even float yourself or other heavy objects. Learn the ins and outs of aerodynamics and the science of air and oxygen.

You could oxidize objects, ripen a fruit, control different gases. Isolate compounds to remove one gas from another. Control the temperature of your air to freeze or heat objects.

Maybe your adult temper tantrum can cause a tornado.

But for now, you need to strengthen those muscles. Breathe. Do the meditation and focus on deep breaths.

Pick a cardiovascular exercise. I prefer swimming, but that isn't much an option in the middle of the city now. Maybe running will work better with what we have." Margie stops her tangent to examine Rayleen's hand. She pulls the water off before taking the bowls and match stick off into the other room.

Returning, she continues. "We're going to talk about the laws of aerodynamics; simplified. The laws of aerodynamics are a scientific explanation for how things fly. It can be broken down into four categories; weight, thrust, lift and drag.

Weight, it's how much you weigh or how much the object you want to float weighs. Easy, right? Drag is the force resisting flight. Weight, how big the object is, the shape of the object all resist flight therefore creates drag. Drag feels like walking through air versus walking through water.

Lift and thrust work hand in hand. They are the forces that get it up and get it going. Good so far?" She stops to connect with Rayleen, who just nods.

I have doubts about a full understanding of the concept, but Margie seems to be explaining it simply enough so that a child might understand. Rayleen hasn't asked any questions, so I can only guess that she is following along, or too nervous of failure to say anything.

"Great. So, you've already been doing all of this naturally; intuitively. That paper airplane. It's a light object, so it doesn't take much energy to get it to fly. Your drag is the weight and shape. Flimsy paper that is folded. Having folds that catch air and hold it rather than letting it pass smoothly. The wings catch your wind and create lift. Your wind thrusts the plane forward.

The airplane, as an object, is better to start with than say a pencil. What I'm getting at is that having a better understanding of the sciences can help you maintain control."

As Margie speaks she pulls out a round object from the side of her desk. "This is a paper lantern. I thought it would be a good way to float something using one of the rules. Hot air rises. Cold air sinks. This paper lantern houses hot air that you will blow inside to make it float. The hot air inside, lighter than the cold air outside, will make it float.

You will have to work at strength, heat and extension." Margie hands Rayleen the lantern. "Lie on the bed and hold this above your mouth. Breathe your magic into it. Hot deep breaths."

Rayleen does as she asks. Margie walks to her kitchenette and makes herself busy.

Rayleen holds the lantern in place above her mouth and blows into it. Mid breath, she lets go and the orange lantern falls to her face. This continues time and time again.

Margie comes over with a steaming tea in hand. She settles into the chair and takes a drink. "Remember, hot deep breaths right inside the lantern. You need to maintain the breath long enough to lift the lantern into the air. Extend to cover a greater distance.

You are working against time here too, not just how long your breath lasts. As the lantern air cools inside, it will drop." Rayleen tries unsuccessfully again. "Try to take the biggest breath you possibly can, and try again."

Rayleen sticks her mouth straight into the opening and breathes deeply for a few breaths; seemingly like trying to inflate a balloon. This time when she lets go, the balloon floats a couple inches above her face. It falls when she has to take a breath in.

"Progress. Good. Try again. Try for higher and longer." Margie grabs a book and starts reading where she takes a book mark out from.

I pay attention to Rayleen, since her teacher won't, but soon find it boring and repetitive. I almost wish for a book of my own to pass the time.

"Margie?" Rayleen's voice is soft and cautious.

"Yes dear?" Margie answers from behind the pages.

"I'm tired and it's not working anymore." Rayleen whines.

"You're out of energy. It's okay. It'll take time to build up the strength and stamina." Margie reassures. "You two are done for the day.

You are welcome to take the lantern with you to practice some more tonight, but don't practice before you come tomorrow. I don't want you out of energy before you even get here."

"Thank you for the lesson today." I wait expectantly for Rayleen to thank her as well. "Rayleen, thank her please."

"Thank you for teaching me magic." She says politely.

"You're welcome. Go along now." Margie pushes us out the door with her words. "I imagine your griffin would like to fly around a bit. Take her out to pee."

We put our winter clothes back on. "Thank you. Have a great day."

"Bye now."

We leave the room to a frigid hallway. I hadn't realized how warm it was inside, and how much I've missed that. There's a certain freedom that comes from not having to wear clunky clothing.

I lead us straight to our room, reasoning that Crystal doesn't likely have to pee after she did so right before we went to Margie's. Besides, Daniel might be angry if we don't go back to him immediately. I have some apologies to make.

The door is cracked open. I turn on the nearest flashlight to illuminate our way. Daniel sits in a very dark room. We had blown out all the candles, and he's neglected to turn on any of the flashlights.

"Can we talk outside?" I ask.

I light a couple candles with a match and turn on two more flashlights. Daniel abruptly leaves the bed and the room.

"How could you choose her over me?" He bursts out.

"What?"

Rage roughens his voice. "You betrayed me for some old woman we don't even know. You chose her over me. You are my girlfriend. You are supposed to take my side on things."

I muster up my best apology voice. "I am really sorry. I didn't think of it like that. I was just thinking that Rayleen needed help with her magic." Tears held back from stress breaks through.

He hugs me to comfort me. I wrap my arms around him, but it's a mixed bag of confusion and joy. Am I really supposed to take his side of things on all things; even when I think he's being stupid?

"I need my girlfriend to not undermine me when I'm trying to do what's best for our family." Daniel's voice quietens with reasoning.

Taking my feelings out of the equation, I work on getting us back to normal. I need that more. "I'm sorry. I didn't think of it like that. I didn't mean to hurt you. I'll do better next time. I didn't know that I was betraying you like that. I'm really sorry."

There's a very short pause to disconnect what I say. Give him a chance to respond but he doesn't. "But, Margie really is helping Rayleen. We figured out that she can only do air magic. And, we got her to float a lantern like a hot air balloon.

Margie's working on the basics with Rayleen and exercises to help her get stronger."

"You trust her?" Daniel asks.

"Yes." I push for sincerity. "And, Rayleen likes her. She's actually a really good teacher. She raised two sons and taught them how to use their magic."

"Okay." His hugging arms lower and uncross. Two forces lift me closer by grabbing my butt. "I know how you can make it up to me."

I playfully push him away. Afraid of Rayleen watching and getting a bad idea of romance. "Later. We need to take Crystal out to pee.

Are you going to come with us?"

Chapter 18

A haze in my head has me dragging my feet. I regret staying up, but I couldn't go to sleep until I had finished what I started.

Jaiden had a sketch hidden under the flipped notebook. A simple child-like hiding place, but a hiding place nonetheless.

She meant to have it hidden from people. People like me, who would go searching through her room. Searching for whatever she might be hiding and lying to me about.

Extra cautious for a private space to view my findings and to do some work had led me upstairs to an open room; third one down on the right. Unlike her, I know where to hide things. Tipping the night stand over, I collect the rest of my work.

My late night work is an improvement on what Jaiden had started.

The simplified version made better through a bigger focus on the pentagram. The words are nice, but people don't remember words as well as they do logos. I don't know even a tenth of the slogans for companies I shop at, but I can recall every logo.

But, I kept the words any way. They will be helpful, to those who bother to read them, to get the message across before people generally recognize the logo.

I made it less wordy however, and stopped the all caps yelling.

Fight for Equality & Peace

I recognize her intention for the drawings. They were obviously made for the rebellion I'm supposed to head; that I'm going to lead. I've accepted that much.

She had a page of information in point form too. Random thoughts. Maybe she was going to make pamphlets out of them. A well informative pamphlet explaining everything perfectly to what we're about; they who, what, where, when, why and how. Like a well-executed plan.

I still have my doubts about leading. Jaiden might be a bit ridiculous thinking that I'd be amazing at leading this rebellion. I have my own social anxieties; it comes and goes.

But, on the other hand, she also might be right. Put my anxieties aside, and I might be the best fit for the position. Who else would it be? Jaiden's made it obvious she can't do it; or won't do it. No one else from our ragtag group would even have a chance at pulling the right strings.

Wouldn't trust James to do anything useful.

Don't know anyone else.

I've had tastes of leadership before. I know I can lead, at least. Theoretically, it shouldn't be too hard apply school council leading to a rebellion. It takes understanding, passion and drive.

Which, had me up all night scheming and creating. Hundreds of hotel notepad pages gathered and drawn up; have either been slipped under the doors of every occupied room or distributed into every box and bag set out for delivery today.

The final handful of flyers, I take out of the room with me. Walking down one flight and right to our assigned rooms, I open the doors and put some of the flyers on the desks in each room.

As the final flyers are set down, I feel accomplished and exhausted. My hand is cramped. I contemplate falling into bed and napping before I have to work, but there is still much to do. Adrenaline will only push me a few more minutes.

The lounge lures me with coffee. I joyfully pay with tip money; an unexpected perk of my assignment. It's lukewarm but tastes like it was burnt. Jules' food is good but her coffee sucks. The liquid empties fast as I look around the lounge for Jerry. He's not here.

There aren't that many people in here. It's after the night dweller's supper and right before breakfast.

A jolt of caffeine wakes me up as it courses through my veins. It's immediate and comforting. With renewed energy, I set the mug down on the counter for Hectre to clear away. My search is over here. I move along.

Jerry's not in the lobby either. I walk around to the diner side to find him discussing with the supernatural that showed us back here; Jaiden's delivery friend.

They stop talking in hushed tones once they realize I'm here. Likely talking business they wouldn't want an outsider to hear. They look expectantly at me. Right to business then. "I'm hoping you have some paints that I could give to Rayleen."

"No." Jerry shoots me down immediately.

"Well, can it be added to a list somewhere; things to find?" The attitude floods my voice as my irritation with him rises.

"I doubt you have the amount of money that would be required to purchase it." He turns, as if dismissing me.

"I do have some money." I defend myself. "But if that's the case, then I'll just go out and find some."

"No. You're not going anywhere." Jerry argues.

"You know what?" The other man interferes with my imminent outburst. "I know where there's some paint. In those little Christmas ornament things we grabbed from that dollar store. Give her something to paint too. They're just taking up space. She can paint the little ornaments. None of us are going to use it before next Christmas, and the paint will be dry by then. She can even pay for it. It's from a dollar store, so a gold a piece."

"That sounds fine to me." I agree. Grateful to him for helping to defuse the situation.

"Fine." Jerry relents.

The other man goes deep into the dining area and comes back a few minutes later with five ornament painting kits. I dig into my pocket and give Jerry a five coin. "Thank you." I say more to the other man than I do Jerry, before I make my exit. Back upstairs with my stash.

I deliver one of the kits to Rayleen's room; just so I can say I did. The other four come with me to my room. I take out the paints and the tiny paint brushes. There isn't much paint here. Seventeen little pods of paint. Mostly, of silver, red, green and yellow. One pod of blue. Another kit switches out the yellow for gold. The one kit of five has black and white. While not what I wanted, I can work with it. The paint brushes are miniscule, but something I can work with as well. Stuffing the paint into the sides of my boots, and the paint brushes into my pockets, I stealthily walk right out the front door.

I walk around the side of the building and out towards the fast food restaurant across the street. The roads around here seem like they were main roadways; three of them surrounding the hotel.

I haven't seen much traffic, except for Jerry's trucks; oh those would be great to attach logos to. I need to find spray paint.

Brick seems like it would be too hard to paint on. That's unfortunately what covers many of the buildings in the area.

The window might provide a great surface to paint on. I rub the dirt and grim off it first with my jacket sleeve.

After drawing the logo a hundred times, I've gotten good at it. My stars are no longer lopsided. The small paint brush paints a thin line on the window. It glides easy, but also too thin. Half a paint section spreads over one image. The paint is only solid where there are globs of it. With such thin lines I have my doubts that the pictures will be seen from far away. I need bigger; clearer.

An idea springs to mind. Across the way is a building with a big grey concrete wall. I bound over to the building. Big and open, on a main road. Marketers would kill for this advertisement space.

Replicating the flyer onto the concrete wall. The little paints don't cover as much space as I would like, but I work with it. The colours show better on this surface and colour.

Splashing little bits of paint here and there. A mosaic of colours creates the large picture. It's not an image one could miss seeing.

I use up all the rest of the paint. Disposing the used up little containers on the ground as I empty them. They have no use now that they only have a miniscule amount of paint in them.

Taking a step back, I see my master piece and have no doubts that this one will not be missed. It's a shame that I had to use up all the paint on one singular work. I'll need to find more paint soon.

Jerry can kiss my ass.

Out of paint, and with no close prospective places to find spray paint, I collect my garbage and go back to the hotel. I'll talk to Jaiden when she gets back. She can find me some.

Breezing back into the hotel, with as much stealth as a half hour before, I go to the lounge to check on when my shift will start.

I get a feeling, when I see so many people, that I should have just gone up to my room. The boss will tell me to come in early, since I'm here already.

An unusual buzz fills the air.

"You coming in early?" Hectre asks me between customers.

"I came to see when you wanted me in today?" I ask innocently.

"Lunch and supper, but I'm not going to argue if you want to start now. That'll be a long day for you." Hectre leaves it with me.

"Alright, I'll pop back in before lunch." Excitement fills me when I get the go ahead to get some sleep. I turn quickly, so he doesn't get a chance to change his mind.

"Who do I talk to about this?" The deep voice cuts through all the rest of the noise. Curiosity turns me back around. One of my flyers is clenched in his hand and held up for Hectre to see.

"Look, I don't know. Half the people here have one of those. Go over there and go talk to them." Hectre points the man off to some people over by the slot machines.

"What do you want to know?" I ask, stepping closer.

"Who's in charge?" He asks pleasantly.

"Me." The immediate area quietens around me.

"You're in charge of this?" He asks for clarification.

The whole bar quietens to a level only described as one to hear a pin drop; to listen to what I have to say. "Yeah, I am. It's a revolution standing for equality and peace. Everyone, no matter the race or species, standing side by side to end the war."

"And, then what?" A girl pipes up in the crowd to my right.

I turn. "And then we work to keep peace. We work to make the world right and fair."

"What makes that any better than what we already have?" Searching through everyone, I can't find who is talking.

I address everyone. "You think this is better? Better than what you had, sure. No one wants to hide who they are. Treated as second class citizen because of how you were born. But, not better than what we could have. We have a chance to set up a new world. Are we going to let the same thing happen all over again? Maybe it's the humans who go into hiding this time. Maybe we just keep them for food. Or, we can do what's right. We can have everyone living in peace. A right to life. A right to freedom. We already have; my friends and me. The last city we lived in, we were able to have that peace. Supernaturals and humans living and working together. If we can do that there, then we can do that everywhere. It's spreading. The idea of peace and equality is spreading. In order to do that, we need to fight for it. We are asking you all to join us. Because you either do or you don't, but we're making it happen either way. Would love to have this go the easy way, and have all of your support."

"Just kill the bitch already." A new voice announces.

"Dude, shut up!" Jules tells him.

"No, I like things how they are." He raises his hand. A glimmer in his clenched fist is held over his shoulder. One fluid flick of his arm and the glimmer comes towards me.

A hand is in the way. I don't see the knife coming at me anymore. Drops of blood drip to the floor and flow down the arm. The arm comes down to hide behind his body.

Lurching forward, the man beside me runs and punches the one who attempted to stab me. A brawl starts with the first punch. One side with significantly larger number than the other. Two ganging up to each one.

This had been coming before I had come in; I reassure myself. The sides are already drawn. They know who they are and what they want.

A hand clenches my hair and pulls me back. I snap my elbow into her solar plexus then throat. She lets go of me to wheeze. I kick her away, but she only stumbles back one step. Hectre knocks her off her feet with a smashing punch to her cheek.

"Get out of here." He practically pushes me out the door with words alone, but everything in me says to stay and fight. Hectre runs past me. Whipping around to look, Hectre is punching down another man.

The violence is escalating. Tables are breaking and blood is scattering as much as fists are being thrown. Weapons brandished and scraping against other blades.

Hands clenched into fists, are ready to defend myself from the next attacker.

"Leave." My head twists to the voice. Jules pushes on me to get me to go. She's probably right. I dash out of the lounge, right by a glaring Jerry on his way to break up the fight.

Nowhere else to go, but back to my room.

The commotion in the lounge brings many rushing to help; particularly from the first floor. Other floors may be unaware of anything going on.

Exhaustion sets in, once again, as soon as I enter my room. No one else is here.

Might as well take that nap now. I don't think I'll be welcome at my shift.

Chapter 19

It catches the corner of my eye first. A multicoloured mural on a concrete wall; Fight for Equality and Peace with the symbol below it.

The imagery is too close to my depiction to ignore and push it off as a coincidence that my paper went missing just the night before.

It doesn't take a vision to know that I'm going to be in a lot of trouble with Jerry as soon as he sees that. I hope he doesn't see it soon. Only time can be good for a conversation like that.

It poses an answer and a question.

Someone I know must've taken the flyer, but who? Sara?

I itch to ask John if he knows anything, but I doubt he would. He's been with me delivering things and finding supplies; all day. He doesn't stop and doesn't careen his head, so I don't think he noticed.

We drive right by, turning down the road and into the parking lot. John parks and we get out to a chill in the air.

I grab the clipboard to return it to Jerry; hopefully without actually having to see him. John takes the grocery bags.

Through the doors of the hotel, her strong voice pulls the two of us to the opposite direction; to the lounge. It only gets louder as we get closer; interspersed with other voices. They talk over top of one another in some sort of disagreement.

"There is no other choice if you're decent person. To choose to enslave someone rather than push for equal rights is the mark of a horrible person." Nique pushes.

What's happening?

"They did it to us! We've been hiding who we are for thousands of years." A deep voice bursts.

"Not one single human alive is responsible for what happened. You can't blame all the humans today, for what their ancestors did thousands of years ago. It's not fair.

It's 2013 and we are in a time where we should have equality. The past couple hundred years, humans have come a long way in equality. Not perfect, not even close, but it's a work in progress.

The rebellion will make equality a work in progress and not just write it off, like you're doing."

Oh no.

With Nique's words, I get a gut feeling that I know who stole the paper. For someone who wasn't interested in leading the rebellion, she sure isn't acting like it.

John touches my arm to gain my attention. He points into the crowd. I follow the finger and spot Sara. John walks off towards her.

I scan the rest of the crowd and don't find any others from our group, but there are some familiar faces. Acquaintances from delivery runs, Hectre, Ziam, and a few passing faces.

My arm is grabbed tightly. Jerry jerks me towards him and towards the kitchen. "We need to talk."

He lets me go, but there's a steely expectation for me to follow. One, which I dare not go against. I look for help amongst my friends, but not one of them is paying attention to me. They are too caught up in the argument to notice.

We enter into the kitchen. Jules looks over their shoulder and smiles a greeting. I return it and wave.

Jerry expects me in the freezer. He closes the door behind us. It's much colder in here today. I hope he's not planning on freezing me to death.

At least Jules knows where I am.

Would Jules save me?

"This is her second speech today. The first one caused a riot and destroyed the lounge. I have no control over those people anymore." Jerry seethes. "Whatever this is, you need to shut it down.

"I didn't do this." I sputter and defend in a loss of words. "I don't know what's going on exactly; I've been out all day."

"She needs to leave, if you can't control her."

There is nothing else in my bag of tricks. No escape and no choice but to bend to his power struggle; lest I risk something bad happening.

"No, I can't control her. I can't control her as much as I can't control anyone else." Reasoning turns to begging. "But, you need to let her stay. I'll make another deal."

"I told you I'm neutral." All composure has been lost. Wild intimidation of power. He uses his size to square up to me, to tower over me.

A mental note controls my actions. A calm and sweet voice will hopefully speak to his reasonable side, and then I can speak to his business side. "And, I told them to keep you out of it. I told them all that you wanted to remain neutral and keep out of it. And that is something that I'll talk to Dominique about, but your hand is forced now.

You said it yourself, that you can't control the crowd. That means they like what she's saying.

So, you essentially have two options. Either denounce the flyer and use a scapegoat and tell everyone that you are against it and kick everyone out that is for the rebellion. Which, looks like you'd be losing three quarters of your business.

Or, go with the news and show solidarity to your new customer base. And, by the looks of that crowd, you're actually gaining some customers from this.

The lounge is packed with people, and I don't recognize most of them. And, chances are most will order from you. They are all bound to get hungry or thirsty eventually; need consumable items. Word spreads and more people will come.

I don't condone her going behind our backs to do this, but it's done now and we have to deal with the consequences. We can make a new deal for the new situation."

The freezer door handle scrapes, scaring me, and the door slides open. It's a bit of a relief, no matter who it might be.

"I want you out; all of you." He speaks over my shoulder. I turn to see who he's watching.

Seeing Nique there is not as much of a relief, rather could be more problematic than anything. She might unravel my work.

"That's a shame, because we're not going." Nique glares at me when I try to talk. "I'm done with Jaiden's deals with you because you're just screwing us over and over again."

"Our deals have been fair a-"

"I'm not done talking, and you're interrupting me." Her voice booms and almost echoes in the small room. She's assertive. "Now. Jaiden's nice and sweet, and it's great that she was able to get us a place here. But, I'm taking over.

Now, you can continue being manager of, whatever it is that you actually do. And, we'll continue working; that's fair. We will work for our stay, and we will be staying. But, we get our freedom back. You don't own us.

You will allow us to hold our rebellion meetings here. I don't care about your association with it or if you just look the other way, but they will be happening. If you disagree, then we'll just take over and kick you out. You know we have enough power and people to do so."

"You can't threaten me. You overestimate your power. You're no stronger than a human." Jerry tries to call her bluff.

"Really? Chad's loyalty is to Jaiden and not you. Did she forget to tell you that? He's on our side, along with his whole gang. Plus all the people out there, and add in everyone I spoke to when I snuck out earlier.

I put flyers in all your deliveries today. How many people do you think will answer those flyers? If you haven't got it yet; you have no choice. This is the new deal. Take it, or you're gone." Nique takes one step back. "Come on Jaiden. We're getting out of here."

There would be no point to my staying, even if I could talk at this moment. Even if I could bear talking with Jerry any longer. Anything I would say would go against the point of Nique's deal. She was making a point. Jerry would no longer hold a position of power of her. Between her taking control of the rebellion and forcing the new deal on Jerry, she is exercising leadership skills.

However, she's also making an enemy out of Jerry when he could be an ally.

I leave Jerry's power grasp and follow after Nique. Out of the freezer, John and Sara wait just outside for us. Ready to rush in at a moment's notice and save us should something have gone awry.

The four of us walk out the door. I speed a little to catch Nique's ear as she turns to go back to the tables. "Can we talk?" I ask her.

"Sure." Nique leads us to all the way upstairs and to an open room. We all settle inside; door locked.

In a moment, I realize I'm still holding the clipboard in my hands. It had been forgotten in the tense conversation. The board is shuffled in my grasp. A sting appears in my hand from where I had been gripping it hard. Red and indented, a line distorts my hand.

"So, what have you been up to today?" I break the silence.

"Not sleeping." She jokes. My head tilts and smile falls. Irritation rises. "Relax. I found your flyer."

"You mean broke into my room and went through my things." I accuse.

"You suck at hiding things." She says as if that makes it right. My eyes almost roll at the insult, but it's also a note for later. "I found your flyer and I thought I would get to work. So, I revamped it and made up a bunch of flyers. Distributed them out to the deliveries and under everyone's doors. Then I snuck out and painted that symbol on a wall."

"What did you do to the flyer that I had made?"

"Put it in the garbage." Nique answers an alternate meaning to my question.

"I meant that you said you revamped it. But thanks."

"Oh. I'll show you." She takes the notepad on the desk, and starts drawing with the provided hotel pen. Nique hands me over that paper once she's finished.

"It looks fine." I personally liked the other version better, but I may be biased. "But you still had no right to make a bunch of flyers and put them in for Jerry's customers. He wanted to be neutral."

"No one is ever neutral. Neutral means keeping your mouth shut, and that's just as bad as being one of the bad guys." Her anger twitches her face. "Look whatever, it's done. And you're welcome. People saw me and my face. Isn't that what you wanted? They're excited about it."

"The symbol could cause some confusion." Sara interjects conversationally and physically. Nique's impending rage explosion defuses. "It's an insignia for the Council. You're basically stating that the Council is behind this." Sara veers the conversation off to a new direction.

My jaw drops. That wasn't in any of my research. I couldn't find the symbol, and I didn't see it when I was on the Council's website.

Is this fraud? Could I get in legal trouble for this?

"Should we change it?" I ask.

"It's too late now. People are already associating the logo with this, spreading it everywhere, so it's done with. The Council might as well do something for us. James started this. We can say we assumed we had the Council's support." My heart drops with Sara's words. If that's true then there might not be any taking this back. I hadn't meant for things to happen this quickly. We were supposed to be in the planning stage, not the doing stage.

"All day, everyone I've talked to, I've told people to get the word out, create identical flyers, and tag buildings. There's even a man who said he could weld a sign together for us. No one said anything about it." Nique says.

"So, what do we do now?" Sara asks.

I shrug when a couple eyes turn to me. Looking to Nique, I let her take lead on this. My hand goes up in motion to her.

"Go for supper."

"Shouldn't we figure out a clear plan for the rebellion before we go back down there?" I vocalize.

"We can do that later. Besides peace and equality, what would we really need to plan? I'm starving. Let's go." She up and leaves the three of us behind in her rampage to the lounge. We catch up to her after looks exchanged and a bit of jogging.

Nique leads us to the edge of a pack. They quieten down as they realize that she's returned. Chairs scrape the floor as they are moved to join the table and make room for us.

"Something wrong?" His English accent stands out in his smooth voice. I see double, as next to him is an identical male with the same contrasting dark hair and light skin.

"No, not at all. Just a little talk." She holds her hand out motioning to me palm up. "Jaiden was out all day and needed to be caught up." She heightens her voice to a level everyone in the room can hear. "I want to introduce you all to Jaiden. She's second in command. If you can't find me, find her and she'll deal with it. She's got as much say as I do."

In part, I'm sure this is some sort of revenge plan, but it's also in alignment with our previous conversation about our roles; just a more high profile public role than I would have liked to play.

The embarrassment of dozens of eyes turning their attention to me is nothing abnormal. It feels like a small switch up from the 'this is my daughter and one day your boss' introduction Jacob used to do to me.

"Very nice to meet you. I'm Cole." He shakes my hand. Curiously and suddenly, his eyes search mine.

"Something wrong?" The identical man next to him straightens on edge. A hand goes under the table; reaching for something.

"Calm down." He lets go of my hand to put it on his identical companion. "I just can't read her."

"What kind of reading?" I ask; treading carefully forward.

"Thoughts. I can hear the thoughts of people I touch. But, not you." He watches me with amusement, while his brother looks at me concerned.

I have no other knowledge on this but link it back to Calli's explanation at our meeting. It's certainly something I should research tonight; a dreamer's mind/soul lock or similar abilities in other supernaturals.

I doubt I'll find anything, but I can start there. Seems like much of my family history was scrubbed from the internet. There's a Marshall's Law that I can only find references to, but never the law itself.

Then there's him; someone who can apparently read minds through touch.

Hectre clears his throat to gain our attention. "Jaiden, can you help me with something in the freezer. It'll just take a moment."

"Sure." I smile to Cole in apology, but I'm thankful that I won't have to explain anything for the moment.

My phone weighs heavily in my pocket. I'll make sure to research something before I have to go back. A washroom excuse will let me bypass without question; or that might be too suspicious.

I follow Hectre passed the bar. Dropping off the clipboard on the counter; glad to get rid of it. We go into the kitchen.

Jules is missing from their post. Food is cooking on the stove and sitting in the warming trays. Leftover food remnants sit on a cutting board next to an abandoned knife. Evidence of the chef's presence and yet said chef is nowhere to be found.

"In the freezer. I'm not familiar with human nutrition needs and Jules has the rest of the day off. Would you mind?" Hectre pulls on the handle.

"Okay."

Hectre opens the door.

The comradery ends when I spot Jerry inside, and a push from behind sends me into the lion's den. Hectre slides the door shut.

"Give me a reason why I shouldn't kill you." Jerry growls ominously. A knife poised in his fist. He didn't take the power struggle too kindly; thank you Dominique. Now I'm going to die here.

My hands go up in defence. Thoughts go to how likely I would succeed in escaping this room alive; all scenarios I can imagine lead to death.

"Because I don't want to die." I answer too honestly. "Self-preservation. And, despite of Dominique's thing earlier. Uh. She wasn't completely wrong, but she also wasn't completely right.

You were being cautious and generous. We obviously failed the test as a whole. However, it doesn't seem like the others have freedom restrictions, and most of those people are complete strangers.

You want the humans to stay inside, and away from supernaturals. That's fair as far as their safety is concerned, but then again they need to take Crystal out and about. Dominique was right, in that it hasn't been a completely fair deal, but deals are rarely fair.

Dominique appears to be most of the issue; right. The ownership of the rebellion she's overtaken is a problem. You don't support the rebellion, or else you'd have relented by now. It isn't fair to you to have your business taken over by a rebellion after you took in some people on a favour. This all means that we need to make a new deal. One that benefits you more than any inconvenience we are."

"I want you gone." He waves and thrusts the knife in my direction, but he's too far away from me for it to be anything more than a vicious threat.

"No. I can't do that. Where would we go? I can get them to move meetings, and keep it out of here and out of your business; that's fair." Dominique would never let us leave now. She's too stubborn for that. "So, you'll need to figure out something else. Maybe something we can retrieve for you, or you can send us on a suicide mission to defeat your enemies, or something."

He retreats into his head. Opting for pacing back and forth a few steps as he thinks. When he has it, I know. He stops and turns to me. The knife points threateningly at me. "James Ellesworn. Get him here. He's got a bounty on his head, and I would like to redeem it."

So, he means to kill him and turn him in, or capture him and turn him in. He's choosing sides and it's not ours. Unless, this could be a test. Something to see if I really could get James here. "Alright." I promise despite thinking I won't be able to get into contact with James; let alone get him here. "It's going to take some time though. He's deep in hiding right now. I don't know where he is."

"You've got time, if we have a deal." He sticks his hand out to shake on it.

I'm not ready yet. "I get James here for you for your part of the deal. We'll continue to work for our stay, but keep our business away from your business. Our group gets freedom of movement.

For my part. I want your silence. No one can know I'm still making deals with you." I summarize all that the deal encompasses.

"But you'll get James here. And, you won't tell him I'm going to kill him." Jerry clarifies his stance; as if I didn't piece that together.

"I promise I won't tell him that you plan on killing him." I word it out completely to help him. "Dominique doesn't like him anyway. He's bad for the rebellion plans. He's got antiquated ideas about what the new world should look like, which aren't in line with what we want." I make up an excuse. Something to excuse why a rebellion working for James, would want him dead and just hand him over. I need credibility.

"Deal. I'll play along." Jerry concedes. I shake his hand. He makes a show of power by squeezing to the point of pain.

"Great." I almost sigh in relief. My heart pounds, but at least it will continue to beat; for now and in the imminent future.

He knocks hard on the door five times in an even beat. The door slides open, not because of Hectre but because of Jules. Utter confusion crossing their features. Hectre is across near the stove. He looks a little frightened.

"Are you okay?" Jules asks.

"Yes, I'm fine." I script out. I keep my face low and dash out.

I escape to the soundtrack of an exclamation. "Jaiden! Hectre? What happened? Jerry?"

Stopping momentarily with my own confusion. The room has been mostly cleared out. Everyone Dominique had surrounded us with, Dominique, Sara and John, they are all gone.

Where is everyone?

A moment's stopping is too much in an escape; my logical brain reasons. Moving along in a quick pace out of the area, I search for any trace of where they went.

It's strange. I can't help but feel like something bad has happened. A pit in my heart knows something bad happened.

Maybe they went back to their rooms; I reason.

My next stop is the three rooms Jerry placed them in. Daniel, Alexa and Rayleen's room is empty. I nearly walk into the one room, but stop when I hear muffled talking.

DeAngelo, Chantel, Kelly, Miles, and Shawn. I list off as I see them; checking them off the imaginary list. Shifts are done at suppertime for the labour crews.

They turn their attention to me. "Have you guys seen the others?"

"No?" Kelly looks uninterested.

"Not since this morning." Miles answer is not helpful.

"Why?" DeAngelo gets up from the chair; concerned.

"Long story. Short version is Dominique, Sara, John and I went to the lounge for supper. I got pulled away to help Hectre move something in the freezer, and by the time I returned, everyone had disappeared." I tell the room.

"Do you know about this?" Miles holds up one of Dominique's flyers.

"Dominique made those. She kind of started a rebellion by herself." As a second thought, I feel the need to inform them of their newfound freedom. "And, made a new deal with Jerry. We all have the freedom to come and go as we please. We still have to work to stay.

Dominique passed those out today, and got the message out, without discussing it with anyone. So, we're going with it.

We weren't aware it was the Council's insignia until after everything was done and passed out. But, it's a bit late to take that back now. And we need to find a new place to hold meetings that isn't the lounge, and preferably not in the hotel.

Anyway, it's weird that everyone disappeared. I have a bad feeling about it. Like something's wrong. I should continue to look for them. Let them know I'm looking for them, if they come back here." I excuse myself. I can't handle any questions at this time. I don't know if I'd be able to hold back the tears threatening to fall.

"I'll help." DeAngelo offers. I pause to wait for him. He grabs his coat. Within the time he takes, no one else offers, so DeAngelo and I leave together.

Chapter 20

"Supper's here." Daniel sets the tray down on the bed, and then hands each of us a plate. A simple spaghetti with a white sauce; maybe alfredo. He returns to the tray and pulls a small plate of raw meat off it. Crystal chirps in excitement. She snaps as it gets down around face level. "Down. Don't bite." He drops the plate on the ground from a couple inches up.

Rayleen and I tear into the spaghetti. Hunger ravenous after lunch was essentially skipped. No one showed up with food at lunch. When Daniel went to check, he found a destroyed lounge and no one willing to help or let him into the kitchen.

Lunch turned into leftover snack foods from our bags. Most of which, ended up going to Rayleen.

The pot steams. Daniel pours each of us a cup of the boiling hot tea. It's going to be a long while before we'll be able to drink it without burning our tongues.

Rayleen immediately takes hold of her cup. "It's too hot to drink right now." I warn her. "You'll have to wait until it cools."

A deep breath in, she blows onto the tea fast. A bit of the tea splashes up. Rayleen adjusts her stream of air a little, until the tea starts circulating.

Rayleen lifts the tea to her lips to test the drink. The liquid fast disappearing as she guzzles it down to half. She blows on it again.

It takes just a moment for me to realize she must've successfully cooled the tea down with magic. A cold breath of air to quickly cool down the hot beverage.

"Do you mind cooling mine down too?" Daniel asks. He holds out his cup for Rayleen to repeat the same spell. Rayleen takes the proffered cup and blows into it. When she gives the cup back, Daniel takes a sip of the tea. "Thanks."

"You're welcome." Rayleen says before she takes my cup and blows into it without my having to ask.

She isn't supposed to be wasting her magic like this, but it is nice to see her do something more than just float things. Super cooling air seems a little more practical than floating a paper airplane within an arm's length from you.

"That's pretty cool. Is that something Margie taught you?" Daniel inquires.

"Mmhm." Rayleen swallows her mouthful of pasta. "She's been teaching me to control the temperature of my air magic. I can blow cold air really fast."

"Comes in handy. Good job. Keep it up." Shocked, I stare at him as though he is an alien. With all the trouble he's given us about training with Margie, he's not allowed to act this nice about it. He notices my stare. Daniel puts down his cup and fork. He clears his throat before he talks. "I want to apologize to you both. I've done a lot of crappy things lately, that neither of you deserve. It's, I've been angry and scared. That doesn't excuse it though. I'd love for you to forgive me, but I understand if that takes some time. I'll do better. I promise that I'll control myself more."

The apology comes out of left field, but don't skip a beat in forgiving him. "Thank you." My hand reaches out to grab a hold of his. We lock fingers together. Squeezing twice to his once.

Rayleen stays quiet and concentrates on eating her food and drinking what is left of her tea. She's less accepting of his apology. It's okay.

Scraping claws against wood is a familiar sound. Crystal is missing from her spot for dinner. I find her at the door.

"I'll take her." Daniel offers. He gets up.

"I'll go." Rayleen puts down her fork. Jumping up and running to the door.

"Coat." I shout after her.

I look at my uneaten food, then back at the three making their exit. I don't want to be left alone. "I guess we'll all go." I mutter to myself.

Twirling one last fork full of spaghetti and release it into my mouth. Not to gracefully eating the large mouthful. Coat on and boots on for all, then we leave.

Daniel entwines his hand in mine. He brings it up to his mouth and kisses it. Hand in hand, we walk down the long way to the outside.

A large ruckus is happening in the lounge. Supper time must be really busy around here.

Crystal and Rayleen run ahead; excited for the running room and fresh air. They know where to go and what to do.

Daniel tugs on my hand in the middle of the parking lot. I'm tugged to him like a magnet and metal.

Lips cover mine in an instant. My eyes close automatically as his lips cover mine, moving in harsh movements. I wrap my arms around his neck for support. The back of my head is grasped by his hand as Daniel forces his tongue into my mouth. I play with his tongue a bit, in a heated passion from buried anger.

I moan, as a heated bubbling grows inside me from the feeling of his hand sliding up my shirt; rubbing my side.

He pecks my lips one last time and pulls his hand out of my shirt. His other hand scrapes at my skin, sure to leave white marks, as it is forcibly removed.

Opening my eyes, I find a rage filled stare aimed in my direction. His hungered look unnerves me. At one point it made me feel special, but right now it terrifies me.

His mouth snarls and clamps down on Daniel's neck. A gargled gasp. Pain filled screech is short lived as his breath dies when a clump of tissue breaks way into Darius' mouth.

Warm blood squirts and splatters over my front; some runs down my face. I can feel nothing else.

A bloody devilish grin as Darius lets Daniel's body fall to the ground. There's no way anyone can survive having half their throat ripped out.

Daniel is dead.

Darius spits out the chunk of meat. A whimpered cry escapes on impact; jumpstarting a wave of desperate cries of pain. White hot pain encapsulates my chest.

His nose flares with each nasally breathe. Eye bore into me, holding me captive to his gaze. My chest rises and falls with each of my own quick breaths. Warm tears falls.

"You're coming with me." My head shakes. I can't voice a syllable. Instead, I look down to Daniel. Blood pools on the concrete; more and more as he lies there motionless. "I gave her to you, I can take her back."

My gaze jolts up.

Darius lunges for Rayleen, but her tiny protector gets in the way. His foot comes down crushing her small body with a squeak. She was merely a road bump in his path.

Darius' body covers all of Rayleen. He blocks her entirely from my view until he turns around.

With all her might, her tiny body struggles in shakes against his grip crushing her to his body.

"I'll return her when you return to me."

He runs.

Chapter 21

Jaiden stalks off with Hectre. I watch them tuck in behind the counter, and go off into the kitchen. There's a slight lure to follow them; purely out of curiosity.

But, I know better, and I don't wish to get caught up in whatever he needs done; cooking, cleaning, fixing, moving inventory, and the such. Jaiden always seems to be finding herself helping with chores around her, even when she has no reason to be; the person everyone calls when they need an extra set of hands.

I wonder what exactly her role was the last time she was here. She never spoke much about her in between; summaries are the best of what she's described.

Of the time, she said she was a delivery girl. But, she seems like one of those overachievers, never content to just be one thing; reaching beyond her job title.

I sit down in a vacant chair across from the twins. Neither of them looks more than human; though I should know better by now. I hadn't even thought to think about what kind of powers they might have; something I'll have to remember in the future.

John and Sara claim seats next to me on the left. Sara reverses quickly to pull over another for Jaiden's return. She'll sit between John and Sara. A buffer, I figure.

I push my attention back on the twins. Dark brown hair frames all around their faces, and contrasts greatly against white skin. Each has a neatly trimmed full beard; trimmed to the same length. Eyes, as dark as their hair, flit around between the three of us.

They mirror each other perfectly in a freaky samesies twin thing.

The one on the left, the one only distinguished by a jean jacket, touched Jaiden, and told everyone he couldn't read her.

I figure, that's a good place to start. "So, you can read minds?" I push for more information.

I'm cautious to be weary of my thoughts. Wondering how many times he's must've heard people thinking that they must not think about a particular thing. Better than the alternatives I suppose; hearing any nasty thought someone might have.

"Only when I'm touching people." He eases my mind; slightly. "Except for, with Connor, I can read his mind anytime I want. He can't read minds, but he's a lie detector." With one brother cleared, the other may have just become a bit of an issue. It isn't said, but I hope Connor has the same limitations as Cole.

The unmistakable sound of crashing plates swings everyone's heads to the source. The room claps, and so do I; it's customary, if not embarrassing.

Jules has her head down, looking down at the food, and broken dishes. A sigh draws up, and down her shoulders. She takes no joy in the broken, and strewn about dishes. I still my hands from compassion; hesitant that it may not ease the embarrassment as much as previously thought.

Jerry might even have repercussions for this. He might force her to pay for any broken dish. Pay for any food wasted.

She bends down to pick up the pieces as the lounge goes back to their own things. As I'm about to rise to help, Sara goes over to help Jules pick up the broken pieces of the dishes she had been collecting from around the room.

It doesn't take more than two people to pick up a tray half full of dirty dishes, so I feel alright with not offering my help, and settle back.

"Jaiden, right?" Cole quietly asks for a confirmation of her name, and continues with a nod from his twin. "It has to be hereditary." He says to Connor. They're already going on about a conversation. I pick it up only at Jaiden's name. Cole had mentioned he could read Connor's mind without touch, perhaps their conversation had been within their heads, and this is the first I'm hearing from them.

"Sorry? What do you mean?" I ask.

They both pay me their attention, but Connor answers my question. "Her mind guard. It's either something she's practiced at placing, or she was born with it."

Cole shakes his head. "No, it has to be hereditary. It was immediate and strong, not something thrown up when I connected. I couldn't get anywhere in her head; not even a peek; not even a knock. Most people don't just have a bullet proof mind guard up for no reason; unless you constantly have something to hide." There is accusation within his words.

I eye Connor up, not daring to lie if he can feel it. It's hard not to notice the attention of everyone else; all eyes on me. They too, want to know more about Jaiden. Maybe she was right in trying to keep to the background. Something I made impossible by announcing her as my second-in-command; whoops.

Too late now. I didn't know about these two when I did that.

"Oh, yeah, it's hereditary." I answer vaguely. I don't want to give more than needed, but I can't make her untrustworthy by telling people she's constantly hiding things on purpose.

"Really? What is she?" Cole pushes further.

I wasn't ready for my vagueness to be questioned, and the word escapes me for what she had mentioned she was posing as. "Umm." I fill in begging for more time to answer. She said to say empath, but would they have that ability?

I can't tell all these people that she's a seer. She doesn't want people to know. And, I'm still not entirely sure if it's safe for other people to know.

Darius might not care without reason, but Sandra might come looking for her if she finds out. She may have been skeptical of me, for good reason, but Sandra's too cunning to ignore the benefit of real prophet. Knowing the future could be dangerous in the wrong hands, and that Jaiden wouldn't last if taken, I can't let them know.

I don't trust any of these people yet.

"Don't know or can't say?" I shut my mouth tighter, but Connor takes his answer either way. "It's a secret then."

Cole takes a hold of my hand lying carelessly on the table. The thought of Jaiden is already in my mind. I try to think of nothing but my hatred of the forced entry to my thoughts; jealous of Jaiden's ability to keep him out. And, try to rip my hand from his vice grip.

"Definitely a secret, but not in a bad way." Cole pulls back. I snatch my hand back, and keep it close to my body. "I apologize, but you were acting sketchy, and it doesn't take Connor to know you were hiding information. It was in my best interest to find out what secret you were hiding. It's hard to trust that strangers have the best intentions with their secrets, especially when they're staring up a rebellion. But, you do. While I believe they may be misplaced, I can respect your wish for it to remain a secret. And, I think, everyone else can too."

Cole and Connor visibly relax with Cole's admission, but the others only seem half appeased; more curious and peeved.

I seethe through my teeth. "Never do that again." Flashing my anger with my eyes, I warn him in an open ended threat.

I don't know how much information he got, but he has to know about Jaiden as a prophet; at the least.

His words let on to more than that. I don't know how the mind reading works. Does he just read direct thoughts, or can he take anything stuck in my head; more? How deep can he dive?

"Shit!" Sara shouts, standing next to Jules, and the collected dishes, gazing out the window.

Tumbling out of my seat, I bump with others, scrambling to the window to see.

Darius is outside dumping a slumping body to the ground, and staring down Alexa.

As some go to the window to watch, others race outside to catch him. I dash to go outside.

The thought flashes that I don't have a good weapon to confront him with, but there's no time to grab anything. I have to hope one of these people have something bigger, and sharper than my pocket knife.

We can take him out here and now.

End this here and now.

A crowd around me covers much of my view. The far distance is more seeable than what's right in front of me. Darius turns with Rayleen entangled in his grasp; running from the emerging crowd.

The people open up once we are out of the bottle neck of the entrance. Resistance releases at this point.

A body lies in a growing pool of blood in the middle of the way. Body faced away from me, yet, something inside me recognizes it as Daniel. Same clothes, hair, and in the right association.

Daniel is dead.

Alexa watches Darius as he leaves with Rayleen. Not one shout or sign of resistance from either girls. Is she letting Darius take Rayleen? Was this part of some plan? The questions switch my aim from Darius to Alexa.

I'm upon her in moments.

"Did you let Darius take Rayleen?" Alexa does nothing but stare at the retreating form. Dead eyes and mouth agape. "Is he kidnapping her?" She's not responsive. "Alexa!" I shout her name in frustration. "Talk to me!"

She's useless. I resist the urge to shake her or slap her out of it. Those things only work in the movies; right? But, they would make me feel better.

A cold chill raises the hairs on the back of my neck with an epiphany; Darius took Rayleen, and Alexa wasn't a willing participant. She's in shock. And, Darius is running away.

I turn to see where Darius was escaping from. He is no longer there. I widen my search, but he is no longer anywhere.

Darius is out of view, but those chasing after him are not. Most have given up already; they are heading back. Others are standing and watching as the opportunity runs away.

There's no way I could run fast enough to catch up with him even as fast as I am. I am no match for a vampire with a head start. I'm not even sure I would be any match for any vampire.

Taking stock of my surrounding in quick moments.

The death of Daniel on the pavement. Someone putting, a barely alive, Crystal out of her misery. A catatonic Alexa stands in shock in the aftermath. Rayleen kidnapped by her cousin's ex-boyfriend; again. Darius is getting away.

Elation turns to sorrow in just a quick moment.

An engine roars. Zippy movements pull it out of the stall. Putting myself between the truck and the driver's goal without a second thought; it stops right before it hits me.

Ziam shouts out a declining window. "Out of the way, or get in." He plays to the best reaction I could have hoped for.

I choose the latter, and get inside the passenger seat. Barely inside, and in the seat, I'm pulled back, as Ziam slams the gas pedal as far down as he can.

Arms fly out in front, and to the door to brace myself. I hold on tighter in the knowledge that I'm not wearing a seat belt.

Suspending myself in spot; my back bumps the seat twice. My stomach lurches in sync with the truck.

Ziam drives as fast as the vehicle will let him. Faster and faster, turning the corner, until we catch up to those in chase. Passing them, we expect to see Darius just ahead, but he's gone.

Left, right, there's no sight of Darius.

"Where is he?" I ask the universe, but Ziam is the only one listening.

"I don't know. Gone." He answers back. The truck slows.

"No." I refuse. "No."

"We can keep going, or swing around. Someone we passed might have a better idea." Ziam stops the truck completely.

I want to tell him to keep going, but I don't know where. We stop in a large four way intersection. Parking lots and sparse business buildings allow for a clear view in all directions; ground and sky.

Not one bit of it gives way to a hint of Darius.

"Turn around. We missed something. You drove really fast, too fast for the others, and too fast for him. He had to have ducked down one of the side roads." We went too fast; that has to be it.

Ziam turns the truck around, and tracks back to John, and three other people. I recognize their faces, but we haven't had our introductions yet; allies of the revolution.

They're stopped. We roll down our windows to speak with them.

Frustration scrunches all of their faces. If I had a mirror to look into, the same look would be in my own features. I can feel the angered rigidness in my jaw, and eyes.

John changes out of his wolf form. Furred skin shifts with the bone underneath.

The transformation looks like it would be nauseating and painful, two expressions John just barely shows as it's happening. It takes away from the oddly funny sight of a humanized wolf in people clothes.

I avert my eyes, not bearing to watch any longer. It's gross and weird. The change feels like something private; something I shouldn't be witnessing.

"I lost their scents. They're gone." I look to him as I figure his talking means completion. The transformation is over, almost, too fast for what it is.

John's regret is written in his eyes. He won't look at me.

Shoulders quake as he catches his breath. The transformation must be exhaustive.

"It was your stupid truck. If you hadn't passed us, we wouldn't have lost sight of him. And, he could have smelt more than gas fumes." The one argues; thoroughly angered by our interference. He blocks my view of John as he comes closer.

I wonder if these three have had their own interactions with Darius. A motivation for their anger, and want to go after Darius personally. Beyond what everyone else had; killing someone outside our doorstep.

It's foolish to think that Darius and Sandra did absolutely nothing for the whole winter. Darius wasn't just stalking Alexa in the shadows or sneaking away with her to make out. Sandra would have attacked us if she had her way.

Four months is a long time. They could have created more bases, levelled cities, and murdered thousands of people.

All four of them try to get closer to the window, to speak with us easier.

"What way was he going? Where could he have gone in the half a second it took us to pass you?" I turn it back around on him. It wasn't all our fault. We didn't see him at all. They're the ones who were tracking him, and lost sight of him.

"Down this road." He tries to defend himself further. "He's fast."

"So, where did he go? Turned down a road? Ducked into a store? He had to go somewhere." I press. "Because he didn't just go straight. And, he didn't just disappear. We were too fast, and we would have caught him. But, we didn't see him at all. I didn't see him after he split the parking lot."

"Let's go back to the hotel." Ziam interjects.

"No." My frustration turns on Ziam. "I'm not going back until I find Rayleen."

"He's gone. There's nothing we can do." He kicks back.

"He has to be close." I say. Further away each second we talk this over and over.

"Or, he had a dragon waiting for him; like last time." John tries to help Ziam with reasoning. "Magic to cover scent."

How does he know that? I question before the answer pops into my mind.

Jaiden.

A short cool down stops the battle between us all. Ziam breaks the silence. "Look, I don't care what you do, but I have to get this truck back. We don't have much good gas left, and Jerry will be pissed if he finds out we wasted too much of it for this. I'm sorry for your loss, but she's gone. There's nothing we can do now."

He's wrong. I want to tell him as such, but I feel like it would be wasted words on a closed mind.

Throwing the door open pushes the four outside back and out of my way. They wouldn't have been hit, but the air breeze touches them all.

I get out through the door, and slam it shut behind me. "I'm going to look for her."

"Dominique." John chastises with only my name.

"John." I dare him to argue with angered tone and glare. He can do what he wants, but I'm going to do what I need to do.

He relents with sinking shoulders. "Head back." John waves them off. "We're going to look around some more. See if I can catch his scent again."

The others file their way into the truck with their goodbyes, and good lucks. Ziam takes them back to the hotel.

I wish to get started, but John doesn't do anything. "So can you— umm. Do you smell in this form or do you have to morph?"

An eyebrow goes up, and I imagine his tongue sticks to the roof of his mouth in distaste from what I said. "My smell is better in my lycan form. And, we generally go with transform or shift." He informs me. He grins and shakes his head. Air blows out audibly through his nose, likened to a snort of laughter. "Morphing sounds like something the Power Rangers would do."

Any other time, I might loosen up with his sign of peace.

"Okay?" I look at him, expecting him to get the cue to change. He's wasting time. I raise my eyebrow in irritation.

John's shoulders rise, then sink with an audible fast breath out his mouth.

Eyes bore into mine. Changes to his face structure grow out towards me. He grits his sharpening teeth. A small growl escapes at the same time his right eye twitches.

An abundance of hair grows from every pore; every spot on his bare skin. He's wolf like, but also human too.

The change happens incredibly quick for what it is; a full body transformation.

Not like what I'd expect. Many movies and shows go with a bone breaking total wolf transformation; the human body changing into a wolf. Not, this. Not something in between; not something more human than animal.

Is it because of his human mother? Is he more human like because of her? Or, are all werewolf transformations like his?

So focused on the physical changes, I almost miss the rest of his reactions to the change. Scowls and near growls of pain. Twitching muscles. Clenched fists. The barest of blood from the new features blends so well, is gone so quickly, it is a near miss.

The clothes look strange on him. So often, more than not, werewolves in movies tend to be naked. They either remove the clothes before that transformation, or it breaks off during the transformation; somehow.

They also look more like actual wolves; or angry monkey face, wolf eared, and fur suit creatures.

He waves his snout around. I can hear him sniffing the air. John walks around the area with intent. Scenting slowly as he walks back to where we had originally crossed him in the truck.

Right towards some restaurants and stores. Down, a little ways, to the left, and to a road between more stores and houses; both named 37th street despite not meeting up in a perfect line.

Left we go, down to the houses. Two blocks down to apartments. A quick, but leisurely pace. Right, left, right. A stroll by housing, parking lots, and trees. All, with no sight and no scent.

A hospital comes up on our right.

John stops walking. I think he might have final gotten something; so far away from our original position.

Hands clench, muscles twitch, and his head tosses side to side. Excess hair pulls into his skin. Somehow, his body knows to keep the human hair exactly as it was in either form.

John turns around. "There's nothing. No scent of them anywhere."

"Try again." I insist.

"No." If he could growl, I'm certain he would be.

I bite my tongue, and resist yelling at him. He's not who I'm angry with; just part of my frustration. "There's other roads. We haven't checked them all."

"The hotel is on the other side of this hospital. Let's just go back, and regroup." He insists.

"I can't give up on her. I need to find her." I reveal to him in a desperate plea. "What if they torture her, or kill her? They don't care that she's just a little girl. They don't care what she means to Alexa."

"It's a big city. We need more people. That's if they're still here." He pulls it back to his theoretical escape plan.

I roll my eyes. "I didn't see any dragons in the sky. That means they're still here. They have to be."

Both his mouth and expression say, "Really?" He approaches closer, and tries to reason. "Were you looking everywhere in the sky? At every moment?"

"Yes." No.

"Okay, so he didn't take off by dragon. Maybe he fled into any of the thousands of buildings around here. Eluded us, and then took off after we were all clear and gone.

He probably had some sort of getaway planned.

He likely had help; a witch or two. He's not stupid enough to come for Alexa without a plan if we decided to attack." John plots out more reasoning. He wants to go back, but I can't.

I slump my shoulders to release the fight, and release the tension built up inside of me. "Please. Can we, just, search a little longer? I can't leave her alone with him. At least I was there to protect her last time. No one is there for her now. They don't care enough to do more than just keep her alive. If they even care at all now.

Alexa was dating Daniel, and he's dead. Who says Darius is going to care what happens to Rayleen now. He could hurt her to spite Alexa. Hurt her because Alexa hurt him. Who knows what he'll do to Rayleen."

He mulls it over for a moment. One final gaze off in the direction I assume the hotel is in, before he looks back at me softly. "Fine. But, just for a little longer."

"Can you, please, transform again?" I ask.

"No. I can't budge on that. Transformations take a lot of energy. I've already gone back, and forth twice in a small time period. The pain worsens when you do them back to back like that. I'm exhausted, and about ready to drop. If you want to keep searching, I'll need what I've got left." John explains.

"Oh." In my worry for Rayleen, I ignored his wellbeing. It looked painful, but I mostly ignored it to get what I wanted. "Okay. I'm sorry." I apologize.

It must take a large toll on the body to change if he's admitting to pain and exhaustion; though I doubt his admission is the full truth of it all. Which means it's worse than what he says.

We walk off in the same direction we had been heading. Silently in a thick tension. It feels like the same air we breathed the week leading up to our breakup.

I look for something to break the tension. I'll start a conversation, and we'll go from there. One of a hundred questions cross my mind. "So, why do you wear clothes in your werewolf form?"

I look between him, and the road; sparing what I dare to not pay attention as I walk.

John looks at me confused, "I'd be naked if I didn't wear clothes." Then, he's amused, cracking a smile, and laughing at my expense. "It's not like we change personalities. We're us. Embarrassment at being naked, and all. Modesty, and all of that."

He pauses to think. "It's certainly easier to run around naked, and the clothes feel weird on the extra hair. But for quick in, and out transformations, the clothes stay on. Besides, you've seen it. It's not like I'm down on all fours all the time, and things aren't exactly covered well down there." He spells it out without actually saying that I'd be able to see his penis. "It's not PG."

I blush from the insinuation. "So, you run around naked sometimes."

"Sometimes. Some packs aren't as modest as others. It's more of a traditional value to be naked when in lycan form. It's a sign of freedom for some."

"So in ye olden days; werewolves-lycans?" I switch questions half way through when I get to the particular word. He's used lycan a couple times now, but I remember Sara and Jaiden also using werewolf.

"Either. There used to be more of a physical distinction that determined which was used, but in modern times we use them interchangeably."

"So, in ye olden days, werewolves used to just be naked all the time?" I ask, confident I can use werewolf; lycan seems odd to me for some reason.

"Not all the time, just when transformed; a planned transformation. And, only those who wanted to. I'd imagine some preferred to keep their clothes on, though there might have been a stigma against that."

"Does it hurt? It looked like it hurt." He said as much, and that it was exhausting, but I wonder exactly how much.

"Yes." John's decidedly hesitant to definitively answer. "It's very itchy. Like a hurtful itchy; all over your body and inside your body. That's the constant through the whole change. Everything else is a quick burning or piercing pain as bones and muscles change positions or shape."

Our search continues through the streets with chit chat passing the time. We spend hours weaving through all the roads we can. Looking for any sign of either Darius or Rayleen, but there is nothing.

Night falls, and it becomes too dark to return or continue. For all his complaints earlier, I take it as a good sign that he wants to continue the search with me.

It sucks that it's so easy to talk to him. Yet, it feels right. I hate him for that. I hate his clan, pack, more for their part in breaking us up.

I wonder, for the thousandth time, if we'd still be together had they not interfered. Would we be married? Would we have any kids? Would I have ended up like his mom, divorced at the first sign of werewolf in our children? Or, would he have gotten up the courage to tell me about his genes?

We finally break into a house for dinner and sleep when it gets too dark to continue.

Deciding on sharing a bed for extra heat, the two of us pile all the blankets onto the king bed, until there is five pounds of blanket to weigh on our chests.

The exhaustion of the day pulls down on me. I manage to hear snoring from the man next to me, before passing out myself.

Chapter 22

We exchange glances. There's an oddity to so many people, all at once, trekking inside.

I recognize Cole from the jean jacket he was wearing; his twin jacketless behind him. He was with Dominique the last I saw her; it's the best clue we've gotten thus far.

I make a mental note to figure out how to tell them apart. The jean jacket thing will only last for so long.

The whole lot of them corral into the lounge.

Flitting between the faces of each person as they pass by, I check for our missing people. Sara, John, and Dominique; they're all missing. Possibly, still outside.

"Outside; maybe?" DeAngelo remarks.

"That's what I was just thinking." I tell him.

I peek into the lounge as we pass, but I don't see who I'm looking for. If nothing else, Cole and the other one are getting comfortable back at the table, so I can ask them when we come back inside. Others sit with them; I could ask any of them.

Cole and his twin are a bit of a worry over what he said earlier. He can't read my mind, but the fact that he was expecting to, and announced as such, could be of concern.

Oh no.

In my hurry to extract myself, I left the other three there to answer in my stead. I hope they didn't tell anyone about my visions; if they got much of a choice in the matter.

I wonder if Dominique is so mad at me that she would tell people out of spite.

DeAngelo stops in his path, not to wait for me, and my slight delay, but to stare at something beyond the doors.

Like a picture, the open doors frame an image. It takes a moment to assess the still. A pool of reflecting dark liquid. Just behind it, a statuesque woman looking into the distance; nearly set perfectly in the middle of the image. A focus is set.

A deep feeling of wrong, settles in my gut.

I move first. There's no sense in delaying it anymore. What's happened has happened. Whatever it is, we're stumbling into the aftermath.

The scene chills more that the cool air I breathe.

Alexa's lone figure is troubling. The blood, could be anyone's but Alexa is rarely without two particular people; both missing from the scene. The amount is too much for one person to have survived the blood loss.

When all others are returning from the end of the show, she's still out here.

I hope I'm wrong.

That Rayleen will come out from behind a truck with Crystal. That Daniel decided to stay inside. That the blood is from some other person or multiple people.

But, I have my doubts in optimism. I prefer to stand firmly in realism. There's no body to tell me what happened, just one catatonic woman who pays me no attention. She wouldn't be this way if something didn't happen to one of her people.

"Alexa?" I tentatively question.

There is no response. Her eyes are glazed over. She's staring off into the distance. I look on to what she's looking at; nothing out of the ordinary.

"Are you okay?" DeAngelo asks her. "What happened?"

"She's in shock." I deduce.

DeAngelo goes in front of her, and places his hand on her cheek. If he does something with his elf background, he doesn't let it show. Either he soothes some of her pain or the touch itself brings her out. I don't know if wood elves have that power too. I forgot to look into aziza.

Her head and eyes slowly focus to DeAngelo, then shift to me. She's an empty shell of a person. My mind flips back and forth between who died, to a theory of both her loves dying.

I peer off to where she had been staring again. No sign of anything. No movement of any sort. Whatever she was looking at, if she was looking at anything, is long gone.

"Let's get her inside." DeAngelo suggests.

"Right." My eyes sweep the area once more. Turning back to them I continue, "of course."

Words catch in my throat with a renewed sight of blood. There are two distinct blood pools, not just one.

What happened? Who died? If not, are they going to die? Where are Rayleen and Daniel? Where is Crystal? Where are Dominque, Sara, and John?

So many questions and no answers.

This exact moment, is not the time to ask them. To push Alexa might bring about another catatonic state.

DeAngelo turns Alexa around, and tugs her in the direction of the hotel. He has one arm wrapped around her back, with his hands on each of her arms.

We guide Alexa slowly up to our rooms. I hurry slightly ahead once we get to the. I reach to grab the door knob for her room.

"No! No. No. No. No! I can't go in there." Alexa rigorously shakes her head. Her body is like a leaf in the wind.

I look at her in a bit of a panic from her visceral reaction. A death of a loved one. Her reaction pulls me back to the days I couldn't bring myself to go into my mom's bedroom; where I had found her.

But, I didn't get a choice. As soon as Jacob figured it out, he pushed me to overcome it; locking me in the room for hours. Until I stopped screaming and crying; stopped begging to be let out.

He continued by making excuses for me to have to go inside, mostly so I could help clean out her stuff. I had to be the dutiful daughter and assist him, lest he think I was acting out and disruptive. I remember a threat to be shipped off somewhere to adjust my behaviour, but I don't remember where.

Funny how death forces long lost thoughts back to the forefront. I hadn't thought of that in years.

I won't force her into that room, if she doesn't want to be in there. I'm better than that.

I have a part answer. "It's okay. We'll go into another room."

DeAngelo guides her into one of the others. No one is here to greet us; might be for the best.

She sits on the closest bed. DeAngelo sits beside her, and takes her hand; a mostly unnecessary touch. He must be working his magic to help alleviate her pain. Or, it's his version of comforting her; elf magic or not.

Maybe even magic from his aziza side? I remember thinking about needing to research the aziza, but never actually doing it. I'll try to remember to do it soon.

"Can you tell us what happened?" He treads lightly, and soothingly.

"He took her." The voice is gravely and small. Alexa looks down at her lap; staring at nothing.

"Who?" I ask for confirmation that she's talking about Darius.

"He took Rayleen." Darius. His name springs to mind despite Alexa's confusion of my question. It had to be him. Who else would just take a little girl? There is a certain wave of relief to know that she's alive.

"Well shit." Kelly loudly announces her presence. Not a surprise from how loud Alexa screamed. Even the humans would have had no problem hearing her. "So, now what? Darius found us; again. I doubt he'll stop at kidnapping little girls."

"He warned me; said he'd do this." Her quiet voice screams into the room.

"Alexa." I try to warn her with her name, but she's already said too much. I realize too late, that I might incriminate myself at the same time. I can envision this going south from here. Like watching a train approaching broken rails and knowing there's no time to stop it.

"He killed everyone in Banff, after he told me to leave. He killed the people at the farm as a gift to me. Said I'd be forced to go with him. He threatened Rayleen. And, now he's taken her. He said he'd return her to me when I return to him. Daniel's…" Alexa chokes on his name. "I have to find Darius. I have to get Rayleen back. I can stop all of this."

Kelly turns on me with a sneer. "What happened?"

"Can we talk in the other room? She's been through enough." I try to sway her. She's hostile and that's not helpful at this moment.

"No! She's getting everything she deserves." Kelly stomps up to Alexa and points her finger. "You knew! You knew he was going to attack and you did nothing. You deserve everything you're getting. I tried to warn you, but you didn't listen."

My mind reals with wonder about what Kelly warned Alexa about. A warning about Darius, obviously, but what exactly.

"Kelly. We don't know what she knew; when she knew it." Miles goes up beside her. He tries to put himself between the two girls, but there isn't enough room for it to be effective. "Now is not the time."

"She knew something; obviously!" Kelly continues to berate Alexa. "Darius came here for you, right? Everything he's done is on you. Every single person he's killed is on you. He wouldn't still be fucking us over if it wasn't for you."

I need to interject. This blame game isn't helping anyone.

Alexa's lost enough. She knows that she screwed up. But, Darius is his own autonomous person, and what he's done is on him. Alexa can't be held responsible for his every action. "You're not helping things. It's done. Rayleen's been kidnapped again, and we need to figure out what to do about it."

"Give her over. She wants to go." Kelly offers.

"Oh, please." Please stop this ridiculousness. "Do you think she actually wants to be with him? Darius is scaring her and forcing her hand. Him killing and kidnapping to get what he wants is on him; not Alexa. She's become an unfortunate victim of his obsession. We can find another way to do this. One that doesn't involve sacrificing a lamb for slaughter."

"Her lamb was already taken for slaughter." Kelly's sharp reminder stabs my analogy. This is why I hate analogies.

We do find a way to do this. That vision, where we failed to rescue Rayleen. She died then and there, but she was alive to that point. This has to be the situation that leads to that.

How many times can one person get kidnapped?

I'm stuck for a response between her retort, and the stare down, and my reluctance to reveal my vision. I'd incriminate myself. If I had told them about my vision, they might've been more cautious.

A dangerous air dares me to challenge her again, but I don't want to take the challenge.

"Where's Nikki?" Shawn asks the room. He walks closer to the rest of us from the doorway. I hadn't noticed him, but welcome the interruption.

"I don't know." I tell him truthfully.

"She ran after him." Alexa's quiet voice answers.

"Of course she did." Shawn rolls his eyes and sighs. I agree with his sentiment. Of course she ran after Darius to save Rayleen; they bonded while kidnapped the first time. Dominique watches out for her, better than Alexa does; more motherly than Alexa does.

"We're is she?" An old lady bursts through the door; the one Jerry said would help Rayleen with her magic. I can't think of her name right now; did he even mention her name to me? I hope she means to introduce herself, then I'll know it.

Kelly runs quickly to the intruder. Readying to attack the unknown trespasser.

"Wait!" I try to interject before Kelly does something to the old woman.

The old lady brings up her hand, and merely pushes Kelly to the side. A force large enough to knock the vampire into the bathroom.

Her hand, discoloured and grey, is covered in rock. A punched force, with a hard value of rock, packs a greater impact; smart and quick. My worry was unneeded; looks like she can take care of herself.

"I'd rather keep this cordial." She admonishes Kelly. "Now, someone needs to explain where Rayleen is."

"Hi, I'm Jaiden." I officially introduce myself, but I have no idea if Jerry mentioned me to her. My hand sticks out to shake her own, but she looks at it with disdain; no time for niceties then. "Alexa's in shock right now, and no one else here saw what happened. We've been able to get that Rayleen was kidnapped by Darius; Alexa's vampire ex-boyfriend, and this region's leader. Darius is still obsessed with Alexa, and knows that he can get to her through Rayleen. He killed Daniel; Alexa's current boyfriend. We have a couple people out there searching for her right now."

She, "mhmms," and examines over my shoulder to Alexa.

Kelly stumbles out of the bathroom, but backs down with a stern look from the elder woman. "She's going to need some water; tea perhaps. Some food; real food." She orders me. Looking from me, she starts barking orders to the others in the room. "We need to get her warm; get her settled and under the blankets. Tissues and possibly a bucket to puke in." She switches gears to be motherly, and caring towards Alexa; kneeling in front of her. "Dear, do you feel nauseous at all?"

This woman has taken control of the situation. I am beyond fine with letting her.

I leave the room to take care of her request. Hoping the tension will be lessened by the time I get back.

Alexa will need to be handled with kid gloves for the immediate future. Which means, it might be best to try to keep Kelly away from Alexa for the time being.

Pressure quells when the room door shuts, then rises when I enter a buzzing lounge. Expectant eyes call me over, but I don't know what I could possibly say to them.

To ignore them all completely after our connected gaze, would be rude. I play dumb to the reason behind the looks, but wave, short a smile, and nod to acknowledge them.

I have my goal and don't wish to stop to answer questions I can't answer.

Hectre averts his eyes. He's the only one who can't stand to look at me; with good reason. I bet Jules has had a talk with him.

He says nothing as I go behind the counter, even though I half expect him to tell me to stop. I'm not sure of the unspoken rules and barriers anymore.

The freezer door is open. My feet stop when my eyes behold the sight. "What are you doing?" Blurts from my mouth.

Daniel's body is being strung up like a deer carcass. Crystal lies deathly still on the ground.

Jules is preparing him to be eaten; he looks like a strung up deer. The question is answered in my thoughts before Jules gets the chance to talk. My feelings about it set before they answer my spewed question.

Jules turns to look at me. "Preparing the body. We shouldn't waste food. Plenty of supernaturals here eat human meat. It would be a waste to bury fresh meat."

They are done for now. Daniel's set in place. They turn me, and guide me away from the freezer; closing the door behind us.

"Okay." I say simply.

The defensive tone disappears; shock in its place. "Okay?"

"I can't argue with the logic." I answer simply.

"Usually humans have problems with other humans getting served up for dinner." They are incredulous. I suppose for good reason. Cannibalism is a taboo subject. People don't just eat people.

"I mean, I won't eat it, but Daniel's dead. Darius killed him, and left him. And, you're right it would be a waste of food to just bury a fresh dead body in the ground." They'll catch no arguments from me, but Alexa can never know.

"You knew him." It's a statement, but I know there is a question attached.

"Yeah. He was with my group for the last six months." I answer simply.

Jules' eyes widen. "I am so sorry."

"It's fine." I shrug involuntary. In my bid to ease Jules' worries, I worry I come across flippant. "That, I mean, sounds so mean, and heartless. Uhm. We didn't get along." To put it succinctly. "I can disassociate well. I'm not sentimental over dead bodies."

They nod. "You were travel companions by convenience, and circumstance, not because you liked each other. You understand the circle of life, and won't let others go hungry just because you knew a person in life."

"Yes." Jules finds a way to put it, in which the words were lost to me.

"It's fine. I don't think you're a cold, heartless bitch." They joke.

"Thank you?" I question partially in jest. I think the bluntness was meant to ease me.

"What happened with Hectre and Jerry earlier?" Jules' question means they haven't talked with Hectre yet; he's ashamed on his own. I search for what to say. "I know something happened. Hectre refused to let me into the freezer; stalled me purposely. You looked pale, paler than usual, and freaked out. Neither of them would tell me anything."

"It's fine." I stall for a moment in time to figure out how much to say. Jules reprimands with a tilt of their head. "Jerry wanted to yell at me for the havoc Dominique has been causing."

"But, Hectre lied to you, and lured you into the freezer to do that, right? I saw him. He asked you to help him with something? Then took you into the freezer to Jerry?" Jules has it right.

My mouth opens and shuts. I can't bring myself to say no or tell a lie. Jules has their answer either way. "Yeah."

"I'm sorry. He shouldn't have ever done that. I'll be having a-ah, conversation with him later." Jules' words and tone promise it to be a loud, one sided conversation.

"I don't want to cause any problems." Their relationship shouldn't take a hit because of me. I don't know how much Hectre knew beforehand. I do know Jerry wouldn't be beyond intimidation to get compliance.

"He was wrong. He shouldn't have done that, and I will make sure he knows that. This isn't on you; it's on him." Jules tries to assure me, but I can't help but feel guilty.

"I'm sorry." I apologize.

"Don't be." They switch gears fast to put an end to this line of conversation. "Were you hungry?"

"No, Alexa seems to be in shock. She was dating Daniel, and was there when he was killed. I was hoping for water, tea, and some food." I tell them.

"Of course." Jules hops around gathering a couple items. They present me a mug with a tea bag in warm water, and a granola bar. "If she finishes this, come back, and I'll give you more. Some people just don't eat when they're in mourning. Shock or not, don't force it down her throat. The tea might go over easier than food."

"Thank you." I move to exit the kitchen. "I'll see you later."

They are waiting for me.

The crowd has moved to perch at the bar; the twins are front, and center. Those not interested, are still intent on watching the ruckus. They stare from their seats around the room. Wondering what's going to happen.

I get the jump on them. "Does anyone know anything useful? About what happened? About where Dominique is?"

"She left with a lycan to search for the little girl the vampire took." One shouts above the wave of responses.

"Which lycan?" I ask to the crowd. I can't pinpoint who spoke before.

"Who do you think?" I locate Sara as she yells. John must be with Dominique since he doesn't look like he's with Sara.

My questions are done. I'd rather excuse myself to get these back to Alexa, but the crowd has their own questions.

"So is this it then?"

"Is she coming back?"

"What if she doesn't come back?"

"What do we do now?"

There are many questions shouted all at once. I can only distinguish a few. They seem to want reassurances that this isn't the end of the revolution. In such early stages, it could be broken so easily.

I hold up the hand that has the granola bar. They quieten. "Dominique will be back. She's just passionate and she cares about the little girl who was kidnapped."

John will make sure she doesn't take too big of a risk. "We will carry on. Nothing has changed. I'm in charge while she's gone. It's why I'm second in command. When she's gone, I'm in charge. You can bring any problems to me." I reassure them.

There isn't much to the revolution at this time; it should be easy. "We are in the stage of getting the word out, and recruiting more people. We stand for peace and equality. It's that simple. Go and do that. This is home-base. Send everyone back here. Check in here."

I want and need to wrap this up. "When Dominique comes back, please send her to me. I will be back down soon, once I've got things settled with Alexa, and I can answer more questions then."

I aim for and collect Sara as I walk through the crowd. "What exactly happened?" I question her as soon as we're out of the lounge.

She shrugs. "Darius was outside. I saw him first. I told everyone he was there. Then, he killed Daniel and Crystal, and he kidnapped Rayleen. A bunch of people ran off after him. Dominique tried to get ran over by a truck, then she got into the truck. And, they took off. Some guys came back, and said Dominique refused to come back after they lost track of Darius. She and John are going to search a little while longer."

I hold my tongue with a question about why she didn't go with them. It would be safer with more numbers. "At this point, I hope they don't catch him. He's had time to regroup. If they find him, he's going to have them out numbered and killed."

"What about Rayleen?" She asks.

"He won't kill her. Not as long as he thinks Rayleen will get him

Alexa." I hope.

Chapter 23

Daniel is dead. Darius killed him.

Rayleen is gone. Darius took her.

He's going to hurt her.

No. No. No. No. No. No.

What do I do?

Daniel is dead. Darius ripped out his throat.

One minute I was kissing him, the next minute he was dead.

Blood. His blood is on me. Burning an itch in each place.

Spots and splashes on my front. His blood.

He can't be dead. It's a mistake.

Daniel can't be dead. I can't do this without him.

Someone took him away.

They wouldn't do that if he was dead.

Too much blood.

Daniel's dead.

I'll return her, when you return to me.

He took her; to get to me.

If I go to him, I will get Rayleen back.

Confusion and pain dampen as motherly arms wrap around me.

Margie is here. When did she get here?

A moment of clarity reaches into my head. Margie is a very powerful witch; she can help me find Rayleen. Margie can help me get Rayleen back.

"Can you do a locator spell?" With all my hope, I ask Margie; plead with her.

Margie pulls away. She looks at me with a sorrowful look. "No, sorry. I can't do that."

Sharp pains in my chest return from previous numbness. "There has to be something you can do. All the movies have witches who can do locator spells. There has to be something you can do."

She shakes her head. "Nothing works like in the movies. Any and all locator spells, anything I could do at this point, would involve blood magic. I don't do blood magic."

"It's for Rayleen." My voice wavers. "You have to do something."

"I don't do blood magic." Margie pointedly spells out.

But she could, if she wanted to. She doesn't want to find Rayleen.

Anger spills over in a hot mess. "Then find me someone who does!" My screech breaks at the end.

"No one will admit to it." She says.

I look away from her to the ground. Refocusing to stare at the blood at the blood on my pants.

"What about a blood attraction spell?" Miles offers. "It's on the low-end of the blood magic scale. We don't have Rayleen's blood, but Alexa's might be close enough with one of Rayleen's hairs to get a little bit of a range. Better than nothing. We could scan the city easier."

I look to Margie hopeful, but she sours it with a scowl. "What is with the people you know and blood magic? I've never heard so much talk about in the last fifty years, as I have in the last couple days." She turns her head to Miles. "No, I can't, nor would I, if I could. Blood magic, in my eyes, is still illegal.

Besides, you'd be better off getting a wolf to chase after them."

Kelly pipes up. "Great, we have two wolves. Where are they?"

"They might be wherever Dominique is. They're missing. She's missing. It's not that far of a stretch. Dominique went after Darius. Maybe, they're out searching still." DeAngelo says.

I don't remember seeing the two werewolves we picked up.

A cloud hangs over most of the memory of what happened. Glaring details of certain moments blare at me, while others are fuzzy or don't exist at all.

"What should we do?" Shawn asks. "Do we stay here? Do we go out and look for Rayleen?"

"We stay here." Kelly commands attention. "There's no point in going anywhere. We don't know where Darius is. We don't know if they found him. And, it's not really our business."

"Kelly!" Miles admonishes.

"No, you're all tiptoeing around Alexa, but it's all her fault. Darius killed Daniel because Daniel was dating Alexa. Rayleen was kidnapped as punishment.

You'd have more luck sending Alexa out to walk around randomly, and use her as bait, than you'd have with anything else. Darius wants her. So we give him her. That's how you're going to catch him." She centers her wrath directly onto me. "Why don't you just go with him? You loved him at one point, you can love him again.

He's just going to keep coming back. He's going to kill more people because of you.

How many people do you think he's killed because of you? I'd say you're at least at a few hundred by now. A whole town slaughtered. A community killed; all to make a point to you.

Darius is not going to give you up. He's never going to stop.

Not one of these people are stopping me right now, because they know I'm telling the truth. They're all thinking the same exact thing. I'm not lying about any of this. I'm not making it up. I'm not exaggerating or being dramatic.

It's your fault.

Daniel is dead because of you. Rayleen is probably next; if he hasn't killed her already."

I can't take this anymore. She's right.

I bolt from helping arms and the room.

Agony.

I cross the hall.

Slamming into the door I wish to open, when my wrist doesn't turn the door knob fast enough. The door swings open, and I lock everyone out behind me.

All composure ends once I crawl into our bed.

My chest uncontrollably heaving as panic sets in as hyperventilation.

Gasping for breath. Tears start falling after they blur my vision.

Daniel is dead.

I'll never get Rayleen back.

Everything hurts.

It's hopeless.

The world closes into this room. Closes into the bed. Time stands still. It means nothing right now. Just this. Just me. Me and my head.

Daniel is dead. He is dead because I loved him. Darius killed him because I love him, because I was kissing him. He did it to punish me. For loving someone who wasn't him.

Everyone in Banff is dead because of me. All those people are dead because of me. Because, I didn't warn them. Because, Darius killed them; because of me. They were innocent. I didn't love any of them. I didn't even know most of them. Darius did it to punish me. Because, he loves me.

Because, he's obsessed with me.

Everyone at the farm is dead because of me. All those people are dead because of me. Darius' gift to me. He actually thought it was a gift. Rather, it was a point. A point he made to me about what he can do. A point about what lengths he will go to get to me.

He did it all to get to me. If I won't go to him willingly, he will make life so unbearable that I have no choice but to go to him.

He's taken Rayleen. He knows I will do anything for her. It's his last point. It's my breaking point.

My wails are loud enough that I know that everyone around me can hear me; I can't bring myself to care enough to dampen my voice.

Stupid demons, stupid vampires, and their stupid extra hearing. They'd hear me even if I were quiet.

The anger brings a reprieve. A moment of silence, where there is no crying out. My breathing evens. The pain exists.

In my silence, there is no outlet. My fingers get itchy; get twitchy.

I've been here before. The urge too strong to resist. I need to release some of my pain; put some of my pain on the outside.

A cheap razor in the bathroom snaps under my pressure. A practiced movement releases the blades.

My pants are pulled off. I sit on the edge of the tub, with my legs inside. The tub will catch the blood; easier to clean away at the end.

I can't see. By feel, I find the old scars. I know how much pressure to push. The blade slides across my skin, in line with each scar. Cutting the tissue, and releasing blood.

It's all my fault.

All of it is my fault.

Another sweep.

I need to bury Daniel's body.

What did they do with the body?

Another line dug deep into my skin.

He's never going to give Rayleen back to me. She's never going to be mine. She's never going to be safe.

Darius has kidnapped her twice, no, three times now. This time, she's alone. Alone and scared.

And, it's all my fault.

Sweep and sting. Blood cools my skin, but not as much as the tub.

Finding Rayleen means giving myself over to Darius. But I don't want Rayleen growing up with that.

I need to keep her safe. I need to give her up.

A scary calm releases the blade from my hand. It clinks to the tub floor.

Nothing more than an empty shell, I slump over in the tub. Just waiting for blood to dry and scab.

Numb.

Chapter 24

All my ire connects foot to rock, and it scuttles across the ground. It doesn't do anything to settle me.

Where the hell is he?

John emerges from the building as I kick another rock. "Sorry, one of the guys had a few more questions." He runs his hand across the top of his head, to pull hair out of the front of his face.

"That's fine." I bite out.

The larger group of humans has held our time for the last hour. Twenty five, twenty six or so, people living in one house. The masses of people we've found today surprises me. They may not be in the open, but look under the surface, and they're there; all types of people.

Habits have changed, rather than feeling free to roam the streets, they hide in the shadows. They only emerge when they absolutely have to. Each time ventured out, means more risk of death to yourself, and those you're sheltering with.

I get the feeling that more people survived than I had originally thought.

Maybe more will come out with the warm weather. A lack of attacks has had to have been noticed. They have to come out to investigate at some point. They'll find no immediate danger, and go further, and farther from their shelter.

Unless, Darius has now decided to set up shop here. Things could get dangerous again.

Out of all the people we've run into, none of them have seen Rayleen; not one peep of Darius, Sandra, or their followers.

While our search finds success on a rebellion front, it's a failure in helping us find the little girl.

John starts to say something, but I shut him down with a glare and a spin to another direction. I know what he would say. He's said it many times since noon, and more times since this morning; an annoying amount of times.

He wants to go back to the hotel, and give up on the search. He wants to regroup, and figure things out from there. I can't. I won't give up on her.

John passes me; in a hurry for something. My heart flutters. This is it.

As he picks up speed, I match it right behind him. Rounding a corner reveals a bloody scene of one.

John runs straight for the body, to help the man out. I'm both disappointed, and relieved that what we've found is not Rayleen.

Weary of a battle just had, fresh blood oozing out of wounds, I search for signs of the perp.

"We need to get him back to the hotel." John says.

I hesitate for half a moment, but I know he's right. "Yeah, of course." I kneel next to the man; demon.

Slashes part his yellow flesh. Many of the gashes across his chest seem superficial. His arm spouts the most blood. A black pool grows beneath him. White broken bone pokes through muscle, and skin.

"We have to do something about his arm. We can't move him like this." John handles it as he speaks. He pops the bone down, removing his sleeve to tie around the wound. The wrap will hopefully hold things together until we can get him to the doctor.

I gag. "How are we supposed to move him?"

"Carry him." John picks up the man, and cradles him to his chest.

"Carry him?" Quickly settled, John starts walking. "We've got to be hours away. We can't just carry him the whole way. Do you even know if you're going in the right direction?"

"Well..." he pauses. "Actually, we're probably about a twenty minutes' walk away."

"What? No." We've been weaving in, and out of the streets for a full day, there's no way we could be so close.

John nods his head towards the park. "That's Rotary Recreation Park. It's a few blocks away from the hotel; to the west and slightly south."

The directions mean nothing to me, but I assume it's the direction he's headed. "Why are we so close to the hotel? I thought we were going to the edge of the city."

"We must've gotten turned around somewhere." He offers lamely, but I suspect he knew exactly where he was going; he's always had a precise sense of direction. "I can carry him there."

"Should we find a car or truck or something nearby?" The heated rage cools with the chill of helplessness. There has to be some way I could help. I look around.

"It would take massive luck to find something that works."

"Why wouldn't it work?" I look back to him confused. All Jerry's trucks work.

"Batteries freeze and die in cold weather. Gas, oil, motor fluids all evaporate or break down. A bunch of things can go wrong when vehicles sit for a winter, or just over time. Give it another six months, and I guarantee nothing parked for the year will work without mechanical work."

"That doesn't seem right." I mutter.

"Going off your vast knowledge of cars." He jabs. John has a leg to stand on with that. He's helped me out a few times.

"Well, you'd think all the apocalypse shows and movies would research the facts, and not coordinate the same lie." I debate.

"Most apocalypse shows aren't taking place a year after; the apocalypse is happening in the movie. Gas is still good, oil is still good, canned goods aren't expired, generators are in new condition, people haven't even had the chance to miss showers yet."

"God, I miss showers. No, I miss my baths; warm, bubbly, wine in hand." I resist cataloging all the things I miss about baths, to try to do something that would help. "Should I run back? Go grab a truck from Jerry."

"It would take the same amount of time for me to walk back as it would for you to make it back, grab a truck, grab us, and make it back to the hotel. Who knows how long this guy has."

We walk silently after that. I check up on the demon now, and then. Look for chest movements.

John carefully, but quickly, walks along. Speed picking up a little when the hotel is in sights. He was right, we were close, but we beat the twenty minute timer. We get through the doors to see some people milling about.

"We need a doctor!" John shouts above everyone.

Lobby people rush us. Lounge people hurry to see what's happening. Two people come forward to check the body. One checks for a heartbeat on the man's neck. "Down the hall. Follow me." The older one says.

We follow the pair down the hall, a few rooms away from Jaiden's assigned accommodations.

The one sets to work collecting items, while the other instructs John to place the patient on a massage table turned medical bed. There is a clear leader in the taller man, he orders the other around to collect things, and do other things. They whirl around, assessing wounds, placing priorities, and conducting surgeries, and stiches.

"Dominique. Dominique." I look to the two attending to our patient; but neither looks like they are calling me. "Dominique." I look to the voice. She's looking at me. "Jaiden's been waiting for you to get back."

Of course. That's why she's calling me Dominique. She heard it from Jaiden. "Where is she?" I ask.

"She's been running all around the hotel; giving people jobs, fixing problems, organizing things. She's never anywhere for more than a few minutes. But, she keeps returning upstairs to check on a... Alexi— the grieving girl."

"Okay, I'll find her. Thanks." The doctors appear to have things under control. With no medical knowledge, I won't be much help here anyways. "I'm going to find Jaiden. Did you want to stay with them?"

John nods. "I'll find you later." I touch his arm before I leave as a bit of a good bye.

I walk straight upstairs; carried on a mission unknown to my conscious mind. A rising magma of heated rage rises up as I ascend.

Each step angers me more and more; the closer I get. As I get closer and closer, there is more of a reminder about Rayleen, and how she ended up kidnapped. Right in that room, is the very reason why Rayleen is gone. She didn't do anything to stop Darius from taking her. Darius wouldn't have taken her, if not for Alexa.

Barging into Alexa's room, I instantly note how dark it is. It takes a moment to spot her lying in the bed. She didn't even bother to get under the covers.

Still dressed in yesterday's blood covered clothes.

"How dare you?" She jolts up; surprised at my return. Alexa returns to her pillow to get comfortable again. "What the Hell do you think you're doing? You're just laying here while Rayleen is being tortured, maybe raped, maybe killed.

Get up! Get up, while I'm trying to talk to you! Make an effort to face me, and what you did." Alexa mechanically sits up. Her legs fall over the edge. Hands in her lap. Expressionless, as she looks me in the eyes.

I go closer. Blood still splatters her. She's frozen in time after the kidnapping.

I suppose we both are, when I think about it. I walk up to her.

"Did you even think about going to look for her? I've been out there for the last day looking for your little girl. She was taken by your boyfriend. You don't get to be comfortable.

You should be out there looking for her. You should be the one searching for her. The one to find her."

"Nique!" Jaiden grabs my hand; stopping it from connecting with Alexa's jacket. The other meets with it, and clenches a fist in the cloth. "Leave her alone. Deal with her when you aren't so angry."

What did she call me?

I know it wasn't exactly my name. That's takes longer to pronounce. Then again, I hadn't exactly been aware of more than screaming at Alexa. Maybe she said the whole thing?

I let go of Alexa, and willingly let Jaiden pull me outside the room. She closes the door.

We look at each other; one thing nagging in my head. "What did you call me?" I question her.

Her face goes paper white. She's terrified. Curiosity peaks my amusement. "Nique." Her voice is small.

"What?" I ask for repetition. Unsure, exactly what she said. Wanting her to repeat it, so that I know for certain.

"Nique. I'm sorry. I made up a nick name when you said I couldn't call you by your other names." Jaiden avoids my eyes, and puts her head down.

Giggles bubble up, and pour out from the absurdity. I put my hand in front of my mouth. "I'm sorry." She's upset, and I'm laughing at her. I apologize. Laughter cannot be stifled by one hand. "I'm sorry. I was mad. I'm over it. You shouldn't have taken that so seriously."

The giggles are done when she can't meet my eyes anymore. I work to ease her worries. "If you want to call me Dominique, Nikki, or Nique, you're welcome to." I don't think anyone's ever called me that before. "I think I like Nique. It's interesting."

Chapter 25

If Dominique's going to take off, for who knows how many days, then I'm going to handle this my way; a methodical sweeping through the grid, and clearing of high priority locations.

Peering at the now gridded map of Red Deer, with marked off important locations and our territory reclaimed; I ground myself.

I look up at all the waiting faces. I focus on Sara directly, and shut everyone else out with tunnel vision. If I am to get through this, I can't employ the common standards of leadership speaking.

Sara's the only one here. She's my friend. I'm just talking to her; at her. No pressure.

With great nerves, I take a deep breath and begin. "The immediate area is cleared. And, by that, I mean this hotel, and the coffee shop at the end of the parking lot; nothing else. We are going to head out west; our first two priority locations are the hotel across the street, and the hospital. We sweep the areas, we clear and reclaim building by building.

Anyone holding refuge in the locations are to be approached carefully. They may be skittish to see us. They might attack, so we need to tell them our intentions clearly and quickly.

It is never our goal to kill anyone. It is not our intention to go into these buildings, and kill first, ask questions later. You should only kill if that's your last option; self-defense.

Each of you will be getting your orders; either supplies runs or land recapture."

"Wait," Bob calls out to interject. I look over to him to address him directly. One on one. "So, what are we doing? Stick a flag in the ground; this is ours now."

"Metaphorically; I guess." I question my own answer. It's better to explain out my thoughts, so there isn't any confusion. We don't need conquerors. "No flag; maybe some flyers. The property's also not necessarily ours. Especially, if it already belongs to someone else."

I'm losing them; I'm losing myself. It's time to restart my answer. "We're reclaiming the perimeter, and the people. If they already have a home set up, we're not taking it for ourselves, and we're not taking their stuff.

It's like recapturing territory, expanding our imaginary safety circle, so we can build a functioning city starting from this hotel going outwards. Getting people to join us, and the new world."

I'm boring myself, and beating the question to death. It's time to move on, back on to my original track. I look back to Sara.

"Supply runs are buildings where the potential supplies are more valuable than the building itself; right now. Like, a restaurant isn't very useful to us right now; a restaurant without electricity. But, they might have toilet paper, cleaning supplies, or preserved food.

Whereas with land recapture, the hotel across the street could, potentially, start housing people by the end of the day. It's somewhere to place people. It can be home base for us.

And, the hospital, I don't need to tell you how valuable a hospital is; we all know that.

We start reclaiming land, we find supplies, we find people, and allies. Growth and strength will come organically." My mind blanks. I can't think of anything else to say.

I decide to start delegating. In a lack of knowing people's names, I decide place leaders in those who I do know, but not necessarily people who could be seen as favoured friends.

"Now... Everyone who has a regular schedule for deliveries, and functioning roles for this hotel; you'll stay here, and keep things running as usual.

Adam, take two people to the restaurant across the street; supplies run. Everything you think is useful, grab it. Box it up. Bring it to the other hotel, we should be done clearing it by then."

I try to think of more things to do, but I can't. We'll need quite a few people to go through the hotel efficiently; that is the priority.

"Everyone else will be reclaiming the hotel across the street with me. If that goes smoothly, we'll clear some more buildings; maybe even get to the hospital today." It's ambitious, but best to be clear with the group.

I don't want to run into a conflict if people expect to be finished for the day after running through the hotel; if all goes smoothly, then it should only take an estimated hour.

"I think we can get to it." Some take that as their dismissal. That sucked. That was awful. I sigh inwardly.

The people left look to me for instruction. "Are we ready to go?" There's confirmation from everyone and zero objections, so I lead the way out the building.

We don't have much for weapons, and I hope we won't need them. It's a fool's errand if we have no luck in that.

Theoretically, I've seen no movement from the hotel, so there shouldn't be anyone in there. Jerry wouldn't leave people there without absorbing them, or gleaning customers from them.

In a moment of silence, my mind wanders to my speech. I wasn't clear enough. I rambled way too much. There was a stutter or two in there. People looked bored.

I don't think I said things properly. Intentions not clear enough.

Do they think that we're on a whole take over the world thing? No. Then again, he said the plant flag territory thing.

Should I have gone through how to approach people? Should I have divided them further into specific jobs? Do I need to talk to them when we get to the hotel and divide them then?

What if some people are there? What if they don't agree to having us stay? We need somewhere to stay if Jerry is going to have another fit. I can't keep making deals with him. How much am I supposed to lose to keep this going? He's at an unfair advantage in our dealings.

He's frightening.

We approach the hotel, and I realize that our plan, and lack thereof, may not work. I hadn't had a good look at the hotel before this point, but it looks like room access for the main floor is from the outside; each individual room has a door to the outside. So, the main floor rooms might not be attached on the inside.

Blinds are drawn on every window. The door is blacked out with something shiny.

I think to wait and divide, but people open up the doors, and bypass me. It's a hallway to stairs, and a door to the lobby.

I remove the garbage bags from the doors to let some light in. Someone put those up, and it wasn't before the war.

The light makes its way down the hall, but not up to the top of the stairs. The hall to the rooms is dark.

"Jaiden?" My name comes from the first open room.

I answer, "Here," as I make my way inside.

"You need to come see this." His voice calls to me.

A wall of stench pushes against me. Stifling a gag makes the second one worse. "Open a window." I choke out.

"You okay?" He asks.

"Yup." There's only one thing I can equate to this putrid smell. "Dead body?"

"Bodies." He reveals.

"Jaiden?" Another voice calls to me from out in the hall; Bob.

"What?" I fear I already know the answer to my question.

"Bodies in here too." Bob answers.

With the discovery of the third room of bodies, I understand what happened here. Mass murder and/or mass suicide; perhaps poison or drugs. All of them are dead in their beds. One family of four. A man and a woman. A single man. Two men. Three women. All about the same level of decomposition.

At the end of the bodies, are empty rooms in various conditions.

Some look lived in, slept in, stripped of necessities, or completely untouched.

I order all the rooms' windows left open. I ready an argument. Would you rather the smell of death linger, and keep whatever little warmth is in here. Or freeze the place out, which outside is honestly just about the same temperature, lose the smell, and we can start gathering warmth again later. But, it isn't needed; no one argues.

Blinds draw open. Doors shimmy open. Until, everywhere has some amount of light.

The smell drifts as the bodies are removed by those with the strongest of stomachs. No one escapes from taking part in the cleanup. I garbage the sheets with a couple others. Some remove mattresses and some remove box springs.

We'll use these death rooms as storage. No one is going to want to stay in them. The smell could linger for months.

A man sits alone in the parking lot; heavily distressed and possibly ill. I sit down next to him in a social and moral obligation. Dropping the bag of sheets a few feet away.

"Why would they do that?" He cries when he notices me.

I think about stating a quick I don't know, but the logical thought process had already run through my head. Perhaps it would give a little comfort to understand why they would kill themselves.

It helps me when I can rationalize it. "They didn't think they had a choice. Middle of winter; run out of food. They might have been too scared to go out, or maybe supplies runs didn't come back. People, other people, probably died first. They didn't want to suffer anymore.

We don't know exactly what happened in there. Maybe everyone decided collectively this was the right choice. Maybe a few decided for everyone.

When people are placed in desperate situations, they make desperate choices. There's nothing we could have done. They've probably been dead for months."

"Do you-" He turns his eyes away and deflates. "Never mind."

"No, go ahead." I insist.

"It's stupid." He scoffs.

"That's fine. Go ahead anyway." I tell him.

"Do you think they would mind if I gave them a death prayer?"

"Of course they wouldn't mind." I tell him. I feel like he has the best of intentions in his request. "Whatever religion or not, that these people were, I'm sure they would appreciate it. If not for the prayer itself, then for the thoughts and good wishes behind it."

"Thank you." He wraps arms around me in comfort, and gratitude. I take it awkwardly and pat his back a couple times.

A death prayer might help him more than the dead, but the living need it more.

He releases and gets up. I do the same, and take the cue to leave. Grabbing up the bag and taking it out back to the large garbage bins.

Swinging the large and heavy lump, I gain momentum for a big heave into the garbage bin.

I'm at a loss for what to do next; that was the last of it. I need a long hot shower, or a bucket of hand sanitizer, but that won't be as likely.

I decide to explore the lobby. It's connected, but feels like a whole separate building. The lobby's two main walls are lined with windows. With the curtains opened it lets in the light of the day, and brightens the whole room. There is hardly a need for lights.

The light casts down on the remnants of the community. People had lived here a while. They had their own system of running things. But, now they are dead, and this building is under new management. I shake a smile off; that's not a good joke.

Tables and food or gathering area - check.

Storage room, no food, plenty of soaps - check.

A useless computer - check.

Another door to the outside - check.

Emptied staff room and rancid bathroom - check

Keys behind the desk - check.

The guest book draws my attention. It's centered in the lobby desk;

opened to a page.

Even in the darkest of days, children are still children. Black pen drawn pictures take up the majority of the back pages.

The last worded page before the pictures contains names from before the war. Nothing from anyone I would assume would have been here at the time; mid-November. The last dated name is from November 2nd. The guest book wasn't utilized often.

I grab a few keys in order; numbers I assume will be for the main floor rooms.

Three keys for three rooms. All empty of bodies. Other evidence of use is covered in dust. Drawers and closet doors left open. An electric razor left in the bathroom of one.

Two rooms speak of a rushed exit. Maybe people parting ways in the attack.

Those who stayed may have relocated to the upstairs. Rooms with an exit to the hallway, and not the outside world.

One room looks ready to receive a new guest. Empty since the beginning, I assume.

"Jaiden." I exit the room to my name called. "Need some help?" There are three people just outside; none of their names are known to me, but I recognize them. Two girls and a guy. They're a small clique; likely travelled together.

I shake my head. "These rooms look empty. Either the hotel wasn't busy, or people left, and took their stuff with them. There doesn't look like there's a generator. There's no food, though there is lots of soap, shampoos, and conditioner. We can either do what they did, and centralize everyone upstairs until we have too many people, and are forced to move in down here, or-"

A hand goes up as he interrupts me. "My nose isn't going to take the upstairs. I can't live in that."

"Pick a key." He grabs one at random. "Congrats, on your new home."

"Thanks." He says with a touch of relief. "Is there anything else to do upstairs?"

"I don't think so. If you're looking for something to do, you can start moving any of your things over, start dividing up rooms, see if they need help burying the bodies." I speak another thought out loud, but more meant for myself than them. "We should probably let others know they can move over now too."

"I can do that." The girl with purple hair volunteers.

"Thanks. Give out the main floor rooms, not the upstairs ones. Try to group people up, as we get more places we can separate, and let people have rooms to themselves, but space is a luxury right now."

The hotel seems cleared. I should go check on the restauarant; they should have been here by now. I should go check on Alexa. And, I've still got to check in with Jerry for my delivery job.

But, I should be here at the hotel. It's early enough in the day that we could go elsewhere.

"You're spacing." The girl says.

"Sorry. Were you saying something?" I excuse myself for being rude. Sometimes, I just get lost in my thoughts.

"Nothing, what's going on in your head?"

"Drawing up a list of everything that needs to be done." I answer. There is quite a bit to be done, and I don't think I can handle it all by myself. "I should see about finding an assistant."

"What do you need done?" The man seems like he's volunteering himself up for the position.

"Sort people into rooms. Get a log going of who lives where, job skills, how many empty usable rooms, list of supplies needs and wants. Take stock of what we have. Make a list of needed items."

"I'll get it done."

I look at the other two for any negations. "Alright."

"Okay, so you want names…" He trails off to ask for more information.

"Job skills, just skills; anything useful." I decide to add some examples to help him out. "You have good luck with keeping plants alive. You once fished with your grandpa when you were a kid, and remember what to do to catch a fish. You know how to hammer nails into wood. You're good with math and numbers. You're a master at karate. You once took a first aid class.

Anything that could possibly be useful. Take stock of the rooms and supplies. And, gather a list together of needed items.

Like if someone has allergies, then we should try to find medication or epipens. Species and dietary needs."

"I can get that done." He says.

"Great, thank you. I'm going to check on other things. I should be back in about an hour or two, and we'll figure out if we should move on to more buildings or call it a day, and settle in." I let them know. If anyone needs me, someone knows what's going on.

As we part, it occurs to me that I should have asked for their names. But, I wonder if they'd be offended that I don't already know them. It seems like a good leader thing, to know the names of everyone. Not that I've gotten much of a chance to find out peoples' names; no official introductions have been made.

I walk over to the restaurant. Through the dirty windows, I see movement inside. One of the windows has a faint council emblem on it; not noticeable if you aren't looking closely. I wonder if Dominique put that there too.

The door is open, so I let myself in. A door opposite to me was broken in. I hope they didn't have to break it, but how else were they to get inside?

"Hey." A guy greets me.

"How's this going?" I ask.

"There are a few things here, but looks like anything good was already taken." He concludes. "Don't open the freezers." He warns with a smile.

Adam comes out from the kitchen area. "You know this might not be as useless as you think. Machines are clean; they weren't open yet; when the attack happened. Freezer and fridge are going to need cleaning. A board put up over the broken window in the door. If we can find another generator, solar panels, we could get this place up and running easy."

As Adam takes hold of my attention, and the conversation, the other man gets back to whatever he was doing before I arrived.

"Yes, eventually. For now, Jerry's hotel owns the only generator we have. They have a kitchen and freezer, and need it there; he's not going to give it up.

If we find another generator, it might be better off at the new hotel, or maybe at the hospital. Then here, for a restaurant. It's not as high on the priority list." Electricity aside, a restaurant might be a good idea to get up, and running sooner than later. "I'll see if I can work something out with Jules and Hector for bulk food orders. Maybe use this as a buffet style restaurant until we can get electricity back.

There would need to be enough demand for it. Which there might be with how many people we have. Jerry will want extra trades since most of us won't be working for him anymore. I'll work on it some more."

"Jerry doesn't do anything for free does he?" Adam asks.

"He's a business man, running a business. They never do anything for free. Even if it appears to be for free, there's always an angle." Which is how most businesses work. Can't make money if you give everything away for free. Charity is great for tax reasons and publicity; the only reasons Jacob ever did any charity.

"So how'd you get him to agree to house refugees?" Adam asks.

"In a trade. All of this has been trades. That's part in why it's so important that we got the second hotel. Less dependence on Jerry, less deals I have to make to house and feed everyone." He goes to say something else, concern on his brow, but I beat him with a question. "Were you wanting to be in charge of a restaurant?"

"Not me specifically. But my wife, Rebeckah, she's a great cook, and dreamed of having one of her own. But, we couldn't afford it before."

"Adam, leave her alone. It's fine. She's right; there are more important things right now." Her voice chastises from the kitchen. I hear her long before I see her.

"Give me a spiel. What are your qualifications?" I ask.

"Officially, none. I never went to school or took courses. My grandma taught me some, and I learned on my own. I used to be in charge of family dinners. Everyone loved my cooking. I love cooking." She finishes talking, but there is too much unsaid, and too many questions that need answering.

"And, you can cook a variety of dishes for large groups. Using whatever we can find to cook up. Not give people food poisoning. You're not squeamish if someone brings you a still bleeding carcass to cook up."

"I don't know how to butcher meat." She says. I assume the rest is fine with her, since that is her only objection.

"So we'd still need to find a butcher, or teach you."

"I could learn; if that helps her." Adam offers.

"Okay, so you'd be fine. Someone brings you a full cow they just killed. You'll need to remove the skin in a condition well enough that we could tan it, you need to remove all the bowels, stomach, intestines, reproductive organs, and such. Hang it, carve it up into edible sections. You'd be fine with that?" I list out the job description.

"Maybe." He waivers.

"We can find someone else, who might have skills in it to either do it themselves or teach you, but you have to be certain if you want to learn." I'm not keen on wasting time if he isn't sure he could do it; butchering is not a job everyone can stomach.

But, Jules could possibly teach him, if he is actually up to it.

"Yes I'd learn. I could do it." He confirms with a new confidence.

"Great, then you are in charge of this restaurant. You cook, you butcher. Congrats, it's yours." Rebekah and Adam's joy is palatable. Rebekah shrieks and hugs Adam. He looks down at his wife with soft eyes and a pleasant smile.

"So, it's that easy. They just get the restaurant. Just like that?" The other man argues, breaking up Rebekah and Adam, and their happy moment.

"Yeah." I agree before Adam takes the bait for a fight. He's angered, but lets me handle it; for now. "We're divvying out jobs. We're going to need a place to eat, someone to make all the food it's going to take to feed all these people. It fills this building with a purpose."

"That's not fair." He declares.

"Give me a pitch. What community beneficial reason do you want this building for? Or, what job do you want?"

He crosses his arms, and tenses up. "I-well, I don't know." My simple question proves to be a tough one. A child's game of wanting something only because someone else got it first.

"Then you have no standing ground to argue." I close the case on the restaurant, but I feel bad. I turn the tables. I'll help him find a purpose. "What are you good at? What skills are you willing to learn? What job did you do before this?"

"I was a day trader," is his only answer.

I resist the urge to sigh. He's going to be resistant, just to be stubborn.

"Great, that's useless now." I inform bluntly. "What else can you do?" His mouth moves as he appears to grind his teeth while he thinks about my question, or grouches from my approach. After he takes a long moment, I decide to help out with some suggestions. "Can you cook? Hunt? Fight? Do mechanical, plumbing, electricity? Can you put a nail into a piece of wood?"

"No." He sneers.

I have my doubts that he'd be that useless. He had to learn something over the last few months. Hunting; at least.

I feel like he's digging his heels in further and further each time I speak. "Well, you have to think of something.

You know you. What hobbies did you have? What did you gravitate towards in school or work? What did you always want to learn to do, but couldn't? Something that would be useful to us." Silence in his answer. "How have you survived since November? You've have to have learned some survival skills." His silence continues. I think he's shut down. My irritation grows the longer he's quiet. "What about a bus boy or dishwasher? They're easy things to learn. They're going to need help around here."

"I don't want to be a bus boy. That's a low level job."

My jaw clenches. Anger sharpens my words slightly. "If you have no usable skills, then you get what you can get until you can learn a skill. We're going to need bus boys and dishwashers, just as much as were going to need chefs and butchers.

Every job is important, and no one is above or below doing any job. I don't care who you are. It doesn't even pay anything at this point. Things just need to get done."

The man pushes on a table to his side. I jump back as chairs crash to the floor, and the table tips over. The motion of his unchecked rage, I can't help but feel was directed to me. That he'd have done something to hurt me, if he felt he could get away with it; with no repercussions. His temper has my instincts pushing me to run.

He walks out before anyone can do anything else.

"Sorry." I apologize.

"No. As harsh as that was to watch. You're right." Adam says. "Should we take the supplies to the hotel?"

"Yes, please." I say.

"Can we leave a few things here? Just in case we can open the restaurant sooner. Then, we already have what we need here." Rebekah asks eager to start on the new venture.

"Yeah." I agree. "Use your discretion. Maybe, a half/half split. If you think that's reasonable for what you found. Leave cooking tools and what not here."

"Sure, yeah." She agrees.

"Great, umm, I'm going to go to Jerry's hotel. There's some people I need to talk to there." I have a thought as I make it to the doors. "Oh, maybe try to find something to cover the broken window before you're finished here. And, see if the office has any spare keys."

"Sure." Adam says.

"Thanks."

I hustle back to the hotel. A few people are headed over from our hotel; likely to get their things. Assistant guy must've gotten the message to them.

I have my own list of people to manage and inform. Miles, Kelly, DeAngelo, Chantel, Sara, Shawn, and Alexa. They all had their jobs with Jerry, now that they are moving out, that deal is broken.

I'll find Alexa last. I doubt she's moved from her room.

Kelly and Chantel are in the lounge. Chantel looks flustered as she tries to keep up with the orders. Jerry pulled her from cleaning to fill in Dominique's waitressing spot despite her lack of experience.

"Hotel's ready for move in. After your shift, grab your things, and you can move in." I tell Chantel.

Kelly puts her tray down on a table. "Fuck that."

"Please finish your shift. Jerry won't be happy if you quit in the middle." I beg.

"Like I care. I'm done. I'm moving out. I don't have to be here anymore. The deal was work while I live here, and I don't anymore."

"Can I leave too?" Chantel asks as she puts down her tray.

"No, please." I switch from addressing Chantel to begging Kelly as I follow her out of the lounge. "Kelly? Please finish your shift."

"No. I'm not working for that ass one more minute. I'm grabbing Miles and leaving." Kelly uses her speed to lose me, and end the discussion.

"What's going on with her?" Sara asks. She's with Shawn coming from the storage area.

I sigh. "The other hotel is ready for move in. I asked her to finish her shift, but she's refused. Maybe I should have waited for the end of the day to tell everyone."

"You've got this by yourself?" Sara asks Shawn. He nods his response. "I'll finish Kelly's shift. DeAngelo was with Miles. I doubt Kelly's going to tell them about the waiting part. Your best chance might be beating them back to the room."

"Thank you." I chase off; back to the rooms to wait.

Kelly, Miles, and DeAngelo barrel down the hall with excitement. "Did you grab your things too?"

"Not yet. I don't suppose Kelly told you I was asking for you all to finish you shifts."

"No, do we really have to?" DeAngelo asks.

"I suppose technically it's more courtesy. Jerry's going to get mad if everyone up and leaves with no warning. We don't want him angry with us, or he won't trade with us. We could make a new deal to have people work for something else like food or supplies. Sara's already offered to take over for Kelly's shift because she walked out, and left Chantel to fend for herself."

"That's up to Sara then. We're going. I'm not spending another minute here." Kelly bypasses me to go into the room.

"Maybe we should finish our shift then." Miles suggests.

"I'll go back." DeAngelo offers a grin. "I'll cover for you, if you want to go with your girlfriend."

I thank DeAngelo and leave them to sort it out. Kelly is going to leave immediately; no matter what I say. Miles might go with her. But, at least all the jobs are covered for.

Miles goes into the room with Kelly to work things out, while DeAngelo walks back down the hall.

I take a deep breath and enter Alexa's room. It's stuffy in here from a lack of air flow. I catch her coming out of the bathroom. We both scream a little from the surprise.

"Sorry." I offer automatically. I did enter her room without knocking; I should have knocked. "You can stop working here, and go find a room at the other hotel. We'll pack you up and go."

Alexa turns and walks back to her bed. "I'm staying here. Darius knows I'm here. If he brings Rayleen back, he'll bring her here. If she escapes, she'll come back here."

"Darius isn't just going to let her go. If Rayleen manages to escape, she probably won't be able to find her way back here." I logic away her reasons. "Staying cooped up in the room you shared isn't going to bring you relief from the pain.

Eventually you'll need to leave.

Daniel is in your memory whether you are here or elsewhere.

Rayleen is alive. You should be focusing on her. You need to get out there, and look for her." She shuts down. I'll let the seeds of thought grow. Alexa's not going to be receptive to leaving because she's still mourning. "You can have a day or two to mourn Daniel, but Rayleen needs you to search for her. Jerry's going to make you start working again."

Alexa crawls into bed. Her body rolls to the side, and pulls the blankets high enough that I can't see her. She means to ignore me.

I'll give her another day. A sigh releases as I leave.

I had forgotten about my stuff. I never really unpacked, so I mostly just need to stuff a few things back into my bag.

"Jaiden!" Jerry's anger stops me at the bottom of the stairs. "Where are my people going?"

His booming voice is drawing the attention of everyone. It bolsters me, and pushes me to stand my ground; bolder than I'd be under normal circumstances. I'm at the end of my patience.

"Not your people; my people. The people I came with who worked to earn their keep. Whoever has decided to no longer live here, are leaving for the hotel across the street."

"It's not just them." He interrupts.

"You mean the people who are free to come, and go as they please. Or, do you mean the people who only worked for you to pay off staying here. They leave, that's the end to your contract.

It's not like I'm taking away your long held employees, I'm taking people who came with me, and who are here because of us in the last few days.

And we're not gone forever, we'll still need to buy food, and make trades for supplies. Some of them might even want to keep their jobs for other compensation. I'm still delivering for you, which will need other compensation since I won't be living here."

"You're taking my staff and customers." Jerry urges. He looks two seconds away from a temper tantrum.

"Work for keep. If they are no longer staying here, they are no longer obligated to work for you." I reiterate.

"We had a deal." He whispers.

I'm incredulous that he thinks whispering is going to have any effectiveness of confidentiality right now. "Yes, and we've upheld our deal. I'm still upholding my part of it. You can't be this upset because a couple brand new workers, that barely know their jobs, are leaving, while the others will just want other compensation."

He grabs my wrist, and pulls me into the hallway. His grip is strong, and I can't break it by yanking or twisting. I feel weak.

With all those watching, I can't help but feel betrayed that no one is trying to stop him.

Jerry pulls me to his room. I death grip to the frame. It's all I can do to keep the door open for an escape. My joints ache to dislocate with his yanking.

He lets my hand go, but comes in a hair's width away. Taking away my ability to open the door. "James?" Jerry's voice is so quiet; I almost don't recognize the word.

"It's going to take longer than that to get in contact with him. It hasn't been long, and he's deep under cover. I'm still working on that. I'm moving across the street, it doesn't change that deal." Agreeing is the only way to placate him. Since none came to my rescue as he pulled me away, I have my doubts of any rescue attempts should I scream.

I won't be able to overpower him.

My eyes flit for something nearby; anything I could use as a weapon. Nothing is close, but I eye up a lamp on the desk. I don't want to get that far into the room.

He's not positioned for a knee to the crotch. I might be fast enough to punch his throat, but I don't know if that would push him far enough for me to leave the room.

"I want something else." His demand clears my thoughts.

"For what?" Hard line pronouncing each word declares my frustration.

"You're poaching all my staff and customers. I'm going to suffer loses because you're taking all my people."

There is no arguing with him. I know this tactic. Jacob used this tactic. Beat the issue to death until you win; at that point it doesn't matter whether or not you were right, because you won and you get your way. He will be dense until I let up, and let him get what he wants.

It's a behaviour this type of man employs to get his way. They are fully aware of what they are doing. But they do it, because they've learned that it works.

And yet, I argue back. Buying time until I can escape, or make him blink first. "People are free to make their own decisions. Shop where they want to shop. Work where they want to work.

You still get to keep the generator, which I'd argue is far more valuable than the short time we stayed. Most are staying for their jobs, just give them food and supplies in exchange instead of the room."

"Hi, Jaiden, are you ready to help me with that thing yet?" Jules pushes open the door, and comes to my rescue. Jerry leaps away. The tightness in my chest eases when I see them. The joy erases the ache in my arm from where the door must've scraped as it opened. "I'm sorry Jerry. I'm going to have to steal her. I only have a few quick minutes on my break to have her help me."

"It's alright we can finish our conversation later." Jerry relents.

Jules grabs my arm, and tucks me into their side. We don't detach until we get inside the kitchen. No words spoken until inside, and the door shut.

"Thank you."

"Okay, what was that?" Jules pulls me in for a tight hug. They care. They must, if I had scared them enough for a long tight hug. "You are lucky Hectre came and grabbed me. Shit." A puff of hot air breezes by my ear when they let out their stress.

Jules pulls away.

"It should get better right away here. We're moving across the street. I won't have to deal with him, and his mood swings about the trouble were causing him; as much." Jules frowns, but I quickly transition to something lighter in topic. "I actually wanted to talk to you, and Hector about food."

"Trying to poach us?" They heard the conversation. How long was Jules listening. Not, that Jerry was being discrete. Half the hotel could've heard our argument.

"No, more like seeing if you can make big batch food, buffet style once we get the restaurant running. We'll trade, and pay for it of course."

"Of course." Hectre surprises me from further in the kitchen. "Jerry won't care as long as it's paid for."

"Great, I'll let you know when I know more about when we might need that." I check off everything in my head. I should have everything now. "I'm going to head back to the other hotel. See how they're doing, and duck out before Jerry can catch me again. Thank you again for intervening; both of you."

"We've got your back. Jerry can be a bully." Hectre commiserates. "Maybe try to get a buddy system going for when you're here. He can't corner you, if you're never alone."

"Thanks. I'll see you later."

Hectre follows behind me as I crack open the door to the lounge. With no sign of Jerry, I speed out of the lounge, grab my delivery list and keys from the lobby desk, and bee line for the exit.

Air rushes out in a sigh when I exit the building alone. The short walk is enough to gather my wits again. I peer at the list. I only have one delivery listed for today.

I run across the street and inside. Walking through the door frame to the second floor onslaughts my nose with a woody smoke. It's light, but certainly noticeable. Like an incense burning.

"Oh good. Korbin is smoking us out. And, he won't stop." My manager complains.

"It's a smoke cleansing." The voice of the man I gave the go ahead for a death prayer calls from the room next to me. Korbin walks out from the room with a charred bundle smoking from the end.

"It's bullshit." A voice calls out from further down.

"Suicide and murder is a harsh way to die. Souls are bound to linger. I'm clearing them out." Korbin explains to me.

"It's better than rotting corpse!" Another voice shouts. I have to agree. While the smoke is bound to me a headache, the smell is better than rotting bodies.

"He can keep it to himself." My manager counters; nose flaring.

"How far have you gotten?" I ask Korbin.

"Almost done."

"Great. Let him finish. I already had to deal with angry departed souls once this month; that's enough for me." All sorts of looks are sent my way. Concern from Korbin being the closest.

He comes up to me and swirls the smoking stick around me. "May I?" Korbin holds up his blackened hand.

"Maybe, I don't know what you're doing." I disclose while half giving him permission.

"Cleansing." His hand comes up, and swipes up between my brows when I don't pull away.

"Thank you. I don't know what to do now." I admit.

"You can keep it or wipe it off. It's meant to cleanse your soul. It starts working on immediate contact. But, if you want to, try to keep it on for an hour. It should clear everything out by then."

"Thank you." I tuck away the thought to research this later. Korbin continues on to another room.

My manager is annoyed, but starts up giving me a report when I ask for one. "We started getting everyone settled and in rooms. I figured it would be easier to get everything else done after people settled. That way we don't miss anyone."

"Okay sure. Did you start a supplies list?" I ask.

"Kara is down there right now." She must've been the woman.

"Great." I acknowledge.

He hesitates. "We were thinking we should get settled here today; instead of expanding out. There is work to do here to get it habitable and running. If we find more people, we should have a way to handle it. It's no good for new people to come, and find us unorganized. Doesn't look good."

Mental exhaustion is starting to show as physical exhaustion, so there isn't any need to convince me to be finished for the day. "Great. That works. We'll expand out, clearing the buildings behind us tomorrow morning. They should be more supplies runs than anything else, and then tackle the hospital tomorrow afternoon."

"Jaiden!" Her voice makes me panic. There's a sense of urgency.

"Here!" It came from down the stairs. I pivot, and rush to the stair well.

"Nikki's back. She's got someone injured with her." She says.

I bolt from this hotel, and run to the other. Down the hall, I go to the medical room. John sees me before I him. There's someone on the examination table, but it's certainly not Rayleen.

"Dominique just went to go find you." John says.

I stare at the broken body. "Do you know where?"

"Upstairs I think?" His answer brings one word to mind; Alexa. "You have something on your face." John brings his sleeve up to wipe away the char.

"Thanks." I exit the room and hall to run up the stairs. My stamina cuts out half way up, and I'm forced to slow a little.

I can hear Dominique before I see her. My stomach drops.

"Did you even think about going to look for her? I've been out there for the last day looking for your little girl who was taken by your boyfriend! You don't get to be comfortable! You should be out there looking for her. You should be the one searching for her. The one to find her."

I round the corner as her hand is raised to slap her. "Nique!" I grab her one hand, and stop it from connecting with Alexa's face. Her other grabs at Alexa's jacket. "Leave her alone. Deal with her when you aren't so angry." I tell her.

She pauses, and looks at me blankly. Her hand lets go of Alexa's jacket, and I pull her outside the room. I hope she hasn't done much more damage to Alexa's mental health.

When we get outside, she talks first. "What did you call me?"

My heart stops. I think back to when I barged into the room. Her nickname slipped out. She's pissed. "Nique." The name comes out quiet; too quiet.

"What?" She asks for repetition.

"Nique." I look down, and begin apologizing profusely, and giving her an explanation. "I'm sorry. I made up a nick name when you said I couldn't call you by your other names." I stop my rushed out explanation when I hear her laughing. Not the reaction I was expecting. I was expecting more anger; possibly.

"I'm sorry." I look up to her. Her hand is covering her mouth, like she's trying to stop her laughter. "I'm sorry. I was mad. I'm over it. You shouldn't have taken that so seriously." I can practically feel how hot my face is from the embarrassment. I look down to the ground. "If you want to call me Dominique, Nikki or Nique, you're welcome to." She pauses for a moment in thought. "I think I like Nique. It's interesting."

"Sorry. I-um." I deflect. I'm still unsure about calling her Dominique, despite what she says. "Did you have any luck?"

"No. We went around in circles. I think John did it on purpose to get us back here. He said he lost her scent from the beginning. Darius had it planned out." Dominique crosses her arms.

I shrug, and think it out loud. "He very likely had a plan. Something in place to lose us while he took Alexa; then Rayleen. You know it's not all her fault; right?"

"I know. But that doesn't excuse her from sitting on her ass this whole time." Nique raises her volume so that Alexa can hear.

"She's in shock; probably depressed." I explain in hopes to get her to stop. "Not everyone reacts the same way as you do or would in her situation. Fight, flight, or freeze. Your instinct is to fight, and hers is to freeze."

"Yours?"

"Flight." I answer quickly. Something happens, and my first reaction is that I want to run far from it. Not that I ever get the chance to actually run away. "Look, Alexa needs to get out, no argument, and I bet you want to be out there too."

"Of course. We'd still be out is we hadn't found that guy." Her voice has a bitter edge.

"Of course." I need to let her get out there. She's not going to bear being held back from searching. "I can handle things here. You can organize, and get people to go out there every day until you find her. But, unless you have a reliable lead, or you gradually have to go out further, you have to be back here every night. Well, not here; at the hotel across the street. We've taken it over. We should get your things moved." I move us to her room.

"You've been busy." She admires with a grin.

"We didn't know when you would be back, so I took over, and started expansion." Simple really. I did what I had to.

"See, I told you you could do it." Dominique knocks my arm with hers.

"I still think you could do better. Connect better with them. I'm not exactly a people person. I've already angered a few people." Jerry mostly, not that he's a new problem, and Dominique would have probably made that worse than it was. But, she would have done better at the restaurant with that guy.

Dominique grabs up her bags, and starts packing everything up.

"Every leader ever, has pissed a few people off. You're never going to make everyone happy; it's impossible." She has a point.

"I suck at the speeches."

She laughs breathily. "Everyone sucks at speeches."

"No, they don't. Some people are naturally charismatic, and can come up with amazing speeches on the spot." I've seen those people. Known some of those people well enough to know they did, in fact, make up the speech on the spot.

"It'll come. You just need to put yourself out there a little more." Dominique hands me a bag of stuff, and takes her own. "Did you tell Shawn?"

"He's working still. He's going to move once he's done."

She grabs up his bag, and throws a bunch of things inside. "I'll pack his things too. I don't want anything to disappear accidentally." When she's done packing up, everything from this room is gone.

"Can we go grab my stuff too?" I ask. I hope my things haven't mysteriously disappeared. I wouldn't put Jerry past it.

She loads me up with two bags, and grabs three for herself. We trek downstairs, my heart blaring the whole way; fearful of encountering Jerry.

My room is easy to pack up. All the bags, managed by the both of us determined to make this in only one trip.

My arms ache by the time we reach the new hotel.

Our rooms designated for us, are both on the upper floor, and across from one another. The manager's thought of convenience due to our leadership has Dominique excited about the closeness.

It seems unfair that we have rooms to ourselves, when others have to share, but I keep quiet because I'd prefer the privacy.

Chapter 26

"Alexa, wake up." I jolt awake; springing up from a forgotten dream. Jaiden has her hand on my shoulder. "Whoa, sorry. I didn't mean to; it's time to get up and eat."

That's it? A heart attack for no reason?

"No." I fall back into the mattress, and sink back into a comfortable spot. The heat seeps back into my back from the mattress.

"Get up. You need to get out of this bed." She tugs at the blankets. But, I grip harder.

"Go away." Holding the blankets to my chest, I roll over. The new spot is cold. Seeping into my bones, it rips away all comfort.

"I'm not going away." It's quiet for a moment. Maybe she's giving up. "Look, I'm sorry for your loss. I certainly understand how rough it is to experience death." Her voice softens for just the moment she hangs on a pause. "But, you need to get out of bed, you need to eat, and you need to dress."

"Leave me alone." I plead. It's too soon to leave this bed; too soon to leave this room and face people. I screw my eyes shut tighter and pull the blanket up further to my chin.

"No. Get up, or I'm throwing this hot bathing water on you." I think she'd actually do it too.

Looking over my shoulder, I confirm she has what she threatens me with. A large bucket is held in her hand.

"Fine." Dragging myself from the bed, I gather the pot from her, and barge into the bathroom. Locking the door behind me, I wait for the other door to open and close, but it never does.

I fumble around in the pitch black. Finding the counter, then the sink, I wave my hand around where the flash light should be.

I click on the flashlight in resignation. All the while I get clean, I listen closely for Jaiden to leave, but she never does. Instead, now and then I hear soft clinks and rustling around.

Is she going through my shit? Is she cleaning?

"Alexa?" Her voice asks tentatively from the other side of the door.

"What?" My voice is on edge. I don't dampen my irritation and anger. She deserves it.

"Well," she starts. Jaiden clears her throat. "I just need to assign you a job for the day? Would you rather clean the hotel, work as a waitress, or work at the front desk for complaints and requests?"

My face scrunches and eyes roll. "I'm not doing any of that."

I got up and I'm cleaning myself; what more does she expect.

"Oh, but you are." I can imagine her snide smirk in my head. "See, you decided to stay here. This means, you're still under Jerry's rules. This means if you don't want trouble with him, and I promise he won't hesitate to kill you, then you have to go to work today.

Or, you could just move to the other hotel. And, the only thing I'm going to force you to do is go search for Rayleen." She breaks for only a moment. "Look, I know you're heartbroken right now and you should have your day to mourn.

Dominique has already gone out searching with a group this morning. So, we're going to move your stuff and you can mourn Daniel for the rest of the day."

She may have some good points, "but what if Rayleen comes back here?"

"We're across the street. People know her and what happened. We have our own people in and out of here all the time.

If Darius is watching you, he'll know we're just across the street. If Rayleen shows up here, she'll know where to find you and you'll know about it.

I wouldn't doubt it if Darius also has other people watching you, if he's not watching you himself.

But you also know, Darius wouldn't just take her, just to let her go; not without a big production for you. He'd make sure you would be watching to play with your emotions for him. If not, he'll show back up with promises to take you to her."

She does have some good points.

I don't want to leave, but I don't want to work here. At least over at the new place, I won't have to clean this place anymore. "Fine."

"Great, you're all packed. Whenever you're ready." So that's what she was doing.

I glare at her after I leave the bathroom. She acts like she didn't see it.

I hate you! I scream at Jaiden in my thoughts.

She passes me a bag of my stuff. I place it on the bed and run around the room to make sure she didn't forget to pack anything.

Then, go into the bathroom to collect the few items in there. Placing those in the bag before nodding to Jaiden that we can go.

I leave the room behind hesitantly, but the further I walk away from it there is a building sense of relief.

All the eyes feel like they are on me. It feels like when my parents died, and I went back to school the next week.

They all knew, but no one knew what to say, so they all avoided me like the plague. Which made it all the worse.

The only person who spoke with me my first day back was the gym teacher. He had noticed people avoiding me, and gave me a little pep talk. Condolences, he had lost his father young too, and that people just don't know what to say when things like this happen.

We arrive at the other hotel quickly.

We go inside and Jaiden leads me upstairs.

Jaiden has a room all picked out. Each room has a name or two listed on a notepad paper taped to the door. Mine has two names on it; Alexa and Rayleen.

The room is small, but there is a window to look out of. It lets in some light; enough to see the room.

There is a funky smell to the room. Like stale garbage, smoke and something else. I wish I had an air freshener.

"It only has one bed, but I thought you and Rayleen wouldn't mind sharing. I also figured you'd want to be close to your friends. Miles and Kelly are next door. The rest of us are nearby." Jaiden goes to leave, but half way out the door she lets herself back in. She closes the door and comes real close.

Jaiden writes me a note at the desk and hands it to me.

I read. *Darius is either around himself, or has someone watching you. He wouldn't just leave with Rayleen, and that be it. You need to get out, and about so there are more opportunities for you both to connect. You need to take the first opportunity you get, whatever it is.*

She's gone by the time I finish reading it. I have questions, which will now go unasked and unanswered.

Does she mean to kill him or rescue Rayleen? Does she think I should go with him? Or is she really saying that whatever happens, I need to jump on whatever opportunity it is?

She probably means to kill him.

She said she would do it, but now she's telling me I have to.

I think he's finally pushed me to a point that I could probably kill him. It's the only way I'll be rid of him.

Jaiden was right. I'm the only one that could get close enough to do it; his guard would be down.

But, if he takes me with him to go get Rayleen, I would be in the middle of his territory. Killing him would mean certain death as soon as anyone else found out about what I did.

Which would mean, go with him and play pretend so I can get Rayleen. And, whatever happens after that, will be with the goal of surviving while trying to get free. But, at least I'd be with Rayleen if I went. I could become a vampire, and get stronger.

I sigh.

I explore my new room while putting away some superficial items.

Someone lived in it before me. There are giant black socks in the drawer, a laptop on the desk, and a suit in the closet. The bed is made, but amateurly; not done by housekeeping.

I find pills in the nightstand; sleeping pills. I read the instructions. Take one as needed. They belonged to Davis Sheperd. I guess that's who was staying here before me. I put them back.

I set to unpack fully once I'm done snooping; a momentary distraction. Setting out drawers for the both of us, I organize our clothes into each.

I stop when I grasp Daniel's hoody.

Dropping it like it's made of lava.

My shoulders droop. Reality sets in.

Daniel is dead. Rayleen is gone. She's as good as dead.

It's hopeless.

Jaiden's making me go out and search for her.

But, Rayleen would be better off without me. Not with Darius, but without me.

All I've done is hurt her. I've gotten her kidnapped twice. Technically three times, if I count the day of the attacks as kidnapping.

Tears fall.

Alone with my thoughts; my only escape is in sleep. I crawl into bed and try to sleep. My thoughts keep racing a guilt ridden self-loathing track.

There is a ticket to a quick sleep right in the bedside drawer.

I wet my mouth with excess saliva. The pill is large. I pop it in my mouth, and try to swallow. It sticks to that back of my throat, and I gag. I swallow again and it goes down.

My throat feels scratchy now.

I lie in bed, and wait for the darkness to take me away from here.

Tears cool my cheeks as I think of Daniel.

He might not have been perfect, but I loved him.

Lost Souls

He didn't deserve to be killed because of me.

Chapter 27

"Well, Nikki was taken with Rayleen the last time she was kidnapped-" Their chit chat goes on beside me. Connor's way of passing time has been questions upon questions. Catch up of our lives to this point; leaving me feeling like he's finding out our every motivation as we walk down a long connecting road.

"Who Nikki?" Shawn points to me. "That Nikki? Your nickname; right?" Connor asks.

"Yeah, Dominique's my name, but I didn't like it for the longest time so I told everyone to call me Nikki." It sounded like an old person's name; I mock myself. Smiling a little, amused.

"I've known her since we were kids. And, I didn't know her name was actually Dominique until a few months ago." Shawn adds. I grin, again, at the reminder. Shawn always has joked that I'm horrible at keeping secrets; jokes on him now.

There wouldn't have been a reason to know my name. My parents respected my choice to call me Nikki. No one was ever around the rest of my family. I went to the same school until high school, and then they had us introduce ourselves. All my teachers knew me as Nikki; the school always had me inputted as Nikki on the class lists. Not like anyone of my friends ever looked at the name on my report card. Nor, which name was written on my ID.

"And, which do you prefer now?" Connor inquires.

I shrug. When people call me Dominique, it no longer provokes distaste. "Either are fine."

"But you have to have a preference." Connor states. "You should make it clear, because Jaiden's been calling you Dominique, so everyone's been calling you Dominique." He adds. "Be honest."

Of course she's been calling me that, but I suppose it works. "I like Dominique now. At times, more very recently, I feel like Nikki was a whole other person. Party girl, down for everything, no idea what to do with my life, boo-yah sort of girl. The kid version of me. But, that feels like it was ages ago now."

"War will age a person." Connor says.

Dominique feels strong. I can handle myself in a battle against the supernatural. Nikki feels like a child's nickname held on as it jingles off my tongue at the bar.

I've actually been enjoying Jaiden calling me Dominique; enjoying hearing the name in a lack of extended family speaking it.

I don't know. Maybe I miss it. Or, maybe I've just grown out of the nickname. Maybe I need a change from Nikki, or I have changed from being Nikki.

"Wait, so, do you want me to call you Dominique now?" Shawn asks. The last time this came up he was adamant to keep calling me Nikki.

"Only if you want to." I leave it up to him.

"Dominique." He scowls a little; like a bad taste. "I'll warm up to it." Shawn sounds reluctant, but I gave him a choice.

DeAngelo and Sara catch up from their side trip to the last building on the block.

"So you and Rayleen were close then?" Connor wraps the conversation back around to the little girl. My heart aches from the reminder.

"Yes." His questioning eyes ask for more of an explanation than that. I indulge before he gets the chance to voice it. "I didn't know her for long before we were kidnapped together. Then, I protected her while imprisoned.

Darius likes to pretend that he'd protect Rayleen for Alexa, but he has no idea what that actually means. He would've let her be raped if I hadn't of been there. He has no idea about basic necessities of a human child."

"Wait!" Shawn grabs my arm, and stops me. He's concerned, and his word comes out angered. "Did something happen?"

There's a moment of wonder before I realize he's asking me if I was raped. "No! No. I practically knocked the guy out who tried. Then Shale came and got us out of there. He'll protect her."

"Okay." Shawn lets it go, but not without his eyes promising that this will be talked about later. I guess I forgot to mention that.

We walk in one direction for a while. Searching through some housing. Each taking a partner or two, to search each house.

We meet up at the end of the block.

Chantel queries. "No offense, but why'd you volunteer to come with us? You didn't know Rayleen."

"More than a little girl was kidnapped, so why wouldn't I try to find her?" Connor both answers the question and digs himself in deeper. He could have let it at that statement, and it would have been reason enough. "Cole and I want to keep an eye on Dominique and Jaiden. Make sure we can trust you all and what you're doing. Cole thought it was better that I go with you. He feels like he didn't make the best impression on you and he wouldn't want to make you feel like any time he touches you, that he's purposely digging through your head for secrets."

"Why would you tell me that?" He could have left his answer at a chivalrous wish to save a little girl, but he didn't. Connor must have a reason to share this with us.

"With my ability comes a sense of black and white to truth and secrets. Most often, it's better to tell the whole truth so that people know exactly what they're getting into. Better than taking part of the blame, either directly or through guilt, when people act on your half-truths and lies."

"Why not have you with Jaiden? It's not like Cole can read her mind. Cole would be better with us for recon; read our exact thoughts. You could tell if Jaiden is lying." Though, I can appreciate Cole not wanting to make me uncomfortable. And, Connor was right; I would have been wearier of Cole coming along.

"I think Cole likes being able to touch her without hearing her thoughts." Connor pauses, and looks up to his head for a moment; thinking about the words he just spoke. "That sounds a little wrong."

"Just a little." I smile, but I can appreciate what he meant. If I had to listen to the thoughts of everyone I touched, then suddenly found someone who I couldn't read, I'd probably be all over them. It might be a relief.

"Neither of us can read her." Connor admits. "And, I don't know her well enough to be able to tell when she's lying."

I'm surprised her ability works with both brothers. "You can't read her?"

"No. She's on complete lock down." He admits.

"So no one can read her mind or read if she's lying." I state to clarify.

"Her mind and soul have natural defenses on them that stop everything. She's very special. Not many out there have both as completely natural iron clad defences."

"I'm missing something." DeAngelo pipes up. I stop walking to look back at him, and the rest of everyone there. Somehow, I had forgotten they were there and that they could hear us.

"Jaiden's a seer, but no one's supposed to know that; or they weren't." Connor blurts out in my hesitation.

"What!?" DeAngelo exclaims.

"No, she's not." I try to recover from Connor's purposeful slip, in a painfully obvious lie.

"Cut the shit." Chantel leers. "You're talking about her mind and soul defenses, and acting like you didn't announce to everyone that she's the real Marshall heir back in Banff. Obviously, she's a dreamer too. There was a good chance with her genetics, this is just you confirming suspicions."

"Okay, well shut up about it. No one's supposed to know. It's safer for her if Darius and Sandra don't find out." I think back to the moment I spoke about her as my sister. Back in the hotel, and in front of friends; Shawn, Steph, and Brad. James heard too. Everyone else was dispersing; I didn't think they would have heard. Chantel came to us after the hotel collapse. "And, how the fuck did you find out? You weren't with us then." I sneer at her.

Her large hand movements make her whole speech a bit dramatic. "Vampire super hearing. People talk, people gossip; obviously." Chantel adds. "No one believes you're the seer."

"That last part's not a full truth." Connor enlightens me. Perhaps he'll be handy to keep around after all. But, what Chantel said, it would explain why no one has asked me about my visions.

"How did I not find out?" DeAngelo asks to no response.

We're caught anyway, so I confirm it for everyone in present company. Who knows how many other people know about Jaiden. People talk; she's right. We should have been more careful. "Fine, yes, Jaiden has visions. She's a Marshall dreamer. She's apparently saved us a bunch of times by altering the future." I don't really know much of what she's done. Nothing more than what she admitted already. But, I can assume there's been much she hasn't said; the girl likes her secrets. "But, this is the last of it. No one talks about it anymore. She doesn't want people to know. I don't want people to know."

"Not completely true." Connor pipes up.

My head swings to stab Connor with a threatening glare. Interrupting him, before he can say anything more, I say, "Do you have to talk?"

"Sorry," Miles picks up. "But, has Jaiden had any visions about Rayleen?"

In all the pretending not to know, I had left it without option to think about what Jaiden may or may not be dreaming about. It hadn't occurred to me to wonder if she's had visions of Rayleen.

"No. I don't know." I answer honestly.

"No, or you don't know." Chantel quips. "There's a difference."

"She doesn't know." Connor informs from his reading of me.

"We don't really talk about her visions often." I tell them. It's been more of a taboo subject.

"Where's she hide her vision journal?" Chantel asks.

"She doesn't have one." I've never seen her write in a journal. If she had one, she might be better at finding hiding places for written secrets.

"What the fuck? I thought all seers kept journals. How else are you supposed to remember all the visions, and let people decide for themselves?" Chantel curses and stomps.

"She was raised by humans. She had to figure it out on her own. She's not going to act like what you think a normal seer should act." Shawn answers for me.

A cold chill runs through my spine. Jaiden wasn't raised by family. She missed out on her heritage, and was left all alone to figure it out.

Was she scared when her dreams started happening in real life? Did she assume she was normal, until told otherwise?

"Well, when we get back, we need to get her to tell us all her visions about Rayleen. And, then we need to force her to start writing her visions down so we can all have a chance at interpreting what she sees." Chantel's rage snarls her features.

"Perhaps not force." Connor cautions. "And, maybe just Dominique should talk to her. But, it would be helpful if she has clues. Even if it has nothing to do with Rayleen's kidnapping and rescue. Whether or not she's had anymore visions of Rayleen, for the future not yet come to be, can tell us plenty." Connor tries diplomacy with us all. He looks to me directly, his voice quietens a little for the shorter distance between us; yet still loud enough for the others to hear no problem. "And, maybe gift her a notebook, and tell her that seers tend to keep vision journals to keep details they may have otherwise forgotten." He gets louder again. A force behind his voice as he talks to Chantel, most of all. "But, it's her choice. No one will force her to tell them anything."

"I want answers. We deserve to know our future. We deserve to know what she's changed. Is she why Michelle is dead?" Her girlfriend. It clicks in why she might be so angry with Jaiden.

Jaiden was a huge part of the rescue effort in the ghost house; no doubt because of a vision. Chantel must blame Jaiden for Michelle's death; she died because Jaiden didn't rescue her.

"You can't blame her for anything." I snap at her. I've had enough of her. Girlfriend dead or not, she can't put the blame on Jaiden for not being able to save her.

"Why not? You said she's saved us a bunch of times. If we can thank her for that, then we can also blame her when people die. She needs to be held accountable. We deserve to know; everyone deserves to know what she is. It's our future too, we have a right to know what's supposed to happen, and have a say in how things turn out." I try to grasp her thinking. Part of it makes sense. If something bad was going to happen to me, then I would like to know. But, that doesn't mean we should force Jaiden to tell us anything she doesn't want to.

DeAngelo goes rigid. "So, what exactly are you proposing?"

"We confront her in front of everyone. No more lies. She doesn't control our future. We force her to tell us every vision she's had that hasn't happened yet. Then, we can decide what to do about it. She needs to answer for anyone's death she caused. That's what a civilized society is about right? It's basically murder by proxy."

DeAngelo knocks Chantel across the head twice. She nearly knocks down from the force. Miles grabs her, and her head lobs down to her chest.

"What are you doing?" My thoughts catch up.

"I was trying to make her pass out." DeAngelo excuses himself.

"I made her pass out. He didn't do any significant internal damage; just a bruise, and a growing goose egg. She might wake with a headache." Miles helps DeAngelo's case, but it doesn't excuse either of them for knocking her out. "We need to keep her away from Kelly. She's the one who told everyone in Banff; I've kept her from revealing to people here; so far. I've had to talk her down from the same rhetoric. If she knows Chantel has the same thoughts, that others will think the same, I might not be able to stop Kelly next time." Miles warns me.

Self-hatred from my stupidity lashes at my cheeks. How could I not know that so many people know about Jaiden, and harbor all this hatred of her?

Are we handling this right? Should Jaiden be straight with

everyone? Should she be telling people what she has visions of?

"Can you make her forget this?" John asks.

I look to Miles then Shawn; can they really do that?

"I don't recommend it. It would involve messing with her brain. I could erase the last day, or possibly the last five years; maybe put her into a vegetative state." Miles says.

"No, but we could keep her unconscious for a day without harm." Shawn offers.

"We can't just put people in comas when they don't agree with us." I try to be the voice of reason. While I don't agree with Chantel, it wouldn't be right to make her forget or to keep her sleeping so that it's convenient for us.

"This is about Jaiden's safety and she doesn't want people to know. We don't need a Jaiden witch hunt whenever things go wrong." DeAngelo reasons. "The Marshall bloodline was nearly wiped out once because people thought they were entitled to their powers."

"We could kill her." Connor articulates.

"No, we can't." I spit out.

"And, you believe that." He states. "Good." Connor pulls his dagger and stabs her through her back. Reactionary, I grab his armed arm before it can slice through her a second time. Horrified at his quick decision and work.

Miles sets her to the ground. "She won't survive that, you pierced her kidney, among other things. She'll bleed out quickly."

Her blood already seeps out from underneath her. I avoid the sight. I can't ask someone to take on the healing of a fatal wound. I wouldn't do it myself; not for Chantel. It's too far away to get her to a medic in time; if we can do anything once we get there.

I let Connor's arm go. The damage is already done. Chantel will die. "Why did you do that?"

"It was the easiest answer, was it not?" He points the tip of the blade as he talks around the circle. "Big guy, there, wasn't trying to make her pass out. I suspect he was trying to kill her. Elf one, and elf two do recommend messing with her brain. I suspect if we did a round of questions, you would be the only one who actually believes it would be better not to kill her, but that could be changed after informing you of possible repercussions of leaving her alive; including Jaiden dying."

Connor wipes his blade off with a cloth he pulls out from his belt pocket. "Protect Jaiden at all costs, right? She could possibly be our greatest asset. A key to winning the entire war, or at least rescuing a kidnapped girl.

We can't let anyone know about her. If someone bad manages to take her and torture her until she's compliant, we're all screwed."

He looks to me, and it feels like his next piece is directly for me. "Seer's visions are public knowledge, with punishment of treason for non-compliance; or it was, because the best defense against a seer is for everyone to know what they saw. You're dealing with a lot of people who still have that mentality.

It might not be the moral and ethical thing to do, but it ties up loose ends nicely.

She can't go back, and force Jaiden to tell her visions. No mob if she refuses. No possible death if she refuses. No death if someone decides she's too much of a liability. No imprisonment for refusal.

They can't intend to drag her out to everything dangerous hoping she might have a vision of it. She's a Marshall. She's a dreamer. The Council nearly made the blood line extinct that way. They learned their lesson and made exceptions for the family. But, I doubt that would protect her right now.

It's easier for her to be dead. It's safer for Jaiden. Tell me I'm wrong." He's not wrong. It was the easiest answer; the safest answer for Jaiden. But, it doesn't mean it was the right thing to do.

Silence greats him from everyone, as his speech sinks in. They look to me for my response. "Everyone needs to swear that they'll keep Jaiden's visions a secret. Connor, can you tell me if everyone is telling the truth?"

"Circle up." He instructs. They each stand in a circle around Connor. "Repeat after me. I swear I will keep Jaiden's visions, and heritage a secret." Connor closes his eyes. His hands are spaced in front of him; grasping at air.

We all repeat the sentence.

"No lies." Connor opens his eyes. "I'll keep the secret from everyone except Cole. But, he already knows from you, and he's not telling anyone."

I nod. There's nothing I can do now, but wonder if we can trust Connor to keep a secret. He says he loves the truth, but says he will keep her secret; that could be a manipulation and a liability.

Shawn and John, there's no question; they'll keep her secret at the very least just for me. Sara loves Jaiden, and won't betray her. DeAngelo is protective over her.

Miles maybe, but he's already said Kelly can't be trusted. Alexa probably knows too, but she's too involved with herself right now. Rayleen's a kid, she probably has no idea.

I'm going to have to tell Jaiden that all these people know. She shouldn't be ambushed if one decides to turn on her. She's needs to know that Kelly could turn on her. Miles has made it clear that we need to watch her.

"What do we say happened to Chantel?" Sara asks.

"She went inside a building and was attacked, stabbed; obviously not survivable. We didn't get a good look at the culprits. And, ran to save ourselves." Connor answers too quickly.

For someone who values truth, he sure comes up with a convincing lie quickly.

Chapter 28

I'm exhausted, and it's not even lunch time. I just want to curl up in my room, and not see another person for a whole week; maybe longer.

I wish Dominique could be handling these things.

Dragging my phone from my pocket, I open it up to see James' SuperData page; to my sent message.

Dear James,

It's Jaiden. We met when you almost ran me over with the truck. I'm informing you that we had to leave Banff because Darius came back, and killed most everyone there.

We are now in Red Deer at a hotel. We are starting up a revolution here, and are gaining speed fast. It would be beneficial to our people if they could get a word or two from you, if you are not available to come, and check on the progress in person.

Please respond as soon as you are available.

People are getting worried that you have passed away.

Thank you for your consideration.

Hope you are well,

Jaiden Kensington

I tag the subject line with Revolution Banff – Alexa, Rayleen, Dominique, Jaiden

If he's alive, if he goes on his SuperData page, I hope he reads my message. It's a long shot, but the best one I have.

The search engine research hasn't been going well. Not one sighting of him has been had. People are speculating he's dead or in hiding.

They would have paraded his head around, if someone had killed him.

Three knocks jumpstart my muscles. My phone flies out of my hand, and falls to the ground with a loud thump.

"Yes?" I call out.

The person at the door tries the door, but I have it locked. "We're ready to go, are you?" Cole calls through from the other side.

I look at the time on the phone; though I should know time means nothing anymore. It's 11:07. I put the phone away as I walk to the door. "I thought we were waiting until after lunch."

I open the door to a darker hallway, and Cole distancing himself from the door. "We had lunch. You didn't?"

"It's fine." I brush it off. I'm not hungry and it's not the first time I've had to skip a meal. All things considered, I've had some sort of food every day, for two or three meals a day; that's incredible in a war situation. I can afford the luxury of knowing that if I skip a meal now, I'll still have one later today.

"What were you doing?" He asks.

"Problems to solve; people to organize; thing to fix; deliveries to make." I summarize, yet leave out the search for James.

"I saw you running around, but I figured you would have grabbed something." He sounds concerned.

"It's fine. I'll eat after we get back." I try to wave it off.

"Which could be late tonight?" Cole reasons. "No, we'll grab you something before we go."

"It's fine; really. We don't need to wait on me."

"We can wait five minutes. No one wants to hear your stomach growl the whole time." He insists.

We walk down to the lobby. Everyone is set to go. Cole calls out as they get up from their seats. "She didn't eat lunch yet, so we're going to be a few minutes."

I can feel their aggravation. I see a couple granola bars, and grab them. "I can eat these on the way. No need to wait on me." I don't wait for a response. I grab my packed bag and go out the doors.

I eat the granola bars on the way over to the hospital. We walk the block; crossing through the buildings.

We try to go inside but the first door is locked. I instruct everyone to split and circle; test doors but not to go inside without everyone else.

Every door we try is locked. Main floor windows are boarded up from the inside or blinds are drawn shut. Light and shadows dance inside. Never quite sure, quick glimpses move within.

Whether there are people inside now can be up to question, but there were people in here at one point. No one would go to the trouble of boarding up windows, and locking doors for no reason. Whoever was inside, meant to stay.

Finally the main entrance on the other side of the hospital is openable. Once we gather everyone, a couple people go in ahead of me. It could be a trap, if people are still here.

Bright white freezes my shell, but jumpstarts my heart. They mean to blind us, and they do a good job of it. I can't see anything ahead. Any darkness now has flash orbs. I close my eyes in a small bid to hopefully be able to clear them.

"HANDS UP!" The choir yells. There's a whole group of them.

My hand shoots up in reflex.

Some of the light fades. I open my eyes. Half the lights are turned off; those pointing at our faces. The spots still blind me partially. But, as they dissipate, we are met with a regiment of serious expressions and various armed weapons.

Forever is but a moment of silence and I break it sweetly. "Hi, I'm Jaiden."

"Is someone injured?" I jump a little from the booming voice. Threatening in its fierceness and lack of apparent concern; though the question itself implies concern.

"No." I answer.

"Then leave." The same voice, same tone answers.

I take a little confidence in those two words; in those before. Would bad people ask for the injured or tell us to leave, rather than shoot at first sight? I keep my voice small but clear; sweet and nonthreatening. "We came to talk to whoever's in charge. We brought-"

"We don't want to talk. Leave now or we'll use force." He booms.

Not to be deterred I continue once he's done. "I brought some things for good faith; some food. I promise we just want to talk. We're neighbours. We just moved into hotel over that way. We're making a restaurant for a food buffet. We come in peace, and would like to talk to whoever's in charge."

There is movement. A woman goes over to the man with the boisterous voice. She answers in his stead. "We'll take you to our chief physician." Relief is the only thing I'm allowed before she talks again. "Only her. And, the bags need to stay here."

"We'll need to pat her down." He's loud enough for me to hear, but he isn't talking directly to me.

They are cautious; perhaps burned in the past. I can understand that. "Walk forward."

I take a few steps forward to separate me from my group. "I'll just take my bag off." I mention before I move. The guns are still aimed at us, tension in the arms of those with close range weapons. I don't need itchy fingers thinking I'm moving for a weapon.

Slipping the strap off my shoulder and into my hand, I set the bag on the floor. The woman comes over to grab the bag. She opens it and inspects the contents with a quick glance. Satisfied with the supplies looks of the bag, she closes it up, and puts it on her shoulder.

The man is in front of me. It feels instant with my distraction. "Arms up. Legs spread."

I do as he says. My gut clenches in trepidation. Flash backs to the vampire gang and the lick on my neck; a violation. The dirty feeling comes back anew; all before he even touches me.

"I have a pocket knife in my pocket; my right side. No other weapons on me." I don't need them to think I'm deceiving them.

The forceful trail rubs each and every inch of my covered body. I look away as he openingly gropes my breasts. Digging his fingers in too thoroughly for what is necessary.

His hands sear a trail in my body. He relents before the touch becomes suspicious to others.

He pulls the pocket knife out of my pocket, and hands it to the woman. "You can get that back when you leave."

His hands grab at my waist. Fingers dip the slightest bit between pants and skin. I want to scream but I can't. No one else will say anything; they can't. Not even if they are noticing what he's doing.

Moving on, he caresses down my butt. Squeezing two handfuls. It's sickening and vile. My cheeks heat from embarrassment.

"Alright. That's enough. She's clean." The woman says.

"She could still have something hidden." He moves on from the area to start running down my legs. Her words are a tiny rescue. I thank her with my eyes.

He finishes the rest quickly and more professionally.

I hope Jules can boil some bath water for me. I'm going to need to scald this disgusting feeling away.

The woman escorts me out of the room, and through the confusing halls. There is life in these rooms and in the halls. People walk around and eye me suspiciously.

We pass by a waiting room, beds, and curtains. A sign that says Emergency lets me know where I am; in a manner of speaking. I still have no idea where I would be, but an exit should be nearby. Hospitals usually have an entrance for the emergency intake.

We enter into an office room after a courteous knock.

"Chief." I wonder if the name is because of his ancestry, or because of his position; possibly both. She said chief physician earlier. "She says she wishes to talk with you. She brought some food and supplies for us." She sets down the bag at the table.

"Dr. Johnston, Chief Physician." He stands intimidatingly tall above me, but disarms me with a smile, and twinkling eyes. His large hand extends to shake mine.

I extend the niceties and shake his hand firmly. "Jaiden Kensington."

Dr. Johnston motions me to sit with a sweep of his hand right before he takes his own chair. "What are you here for today?"

The pressure clears my mind, and I can't think of anything smart to say. The silence can't go on too long, so I start with the basics. "Well, I came to talk, my group and I came to talk; to see if there were people here. We brought some supplies as a gift; just in case people were here."

"Would you like some tea? I was just about to enjoy a cup." The prospect of tea is nice; it's supposed to calm a person. Does he know I'm in need of calming? Likely, he is a doctor. I'm sure they are used to the signs of all sorts of nervous people.

"Yes, please." Dr. Johnston pours me a mug of tea half full, then his own. "Thank you." The mug warms from the tea, and in turn, warms my hands.

"You weren't expecting people to be here." He wonders.

"Not completely." I answer honestly. "No one has seen anyone out and about here, so we came assuming it would be empty, yet hoping people might be here."

"Why?" He asks.

"Doctors are always useful in an emergency." I realize my faux pas too late. "Umm-"

"So you mean to overtake us and use us." His accusation chills me, his body tenses and grows in intimidating illusion.

"No, no. Not at all." I panic. All the words rush out. "We're trying to build a full functioning society. We're going out, and expanding our safety zone circle, adding people to our society and as allies.

I'm not here to take over the hospital. I'm here to say, join us, help us, we can be neighbours, best friends, whatever. Give and take. Trade and barter.

We've got rooms you can choose accommodations; if you wish to have a room away from the hospital. Warm and cold food. We're working on getting electricity. There are plenty of toiletry supplies; shampoo, conditioner, soap, toilet paper.

You have knowledgeable doctors and medical supplies. That's always needed in a society. If anything ever happens; accidents-umm.

We've got a pregnant lady, I'm sure, would take comfort in knowing she can come to the hospital, and see an actual doctor for delivery."

He puts up his hand to stop me. I hope I didn't screw this up. Dominique should be the one handling these types of this; she's better at charismatics.

"Would you like a tour of the hospital?" He uses his sweeter, softer voice again. "We can talk more, and you can see what we do here."

"Sure, yes. Please." I smile sweetly. Up from my seat, I figure it would be rude to waste the tea he gave me, so I take it with me as I follow him out the door.

Staring at his back, I notice the striking white of his lab coat. How is it so clean after all this time?

We even out our pace to walk side by side. I sip the tea, and discretely wipe away a few drops when a few drops slide down the corner of my mouth.

"The first floor is mostly empty. It's our first line of defense, so anyone well enough to patrol takes a shift watching the doors and halls. Make sure no one gets in undetected.

From time to time, we've had guests. We keep them down here, and away from the other patients and priority staff.

We'll go up these stairs to the second floor; where we live."

Dr. Johnston takes the lead up the stairs, and holds each of the doors open for me to get through. I thank him each time.

I hear the cry of a baby, and it surprises me. Though, I guess there would be many people who would still have to have their babies in war. Anyone before the war, isn't just suddenly not pregnant. And, there would be those who might've gotten pregnant after.

Birth control would have mostly disappeared, or been hard to find in the moment. Woman's defence would be used up very quickly. My pharmacy only allowed me to buy three months at a time. I was out of pills before we even got to Banff for the winter; a terrible turn of events for my heavy flow and unpredictable timeline.

"Chief!" A voice calls from inside a room.

"What can I do for you Mr. Hall?" Dr. Johnston detours into a room. I follow after a moment of hesitation.

"You need to do something about that baby! She keeps screaming. I can't sleep." An older man lies in the bed. He has a cast around his leg and a dark purple bruise over his eyebrow. I want to ask what happened, but I don't want to be rude.

"Please bear with us; for now. She needed some sun. She will calm down soon. We will make our way there and roll her around."

"Can't you sun her somewhere she won't disturb the rest of us?"

"It's good for her to be around the presence of others." The Dr. explains.

"Why? So she can kill more of us?" A baby killing people? I want to ask Dr. Johnston but I don't want to misstep in front of the patient. "Who's she?"

I wave quickly.

"Jaiden, you will be seeing more of her around here. They have moved in across the street, and wish to be trading partners." Dr. Johnston explains.

"Do you have any mints?" Mr. Hall asks.

"Possibly. I'd have to check with those who take inventory. If not, I could be on the lookout for some. If, that's okay with your doctor to have mints." I look to Dr. Johnston for approval, but he's looking at Mr. Hall. I look where he's looking, and see that the elderly man has a crook of a smile at the edge of his lips. The grumpy old man is barely smiling at the thought of some mints.

"I'm sure we could allow a few mints here and there. We'll need to watch those blood sugar levels; of course." I try to commit it to memory; Mr. Hall might be diabetic. Sugar free mints would be best, if I can find them.

"Thank you, Miss."

"You're welcome." I answer sweetly.

We exit the room. Hushed, Dr. Johnston says, "You could be good for morale around here."

"In dark and absence, even the tiniest mint could keep joy going." I agree.

"True."

We bypass a few rooms and some medics doing their rounds. They look at me strangely, but neither do they ask about me, nor does Dr. Johnston explain. He will later, I bet.

The screaming gets louder. My heart clenches for the baby. Why isn't anyone stopping her screams? Why did Mr. Hall accuse her of murder?

We enter the room to see her near the window. Light shining on her and focusing everything onto her. She doesn't look dangerous. She's tiny. Barely older than a month; if I had to guess.

Dr. Johnston grasps the cart she's on and rocks her. It does nothing. She's crying inconsolably. Her face is red from effort.

I wonder why he won't pick her up. "May I?" I motion reaching out to her, without getting close enough to actually do so.

"No." He puts his hand out to physically stop me from getting too close. "You don't want to touch her. She's a succubus. She killed a few people before we figured out what was happening."

"So, no one touches her?" I confirm. No wonder she's crying so hard.

"No."

"And she's stealing the whole soul, not just partial?" To kill them it would have to be the full soul. Or, maybe she just brings them to the end, and they die naturally after that. Or could the trauma kill them without their complete soul?

"It appears so."

I swallow down a lump from sympathy. "How long has it been since someone touched her?"

"Two weeks." He reveals; my heart aches for her.

"I had a succubus friend." I admit. "I'm no expert, but she was able to turn it on and off, and she could pick and choose how much of a soul she consumed. Maybe as babies, they haven't learned that control yet. I would like to try something; if you don't mind." I resolve to quieten the heartbreaking screams. I hope whatever I've got going on with me, will protect me. Calli said it might've killed us, but maybe a baby wouldn't be strong enough to do that.

Dr. Johnston looks about ready to pull me away as I go closer, but he doesn't stop me; if I die then it's on me. I put my hand on the baby's head. "Hello darling. Sweetie, we need to talk, okay?"

Dr. Johnston tries to object, but I've resolved to this. Nothing seems to be happening. "You shouldn't do that. She'll kill you."

I place down my tea on the cart to free up both my hands. I explain things for both of their sakes, as I try to calm down the baby. "I'm going to pick you up. Don't try to take my soul; that won't end well. I have a natural defense mechanism on my soul that isn't going to let you take it. Okay? Deal?" I pick her up carefully. I hover above her bed just in case I have to put her down quickly. I'm still not sure what might happen. It could be nothing, or I could kill us both; or anything in between. "Shhh. It's okay."

Nothing seems to happen, besides her quieting down slightly. I wrap her in tighter. Her cries become manageable enough that she opens her eyes. I swipe her brow and dry her tears.

Dr. Johnston looks like he wishes to say things, but keeps quiet lest he break the calm. There is relief there.

"You just want a cuddle, eh? Sounds like it's been a while." A little more confident, I bring her away from the bed, and face Dr. Johnston.

A smell makes itself known to me. "Do you have diapers? She smells like she needs a change."

"In the cart." He grabs a diaper and wipes, and sets them out in the bed.

"Okay, I'm going to put you down for just a minute while I change your bum. I'll get you a nice clean diaper and you'll feel much better." I explain, but I know this isn't going to go well. To have someone finally be able to pick you up, then they put you down immediately, would anger anyone.

Her screams double in effort as she's pulled away and placed on the bed. I pull on the diaper straps and open up the diaper. Gagging on the smell and sight. Green and orange poop mushed in everywhere. I hold my breath and start cleaning. Wiping away the mess reveals the worst bum rash I've ever seen. Her entire diapered area is red.

If people can't touch her, then she hasn't been getting proper bum changes. No matter how hard they would be trying.

"Do you have any rash cream?" He already has it in hand, and holds it for me. I take a wipe and dip it inside. Getting a huge dollop on the wipe, I spread it all over the red. It looks painful. I put the diaper on her, and pick her up. She grasps my hair hard, not wanting to get put down again.

She's naked, except for the diaper, so I need to ask. "Do you have any clothes for her?"

"We have things we could make work. We've been keeping her naked for easier access to change her diaper. An almost impossible task when you're worried about touching the infant."

"Does she have a name?" I ask.

"No. Her mother died in childbirth. There was no father around." That explains that, I reason. Maybe the mom was human, and the father succubus, or bot succubi and the mom died of normal childbirth afflictions.

"And, no one else has named her?" I ask, knowing the answer. I look to the baby clinging to my chest; still screaming her pain out. "Well, we can't just not have a name for you? Do you like Calli? She was my succubi friend. Calista actually, but she liked to be called Calli instead. It's a cute name."

"What happened to Calli?" Dr. Johnston asks.

"We had a community before we moved here; in Banff. We were attacked and she was killed." I tell him. "We lost ninety percent of our people in the attack."

"I'm sorry for your loss."

"Thank you." I rock and bounce Calli to try to sooth her. Eventually she calms to whimpers, so long as I keep moving.

A needle in my brain pokes between my eyebrows. I attribute it to Calli's tiny hand on my face. It started only a moment after.

I pull her away slightly to look at her in the eyes. "Now, now, none of that. Or, I'm going to have to put you down." Calli's tiny head lurches forth and both grabs at my chin. I pull her away, back to look in her eyes. "I can feel you trying to get at my soul, so stop it or I'll have to put you down.

Wouldn't you rather have some cuddles?

You're not going to get my soul no matter how much you try, but you are giving me a headache from trying. You're going to have to learn to control that, so you can be held by others too. It's not nice to steal people's souls until you kill them. I know you need it because you're hungry, but you don't have to kill people for it.

Calista said she could sustain herself just taking a few years at a time, so I think you could be able to do the same once you learn to control things better."

Calli moves her hands to grasp at my hair. Her cries start again, but nothing like before. I set her head at my shoulder, and pull her close. Rubbing her back.

The blanket in her bed seems clean enough, so I wrap it around her back. Rocking back and forth, she starts to calm down. Her body goes limp and I'm aware she's likely asleep. I try to lean back to see if she is, but I can't get the right angle to see.

"What are you doing?" The lady from before is at the door.

"Shhh, I just got her to sleep." I explain in a hushed voice.

"It's okay. She seems to be okay." Dr. Johnston calms her.

"Are you a soul stealer?" She asks me.

"No, but I just had a friend that was one." I try to keep my voice low, so not to wake Calli.

"Jaiden seems to have a soul defence, so the baby, Calli, can't steal it." Dr. Johnston explains.

"What are you?" She asks rudely; like she's accusing me of something.

"A product of a one night stand and my mom was human. As far as

I know, she never told me if she was anything supernatural. But, she died when I was a kid, so she might not have gotten a chance. Basically, I don't know." I explain; 99% truth and 1% lie.

I can tell it wasn't the answer she wanted, but it's as good as she's going to get. "Well, here's her bottle. It's feeding time."

Dr. Johnston takes the bottle from her. "It might be best to let the little one sleep."

"God knows she needs it." She huffs. "Chief, Fredrick wants you to take a look at his foot. He believes it's become infected, and he won't accept anyone else. And, her people are starting to get anxious. I think they think we did something nefarious with her."

"We'll go see her people first, then I'll attend to Frederick, and finish our tour." Dr. Johnston sets out the plan.

The nurse leaves us alone. I feel awkward just standing here, not sure where to go or what to do with Calli. "Should I try to put her down to sleep, or should we take her with us? I don't mind walking around with her, if you don't mind." I know the chances of a successful transfer to the little bed won't be high. Her little hands are wrapped tightly in my shirt and hair.

"Now that she's found a person who can hold her, I don't think it would be wise to rob her of that. Babies need to be held to thrive." Dr. Johnston leads us down a different set of stairs.

"Dr. Johnson-"

He interrupts. "You may call me Chief. Everyone else does."

"Chief, if you don't mind my asking, how many staff, and patients do you have here?"

"Two hundred twenty three total. Thirty six staff, and one hundred eighty seven patients and former patients." The total boggles my mind. With that amount of people, it's impossible to think that we haven't seen them out and about. The amount of food, alone, that amount of people needs is huge.

"There are still patients? Are they critical?"

"Many critical patients died soon after the generators failed. There are terminal illness patients in our care, and a wide range of patients with disabilities, illnesses, and healing physical ailments." Chief answers.

"Do you have any healing able supernaturals on staff?" I ask.

"No." He looks to me like it's an odd question.

"We've got a couple elves that have medical healing abilities. It works through an exchange of energy. Like, my friend had some bruising on her ribs, and we were worried it would slow her down too much. So, Shawn and I exchanged and took on some of the bruising for ourselves. It reduced her healing time significantly, and all of us were better in a portion of the time it would have taken her to heal.

The exchange can work with people and animals. Not exactly something to be taken lightly because of the exchange, but the abilities could come in handy for a hospital; if they are willing or able to help. And, if you are willing to let them."

Chief ponders for a moment. "I'll consider it, but I would want to speak to them more about the mechanics."

"Of course." Better to get the information straight from them anyway. I'm not entirely sure about the whole process. "They aren't with me today. They are out with the same friend who had the bruising. A little girl who was with us, she went missing; kidnapped. So, they are trying to find her."

"That's awful."

We walk into the room, and in sight of my group. They look relieved that I'm okay. "Well, I know you weren't gone that long." Cole says.

"What?" I ask. What's that supposed to mean?

"You leave and somehow come back with a baby." His joke clicks in. We're in a hospital and I came back with a baby.

"Oh, she's a succubus. She seems to be having trouble controlling her soul eating powers. No one's been able to hold her without dying."

"Baby succubi do. It gets better as they get older; from almost no control when born to gradually better as they figure it out. I don't know how long that takes; but I do know it gets worse when they are upset. Other succubi tend to be the only ones that can hold succubi babies. They also control feed souls to the babies. They need the souls to live."

"She consumed souls from three of my nurses, would that be enough to sustain her?"

Cole shrugs. "For a while. Hopefully, until she can control it and take parts. Are there no succubi here? Where are her parents?"

Chief shakes his head. "There was never a father. The mother came to us in labour. But, she died before she got the chance to say anything." He turns his head to me. "Can you feed her souls?"

"Oh, I'm not a succubus. I don't think so anyway. I-"

Cole interrupts. "Jaiden, do you know any succubi around that could help?"

"No, none." I think out better solutions. Others might know. "I could ask Jules if they know any that come through the lounge. Or, Ziam, if he's done deliveries to any he knows of. We can try to find someone."

"Where would you get the souls?" Chief asks.

"The older succubi would feed what they've already collected, at first. Then, I guess, volunteers would offer up portions of their souls." Cole reasons.

Chief doesn't appear pleased with the response. I know why. It sounds like he's lost three nurses to Calli already. "People don't have to die to feed her. My friend only took one or two years off people's souls.

Which doesn't equate to life; necessarily. A soul has its own life span. A soul might have a four hundred year life span, and go through five bodies before it expires. Two years isn't much on four hundred years, though if they are at the end of the soul years, then two years could be a lot.

It would have to be voluntary, with people knowing the risks involved."

"But she took three whole souls already. So shouldn't that be fine to last her?" He asks.

"They need to continually consume souls to survive. But I don't know what the rate would be. Or, if babies are different.

Even after a feast, you're still hungry the next day. But theoretically, that feast could give you enough nutrients to last you a few days." Cole veers us off track to ask me a question. "So, are we taking the baby back with us?"

"We'd prefer you to leave the baby with us. We don't know you. I can't in good conscience let you take the baby out of here before seeing more of your company and operations." Chief looks abashed; like Cole spoke something offensive.

"That's fair." I tell him with a smile. As much as it'll hurt Calli, no one should fully trust a complete stranger with a baby. "We weren't completely done yet either. We just heard you were making a commotion, and wanted to show you that I'm fine."

"You were taking a long time. Wouldn't have worried if we knew you were just cuddling babies back there." Cole jests.

"I'm fine. In fact, if you would rather go back to the hotel, and relax for the rest of the day, you can." I dismiss them, and most immediately take me up on it. Leaving behind any supply bags we had brought for intended gifts.

"I'd rather stay; if that's alright." He looks from Chief to me. "Dominique scares me, and I'd rather her not hear that I left you by yourself with strangers." I chuckle while he explains to the doctor why that's funny. The guards tense, but don't move to raise their weapons again. "Dominique's her, very protective, older sister."

"Relax; you can put the weapons down." Chief extends a hand, and welcomes Cole. "Doctor Johnston. Call me Chief."

"Cole." They shake.

"Chief! Frederick is seizing." A voice shouts immediately after a door thrusts open.

Chief runs off without another word.

The awful man from earlier comes up to us. "We'll have to cut this short; I'm afraid he'll be tied up for a while. I'll inform all the staff that your people are welcome back with escort by you or Cole; until we can recognize your peoples' faces."

"Thank you." I smile sweetly. He turns around to join with the other guards again.

I'm left with Calli in my arms and a question of what to do with her. I don't have to wonder long before a man in scrubs rolls a cart to us. Carefully, I set her in the cart and cover her fully with the blanket. She sweats a little from the extra body heat of lying against me. He wheels her away without a peep from her.

Cole and I exchange glances before we move to leave. "Bye, have a great day." I wave at the guards before we leave.

We are far enough behind everyone that we don't make the effort to run to them. Cole seems happy taking a leisurely stroll back. I don't want to take my normal fast pace and appear like I'm trying to get away from him. I don't want to appear rude.

"I know your secret and I'll keep it a secret. You don't have to worry about me telling people." Cole blurts out.

What? "Excuse me?"

"I read it in Dominique's mind when I questioned her about your mind block. I both do and don't understand why you want to keep it a secret."

Of course.

So, he did end up reading Dominique, and was able to find that out. I wonder what else he knows.

I respond, but only to the last piece. Hoping to give him a good reason about why we'd want to keep it a secret. "I was treated like I was insane. Jacob, my dad, not biologically, wrote me off as being insane. Put me in a mental ward, until long after I convinced the doctor it was a joke.

I had to figure everything out on my own, including keeping it a secret from everyone.

Then I found out about supernaturals, and let the secret out to a few people. One of them became forceful about knowing my visions, and it scared me.

Dominique was kidnapped by Darius when they thought she was a seer, and tortured to comply."

"Which of course, would make you hesitant to tell anyone else." He surmises.

"Yeah. I've thought about it, but at this time at least, I think it's better to keep to myself."

"Okay." Cole nods. He keeps his head straight and just walks from there.

"You touched Chief." Their hand shake. "Do you mind telling me if he's good, has good intentions with us?"

"Yeah. He's good. He likes you. You turned his thoughts around with Calli. You named her after a dead succubus?" There is a tease with the question. He's judging me.

"She was a friend." I defend the move. "We met when she was trying to steal my soul. She told me about the soul shield then. Said I could have killed her, or both of us."

"While she was trying to steal your soul?"

"Yeah. I woke up when she came into my room. Then she fed me her blood which was supposed to knock me out completely, but it didn't. I don't know. I shot up when she kissed me. She yelled at me for not warning her about what I am. It was a whole thing. But, then I recognized her from a vision and knew we would be friends, so…"

Cole looks to me, then back to his path. He pauses speaking for a minute. "I have so many questions. I wish I could read you, makes conversations go a lot faster."

"Not as fast as seeing the conversation before you have the conversation, so you don't even have to have the conversation." He laughs at my joke. "That's got to be frustrating; not being able to read my mind."

"Gods, yes!" He grabs at my arm and nudges me sideways. "Don't get me wrong. It's refreshing not to have to worry about touching you, and hearing things I don't want to hear, but I have so many questions I need answers to, and it would be so much easier and faster if I could just look into your head."

"It's frustrating when you are used to operating a certain way, and someone comes along that you can't do that with. That's why I worry about people finding out too. That I'll tell people, and they'll change things in ways that I can't control. If I can change things my way, then I can mostly control the outcome."

Cole nods in understanding. "I touch people, and find out their deepest darkest secrets. I can find out the truth in an instant. You learn everything when you can enter someone's mind. It's weird to have to take everything as you speak it, and know it's never going to be as full of a truth as I'm used to. If it's even the truth."

"The best lies are 99% truth." I want to take that back as soon as I say it. I know instantly it was a mistake in earning his trust.

"That's not helping."

"So, you really get absolutely nothing when you try to read my mind." I ask for more information. How good is my mind shield?

"No, you are on complete lock down." He reassumes me. "It's like I run into a wall and bounce back."

I wonder. "Is it possible to let you read my mind?"

"Maybe, but I doubt it. It's your body that's putting up the defense. It wasn't learned, it was something you were born with. If it was a learned thing, then you could control it."

There are advantages and disadvantages to that. "Hmm, it would be handy to get a message through if I needed to."

"No." Cole rebuffs harshly. "If you figure out some way to pull it down, you might not get it back up. Or, you might leave holes in it, and be vulnerable to anyone who tries to probe in there."

He has a good point. "Probably best not to tamper with it then."

"No. It's your body's natural defence against people being able to read your visions. Best to leave it alone."

"Are you okay with me asking questions, now and then, about what you read from people?" I ask, knowing that I have an issue with that very same thing sometimes. People asking me about visions, that I don't want to talk about.

"Yes, depending on what you ask."

"Okay. Fair enough."

"Was there anything you wanted to ask me?" He asks.

"No." Not even a moment later, something else does pop into my mind. "Well, I mean I'm curious about some things, but not enough to ask until I get the chance to ask the other people involved."

"Like what?" Cole's eyebrow crease together in curiosity.

"You touched Chief. Did you find out anything about their history, and what they've been doing since this whole things started. But, I also don't know if I want to know your answer until after I've had a chance to talk to him."

Cole grunts in negative. "I didn't dig that deep. It was just a handshake. He was just thinking about immediate events, and I left it at that. Stay away from Derek; the big thug that gave you the handsy pat down. You don't want to know what he was imagining."

"Oh, I could guess."

"I doubt you'd guess necrophilia."

Horrified, I misstep. I catch myself, and continue like it hadn't happened. "Nope. Got it. Stay away from Derek." I wonder how his ability works. Is it like my visions and like watching a movie? Is it just hearing thoughts? "Do you see things? Well, I guess see isn't really the right word."

I go to rephrase the question, but he beats me to it. "I see things when people dream visual dreams. But, on the regular hearing thoughts part, depends on how vividly the person is thinking. It's not usually actually seeing things, but such a vivid thought impression that I could almost see what they are thinking about. Kind of, like, whatever plays in their mind is what plays in mine, so usually just their voice playing their thoughts."

"You can dig deeper though too." There is a question within my statement. He mentioned it earlier.

"It's harder. Easier to ask questions and it brings those thoughts to the surface. But, yeah. If I had time, I could dig into someone's mind, and find out everything they've ever thought; experience their memories and dreams. If it's in there, I can find it. But, I have to be touching them the whole time; that gets awkward after a while." I could imagine.

"Quite the thing to be able to do all that." It seems like a terribly invasive ability. "How do you strike a balance between what you should know, and what you shouldn't know?"

"What do you mean?" Cole asks.

"Any type of relationship would be unbalanced; if you can know everything they are thinking with a touch. You find out your boss is having an affair when you bump into him around the corner. What do you do with that information?"

"Leverage him for a raise." I nod at his quick answer. That's certainly one thing a person could do. "I'm kidding. Unless, I really have to. Or, he's an asshole. I treat the information like I had stumbled on the information through eaves dropping or accidentally seeing a text on their phone.

Sometimes I ignore it. Sometimes I judge them from afar. Sometimes I have to do something with the information I find out.

You know. It's probably the same thing you do with your visions; I suppose. Life goes on, generally, as normal. Like I didn't hear the thought. But from time to time, I do use them to my advantage.

I purposely touch people to know some things. I purposely avoid touching people, so I can't know what they're thinking. I get by easily by telling people that I'm a huge germophobe, and people generally respect that.

It does make some relationships hard, because you're dealing with the absolute truth. It's hard to have friends when you hear them think mean things about you, while being nice to your face. Or, having them think and do that to other friends.

Hard to respect a friend when all their nasty secrets are out in the open.

I've had to drop a few friends because of it. One, I reported to the police and he got arrested for child pornography.

It can make you depressed, knowing that so many people are terrible people on the inside. I can't have the illusion that others take for granted."

I guess when he puts it that way, there isn't much room to judge him harshly.

"The best way to make things happen like they're supposed to is to pretend I didn't dream it at all. I change things when I want to or need to. When it gets too much, I exhaust myself to the point I don't dream, or don't remember my dreams.

I guess I could go for a nap if I wanted to make a vision come, but I don't control what I see. Sometimes it's something important, sometimes it's painting my nails.

Sometimes I see terrible things, and stop them from happening. No one knows, so no one cares. Someone could do something terrible, but I stop it. I'll always have the memory of it, while they don't. I know what they are capable of, but they didn't actually do it in real life." I commiserate.

Chapter 29

A gasp of breath.

A racing heart.

Panic.

I sit up and take a look at my surroundings. Daylight fills most of the room. There is nothing out of the ordinary.

Maybe it was a nightmare that woke me in such a way. But, I don't remember dreaming anything. I don't remember anything since I fell asleep.

I lie back down and beg to fall asleep again. But, I have to pee and my stomach is in pain. I get up and go to the bathroom.

When did I last eat; let alone have a proper meal? It would be easier to tell that, if I knew how long I was asleep for. The sun is shining, but is it the same day, or the next?

It's colder than I would like in here. I miss the warmth of my blankets.

The person in the mirror is haunting like the undead.

I should shower and dress. It would take a trek, a trade, waiting, and a trek back lugging a pail of boiled water, in order to bathe. The effort in that sounds impossibly exhausting. Dressing, that too, I can't bring myself to put forth the effort in.

I weigh the options and find that foraging for breakfast as is, is all I have energy for. My mind is hazy and heavy; like I haven't slept in days.

Drowsy. I give my head fog a little shake. I probably woke up before I was supposed to. The pills are still working. I'll go downstairs, and eat something, and feel better.

I slip my feet into my shoes. My heels fold in the back; I can't bring myself to reach down to put them on properly.

I leave my room, and encounter a tense voice yelling at someone. Jaiden stands outside a doorway at the end of the hall. A bit of a crowd is forming around her and at the doors of the rooms.

"You don't need baby clothes for a baby you don't have. There's a baby at the hospital that needs this right now. The pregnant woman at Jerry's is going to need clothes in two months."

She's in a mood.

I can't bring myself to care about what is happening. I need food. Closing my door quietly, I walk towards the exit; thankful that the drama is not blocking my way. The noise swallows my sigh and deafens my steps.

"You're not even pregnant. You don't even have a boyfriend. You can't keep baby clothes, for a baby you might maybe have one day; likely years from now. Just because you think the clothes are cute, and you don't want someone else to have them."

I close the door to the stairs. I can no longer hear her ranting.

The lobby is empty. It would seem Jaiden's commotion is attracting all the attention. It's for the better, I decide.

Food is lain out on the counter. Unopened cans of fruit, vegetables, and mystery items. Granola bars and fruit snacks that I doubt contain any actual fruit traces. I grab a granola bar, open it, and steal a bite.

A plate of meat cubes is steaming fresh. I take a moment to wonder what it might be. It's a dark meat, but I doubt it's cow.

Picking up a cube, I slide it into my mouth. It tastes more of the barbecue sauce than it does any actual meat flavour.

One, two, three more cubes, before I figure I've had enough for my portion.

A vat is filled with a familiar warm liquid. My nose scrunches at the smell.

I avoid the fucking disgusting needle tea Jaiden forced down our throats all winter. I'll risk scurvy.

"Oh!" I jump at some woman's sudden entrance. "Hi, sorry. I didn't realize anyone would be here." She stops. "You're that girl. Sorry, I've forgotten you name."

"Alexa." I say regretfully. I know that tone and I know where this conversation is going. I've heard it a thousand times since my parents died. No amount of bracing can prepare me for her words. Tears sting the back of my eyes.

"Alexa. I'm sorry. I just- I watched from the window. I'm sorry about your boyfriend and Rayleen. It's a mess what happened. I wanted to give my condolences, but haven't really gotten the chance until now. How are you doing?" I can practically see her mentally kick herself as I waver. Tears fall. "Right, stupid question. Your life sucks right now."

I look up; almost as if that will help the tears from leaking from my eyes, I fail miserably as she hugs me. Instant sobs cry out from my throat. We both fall to the ground on our knees. Somewhere inside of me knows I brought us both down by the collapsing of my knees.

"I lost my husband a few months ago. My children in November. I know what you're going through, or at least can sympathize with it. I was broken, each time, am still broken but eventually you're going to dig yourself out of these feelings.

Eventually, you're going to be able to smile again, a smile that touches as deep as your soul. And then you're going to break again. A cycle, until the hurt gets further and further apart.

It's alright to feel this way; be depressed. I know you blame yourself. Grief is hard, and it sucks. Everyone acts differently. Mourn how you need to mourn and remember we'll be here when you come out of it.

It'll get better with time. It won't hurt so much, as much. I promise."

"I can't." I choke. Suddenly her arms are strangling me inside. I forcefully pull out of her hug and stand up. "I'm sorry. I feel sick. I just want to go lie down."

"I'm sorry." She apologizes, but I'm already gone.

Jaiden continues. "A wealth of material horde gets you nothing. If I hear anyone else is hording anything, I will confiscate their stuff, and make sure everything is divided up to those who need it. To horde items that others need, and you don't, when others have nothing is incredibly selfish."

I close the door on her tirade. Someone's gone power hungry.

In the room, I stand still.

I can't bring myself to do anything. My existence is tiring me. The drowsiness hasn't left. I just want to sleep.

I remove my shoes and lay on top of the covers. Soon, giving up hope that I'll sleep on my own, I dig into the night stand once more.

Another pill washes down with freshly collected spit.

My limbs feel like lead. I can't bring myself to maneuver under the sheets. I wait until I fade away.

Chapter 30

Jaiden's not in the lobby, but Cole is. If he's keeping tabs on her, then he should know where she is.

"Hey, where's Jaiden?" I ask.

He turns a bit, and I see he's finishing a mouthful of something he's picked off the buffet table. "You might want to leave her alone. She's had a bad day."

A thousand scenarios cross my mind in a jiffy, and in each one she's been hurt. "What happened?"

He shrugs. "Every time I've seen her, she's just gotten angrier, and angrier. She even yelled at people this afternoon. The last time I saw her; she had a bottle of wine, and was headed back to her room."

"She's fifteen, who gave her a bottle of wine?" My anger gets the best of me for a moment. It clicks after I yell, that no one would have any reason to stop her. "Never mind, I forgot where I was for a moment. I'm going to check on her." I turn slightly to the see John. "I think it's best I do that alone."

John just nods and goes off to eat.

I trek upstairs and to her door. For a moment, I think about knocking, but I brush it off. If the door isn't locked, I don't want to give her the chance to deny me a talk.

The door stops by the short chain. "Let me in."

After a moment, Jaiden pops into the gap to close the door. I hear sliding metal before she opens it again. She doesn't say anything as she goes to a spot in the middle of a semi-circle of papers and maps. A lantern lights up her room significantly.

I don't miss the wobble in her step; a wave in her beeline. Nor, the rosy glow in her cheeks.

"I heard you had a bad day. You yelled at people, and disappeared with a bottle of wine." I see the wine on top of the TV stand. On examination it appears empty. I pick it up and confirm it.

Do I have to worry about her turning into an alcoholic?

"People are dumb." Wine makes Jaiden insult like she's five years old. Actually, I know five year olds that can insult better than that.

"Was this full?" I question her. I don't feel like babysitting a drunk tonight. Although, maybe drunk Jaiden is more fun than sober Jaiden.

She lifts up a juice glass of the red wine. "If you want some, you'll have to share. This was the last of it."

I take the glass from her, before I call her on her diversion. "That didn't answer my question."

"No, it wasn't full."

I sit on her bed and examine her papers. Two maps on either side of her; each with their own scribbles. Printer paper and notepad papers surround, layered, and scattered around the maps and her. Each paper is in reach from her centered spot.

She's got a bunch of lists of all our names; each with their own purpose. I get as far as the titles of strengths, skills, food preferences and allergy list, before I stop caring what those ones contain or what the other lists contain.

One list each for needs and wants. Desirable professions, and skills list with checks in very few of the areas.

She shuffles some of the papers around, and I don't care enough to figure out what else she's been doing; it looks boring and tedious. I'm not entirely sure it's necessary.

"Do you want to talk about your day?"

"It was fine."

I raise an eyebrow, but she's not looking to see it. "Either you can tell me, in detail about your day, or I'll drink the rest of your wine."

"Have it." She waves off at it.

"I was bluffing; you have to tell me anyways." I pry.

"Then, I want the wine." She holds out her hand to take the glass back, but I take a few gulps to finish off all that's left.

I offer up the glass when I'm finished. She takes it and brings it to the tiny kitchenette sink. "You've had enough and I don't feel like helping you nurse your first hangover tomorrow. Now tell me about your rotten day."

"It wasn't all rotten, just the afternoon, and much of the evening." She points to her map. "We've got this entire section covered and gone through. These buildings didn't have anyone left alive, but there are some useful bathroom items, cleaning supplies. I'm sure the odd thing yet to be discovered will be great. The offices and clinics had some things in them, medical things, and office things. People have started putting in requests for what they'd like to use the space for.

I got things worked out with Jerry, and have designated workers at the hotel in exchange for food and supplies.

The hospital is inhabited. I met with Chief, Dr. Johnston, and he gave me a tour. I'm not so sure about them joining us per say, but they want to be friendly. Chief said that we're welcome to go to them for anything medical, but for now, he's asked that visitors are escorted by Cole and me, until they can identify who's with us and who isn't."

"So they're just there if we need them." Jaiden nods to confirm. "That's great."

"One of the better scenarios it could have been. And, I was going to see if we could bolster relationships more. Make sure that we bring them things every time we visit or need their help. We'll need brownie points stocked up for when we need medical services.

They'd likely keep more to themselves until they know us. Understandable caution. There are two hundred and twenty three people there; way more than we have combined with Jerry; I'm sure. They have plenty of bedrooms in the hospital. Unless they want a change of scenery, I don't think many are going to need places right away. Which leaves more rooms for our people at the moment. More potential rooms for the future, if Chief agrees to house some people."

I search what she says for anything that would lead to this mood of hers. Unless she's a closet alcoholic, and this is the first I'm seeing of it, something else had to have happened that she isn't telling me about. "So, the bad part?"

Jaiden sighs with reluctance. "Started after we got back from the hospital. I had a bunch of things to do, fires to put out, but nothing too bad; really. But, it just seemed like it was one thing after another. And, it was dumb things. Like, Max would have made us all pass out; maybe die. Because, she's dumb.

She decided to make a stronger all-purpose cleaner by mixing a bunch of different types of cleaner together. Three other people were trying to assess her lightheadedness while they started feeling faint themselves. None of them thought anything strange of it; four people getting faint and passing out in a small room, where there are empty poured bottles of cleaner in a pail. I went in and figured it out immediately. We had to dispose of all that cleaner because we weren't sure it could be safe to clean with after that.

And, then I had to go to Jerry's and inquire if there were any succubi that frequent there. But, there's not."

I interrupt for clarification. "Why do you need a succubi?"

"Because there's a couple week old succubi baby at the hospital, and I'm the first person in her whole life that's been able to hold her without dying. Someone figured out she's a succubi, which means they have supernaturals there that should know better. It took me a few seconds to find out that as long as there's no skin to skin contact, then the baby succubus can't steal the soul. They should have known that and held the baby instead of leaving her to lay in a- thing, all day. She had the worst bum rash I've ever seen."

I didn't see a baby anywhere in here. "So, where is she?"

"I had to leave her there because they don't trust me enough to have her come with us. Which is fair, but hard to do. But, that wasn't really what got me going." Jaiden says, but I don't entirely believe her. "People from Jerry's pulled me aside. There's a large group there that want to come under new management; having us overthrow Jerry."

"Well, let's do that." I don't see the problem. That's a good thing.

They are starting to defect to us.

I can feel her internal groan. "We can't do that right now. We don't have enough people. There won't be enough people there wanting to overthrow him. Besides, overthrowing him, and taking his business, wouldn't that make us bad people? Besides that, he has a bunch of off-site people and storage, and suppliers, and who knows what else, that could cause us problems. He might have enough people to completely wipe us out.

We can't afford war with Jerry right now. It'll make it appear like were willing to conquer people who don't agree with us. Taking half his people, even a quarter of his people, will create war. He will retaliate. We need to show the hospital how we actually want to run things, before we end up in a war. Chief might shut his doors to us, if we cause any issues. And, Jerry's got connections that we don't know yet. Where he's getting all the things for the hotel, and his delivery company? If we get rid of him, we might not have access to food through the winter."

"You're already thinking about the winter?" I ask. It's barely spring.

"Of course I am." Of course she is. "Speaking of, down here, there's a farm museum. If you are going to be in this area sometime soon, can you check them out? Take a quick look at what they have. I'm hoping people wouldn't have remembered it enough to scavenge from it. I'm hoping they'll have farming equipment someone can try to get running, like old things that don't need gas. Other important useful things. More importantly presently though, I'm hoping they might have seeds."

"You want to make a garden." She's thinking long term. What happened to the plan to move south? Red Deer isn't exactly as far south as I was thinking. It still snows half the year in Red Deer.

"If we can get a garden going this year, even if it's not much of one, then we can get more seeds so that, next year when we're running out of canned and preserved goods, then we'll have a good amount of fresh stuff."

"Okay." I agree.

"So anyway, I had to stop them, and tell them to lie low for now." She switches back to our previous conversation with a quick pivot.

"And, then Jerry confronted me because he's hearing rumblings of revolution, and thinks it's losing him business, and thinks his staff is going to rise up against him. So I had to deal with him, and lie to him, and reassure him that that wasn't happening. He's on edge."

"This confrontation makes you think he'd start a war over it. Is it safe for you to go there?" I wonder out loud.

"I'll take Cole next time. I don't think he'll do anything, but Cole can read him, and find out if he's planning anything. Speaking of, he read you and knows everything. He says he won't talk."

Drunk Jaiden talks fast and jumps around a lot. I can't help but wonder if this is a peek into how her brain works normally. Maybe Cole is lucky he can't read her mind. He might get a mental whiplash.

"Yeah, sorry. He told me after he read my mind. I didn't think he'd tell you." Not that that would help excuse it much in her head, I'm sure. "If it makes you feel better, Connor was sent to me to supervise me; make sure I'm telling the truth about what we're doing. Cole was sent with you because he finds it amusing that he can't read your mind."

"Yeah, he told me that." Jaiden switches gears again. "So, umm, yeah, I got back here, and find out that the manager I set in charge was basically doing no managing. I had to deal with getting that all set up, and do everything that I asked him to do. He has no common sense. I had to redo so much work.

And, I found out that people have been raiding and hording. I found out because I wanted to find some baby clothes and stuff. One of the girls, who doesn't have kids, is not pregnant, nor does she have a boyfriend, was hording a bunch of kid things, and baby clothes that she thought were cute, and didn't want someone else to get; for a kid she might, maybe, have eventually.

Meanwhile the kid in 7B doesn't have any toys. So I confiscated a bunch of her things, and gave it to the kid, and took some baby clothes for the baby at the hospital." She shakes her head, and throws both hands up near her head. "I just don't understand people. And, that's when I started yelling. Because, somehow I was the one being unreasonable."

"I wish I could have seen that." I admit.

"No, it's not happening again. There were other dumb incidents like that. And, that's when I decided to grab wine and haul myself up in here, and avoid people. So, how was your day?" Her last sentence throws me. Her gruff exasperation is immediately replaced with a cheerful nicety.

I laugh at the break neck switch. "Shitty. We had some problems. Chantel chased after someone, and they killed her."

Jaiden's face drops. "And, you didn't start with that? No, hey Jaiden, Chantel's dead. You were like; let's talk about Jaiden's bad day. What happened?" Drunken Jaiden is sassy. I wonder if she's normally that sassy, and she just keeps it inside. I think I need to get Jaiden drunk a few times to test out my theory.

I can't help but grin, though I know it hurts the news I'm trying to deliver. I force down the smile. "She chased after people, after they attacked us, and they killed her."

She creases her eyebrows. "Is everyone else okay?"

"Everyone else is fine." It takes me a moment too late to realize it's obvious that if we were attacked, we might have injuries too.

"Do you think it was self-defense? You guys might have startled them, and they attacked. Do you think it was Darius or another possible enemy group; like malicious intent? Should we mark the area for possible threats?" Jaiden stares at me intently.

So many questions; I was not ready for follow ups. "No, I think it was self-defense. He was alone, or seemed to be."

Her eyes narrow, and her head tilts a little. She scurries to grab a pen and paper to write something down.

What really happened out there? You went from group attack to one person?

She passes me the notepad and pen. Jaiden circles her pointer finger around, and then taps her ear. Holds her hand like she's holding a pen, waves it like she's writing and points to the notepad. I get the idea that she doesn't want to chance people over hearing.

I suppose I should tell her the truth then, if she's already suspicious of the lie.

Chantel was going to out you. Send a mob after you if you didn't tell everyone your visions. Connor killed her. Everyone else with me knows, and will keep secret. Kelly told everyone in Banff that you are a Marshall dreamer. Miles is handling her, but you need to watch out for her.

When she's finished reading, she looks up to me unimpressed. I take the notepad back.

Have you had any visions about Rayleen?

She hesitates, then sighs. Writing up a longer message.

There was one. We were rescuing her. They killed her in front of us. Too dark to figure out where it was. Dark long hallway. Lots of doors; rectangular window set to one side. Looked through window of one door, and saw her. Big room.

Guards were alerted to us, without seeing me in the window. Killed her then, before we had a chance to run in.

I grab the pen and paper for clarification. *House or commercial building?*

Definitely, not a house. She writes.

"Well that helps narrow down some things."

She silently shushes me with a finger held up to her lips.

I mouth to her. "It's fine."

She continues our conversation in silence. "No it's not. Someone could hear you." Jaiden motions to her ear to emphasize.

I mouth. "You should have told me. We've wasted so much time looking through houses. We could find her faster with this information."

She scrunches her face in confusion and mouths, "what?"

I repeat it, but she doesn't figure out what I'm saying. I write it out to her. Adding an extra line to insult her lip reading skills.

I said. You should have told me. We've wasted so much time looking through houses. We could find her faster with this information.

You need to work on your lip reading.

Sorry. Jaiden apologizes. *I thought I'd let things happen as would be, and change in the immediate moment. It's easier to do that, because now we're working on a timeline that I have no visions for.*

Telling you changes things. Changes the future.

I hadn't thought of that. I show her the message. Once I'm sure she read it, I write some more.

You know, I've been told that prophets keep vision journals. Dad had one. I found it last week. Maybe you should keep one too.

I wish I hadn't dropped that.

She shakes her head. *I don't know. What if someone finds it?*

I counter. *What if you forget a vital detail in a life or death vision?*

Am I going to have time to read a journal in a life or death situation?

She makes a fair point. Though, she could just read her entries over now and then.

Jaiden takes the paper from me. She crumples it up and puts it in her pocket for later disposal.

"I don't know. I'll think about it." The way she says it makes me think she won't think about it at all. She seems to brush off the thought too quickly and easily. "Otherwise, how'd today go?"

"We didn't find anyone or traces of recent activity. We covered probably this whole area." I show her where we've been, to the best of my knowledge. She marks down on the other map.

I realize that the other map details where we've been for our search for Rayleen. There's an arrow for the last known sighting. D and J initials following where I can only imagine was where John and I went. Then, where we've been since my return.

"What about stuff? Are things raided or looking untouched?"

"It's sort of 50/50, but in grouped areas. Like one row of houses looks untouched, and the next will have obvious signs that people have been there broken in, and taken things from every house. But, we haven't found any more people yet." A clear reminder chimes in my head. Except, when John and I were out. "Oh, umm around here, maybe, there was a large group. Maybe ask John. He might know exactly where it was. Do you think we should we go grab them? It was about twenty five people in one crowded house. They were interested in the revolution. I'm sure they'd join, but they'd need rooms."

"Yeah, John showed me. They were here." She points to a circle. "If you want to grab them, I can take care of the rooms." She makes a note down on another sheet of paper.

"So, where are you going next?" I ask her.

"I wasn't too sure about that." She points to the other map. This one has a circle around the block Jaiden's said she's cleared. Jerry's name on his hotel. Chief written on the hospital. Chad's name I recognize, but there are other names I don't. Stars at different locations. "It's a lot of houses in the areas all around us. Which is good and bad.

We're going into spring and summer, while stores will have winter stock. So things like summer clothes; it's the houses where we're going to get those things.

We could start spreading people out into these houses. But I'm afraid of expanding too fast with too little people."

"There are lots of people. We'll be fine if we start spreading out. You wanted to get this grocery store right?" I point to the map, just a little beyond Jerry's hotel.

"There's not likely going to be anything there. Jerry had to have raided it to nothing, by this point. There's no chance he wouldn't have sent someone there after moving to the hotel. Not to mention everyone else since this began."

"But, the building is there, we could start using that as a market place. Somewhere to dump shit, instead of dragging everything back here. Somewhere people can start trading things." I throw the thought out there.

She points her finger at me for just a moment. "I may have wrecked that already. Remember the hording thing. Well, that was prevalent amoungst many of the people. Fights were starting to happen, so I told everyone nothing has value, and it's community property. Whoever needs it, gets it, and if we start having issues I'll confiscate found items, and start dividing it out myself. Because, it's the people who go out, and explore that are then going to own everything; otherwise. Those who stay close to the hotel to do other things won't have anything. And, it selfish to hoard something that others need."

"Okay, well we can still do that, but maybe just with needs, and if things get out of hand. Free trading market for wants. Like food, water, clothes need to be shared equally as required, but you can find a bird house at the market, and trade something for it. Nothing says that we can't go back, say we made a mistake, and change things for the better."

Jaiden nods, processing the information before she moves on to another thing. "Okay, so how do we decide who gets the houses? It's not like a hotel room where you might get some clothes along with your bed. There's a possibility of everything in those houses and hard to move everything. Food, clothes, hobby items, tools, blankets, anything you could think of to trade for.

Do we randomly pick people to win the house lottery, do we choose based on skill? This house has a load of tools, so the handyman gets this house as long as he opens up a shop in the garage. Do we choose based on families, and the amount of bedrooms in a house? What do we do if someone disputes how it's chosen?"

"Breathe." I interrupt. I wait for her to take a breath. "I think you're over thinking things. All of this doesn't need to be as complicated as you're making it. I like the idea of the handyman getting the house for a shop. Think usefulness right now. Everyone is going to win the house lottery eventually, so it's not going to matter what's in those houses unless it can help people as a whole.

When you go out tomorrow or the next day, take your papers with you, go to the houses, and figure out who could live there based on the house contents and the skills people have. You're great with logic, use your logic, and you'll be fine. It'll be fine; I promise."

"And, if someone has a problem with it?" Jaiden said lowly.

"We'll figure it out then. Don't worry about it right now." She's complicating this too much. Thinking about problems that don't even exist. Nothing says that anyone is even going to have a problem with it.

"But-"

I cut her off. "It's just as likely that no one will have issues with it, as will. So don't worry about it right now. We can always address issues when they show up. If you can't deal with something during the day, I'll deal with it when I come back. Okay?"

"Okay." Jaiden repeats.

Chapter 31

I have to remember not to talk so much when I'm drunk. For the thirteenth time this morning, I berate myself for my actions yesterday afternoon and evening.

Nothing more so, than telling Dominique about the vision with Rayleen. I could have saved her if I hadn't said anything, but now I have no idea what's going to happen.

If she dies again, it's my fault.

Clicking the side panel into place, I declare "there; fixed."

"Thanks. I didn't realize that opened." Helena's cheeks redden.

"That's fine. I didn't know it opened until Jerry showed me. That's how it goes. But, you'll know now for next time." I comfort her embarrassment; Jerry had waved mine off as common sense I should have known. "Let me know if you need anything else."

With my hurried steps, I aim to the infirmary; through the lobby, by the stairs, and down the hall. My next stop in my ever lengthening list.

"Jaiden." My shoulders slump at his irritated tone, and commanding call.

I guess he's back. I shoulder check and glimpse a blur of chestnut brown hair, before turning back.

"The minute I know, you'll know." I reassure Jerry.

At least with his return, I can get back to doing more important things. But, I can't help the disappointment of his living status.

"We need to talk." He grabs my hand to make me turn around, and nudges towards his room right as I would have passed it.

On the offensive, aggravated by more than just his actions this moment, I snap at him. "Unless it's something completely new, then no we don't. We've talked everything else to death already.

And, if you don't mind, I'm busy fixing some of your problems, because you disappeared and didn't tell anyone where you were going."

Yanking my hand from his vice grip hurts, as his nail scratches down my finger. His grabbing strength unnerves me. I turn, against my better judgement, and calmly but quickly walk the rest of the way to the make shift infirmary.

I knock on the opened door, and address both doctor and nurse. "How's our patient?"

"Awake." The doctor announces proudly.

Great job Doc; saved his life. Maybe, I should offer them medical supplies; something I could trade Jerry for. I put it on a mental note to talk about later: talk to the doctor about needed supplies without Jerry: talk to Jerry about a trade to my benefit: talk to Chief about procuring those items in a trade to his benefit.

Jerry already owes me for helping him out today, maybe I could bundle that in and trade for something larger.

Our patient smiles when he locks eyes with me, but it doesn't last long. His body immediately tenses as Jerry comes into sight. Eyes widen for a moment, before he shuts down his emotions behind a mask of indifference.

He's terrified of Jerry. I can't have that. He won't tell me anything that way. What did Jerry do?

"That's wonderful. Very glad to see you awake. You look busy though, I'll come back later. Once the patient gets to relax for a little longer; we wouldn't want to stress him out too much now that he's clearly on the mend.

Jerry, follow. We're going to figure out how much you owe me for saving your business." I walk out, confident Jerry will follow. He'll certainly have something to say to me after that.

He holds his tongue long enough to make it into the hall. "I don't owe you anything."

I turn and imagine slapping him with my hand; instead I'll sting him with words. "You had some pretty big fires, ones that could have seen your hotel and business burn to the ground today. Because you decided to take off in the middle of the night and not tell anyone. I didn't have to help, but I did; therefore you own me."

"That's inconsequential. I didn't ask for you to step in." He throws his whole hand, pointed at me, to make his point; though I feel like it's more of a threat to hit me.

"No, but your people did. You disappeared without notice. You didn't leave anyone in charge, and by your design, no one knows what to do but you." That gives me an idea. "My exchange is for knowledge anyway, so it's not going to actually cost you anything physical."

"What do you want to know?" He's intrigued, but cautious.

"The inner workings. I want to know how to run things properly, for if you disappear again.

Sure, I superficially could run things for a few hours, maybe a day, but if you run away for a couple days at the wrong time, you'd lose customers, and be thought of as unreliable. Your name and brand would be ruined, and that's not something you can build back easily.

That means that you need to tell me everything. From where you get the supplies, to the customer list, and who gets what, and why you were attacked at the last location; in case I need to worry about another attack." Everything but his voice defies my. Arms cross, he steps back, scoffing at the thought of my request. "Or, I could trade for the generator, or a bunch of food, blood products-"

Jerry mulls on it for a minute before coming to a decision. "Fine. You have a deal." He leads me a couple doors down to his bedroom. I stick a shoe as a wedge in the door; cautious of being alone in his room with him.

There's a coffee maker on the kitchenette I position myself near; a convenient weapon if needed.

Hidden under his desk is a safe. He pulls out a key from his pants pocket, and unlocks the door. "I keep everything in here." Jerry removes a stack of papers. He fingers through them, separated by folders or paperclips. The top bundle is handed over. "Warehouse locations and passwords; who are supposed to be there on guard."

I thumb through the papers. Each paper is one location. I memorize The Superstore location: Lazarus, before he hands me more papers.

"Profiles for all the regular deliveries." He says. Another stack gets placed on top. "Accounting of trade, catalogue of debts." The last of the papers on top again. "Day to day runnings. That will give you instructions on what to do in the event I'm away again."

He grabs all the papers back, tugging them from my grasp before I can protest. I seethe inwardly when my hand stings.

Jerry puts the papers back into the safe, and locks it up. "That's not the deal." I call him out.

"You'll have a key to the knowledge, and can look at it when needed." He hands me the exact key he had used to open, and closes the safe. I don't miss the combination system; he can still get in. "I'm not going to hold your hand, nor will I show you all my cards.

You won't need any of these. This won't happen again."

"Why were you gone?" I question.

The key is at least something. Maybe I can sneak back in here later. I hope he doesn't move it. He's probably going to move it.

"I was handling some things." He's being vague on purpose.

Jerry half provided what I asked for, why would I think he would be compliant answering my questions.

"Why did the other location was burnt down?" I press on a whim.

"Turf war. A rival gang didn't like that I sold to people they considered their customers." Jerry's reluctance has me questioning the complete truth of his answer.

"Where are they? What's their territory, so I know where not to go?" I press on.

"Follow my lists, and you won't have to worry." Not what I meant.

"We're looking for Rayleen. What if we accidentally go into their territory, and they are provoked into an attack? Think it's you?" A sudden knock at the door disrupts me and makes me jump a little.

"Jaiden, there's some people asking about Alexa." Hectre interrupts.

"Can you show me?" I walk away from Jerry without a word. He may have given me access to the knowledge I want, but he's already proven he won't make it easier than that.

My hand stings while slipping the key into my pocket. I look at my hand, and spot an inch long paper cut. Folding my fingers on the flap of skin. I put pressure on it. I hope it doesn't bleed much.

"Do you know who they were?" I ask Hectre in transit.

"No. But, they're recent customers. Every day since-" He trails off but I finish the sentence in my head.

Every day since the attack and kidnapping.

If people, Hectre only recognizes from the last few days, are asking for Alexa then they must be with Darius. There's simply no other reason for unnamed people to ask for her. The fact that they weren't seen around before the attack, but have frequented the days after, can't be coincidence.

Just inside the doors of the lounge, Hectre stops. "Them." He points over to a booth in the corner.

I walk over to them, and smile brightly. "Hi, I heard you were asking about Alexa."

"You're not her." He dismisses me to drink his blood.

I won't let their obvious displeasure break pleasantries. I need this to go right. If they are Darius' spies, then they'll need to know she's around. That she's looking for them. "No, I'm not. She's out looking for someone right now. She goes out every morning, but is always back by evening, and through the night. Often comes into the lounge for breakfast.

Should I tell her that you were looking for her?"

"No. We'll come back. Thank you." The woman replies in his stead. I don't miss the hard glance down to my injured hand.

"Great," Hectre interrupts. "Can you come to the kitchen with me? Jules is in there too."

I smile and nod a goodbye to the table. "Hope you have a great day. Enjoy your meal."

Hectre leads the way back into the kitchen. Jaded me half expected this to be a rouse, but Jules is indeed in the room; cooking twenty things at once.

"She was with Jerry." Hectre says.

Jules quickly looks our way. It's all they can spare at this moment. "You okay?"

"Yes." I answer. Curious of Hectre's rescue attempt, I wonder if Jules was behind it. "Did you send him after me?"

"No, I went looking for you because of the people asking about Alexa. Didn't figure it was safe to go to her first.

But, then I saw you with Jerry, and thought you might need a rescue." Hectre answers instead. He squares up and looks down. His voice goes softer and bashful. "I want to apologize for my part in, you know. It was wrong. I should've never agreed to it."

"That's okay. It's no problem." I accept the apology immediately. I'll be weary of him still, but he's working his way to being half way trusted. The benefit of doubt allows for forgiveness when it's likely that Jerry forced him in some way. But, it is also for that same reason, that I can't put full trust in him. "I was with Jerry because he's going to show me how to run things; if he's ever gone again."

"Why?" Hectre asks.

"I traded the knowledge for helping out this morning." Sort of.

"Why?" Jules repeats.

I weigh the risk in them knowing my reasons. If Hectre's to be trusted, I'd rather figure it out with this, than with something more important.

It's not anything Jerry couldn't figure out himself. A natural progression to knowing such information. "If I find out how to run things from A to Z, then my next cash in might be for access to his supplier. I might better be able to help run things across the street."

"Smart. So, do you need to go back? Should we come check on you in a bit?" Jules offers up Hectre for another rescue; no way they'd be able to with how busy they are.

"No. Thanks though. We were done. Jerry writes everything down, and he gave me a key to the safe he keeps the information in, and gave me a quick run through.

I'm going to go to the infirmary, and then back to check on my people." I give them the simplest version of my To Do List. "Thank you, again. I'll see you later."

Walking back to the infirmary, I find the patient out cold, and tied in place. "He tried to escape after you and Jerry left."

"Did he say anything; any reason why he would suddenly run? He looked comfortable and relaxed," before he saw Jerry.

"He was biding his time. Waiting for the right distraction." The doctor offers with a shrug; it's just a guess.

I don't believe that fully. He was terrified of Jerry. Relaxed, until he saw Jerry. Terrified enough to run while still healing from a major wound. I wonder if he's part of the rival gang. Did Jerry have something to do with his wounds?

"Can you grab me when he wakes up?" I ask. "I want to talk with him. Dominique is asking about his progress. She found him, and brought him in."

"Of course."

"Thank you." I say before I beeline out the door.

In spite of the lack of traffic, I stick to sidewalks and crosswalks. The large office building was cleared this morning. What am I supposed to do with a building like that? Temporary housing?

Not the problem right now. Maybe I'll just ask for suggestions later. Someone has to have an idea; even if it's just ransacking for parts.

My main focus is on the seven apartments we're tackling today. Ambitious, it seems, with our progress thus far, but we're growing. Too fast and out of control; my mind surges the thought to the forefront.

Dominique sent back twenty five people, and I require accommodations for them all. The hotel is full. The other apartments are full.

Three of the buildings are being set aside for the hospital. A growing number of people are sending in their requests to live elsewhere.

It makes sense for doctors and nurses to have accommodations at the hospital, so it's mostly the healed patients that are looking to leave. Some, even asking for escorts to their own houses or asking when we'll get to that territory; wishing to get their own house back.

Seven apartments in a line. Seven apartments neighbouring the hospital. In reach and not too far; I try to convince myself. We'll be spread out, so no one can attack all of us at once. They can't kill us with one blow. It's a good thing.

These new apartments square off our territory nicely.

People are already slated for each apartment; or should be if my manager has done his job right.

I'm here for, I don't know, to be the killjoy and supervise.

Confiscating items, like the barbeque and propane tank I see on the second balcony in from the right. That's something better off as community use; maybe at the restaurant.

The angered faces of earlier grate every nerve I have; many were not happy that I'd be coming around, and making sure community useful objects would be removed. People aren't used to having to share.

Communism they declared; as though it was a horrible fate. Worse, when I agreed communism would be best. For now, I clarified politically.

Vast wealth does only one person good. We can't live like that when the wealth of one means the death of another.

I enter the first building. Room by room, I knock and enter; people already settling in their new homes. A quick greeting, introduction, motto, and prepared chit chat while I look over the apartment, and jot things down.

Find anything interesting or useful that would be better off with someone else or for community use? Most point to clothes they'd have no use for. Jokes about various electronics as paperweights; only funny the first couple times.

Some have questions about the invasive questionnaire of the manager. Invasive, meaning my list asking for their name, species, food preferences, allergies, and skills.

Name, I need to know what to call you, and catalogue who lives where. Could be handy in emergencies.

Species, because there are species specific needs, specifically because you are that certain species. Vampires require blood, so making sure there is enough of a blood supply: volunteers or supplements. Sunblock to travel outside during the day, or switching them to night jobs or interior jobs. Because different species have different skills they are inherent to. Higher strength might be better for moving things or construction.

Food preferences and allergies, because I don't want people to die because they ate the wrong thing, or haven't been eating the right things.

Skills because I need to know job usefulness. I need to know if you know how to hook up solar panels to a building, or if you know how to get blood out of clothing in a way that in undetectable to all beings.

Most are eased with my explanations and I mentally add informing my manager to give compulsory explanations when asking for the information in the future.

The knocked door opens. "The barbeque?" He asks.

"The barbeque." I confirm.

"I thought so." He sighs. "I've already said my good byes. Gave it a hug. Told it I was sorry I wouldn't have any steaks and coconut shrimp to grill on it." He jests and I'm glad he's playing fun with this. Better than a fight. "Where do you want it, at the hotel?"

"I was thinking the restaurant. We're turning it into a buffet and central eating spot." I admit. "Does it have wheels?" Would make it easier to move if it has wheels.

"I didn't think to check." He moves to check, but I stop him.

"That's fine. It doesn't have to go right now. We'll move it once we get everyone settled more. And, get everything figured out fully."

"Did you want anything else?" There is a sour tone, and I wonder how much of the barbeque dramatics was him taking a jab at me, and how much was him understanding why I'd be taking it. Maybe I read him wrong.

"I don't know." There's no way of knowing exactly, without tearing apart the apartment. "You've been here longer. Anything you won't need, that someone else would be better off with?"

"What aren't we allowed to own?" There it is; his feelings about this process conveyed in a sharp toned question. He doesn't want his stuff taken from him.

It's funny how attached people become to things they've barely owned for a couple hours; things that were given to them free by places taking them in.

I've had this same talk half a dozen times in the last hour. It's becoming easier to repeat what I've already said, rather than come up with it on the spot. "It's not exactly that. It's usefulness. If you have no reason for something, then it should go to someone else. Children's clothes when you don't have a child; it's better off to go to a child that can use the clothes, than to sit in drawers.

If it's better off to better the whole community, then I should take it for a communal space. Like the barbeque, where it could stay here and feed only you, or we could take it to the restaurant, and feed ten people with the same amount of propane used."

"Makes sense." He relents before I need to bring up more examples. "So do I have to pay for the food at the restaurant?"

"No, not technically." I refuse to make the mistake of telling people it's free with no strings attached. There are always those that will purposely take advantage of the system. Note to self, find an identifying system to ensure locals are the only ones getting free food. "It's free in the sense that you can just go there around main meal time, and grab whatever food you can eat.

But, I'm also not saying you can laze around all day, and just take food. Be a productive citizen of the community, contribute, and we will hopefully be able to provide everyone with their basic needs."

"What do you count as basic needs?" His simple question is surprisingly hard. What are the very basic needs to live, that we could almost guarantee to our people?

"Very basic food and shelter." I draw out a bit as I think of needs we could provide. "Some semblance of order and security."

Uhm…

"What about wants?" He moves on, much to my relief.

"There are intentions to eventually install a trade market area, where you can trade want items. That's planned for the grocery store across the street."

His excitement at me mentioning a trade market, defuses at the end. "Why there?"

"Got a better idea?" I ask.

"They were saying the office building next door is empty. I was planning on asking you for something else.

But, a market sounds like a better idea." At each sentence he pauses. He half talks to me, and half to himself. His mind wandering at the prospect. "The building is practically all windows, so you wouldn't need as much light source as the grocery store. The cubicles would be great for individual vendors or stores."

"Huh. Yeah. That's a wonderful idea." I exclaim, wishing I had thought of it myself. "What were your skills?" I hold out my hand and shake my head a little. I'll get straight to the point. "Never mind, round about, do you have management skills? Like, could you build up the market; manage the market?"

"I was a district manager. I'm practically made for this job." He knows what I'm getting at with my question.

"Great. The job is yours." Quickly, I think of some parameters. "You'll manage the market, and report back to Dominique or myself. We get final say in how it's run, but your input will be greatly valued.

We'll need to sit down and talk about it. Evenings would be best, so that Dominique can be there." Anything I'll need from him. "Can you get me a list of things you would need? I can try to find you some people based off the skills list, if you can get me a list of jobs that would be required; if you don't already have people in mind.

Basically, a game plan for getting it up, bare bones, to get people trading as fast and as reasonably possible." In an afterthought I add. "Maybe it would be good to have a section or a level, or something, for community items that are up for grabs?"

"I can work with that." His attitude has lightened considerably.

"Maybe, get me your ideas in a few days. That'll give me time to set up a meeting with Dominique; make sure she's back for it."

"Certainly." He agrees. His mood light and airy again.

"Wonderful. I should get going. I have to do this about fifty more times by the end of the day." He walks me to the door.

I leave, certain that he is a bit more amicable than when I first arrived.

When the door closes a realization swipes at me; I don't know his name. I look at him door; 2B. I'll look at my manager's list for the name of the man at 2B. That way I don't look like an idiot when we have our meeting.

The rest of the suites in this building go well and smooth. Word spreading that I'm not some dictator; I suppose.

Some are helpful, even.

The girl on the far end acquired the home handy man tools from next door. A framer who dabbled in other house building professions. At the very least, a framer that can do basic handy man odd jobs. I told her I'd leave the tools with her, rather than take them. They'd be better use with her, ready to use, than in a supply closet at the hotel. There weren't much there but basics for one person anyway. She'll be good for construction projects.

Down one building and onto the next.

A man blocks the glass door; glaring at me. I knock and smile, knowing he can see me. He knows I want inside.

I dread dealing with this tank of a man, an immediate opposing force, but I try to give him the benefit of the doubt. Maybe, he's playing guard. I don't know him, and he doesn't know me. He's being cautious.

He opens the door a crack.

"Hi, I'm Jaiden. Can I come in?" I ask pleasantly.

"No." His voice booms at me as large as he is. Every instinct tells me to run; danger.

"We haven't met yet, I'm the leader-"

He interrupts. "I know who you are. You aren't getting inside."

"Why not?" My voice is still a bit sweet; I make sure I don't waiver.

"There no need for you to come inside. We don't have anything you want, and we're all good here. Move along little girl." He moves back a little, readying to shut the door.

"That's not how this works." I tell him.

"Look," he pauses the exact time it would take to say one word. "I'm not letting you inside no matter how much you throw a temper tantrum. Power's gone to your head, and you need to be stopped. If you force your way in, you might as well be shooting guns at a peaceful protest. Everyone will turn against you. So turn around and run home."

He shuts the door, and as if given permission, I walk away. I look back, afraid he might come after me, but he's returned to his position. My chest tightens and blood boils. What just happened?

He was with the new group of twenty-five, so he wasn't there yesterday. People are talking about my outburst as though it was a power induced temper tantrum. Of course they are.

They're gossiping and spreading false conclusions. Dangerous consequences have already sounded their warning.

I knock into a chest. Looking straight and then up, when I realize he's are taller than me. "Sorry." Renzo, my mind places name to face a moment too late to not be awkward.

"What's wrong?" He's concerned. I hope I don't look as freaked out as I feel inside. I swallow through thickened honey.

"Do you know where Cole is?" Cole could read him: tell me if he's a real danger.

"Last building. Or, he might've gone back to the hotel." He's unsure. "What happened?" He looks over at the building I just came from. I wonder how much he saw.

"Guys next door refused to let me into the building." I point my thumb over my shoulder to the building.

"What? Why?"

I shrug. "Said it was their peaceful protest against me as a leader. Said the power has gone to my head, and they are tired of my temper tantrums. That they have nothing for me to take."

Renzo pulls my hand to the next building's entrance, but let's go to open the door for us. He ducks inside and holds the door. I follow him into the lobby.

"HEY! Jaiden needs some help!" He shouts loud enough to make me cringe twice over. Once for the decibel level and once knowing he's going to make a big deal out of this; I shouldn't have said anything.

They come barreling down the halls and down the stairs. A few of them inquire immediately. "What's up?"

Renzo looks to me to answer, but I don't open my mouth fast enough. "Guys next door refused to let Jaiden inside, and threatened her. Let's go over, and force our way in."

Each one seems keen to help, but I have reservations against such an immediate and drastic action. "No, wait, I haven't figured out what I'm going to do about it yet."

"Nothing to think about. We're all cooperating with this. They have to too." Someone reasons. There are nods from everyone who agrees; which is the lot of them.

I need to convince them to stay here, so I explain my thinking; explain this needs to be handled with diplomacy. "They compared me forcing my way in like someone shooting bullets at a peaceful protest. They're already talking about my temper tantrums, and saying the power has gone to my head. That if I go in there, everyone will turn against me. We can't force our way in. We have to handle this delicately, before there's uproar."

"Jaiden, it sounds like they're just trying to bully you to get what they want. Anyone with a level head can see you're trying to be fair to everyone. They're just making noise, hoping you'll bend to what they want. You give in; those people will do whatever they want." It's certainly something to think about, but it still doesn't mean we should force our way in.

They start to leave. "Wait."

No one answers me. The crowd evacuates, and goes for the next building. I need to supervise this; maybe I can mediate.

I get to the front as Renzo bangs on the window. "Open up or I'm breaking the glass." Renzo warns.

The tank opens up the door a little; enough to placate Renzo, not enough to leave himself in the open. "Can't fight your own battles little girl. You have to bring your army in to threaten us to get what you want." He doesn't acknowledge Renzo or anything he says. Instead, he focuses on attacking me; I feel like the weakest link. I am the weakest link.

"Does it make you feel good to pick on girls smaller than you?" Renzo eggs him on.

Another man moves, walking up beside Renzo. "Smells like you're trying to hide something. Or, do you have another explanation for the fresh blood on you?"

The door wrenches open. I slide to the side, to avoid an attack. But it wouldn't have been needed. The man is thrown to the dead grass, and pinned by two, while another places himself in front of me.

"I need a knife." One guy exclaims.

"Don't kill him." I plead to the mob.

"Why not?"

"I don't know." The words slip out before I can take them back. The pressure of the situation isn't doing well for my thought processing. "It would prove his point wouldn't it?"

"He tried to kill you."

"He's got blood on him, likely the real reason you weren't allowed in there."

"He's dangerous."

Multiple people supply their own answers. All of them not completely wrong; just not the way we're supposed to be handling things. I'd kill him myself, if I wasn't worried about upsetting the balance of things, and being an example for what we're working towards.

Perhaps it's too ambitious too soon; trying to get back to all life is precious, when the rest of the world is fully operating on a kill all threats mentality. Especially, since there is no semblance of peace in sight. War is still raging. This truly worldwide war is only in the beginning stages; ramping up daily.

But, diplomacy wins. "Just wait, please. We don't want to jump to conclusions. Innocent until proven guilty."

"Three on him. He moves; kill him." Renzo lets go of him position to be replaced. "Everyone else, inside. Shield her. We have reason to believe that they might try to kill her."

It feels like a surreal dream. That people would want to kill me because I'm trying my best to ensure the survival of everyone; make sure we thrive as a whole.

Rhetoric. Lessons for everyone; what we stand for, how we should act. Laws to be made on how things are run and consequences for lawbreaking. We need to make sure everyone gets this lesson; old and new comers.

Reel in my behaviour. No more yelling or outbursts. People can't see me crack or they will use it against me. I'm out of practice, but I'm sure I can fall back into place.

I'll need to tell Dominique about the attempt. She'll have an opinion about it. There will be less yelling, if she hears about it from me first.

I'm not cut out for this. A few days in and people are already trying to assassinate and mutiny against me. The people are proving that I'm a horrible leader.

Who leaves a fifteen year old in charge? Idiots do.

They circle around me in the halls. It's cramped and suffocating. I wish to push the bodies out to an arm's length away, but it's not possible. I allow it, only because I get why they're doing it.

It isn't long before we meet with a crowd in the hall. They were waiting for us. Our commotion drew them together.

"Is he dead?" One asks; he's new too.

"No." I tell them.

"Not yet." Renzo clarifies. "Why'd he have blood on him?"

As though we signaled an alarm, one by one, they lunge down the length of the hall. They paint themselves guilty before we have a chance to talk it out. Cut down easily by two daggers, and a set of claws.

One left at the end of the hall throws his hands up. Renzo stalks up to him with his dagger ready.

I stop him with my voice; too far, and guarded to do much else. "Wait! He's not attacking. Let's hear him out."

"I didn't do anything. I didn't want to do anything. I'm so sorry. I had no choice." The man blathers. I recognize him, though I don't remember his name. He's new.

"What did you do? What did they do?" I ask.

"They- there was a family living here. We were told to leave. They had a gun and threatened us; of course they would. It happened so fast. He turned the gun on the family." I notice people are leaving my sides as they search the rooms around us. "Six bullets but eight people. Then someone took a kitchen knife, and killed the mother and baby hiding in the nursery. They all took knives to make sure they were all dead."

The three from outside return to us. I notice as one walks by me with his knife to the side. It glints red, and I know the large man must be dead.

He stabs the man. I do nothing, because I am unsure of his story. Something about it didn't seem right. He could just be trying to save himself.

People threaten our people with death for not leaving. It escalates, and our people manage to kill theirs before they would do it to us. We managed to kill everyone, so they can't kill us.

A family defending themselves from invaders asks the invaders to leave while holding a gun to show they're serious. The invaders kill the family. Slaughtering even the mother and baby cowering in the closet.

Somewhere between the two is the whole truth.

Renzo asks calmly. "What are you doing?"

"He's just as guilty as the rest of them. They all participated. Not a single one held back." He confirms my suspicions. "They left quite the blood bath, I'm told."

No one talks; silent from the implications. Our people, most of them new, killed innocent people because they wanted to take over their house, and weren't invited with open arms. A baby is dead because I couldn't control these people.

I should have been here. It wouldn't have happened if I was here. Maybe, it still would have. Maybe I would be dead too.

Detaching, I discuss the next steps. "We'll need to take care of the bodies. Move them out. There's going to be a lot of blood. Jules, Jerry's hotel is going to want the bodies; if they can still use the meat. We can trade the meat for other things."

The people return from empty rooms. Bloody footsteps from the room, the offenders had guarded, tell me where the scene will be.

"You don't have to go in there." Renzo tries to stop me.

"I don't ask anything of you, that I wouldn't do myself." I pause with my hand on the door knob. "Can someone go tell Jules that we have bodies for them? Prepare them to receive a bunch of bodies in various conditions."

I don't look to see who decides to go. I'm in the room before another can tell me not to. Before my nerves win and I run.

I'm proving a point.

There is no controlling of expression when my mouth drops, and hands fold together to cover the hole. Breath caught in my throat.

One. Two. Three. Four. Five. Six.

Forcing my hands and mouth to comply, I return them to a regular state. Breathe.

My breath catches from the smell. Iron, the room smells like a penny. I half think I'm imagining the smell, because none of this could be real. That we have, had, people in our group willing to inflict this sort of horror.

This hits harder than the farm near Leduc; though there was more carnage there. I expect that sort of thing from Darius and those following him.

I don't expect this from my own; though maybe I should. It would be naïve to think that any one of them isn't capable of this. Look how easy we mowed down this rebellion. It's the same thing, but we justify it so we can live with it.

Most of us have likely done a version of the same. Killed people only trying to defend themselves.

Only one name comes to mind, one person in the hundreds I've come across, who hasn't killed anyone to my knowledge; Dominique. I stopped her from that fate.

I reason that it somehow makes her better than us. Like she hasn't been tainted by this world.

Remembering myself, I turn around. No one is out in the hall; not even the bodies. I was left to myself in my shock.

I need to bring someone. I have to help. There are two bodies, I know I can handle myself. A little girl shielded by her father. I roll his body off her legs. Close her unaffected eye.

Shot in the head and stabbed in the chest multiple times. Monsters inflicting harm because they liked it.

Dead weight really is heavier. There is no help from the person. Her body hasn't reach rigor mortis yet. It's warm and limp in my grasp, and I have to jolt her a few times to get her in a position I can carry her in.

Draped across my arms, I leave the room and apartment.

The others are just ahead. I can see them, but it's too far to think I can join them by picking up my speed by anything less than a run.

It's a longer walk back to Jerry's hotel.

Blood soaking my front chills me, discomforts me.

What's done is set as a simple order; by the time I get there Jules has already set them up with what to do. A pile in the freezer; a couple are helping to hang them from what they grabbed. The rest are returning for more. I lay the girl down and dash out.

"Jaiden." Jerry stops me as I exit the lounge.

"We're bringing in over a dozen bodies. Jules will catalogue, and we'll figure out what you own us later." I explain to Jerry. "I have to go help them bring more." I don't allow him to command my stay.

Against the flow of carried bodies, I return to the room. The living room is clear, but I can still see the bodies there.

The grandfather ahead of everyone else; the man with the gun. His face was destroyed, and a circular wound to his neck.

Grandma, presumed to be his wife, dragged herself to be closer; was stabbed in the back.

Mom and dad were trying to protect their child. Mom's arms are wrapped around her teenage son. He was taller than her. Her bloody hand print is on his cheek. I think he might've died first. Dad didn't quite make it to his daughter before he died; lain across her legs.

If it's not enough that I can still vividly picture their bodies, the blood pools tell their tale.

There was mention of a closet. Following the bloody footprints to a bedroom, I find an open closet.

A mom clutches her baby. Stabbed through the chest; the both of them.

My chest hurts.

With no help, I'm stuck with carrying the baby's body or none at all; none isn't an option.

I won't ask of them, what I won't do myself. It's become a new mantra. At least they'd never be able to accuse me of getting them to do the dirty work while I keep my hands clean.

Peeling away the mother's grasp, I cradle the bundled baby; the bundled body. Tears fall down my cheeks but I don't cry.

I walk in tunnel vision. There is nothing but my goal. I don't look down, afraid of memorizing the details of the body.

Down the side walk, through the hotel doors, through the lounge, into the kitchen, and stopping inside the freezer.

"Oh Sweetie." Jules rushes to me. "Let me." They take the baby from me.

Quite a sight I must be, I muse.

"Thanks. There's one more left. Someone will be right over with it." I ensure I use it, rather than her. You're supposed to detach pronouns when people die; it helps. It's a body and nothing more.

Jules turns to put the bundle down and I dash out. I'm not interested in talking this out right now.

I return to the crime scene; closing the door after the last body.

Staring at the hall, I state to myself, "We're going to have to clean this up before people can live here."

"We'll get it cleaned up. Go get cleaned up so you can continue your walk about without terrifying people." Renzo tells me.

"Are you sure, you don't want me to help?" I ask for curtesy sake. I don't really mean to help, unless they ask me to.

"No, go. You can't go around greeting people looking like that. We've got this. You have other work to do." He assures me.

I turn. Walking in a daze. The images won't leave my head.

My jacket is stiffening where the blood is drying. My entire front is darkened with their blood. My shoes dipped. My pants splattered.

A moment has me entertaining the idea of stripping down to my underwear, and getting hosed off outside; like a child covered in mud denied entry into their parent's house until somewhat clean.

I roll up my pant legs, and remove sock and shoes instead. I carry those with me. I wipe my feet in a patch of snow. Climbing the stairs, I reach the top and open that door. It shuts loudly behind me.

I drag myself to my room, but am met with an exclamation before I reach it. "Jaiden!" Cole catches up with me in a hurry.

"It's not mine." I reflex.

Cole's hand hovers out, ready to grab me. His fingers close and arm retracts when he remembers he can't read me. "Give me more than that. What the Hell happened? Why are you covered in blood?"

"We had some trouble. A group, part of the new twenty-five, found a family living inside one of the buildings. They killed them: baby, children, parents, and grandparents. Then they attacked us when we investigated, so we killed them." I sum up.

Cole's mouth drops open slightly. "Are you alright?"

"Yeah. Nothing happened to me." He's looking at me incredulous.

"The blood, right, I had to carry the girl and baby to Jerry's for food prep."

"Dominique's going to kill me." He smiles a little towards the end. I'm not sure if he's serious or trying to lighten the mood; possibly both.

"She's not going to kill you." I assure him.

"Have you seen you? Obviously, not. She's going to kill me. I should have found you when I was done. Not come back here to relax." He apologizes with everything but a sorry.

"She's not going to fault you for relaxing. But, if it's going to eat at you, then you can come back with me when I'm finished. I've just got to change, and clean up a bit."

"You're going back?" Cole exclaims.

"I need to finish introducing myself. People had a ton of questions. A lot of angry people who didn't understand things. I have to see if there's anything we should take for community purposes." I explain.

"I can do that. Take a break." He insists.

"No. Without Dominique here, that lies with me. I need to be the one to do it." Leadership needs to be introduced to the people.

"You're impossible."

"Not the first time I've heard that." I open my door to slip inside the room. "I'll be back in a moment."

Closing the door, I immediately remove my jacket. I lift my shirt away from myself; trying to keep the blood to the shirt, and away from my face and hair.

With clothes removed, I look over the blood on my skin. Baring taking a shower or bath, I wipe myself with a little water from a water bottle, and a soap bar. My arms and stomach got the worst of it, and take the most cleaning.

When I deem myself clean enough, without a shower, I put on all new clothes. I leave the room and go next door. Without a word of explanation I steal a pair of shoes from Dominique, and then join Cole in the hall. His expression has solidified.

"Ready."

"Did you get the blood scent away? Our people won't care, but the new ones might." Cole responds with a frown.

"I soaped. That's the best I can do. If they ask, we'll tell them the truth." Once away from the building, and hopefully out of ear shot, I confide my worries to Cole. "Could you be on the lookout? One of the new guys had mentioned about my fit yesterday. Said that people were looking to mutiny against me; right before he tried to kill me."

Cole darkens. "Until we figure it out, you need to take me wherever you go. It's not safe for you until we figure out who's all behind this."

"It might've been everyone that we killed, but there might be more. I can just try to stay in crowds, until we figure it out. There's no need for you to have to follow me around all day. I'm sure you have better things to do."

"Than play body guard to the Queen; I think not." His voice takes on a mocking accent. I pop an eyebrow at him. "I'm kidding; sort of. Everyone's got their job, and I'm a wonderful spy."

I smile and agree silently. What's better than a spy who can read thoughts?

We continue ticking off rooms and apartments.

My cleanse was not enough to clear all the blood; splatters in my hair the biggest tell of all. Those with sensitive noses all detect the blood, a few without spot the remnants in the tip of my ponytail or the spots at the top of my head. Word travels fast, and we find ourselves explaining the events to everyone.

Most are sympathetic. One tells me that tank, Larry, and his lackeys were prone to do such things. She was sorry she didn't mention it because she didn't think he'd continue due to the new circumstances.

Some, Cole read, are dubious of my ability to lead and control the people. They worry for their safety. I look too young.

Nothing I hadn't already assumed. Cole tries to assure them that I would take care of everything. That I'm a wonderful leader, and I've done wonderful things to assure our survival.

The moment he starts talking me up, is the moment I realize this person in front of me needs special attention. People I need to be careful with, to ensure they don't revolt.

We take so much time talking that there's barely any inventory being done. I don't push on items, because I don't have the energy to deal with the fallout.

I let them tell me about what we can take, and suggest items like clothes, books, pots, and pans, extra dishes. I go over the same rhetoric from the earlier forty times.

The hospital people are more receptive than the new people from the house.

Our last room can't come fast enough. Mentally and physically exhausted, by the time a woman in scrubs opens the door. "Oh, hi. Jaiden right?"

"Yes, and this is Cole." I motion to him.

"Right, I'm supposed to know the both of you; to let you in the hospital with people. Hi. Kate." She motions to herself.

"Chief said our people would need to be escorted by us until you can recognize us." I add, ensuring we're on the same page.

"Mm, yeah. We're working on some identifiers, so that you don't have to come. We realize it would be ridiculous to expect people to have to find you before the can get medical aid.

Like sorry, you're bleeding out, but you need to find Jaiden before we can treat you. That doesn't quite work."

"That would be great. Maybe a code word?" Cole suggests.

"Yeah, maybe.

Oh, right. I'm supposed to let you in.

I'm going to show you the plants, and then I have to go. I was on my way to the hospital." She lets us inside and starts walking backwards slowly. "Might've had a witch living here, or a human practicing, or maybe they just liked plants.

The plants are still alive; they don't look wilty, so whoever lived here hasn't been gone long. Maybe up to a week.

Are you sure this place was empty?"

Cole and I look to each other, then back to her. "As far as we know, no one was found here. I'll make sure to ask my manager, he was supposed to be watching over the operation. We certainly would want to take anyone's home from them." She nods at my explanation.

I'll have to talk to him anyway. That family was living here, while he said it was empty.

"Anyway, they're in here." She leads us to one of the bedrooms. "Sage, Basil, Mint, Ivy, Lavender, Jasmine, Peonies, Lemon, Bay, Chamomile, Calendula, Dill, Marjoram, Parsley, Rosemary, Ferns, Grass." She reads labels prettily written on the pots. "You may recognize most of those as spices.

But, if she is gone and I'm going to live here, these can't stay. I kill plants. Do you have a herbologist, or gardener, or anyone with a green thumb? Maybe the kitchen can use some of them."

"I don't know. I haven't come across anyone?" Cole shakes his head when I look to him for an answer. I haven't seen anything on my big list.

"If you don't, then you'll want to talk to Marcus. The man loves his plants, and they love him."

"Great, Marcus. Do you know where he is?" I ask.

I don't remember a Marcus, but that doesn't mean much.

"Hospital. He's a patient. But he's up before dawn, has his supper at three, and is asleep by five. Come by tomorrow morning, and I'll take you to him." She offers.

"Thank you. Early morning, or late morning?" I ask for clarity.

"Whenever you wake up should be fine, but the earlier the better. I'll stay up after night shift to take you." I nod.

I'll try to make sure it's as early as possible.

"Thank you." We leave out the door and apartment together.

"See you tomorrow morning." She says.

Cole and I walk silently back to the hotel. I try to go through to the stair way, but Cole stops me. "Supper." He reminds me that we've missed eating. I haven't eaten much since yesterday, so it would be good for me to eat.

We walk through to the lobby from the stairwell.

Dominique is back. I hear her laugh before I see her. Loud and boisterous, slightly infectious. It sounds like they had a great day.

DeAngelo sees us first. "Jaiden!"

Dominique lights up seeing us. "Hey, the farm museum was a great idea. So many things there!"

"We were talking." DeAngelo starts. He and Dominique share a look before he gets back to it. I'm nervous for a moment, thinking they have bad news to share with me. "And wondering if you might consider planting some people there. There are too many good things there to give it up, and too many things to haul over.

We'd love to take you out there and show you. Help you get an idea of what exactly is out there."

"Does the risk outweigh the reward, or the reward outweigh the risk?" I ask.

I'd already thought of this outcome. That the farm museum might have too many things to move over. That we'd be crazy to leave it open to others for the taking.

"Reward far outweighs the risk." DeAngelo confirms.

I nod my understanding to him. I think out loud. "We'd have to put enough people there, so that they could fight off a small gang. Umm, figure out a warning system, so people from here could come help in the event of an attack."

"We need people we can trust, or this would be the perfect opportunity for more traitors." It's my turn to give Cole a look in retaliation for mentioning that so soon.

"What traitors?" Dominique pins me with a concerned glare.

"Traitors that killed a family in the apartments warned Jaiden there would be a mutiny against her, and attacked our own. We killed them, but we're still trying to find out if they we're the only ones." Cole explains bluntly.

I watch as each person around the table goes wide eyed and mouths drop open in various degrees.

"What?" Dominique asks for more of an explanation from me with only one word and deeply concerned eyes.

"Some people think I've gone power hungry, and want to replace me with another leader. They think I'm childish, and throw temper tantrums. I'm handling it." I try to brush it off.

"Do you want me to stay here tomorrow?" She asks.

"No, no way." My first instinct is to say no. She has better things to worry about, and spend her time on, than me. I try to reassure her. "Go out. Try to find Rayleen. Cole is going to help me and I know a few others that have my back.

Someone's always around; I'll make sure of it."

"She won't leave my side, I promise." Cole adds.

"If she dies, I'll kill you." Dominique growls her threat.

"I wouldn't expect anything less." He sends me a look to say I told you so.

"The farm-" I draw their attention back to that topic. "-can you spare someone from your group to head it?" It's best to have someone we know and trust.

"Actually, DeAngelo already packed his bag, and was going to move out after he ate." I note that another person can now take up his room, and will add it to room vacancies later.

But, one person won't be enough.

"Too good to leave unprotected." He reasons.

"You can't go by yourself. You need to take some people with you. At least, see if you can grab five other people. Can you wait until morning? I don't like the idea of you all going out while it's dark, and you haven't got anything prepared."

"It's not a complete mess. There's a house ready for us. We could survive the night, and then some." He assures me.

That shouldn't be too bad then.

"Someone needs to come back in the morning and report in. Get provisions.

In a day or two, I'll need a brief catalogue of what you have. See what you could send over here. Like, if you have two axes, send one over here. Just in case something happens, a raid won't take everything." I'll save the plant discovery until then; after I've talked with Marcus. I'll need to talk to him about splitting the plants to send some over to the farm. "Right in the morning, first thing, I'm supposed to go to the hospital. So if I'm not here, I'll leave a note. And, get them to leave me a note."

"You got it."

My chest starts to itch from being put on the spot for so long, all day. I'm beyond ready to be by myself. "K, I'm exhausted. I'm going to go to bed."

"You haven't eaten supper yet." Cole reminds me with concern.

"I'm honestly not that hungry after this afternoon." I don't leave it open for discussion. I wave briefly and start towards my room.

"She had to carry the bodies of a child and baby. She was the first in the room to see the massacre. It was a complete blood bath in there. They were ruthless." A chair scrapes. "Let her go. I think she needs some space." He pauses. "It's not your fault."

I go upstairs and to my room, and properly and thoroughly clean myself from head to toe using up all the water I have.

Red and pink drip. Flakes of solid goo scrape off. I use up all the drinking water in my room, because I can't go to the other hotel to get proper bathing water.

I can't face anyone, and their sympathy or questions.

I want to be alone. More alone than one can be in a hotel. Alone enough that no one could see or hear me. Somewhere deep in the middle of nowhere.

Clothed in fuzzy pajamas, I set myself in bed. Ready for sleep after a long and exhausting day.

In a time when my heart should slow and my mind quieten, they do the opposite. My breath quickens to compensate for my shaking heart. I'm not in control of either, as images from today flash in and out.

I can't breathe. The breath going in and out doesn't have time to do anything inside my lungs.

Suffocating on air. My thundering chest hurts. I sit up and lean against the headboard on the slim hope that it might help. Instead, the movement brings a dizzying nausea. There's no time to think about if I'll throw up as my forehead moistens, and my head feels like it's in hot water.

I know that I need to get this under control before I end up throwing up or passing out.

Hyperventilating remedy, I need to hug a pillow. Pulling in the bed's pillow, I put it so it covers my torso with the end sitting chin height. My arms wrap around it and I close my eyes.

In my mind, I imagine my own body wrapping their arms around me. Telling me that everything is going to be okay. A rough day needs to be let out of my system and it's trying to do that all at once. We just need to match breathing, until mine becomes even.

In and out. One and two. Slower and slower. Focus on getting air into the lungs; good. In and out.

As the panic recedes, my breathing slows, and the pain releases in tears.

My body quakes from internalized crying. I mustn't make any noise. I don't want to bother anyone with my crying.

My pillow friend continues to hug and my mind's voice pep talks. Let it out. You need to let it out. Don't bottle it up. Today was horrific, and you managed to stay strong through it all.

Finally calming down, I release the wet pillow and blow my nose in a tissue.

Crawling back into bed, I pull up the blanket over my head and twist it and myself around until the blanket has me in a firm hold. The corner is wrapped over my eyes to keep them close. Digging my arms inside the cocoon before I finally call myself settled in; safe and cozy.

After its antics, my mind refuses to shut down. My body steps in; forcing it to be quiet through exhaustion.

My trapped body stills, knowing that it would ache should I try to move anything.

"If you want respect in this world you have to be more ruthless and callous than a man, but I think you already know that. You just need a bit of long lost confidence. You need to reclaim yourself, and channel your buried rage into thriving." The woman advises. She dips her

hand into the bag of chips.

"And what you do is thriving?" I counter.

She shrugs. "Better than surviving. You know this is better for everyone. You have the most to benefit from this, and in a couple days you'll be home and, most importantly, away from that creep. Just don't eat the cherry pie tonight. I wouldn't want you to get sick."

Chapter 32

Fuck Jaiden!

Fuck Nikki!

Bitches; the both of them!

While part of me can reason they may have a bit of a point, that it's a better use of time to search for Rayleen, I hate the both of them. This isn't searching for Rayleen; not properly. This is a waste of my time.

Nikki doesn't even seem like she's actually searching for Rayleen. There hasn't been one mention of her name.

If we really were looking for her, we wouldn't be bothering with searching out and helping people. Our errand this morning has cost us most of the morning. Not one time, has one of them mentioned anything about Rayleen to the new people. I had to ask myself. No one knew anything, so it was a waste anyway.

Nikki returns to the truck. She opens the door. "Jaiden's at Jerry's, and most are already gone already. Someone's going to talk to her, and figure out what to do with these guys. But, someone should stay behind and help."

"I'll do it." I volunteer. It's better than continuing on with these people. I'm ready to go at it on my own. Maybe I can, if we get this done fast. Pass these people off to someone else, and I can go out searching by myself. Actual searching, not this having to run errands bullshit.

"No, I think Miles can do it." Nikki refuses.

Miles sends me a sympathetic look, before he gets out of the cab and around to the side, to usher the new people inside. They carry with them all their belongings into the lobby of our hotel.

All these people lived in squalor conditions in one house. Now, they are our problem. For some reason, Nikki has made them our problem.

The hotel is right there. How much trouble would I get into if I jumped out right now, and just went back to bed? Not that I could with a person on either side of me.

Miles had been a convenient choice. He was next to the door. We are able to get some slight elbow room now that he's gone though. There are still more people in here than there are seatbelts.

Nikki gets back inside. John starts the truck back up, and we go out to the right on the main road.

Nikki rustles a map. After a quick examination, she's got things figured out. "Okay so I think we need to take a right at the huge intersection down there. No wait. One after. No…"

"Do you know where we're going?" John asks. He stops the truck, so he can get a better look at the map.

"Here." She points on the map to a circled space. I can't see what it is from here, but there are a couple buildings within the circle. Maybe they have a lead on Rayleen.

A bubble of excitement fills in my chest. I try not to be hopeful; leads don't always pan out. The thought that it could very well be another group crosses my mind, and deflates the bubble.

"Okay." John takes the map. "Hey, you were right. We do have to go right, but four intersections down."

John drives us to where ever we're going. I wonder the whole way, if this is another errand, or if we're actually going to start searching for Rayleen. Flipping back, and forth.

I hope the latter, or I'm going to rage.

We drive and turn, drive and turn. We go into a residential area, but it quickly turns into a farm in the middle of town; if the green tractor on a pole is any indication.

We pull up on the road. The chain link fence has a gate, but it looks chained up.

Sunnybrook Farm Museum, a sign indicates. So, not a farm, a museum for farms.

It looks quiet and abandoned. No one's here. If Darius' people were here, there would be more of them. They would have people out patrolling. People would have ambushed our truck by now.

So why are we here?

With dread, I bet it's not to search for Rayleen.

"What is this place?" DeAngelo asks. I want to know too. The answer better be worth it.

The door opens and we are to start getting out of the truck in due order. Cold air seeps into the truck's warmth.

"A farm museum. Jaiden asked us to check it out. She thinks there might be important and useful things there. Doesn't think many people would have thought of scavenging from it." Nikki leads the charge out. She hops the fence after making sure the gate really is locked.

I reluctantly follow after sending dirty looks to everyone. A quick search, I reason, and then we can finally look for Rayleen.

The dirt road has splotches of mud I make sure to avoid.

They fan out in a rush to explore. A werewolf in Sara's clothes runs far ahead. Shawn and DeAngelo run off in their own directions. Shawn to the left and DeAngelo to the buildings ahead on the right.

Some other guy checks the door to the first building and announces, "It's locked."

John and Nikki forge ahead together. I trail a bit behind them. Looking around, just to look busy. Disinterested in why we're here, but not looking for a fight by going back to the truck.

There's farm equipment by the hundreds, but I doubt any of it would work. Museums aren't known for their working relics.

"Way to go Jaiden! Holy shit!" John exclaims peering through a window. He pulls away. "We have to take some of this back with us." Dread fills me immediately. They're going to turn this into a whole day's job. If not, more.

"Jaiden just asked us to scout it out before we look for Rayleen." Nikki says.

"But, what if someone else has the same idea as her. We could come back in a few days, and it'll all be gone." He argues.

"We could have people stay here." DeAngelo suggests.

"No, that's too far away from the hotel. If anything happened, there would be no way of knowing you were attacked." Nikki tries to shut it down.

"This place is a gold mine, and you don't leave the mine after you've discovered the vein of gold. There's too much to move over." DeAngelo argues. "What if we moved everyone here, and around here?"

"We can't move the hospital." John points out.

DeAngelo looks around a bit with a swing of his head. "Well then, make a separate outpost here. This place is too good to give up. If we discovered it, then someone else could too. We could make a whole working farm here. Be able to feed everyone."

"Talk to Jaiden about it." Nikki gives up with a wave of her hand. "She'll know more about how doable it is."

"Isn't it your call?" I quip.

The hard glare she sends my way is worth it. "She's dealing more with that side of things. She'll be able to tell more realistically if it could be done. Who we can spare. Who's suitable to come out here. What vehicles we can give up."

"You mean that Jaiden's really the one in charge." I dig with a sharp edge.

"She's handling those things while I try to find Rayleen."

"This isn't looking for Rayleen! This is going out on an errand for Jaiden." I release my angered thoughts to hurt her, and I know exactly where to poke. "What have you done to lead the whole group since this started? Nothing. You've just been out gallivanting around, and having a merry old time, while you pretend to look for Rayleen. I bet you don't even care to find her."

"Shut up!" Nikki stomps over to me, pointing and towering closely over me. "I've done more to try to find her than you have. Your little girl is out there being held hostage by your psychotic ex, and all you want to do is stay in your room, and mourn your fuck boy. You care more about him than her, or else you'd have been out here from day one. You would have gone with him in the first place."

I open my mouth to shout something else hurtful at her, but the pain in my heart freezes my mind. I can't think of anything to say, if my body would even cooperate long enough to say it. Her words echo in my head. I can't help but to think she's right. I should have gone with Darius when he took Rayleen.

Tears well in my eyes. I turn around so she can't make it worse.

"Maybe we should split off." DeAngelo suggests. "Alexa can go with some people to search for Rayleen, and we can finish up here."

Nikki nods. She looks around. "John, Connor, Shawn, and Alexa, start walking back to the hotel. Search all the buildings between here and there. If you're not finished by supper, note where you are and head to the hotel. DeAngelo, Sara, and I will stay here and ferry some things back to the hotel, then come find you, and help finish up; if there is time."

I don't wait for the others. I'm over the fence, and headed back the way we came before anyone else.

"Hotel is that way." John calls after me. I turn to see him pointing another way. Turning around, I catch up with them to walk back to the hotel. Maybe this is more of a direct route than the roads we took to get here.

This feels better; renewing my energy and spirit. On the ground and physically searching for Rayleen.

We pair off almost naturally. John and Shawn, and Connor and I. John turns into a werewolf as Shawn runs after him. They disappear and reappear now and then. Going too fast for a thorough search of each building, I snide.

We search quickly. Looking through buildings with open doors and broken windows; peering in windows without.

I keep quiet as we search, until Connor tells me, "we'll skip the houses."

"What? Why?"

He shrugs and brushes me off. "They wouldn't be able to fit too many people in a small house. They have to be in bigger buildings; not houses."

"That's stupid. Darius could be keeping her in a house, with just a few people. Maybe they took up a whole compound of houses to fit everyone. Or, maybe it's just him, and a couple others. Is this how you usually search? No wonder you haven't found her yet." I grumble. Tears sting in my eyes.

Connor turns and walks up to me. "We haven't found anything because there isn't anything to find. Darius covered his tracks. He planned to take Rayleen. He could be anywhere. He could have flown her across the entire world by now.

Be glad we haven't stopped the search altogether. We are looking for her, but we also have to be smart about this. If we need to help people out here, or look over somewhere Jaiden's asked us to that could help all of us survive, then we'll do it while keeping an eye out for Rayleen.

Rayleen's dead for all we know. Don't delude yourself into thinking we can search forever when it's very likely that she's already dead."

Darius wouldn't kill Rayleen, would he? Could he be mad enough at me to do that? He's threatened it before.

His words repeat back to me in a menacing taunt.

I gave her to you. I can take her away from you.

Chapter 33

"Dominique!" Jaiden calls over from Sara to get my attention. At least they survived the night. Good to see her alive and well. I stop in my tracks. She must want to talk.

They split off. Sara waves at both of us, before getting to her truck. Jaiden comes over to ours.

I look for any trace of what she went through yesterday. I didn't expect her to be up and about, smiling, acting like nothing happened yesterday. If she wants to pretend like nothing happened, then I will too; for now. We should talk about it.

"Good morning. Where's Alexa?" She asks.

"I don't care. If she's not here, I'm leaving without her." I deadpan; tired of Alexa's attitude.

Jaiden hushes her voice. "You're early and purposely trying to leave without her. I know she's being a pain, but Darius needs to see that she's out there."

"Yeah, yeah." Better for her mental health to get out there rather than stay cooped up in her room. Better if we come across Darius. Better if Darius has spies watching. Cole went over this last night. I assume it's come from Jaiden. She's been talking to him through the day. "I know." I relent. "I'll wait for her; a little longer."

"Thanks. Good luck out there."

"Thanks. You too, and stay safe." I emphasize the last two words.

I decide now is best to give her the little ring; before she runs off. I had saved it to a point. But, now that things are alright with Jaiden again. I think it's time to give her mom's ring. "I have something for you." I dig out mom's opal ring from my pocket. It's cold and almost unwelcoming. "It was mom's; a family heirloom. Only October babies can wear opal; or they'll be cursed with bad luck. She wanted you to have it eventually. So, here."

"Oh." Jaiden pauses deeply while staring at the ring. "Are you sure? She was your mom; your family heirloom."

That stings. "You weren't with us long, but she already thought of you as her daughter. You were family the moment we knew about you. Besides, I'm an April baby. If I wear that ring, I'll be dead with in the year; or wish I were dead from the curse it would bring to me." She out stretches her hand, and picks up the ring.

"Thank you." She tries it on a couple fingers before it fits snuggly on her pinky finger. I guess mom and I have skinny fingers compared to Jaiden. But, I'm glad it fits one of them. I can't imagine trying to find someone who knows how to resize a ring. "It's pretty."

"It's good luck; for you. I think you could use a little extra."

"Thank you, so much." She looks behind me to Alexa. "Alexa's here. Guess you're good to go."

"I guess so. Stay safe." I remind her.

I sigh when I see Alexa climb inside the back of the cab, followed by Miles. I hope she's in a better attitude today. I don't feel like fighting it out with her again.

Our truck is a bit roomier without DeAngelo and Sara, but I'll miss the two extra people searching. Especially, Sara's nose when transformed. That's one less person who can sniff out the area. The more people the better, anyway. Maybe I should ask Jaiden if there is anyone she can spare to replace them.

John drives us up the road, and sticks the truck on the corner of the intersection we would turn to go to the farm. "We're going to go left and right, and search the buildings on either side of this road." Mentally I roll call: Myself, Connor, Shawn, John, Alexa, Miles. "Split in half. Connor, Alexa, and I will take the left. Shawn, John, and Miles take the right."

I leave the truck and look over to the mall. By either some trick of light or actual movement, I think I see a door move.

"Let's go." I walk towards the mall, eager to check it out. Movement usually equals living things. A large mall like this might have people inside. I don't think it would be Darius though. The type of doors Jaiden would have seen wouldn't typically be in the mall; unless there is a back hall system with them there.

"Why here?" Alexa asks.

I warn her mentally not to mess with me today.

Be nice, I remind myself. Alexa is purposely trying to push buttons. She's lashing out because she's in pain. My thought voice turns into Jaiden's as her psychology and reasoning echoes in my head. "Because Darius fled south he could be around here."

"We're just here because of the farm, are we going to check in with them?" I don't appreciate her harsh tone.

"No, Sara reported to Jaiden this morning. They're fine. We don't need to check in on them." I curb irritation; she wouldn't know that.

"So, why here?" Alexa continues.

Nice isn't working. My voice heightens. I turn on my heels to confront her. "Why not here, Alexa? Have you been having secret rendezvous with Darius again? Do you know where he is? Because, that would make this so much easier."

Boldness fades to bashfulness. "No."

"Then, shut up." I tell her.

"Dominique?" John catches my attention in a shout. He's returned from the short distance we've separated.

"What!?" The word comes out snappier than I meant.

"Not to completely derail today, but we're going to take the truck do some shopping at the Canadian Tire." He points his thumb over his shoulder.

I trust his judgment. If he thinks it would be better to shop, than look for Rayleen, then there has to be something good there. "Yeah, fine. Find us when you're done." We'll do the left side up and right side down. I'll try to remember to switch half way.

The guys take the truck, while we walk to the mall. Doors are locked. With their many entrances, we'll need to try them all. One by one, we find each to be locked.

Thud. Thud. Thud. Alexa bangs on the next door. "Open up, we want to talk." She yells loud in hopes of her voice reaching through to the other side.

Out from the darkness a man waves at us through the window to back up. I pull Alexa away. Once we're far enough, he opens the door.

"Weapons stay at the door." He commands. "You'll come inside, unarmed and speak with Bower."

I remove my pocket knife. The man looks amused that such a small thing would be my weapon. Alexa has nothing. Connor pulls a gun out and removes the clip.

"Can we put them inside the door, so they aren't stolen by any passing by?" Connor asks.

"Sure." He answers.

We go inside the doors and put the weapons down on the floor. "You can see Bower now." He beckons us with a pulling motion of his hand.

The man walks ahead of us, while we are joined by others. Armed men and women walk alongside and behind. Our escort is cautious, as they should be. Light dims the further inside we get.

Inside even further, we enter two lines of people. They don't appear to have weapons, but that could mean nothing. Our escort has plenty, but they stop at the beginning of the lineup.

At the end of the line, is a flashlight on the ground, shadowing Bower's face in a menacing horror vibe. "Why are you here?"

"We're looking for my niece." Alexa blurts. "A vampire took her. She's six and a half years old. Long red hair, blue eyes. About this tall. Her name's Rayleen. We've been looking all over for her. Have you seen any sign of her?"

He looks us over before he adjusts the light to a less threatening position to the side. Everyone else lights up their own lights. Bower's position relaxes. Alexa managed to immediately disarm him and earn his trust. "I'm very sorry. It's terrible when the children get involved. We haven't seen her. I'm sorry for your loss." He pauses a moment. "A tissue, please." I look over to Alexa. In the dim light, I can see a shimmer down her cheek. I put my arm over her shoulder to comfort her. "Was that all?"

A woman comes up with a single tissue and hands it to Alexa. She wipes up her tears before clutching the tissue in her hand.

"I mean, since we've found you, we're trying to build a community." I take the chance to make the connection. Since we're here, I should do my part too. "We've met and joined with a few groups already. Trying to help each other out. Trading between each group."

"Where are you located?"

"Hotel up the road." I advise.

"Jerry's people." He announces a scowl.

"No!" I put both hands out like a shield from impending attack. "Across the street. We made a deal with Jerry when we first got to town, then moved the Hell out of there as soon as we could. I never liked him; asshole. He's shady and makes unfair deals." My distaste for Jerry may save us a little. I'm a little surprised from the immediate hostile reaction. I need to know more.

"Alright. At ease." He commands his people. I look behind me to find that everyone has a weapon brandished, and is ready to take us down. "We made deals with him too. Until he wanted what we had, and we wouldn't make a deal with him. He slaughtered everyone at our hotel, and took it from us, then took some of our outposts, and tried to sell our supplies back to us. Jerry is evil and ruthless; watch your back. If I we're you, I'd move your outpost to somewhere he can't find you."

"If he's done so much to you, why haven't you moved further away?" I ask.

"We've fortified. We had guns on you the moment you started walking up." Bower admits. If Jerry came near, he'd be dead.

Connor speaks. "We'd still like it if you'd become allies. Dominique leads us, along with Jaiden. Everyone is welcome, as long as you like inclusivity, and help work towards peace."

"We'll consider it. We'll contact you. Don't come back until we have done so. We might shoot next time." Bower's warning hangs in the air. I'm not sure where that leaves us. He may not believe we're telling the truth. If he hates Jerry so much, he might not want to take the chance with us. I'll have to warn Jaiden.

"Great, well, it was nice to meet you." I offer a pleasantry.

"Likewise. I hope you find Rayleen alive." He looks to Alexa.

"Thank you." Alexa manages a low whisper.

We are escorted out of the building. A large click signals their locking the door behind us. I walk a ways away. If they have guns on us, it's possible they may be able to hear us as well.

Behind the mall, is a large residential area, but a line of commercial buildings go in the right searching direction. We search twelve buildings from the outside; half of them are restaurants. Ending the residential area, I decide to start turning back around. I try to remember 19 St to be able to tell Jaiden later.

It occurs to me, as we search another section, that half the buildings are restaurants. Why did we ever need so many places to go buy prepared food from? How did all these places thrive so close together?

We walk across the street to the giant shopping store. The doors have been left open. Chills go up my spine as I see mounds of bodies where the shopping carts should be just inside. Choking on the smell of decay I turn back around to leave.

"Do you think could be one of the outposts Jerry took from Bower?" Connor asks.

"Maybe. Was he telling the truth about all that?" I break my silence on the Bower mall.

"Yes. He was telling the truth about it all. No sight of Rayleen. Yes, Jerry did that. Yes, they will shoot us if we return unasked." Connor summarizes. "I'll go. Run in quick and take a look." Connor readies his gun and runs inside full tilt. I can't leave him by himself in there, facing whatever might be lurking inside.

I chase after him, but he's topped just inside the inner doors. Far enough that the light still hits us, but not far enough that the smell leaves us.

There is no point to go further, certainly not without flashlights. But, I doubt there would be anything here. The shelves are stripped. Even some of the shelving has been taken. It must've been Jerry. This must have been one of the Bower outposts. Jerry killed his people and took the supplies; it checks out. They location would make sense. The bodies makes sense.

We leave dejected.

Alexa meets us outside. "Anything?"

"Nothing." I tell her.

More bodies at the entrance of the construction store leave us hesitating to go inside, but we have to. Like the other store, there are bodies piled near the door. Unlike the other store, it doesn't look like everything was taken. Food, hygiene, and clothing were more important than taking construction supplies. But in cruelty, they couldn't leave the people alive.

The hours pass as we make our way back to the Canadian Tire. A slew of vehicles and people packing things up in there greet us. A moment passes in worry until I see people I recognize.

We go inside the building, bypassing all sorts of items and people going out the door.

Camping gear, camping stoves, propane bottles, car batteries, and all sorts of fluids, knives, clanking heavy tool bags, solar panels, generators, shovels, candies, and pop. And, more.

At the beginning of the streaming people is where I find Jaiden. She controls the show as she walks through, ordering items to be taken, and which location it's going to.

"Can you check how full the vehicles are getting?" She asks someone in the crowd around her.

"Just came from there. They're getting pretty full." I answer.

Jaiden does a double take. "Hey." She looks surprised.

"Stripping this place?" I ask.

"No." She turns back to the other people. "Okay, then you guys can grab whatever hand tools you can. Try to disperse them evenly between the trucks. Thanks." She lets them go, before paying attention to me. "Just taking what we need immediately. A lot of this stuff is useless now, or it would take us years before we'd need it. No point in taking any of that, yet. But I am taking anything I can think will be of use now, or within the next year. A lot of it we are moving to the market, so we aren't just loading up the hotel. We can sort it more there later."

I nod to let her know I was listening, before I tell her, "We need to talk."

"Sounds serious?" She looks between all three of us for some clue to the news.

"It's about Jerry." I start.

"Then, it should wait until tonight. We can about talk it later." Jaiden moves along; back towards the front. One dark section has no movement in it. Christmas. It doesn't look like she touched the jolly section.

On the aisle end, I spot some globes on sticks. They have solar panels attached to them, and different Christmas characters on top. "We should take these lights for outside; they're solar powered. Who cares if they're Christmassy?"

"Sure." She helps me grab an arm full; Alexa and Connor grab the rest. We venture out to the trucks. "Half in that one, half in this one." We do as she says, while she splits hers between two trucks."

Jaiden counts the people. Then, goes back inside without another word. We'll talk later then.

I look around before I spot someone familiar. I walk over to John. "Hey, you made it." He smiles sweetly.

"Yeah."

"We're packed up, just about to head back, and drop this off; then we were going to find you. But, now you can help us lug all this into the hotel." He cheerfully tries to sell us on the idea.

"Yay." I say sarcastically. He chuckles.

"Jaiden, are we coming back again?" John shouts around me.

"No, no, this is the last round. No one comes back tonight. It'll be too dark by the time we unpack. And, we should get some time to actually organize things tonight." She goes over to a man at the truck beside us. "Henry, I'll come by the market tomorrow morning to help you sort some things out. Nothing's up for grabs yet, but note down if anyone requests any of it, and what they need it for; if it's not obvious."

What market? I ask myself. That's right, she mentioned a market. Did she take over the store already?

Maybe Alexa was right; a little right. If we have a market, as leader, I should have known about it being up and running.

We load up into John's truck. I'll have some questions for Jaiden when we get settled. She goes into another truck after talking with each driver.

All our truck's loot unpacks into a spare room upstairs; one of the dead people rooms no one wanted to sleep in. With six unpacking, it doesn't take long to finish off our truck. Alexa, slipped away unnoticed sometime after the last load up.

There's a buzz of excitement for all the things we found. Gadgets aplenty to make life easier for us. I'm excited about walkie talkies and electricity.

The only things grumbling are our stomachs. We go down to the lobby for supper. I find Jaiden around the wall, tacking notes up to a board.

Community Board with a request box, a map, and sections for jobs and housing. She's already got some job and relocation requests posted.

"That's great." I comment. She jumps from surprise. She must've been concentrating hard not to notice our elephant stampede; lost in her head again.

"Hey. Thanks. I got the idea while I was talking with Sara. A place people can come, get jobs assignments, catch up on news, and territories, where people can request things to get done."

"It's a great idea. Did you eat yet?" I ask. She seems to have been forgetting about that. I know she certainly didn't eat last night.

"No, I was waiting for everyone else."

I'm a bit sad our loot find today wasn't a large amount of food. At least we added to our collection some what. Chips and chocolate were a nice find. It would be nice to have something new meal wise. Can't wait for the farm to give us fresh vegetables. I avoid the mystery meat chunks, and grab from the canned corn, beans, and mushrooms.

We all sit down to our family supper. Some from our building has taken to making family supper a constant. The company is warm even when the food is bland. I wonder about the food at the restaurant, if it'll be any better. But, I'd miss the small comforting feeling of just us.

Besides, I'm afraid Jaiden might get too busy working and answering questions to be able to eat.

Our jovial talking gives way as the people dwindle in numbers. Soon, there aren't many of us left; talking into the late night over beer.

"So, how'd the search go?" John asks.

"No sign of Rayleen. But, we did find a large group at the Bower mall. They're open to being allies, but said not to contact them again until they've contacted us. So, I think that means they plan to visit us whenever they want to make nice."

"How many were there? Did they seem friendly?" Jaiden asks in such seriousness that I can't help but smile. She can let loose and laugh and play, but the moment work is discussed she's all business again.

"At least thirty in the room, but we were barely let in the entrance. There could be more than that. But, they didn't have nice things to say about Jerry." Connor tells her. Cole grabs at Connor, to see his thoughts.

I look around. Cole, Connor, John, Jaiden, and Shawn; the trusted inner circle. It should be fine to talk about now.

"No one ever has nice things to say about Jerry." John adds. "He's an ass."

"He killed their people for the hotel and supplies locations, and then tried to sell the supplies back to them." Connor tells.

"You think the store massacres were Jerry too?" Cole asks me, though it sounds like he knows the answer.

"Yeah." I say.

"What happened there?" Jaiden asks.

"Dead people in piles. Supplies gone; stripped down to the shelves." Connor answers.

"You can't keep going to Jerry's." I tell Jaiden.

"I stop, and he might do the same to us. Just trust me when I say I'm handling things, and leave it at that. So everything was gone?" She switches back topics.

"No, the one store had construction material we could see from the doors." Connor responds.

Jaiden starts talking again before I have a chance to swerve the conversation back. "Good. I'll let the farm know tomorrow. They'll need a bunch of material to fix some things around there. Henry wants a meeting tomorrow evening, to discuss market rules." She looks to me with the last bit.

"What market?" I ask simply.

"Not yet. Henry is setting on up in the windowed building across the street from the restaurant. I told him you should be there to help set rules. Tomorrow evening?"

"Sure." I bring the topic back. She's not getting out of it that easy. "Jerry's dangerous. You need to stop going over there."

Jaiden pauses before she answers. I can feel the eye roll buried inside her. "I bring Cole with me. Besides, what do you think would happen if we stop being useful to Jerry?"

"When." Cole corrects.

"When, exactly, which is why I'm handling it like I am." She insists she's handling it, but it doesn't seem like she's doing much.

"We're- she's working to slowly over throw him. People are going to her rather than him. She's gathering information about the inner workings. Supply warehouses, passwords, and regular customer locations. Debts owed." Cole explains.

I speak directly to Jaiden, but I don't know how much good it will do. I don't know how far she's in with this. I have a feeling I won't be able to stop her, so I think it better to warn her instead. "You need to be careful. If he figures out what you're doing, he'll kill you."

"We'd be dead either way. But, at least like this, there's a chance his lackeys won't listen, and we can turn it around on him. But now, I guess if we take the hotel, we should offer it to the Bower mall people." Jaiden switches conversation topics again. "Moved patient dude to a room here. He's not talking but he stayed so that's at least a sign of intrigue. Maybe he was from another group Jerry's made enemies with. It would be worth a shot to try to talk to him."

"He's awake?" At least that's one piece of good news. "Maybe John or I could try to talk to him. Maybe it would help since we brought him in."

"Maybe, but wasn't he unconscious the whole time? Anyway, he was freaked out by Jerry, so I guess we have that to bring up with him. Now that we know what Jerry's been doing." She says.

"Worth a try." I shrug. "So, Jaiden, what were you doing today?"

"Ran around, took care of problems, and you know the rest."

I expect more, but she doesn't offer anything up. She even takes a few peanuts and munches on them. "That's all you're going to say about today?"

Jaiden shrugs while shaking her head. "Nothing really noteworthy."

I look expectantly to Cole for an answer. He would have been with her the whole day. "We spoke with Marcus about a bunch of plants we found. He's going to split and grow them. He's too sick to move, but Chief says he can handle things from the hospital.

Squashed a little rebellion, who were mad about yesterday. Thinking Jaiden was taking out and killing new people who don't agree with her. But, we explained things and it helped.

Solved some minor issues for us and at Jerry's. And, worked with Jules to figure out food for us. We made a delivery to Chad. And the Canadian Tire stuff."

I look at Jaiden, while pointing at Cole. "See, that's how you recap your day. Don't give me the 'oh, it was fine. Nothing happened.' Details woman. I want details."

But, she isn't giving me much attention. She's looking towards the door with her eyebrows creased.

The door opens. A baby's screaming cries fill the room. Jaiden jumps up from her seat to go to the doors. Entering, is a hospital wheeling cart pushed by a large indigenous man.

"Hey Chief." Jaiden greets. She scoops up the baby, and starts rocking her back and forth, shushing and telling her sweet things to try to sooth her.

"She hasn't stopped crying since she woke up. Do you mind?" Chief tries to speak above the screams.

I watch Jaiden struggle to get the baby to calm down. Her face is red. Snot and tears run down her face.

It's hard to watch her try to calm the baby with no success. I reach out with both hands for a hand off. "Can I try?"

"No!" Jaiden, Cole, and Chief say at once. I step back from the fierce rejection.

"Calli, the succubi baby." Jaiden explains simply.

"Oh right." Soul sucking baby. No skin to skin touching allowed. I stretch out my hand to shake the man's. "Hi, I'm Dominique. Co leader."

He takes my hand in a firm grasp, and shakes it up and down for a moment. "Chief physician, Doctor Johnston."

We watch as Jaiden switches the baby into another position. She cradles the baby's head with her hand, and Calli's body lies along her arm. He legs and feet tuck into Jaiden's chest. Jaiden's other arm helps support the baby, as she starts bouncing her arms up and down.

Like an off button is pushed, the baby stops screaming.

"Where did you learn that?" I ask.

"Something I used to do for my brother when he would cry." I forgot she had a brother. She only mentioned him the once.

"I wish to thank you for what you sent over. They said you didn't want anything in return." The doctor thanks us.

"It really was no problem. We found a Canadian Tire that was practically untouched. We grabbed up the same type of supplies for us, and I thought you might be able to use that stuff. We have walkie talkies now. I don't know what range they have or if they'll work too well, but I gave you a couple, so we can have some communication back and forth without having to walk over." Jaiden brings the baby closer, now resting against her chest. I go to sweep the baby's hair, but pull back when I remember. I pat at her clothed back instead; hoping that's alright.

"That's wonderful. Thank you." He pauses a moment. "Were you able to find any succubi?"

Jaiden shakes her head. "No luck, yet." Jaiden focus on the baby clinging to her chest. Wiping away some of gunk left over. Calli fusses, but nothing comes from it. Her hand grips Jaiden's shirt tightly. Like, she's scared Jaiden will be taken away from her.

My heart clenches for the poor baby. I do my best to stall for whatever time she needs. "Did you want a tour? Something to eat or drink?"

"A tour, please." He smiles.

I look around the room. "Well this is pretty much it; the lobby. Main hang out, meeting room, and some meals. Jaiden just made this great Community Board. I can show you more there."

Chief walks over to our board to look it over. When he gets to the map, he holds his hand up to point at the different locations. "This map. Are these different groups you've found?"

"Yes, oh, we need to add the Bower group. We just found them today." I remind myself.

I do that as Jaiden talks. "There's Chad and his vampire clan, Jerry and his delivery business, us, where the market will be, you, our farm outpost, and now the Bower group."

"So there are others out there." He sounds like he speaks more for himself, than for us.

"There has to be. We can't be the only people who survived." Jaiden says.

"That's true." Chief answers.

I watch as Jaiden rubs Calli's back; rocking back and forth. "Sorry, so really, no one could touch her?"

"Until Jaiden. We weren't taking chances after what happened."

"Poor girl. How can a baby not be held?" I ask without expecting a response. It was good of them not to kill her after she killed the three nurses. But, not holding or touching her was still rough.

"They don't. They need to be held to thrive. There are numerous lifelong benefits to babies being held. Numerous health issues when babies are not held enough." Chief spares us the vast medical knowledge to pare it down to just that; I'm sure. "At least we now know we're safe as long as we don't touch her skin."

"So, I guess you're mom now, until we can find another succubi." A baby could complicate things. Though, if anyone could handle it, it would be Jaiden. I'm out and about looking for Rayleen. Jaiden supervises things here. A baby could tag along with her, and it wouldn't put anyone in danger.

"If, we can find another." She emphasizes the 'if' hard. "If not, we'll have to start playing Russian roulette with how long someone can touch her, to not die, and to only have a little bit of their soul taken."

"How long before you think she can control it?" Chief asks.

"Could be months to years. It's something they learn as they go along, but has varied times depending on the baby. She might do it sooner from necessity, or later because another succubi isn't showing her." Jaiden's answer doesn't hold much for confidence.

"Did Calli, older Calli, you had to make that confusing didn't you? Did Calli ever tell you where her family was?" I ask.

"No. She had no idea. They all wandered about. Never staying in one place too long. Most succubi were like that, so they didn't attract attention. She had lost track when everything happened in November. That's why she stuck with me." Jaiden excuses herself softly. She walks to the cart and grabs a ready-made bottle to feed Calli with. She sits in a chair and gets comfortable while tips the bottle into the baby's mouth.

I start up a conversation with Chief to pass time and learn more. "What about you, Chief? Were you working at the hospital when everything happened?"

"Yes. I was in my office doing paperwork, eating, and watching the news. There were just some weird reports. Then in a steady pace our emergency room quickly filled up with wounds and what appeared to be mass hallucinations. It was quite unusual. Then, some of our nurses and doctors who were off started arriving to help with mass casualties. They were uninjured and reporting the same hallucinations."

"But, they weren't hallucinations." I say.

"No, unfortunately not." He adds.

We all would share the same sentiment in that statement. I wish it were all a case of mass hallucinations. The reality was worse.

I take a page out of Jaiden's book, and change the topic to something more pleasant. "Shall we continue?"

Chapter 34

Strawberry hair whizzes by me. I grab at her with a hushed, "Ray!"

The moment's pause sends Dominique's hands crashing into my back. I brace for a harsher collision that doesn't happen. She looks unsettled when I glace up at her.

I pull Rayleen towards the stairs with us. Up we go, winding up clockwise.

Stairs were purposely built in such a way, so that the right handed swordsman defending the castle will have the advantage over a right handed ascending invader. We, are at the disadvantage should anyone come down; Dominique should have been in the front with her sword.

The stairs open up to a walkway. The crumbing roof inciting fear that each step might send me crashing into the floors below. The railings are gone here and there as they've fallen through the years.

Heat from a fire blast aimed at another dragon and its rider, warms the top of my head. A dozen dragons, or so, tear at each other.

Fighting people crowd the courtyard to the left. The right looms a moat; and whatever creatures hide in the man-made depths.

The dragons are a complication. Hiding in a guard tower will be a death sentence if one of them hits into ours; or breathes fire to it. The walkway is no longer an option for hiding and escaping.

"Jump." Dominique suggests.

"No." Just as quick as I say those two short letters Rayleen jumps

down to the moat, Dominique pushes me towards the edge with enough force I won't be able to stop myself, so I follow through with a jump, and she follows beside me. Stomach up to my heart, I pull a quick breath in to fill my lungs in the small space remaining. Hand over mouth, and pinching my nose, as I plunge inside; eyes closed. My lungs fight to release the air in the cold, but my hand refrains. Swimming up towards the surface, I search for Dominique, and where she should come up, to find her already up. "Seriously!" I vent my frustration.

"You're fine! Swim." She answers back before she starts towards the shore. Her hair has fallen out of its bun from the impact.

Miles is there pulling Ray out of the moat. Dominique lifts her hand up for his help. I grab onto the rocky edge, and pull myself up with my arms until I can get my leg up. As we all stand up, I look all around.

"You jumped?" Miles chides.

"I was pushed." I complain.

"Yeah, and I got as close to a 'fuck you' as Jaiden gets for my efforts." I glare at Dominique; part in jest and part serious. I'm still annoyed she pushed me in.

"And that's her Shut Up glare." Rayleen jabs.

I bite my tongue to keep from smiling or laughing. I think I'm going to chalk that dream up as an unlikely situation; or just a dream.

Well… maybe I should analyze it and remember it; just in case.

Ray, Rayleen, was older and taller. Just about as tall as me; coming up to about my chin height. She had to be about ten years old, give or take a year or two.

Dominique's hair was longer by about six inches; reaching near the bottom of her back.

We were somewhere with castle ruins, Europe likely, which is odd; to say the least. Why would we be in Europe? How would we get to Europe?

Are there any castles like that in North America?

There was chaos. Dragons ruling the sky and people fighting.

We didn't appear to be in any sort of armour; unlike the others fighting each other. Largely ignored, I wonder if we were supposed to be there, or if we were indeed sneaky enough to evade the others.

Which side might we have been on?

Miles was there at the very end. Pulling us up from our frightening leap into the moat. Didn't see anyone else I recognized.

Is this community for naught? Or, could we have been temporarily travelling?

I'd hope the latter. I wouldn't want to do all this work creating a community to have it ripped from us; only four left out of us all.

Whenever this would happen, has to be at least four or five years away. Anything could happen in that amount of time. Like, somehow, we end up in Europe.

Dominique looked great, more grown up and mature. Confident. Still full of joy.

I wonder what I looked like.

Grabbing my phone out from behind the curtain, I turn it on. Going immediately into my SuperData messages, I'm disappointed to find that nothing new is there.

I go over my message and picture sent.

Was asking James to prove he really is himself with a picture, going too far? No, he asked me to prove I am me, so I can ask him the same. You never know who might have hacked his account. It's not like I'm using my own account; I'm still lurking on Sara's.

It's a funny thing; that after everything I've been doing to find James, a long shot message to his SuperData page is what finally might have located him.

It's 5:13. Sun won't be up for another hour and a half or so.

I sit in my chair, curling my legs up for comfort, and catch up on world news.

The Council social page boasts successes on many fronts. More check points are going up everywhere. More people are joining the cause. Slaughter barns are giving human parts to those who eat such things.

The first Utopia is up running and successful. Idealistic pictures depict a full functioning town; electricity, clean water, and gas. The residents boast a lack of humans, except for the butcher shops, and blood banks. Currency has been restored, and thus shopping, and paid work as well.

It looks lovely on the surface; except for the slaughter farms.

Another initiative claims to be reclaiming land. Videos show teams of magic folk burning, tearing down, and burying buildings. The building disappears in a sped up video. A home burning so bright, nothing is left but the basement pit. Dirt moves in to fill the hole. Grass seed thrown up from the bag to cover the space. Water pouring down to drench the seeds. Green grass growing up and taking over the brown. In a matter of two minutes, the space goes from house to lush grass.

Below the video, two pictures claim to be before and after shots. A city, then a field.

They are erasing the excess. I can't exactly argue with that; in basic theory. If half the population is dead, we're going to have too many ghost towns to deal with. Although, I would hope they are pulling out anything that might be considered valuable to future people.

I would also hope that it's not going to screw up the environment. Leaching poison into the soil and ground water.

Once I have enough of the propaganda, I turn off the phone and stick it back behind the curtain.

Time to get up and go downstairs. Busy day ahead. I enthuse.

I pull out an oversized black t-shirt and jean pants. My belt keeps the pants up. A double layer of socks and my winter boots since it's still too cold outside to be out there for a long time without the extra warmth.

A sweater will keep my top half warm. My winter jacket hangs in the closet if it decides to get too cold.

I brush my teeth and comb my hair. Deodorant can try to keep me from smelling, but I soap and wash my pits first to help. The stench of some of the residents has me extra sensitive to my own smell.

In spring and summer, we can have water from the river to help keep our hygiene in check.

When I'm done getting ready, I grab up my papers from my desk and leave.

I listen to what is beyond my manager's door. I can't hear anything so I slip a paper under the door; his instructions for the day. It's too early to be waking anyone up.

Down the stairs and to the lobby. No one else is up yet; I enjoy the peace. Breakfast hasn't been made. I hadn't heard anyone else moving about.

I pin my requests to the board.

Electrician: Hook up generators and inform Jaiden about the generators/power produced expectation. Every location.

Electrician: Solar panels hook up at the farm. Inform DeAngelo and Sara about panel care, and power expectations.

Farmer/Gardener: Relocation to farm outpost area with knowledge, and ability to tend to garden and farm. Report to manager for relocation.

Veterinarian: Care and rehabilitate farm animals. Report to Jaiden.

Labourer: Market place. Report to Henry.

School: Looking for specialized skill sets to be taught on drop in basis. Need skilled people who are interested in teaching to let leaders know. Name, location, and skill(s) on paper put into box attached to board.

I vaguely register that the room's conjoining door opens, and shuts as I work on pinning my papers to the board.

"Morning! Did you eat yet?" Cole chippers away.

"Not yet." I look back to my board, searching for anything else I may have forgotten.

"Eat, then work." He patronizes. "How long have you been up?"

"Not long." Under an hour, I think.

"Long enough." He patronizes. Cole waves a hand to motion at the board.

I relent. He won't stop until I eat. We grab the easiest breakfast, dry cereal, and set down to eat at a table.

"So, market then farm. Do we have anything else on the agenda today?" Cole asks between bites.

"I have to talk to my manager when we get back. I wanted to do that this morning, but I think he's still sleeping."

"So wake him up."

"Mmm, na." I finish swallowing the food in my mouth. "I just want to catch up, and go over some protocols with him. But, I can do that this afternoon or evening. He's already got his list of things to do today. If there was an emergency he would have told me last night, so it can wait."

"We going to Jerry's today?" I catch a hint of distaste in his question. Cole may be understanding to why I'm working on infiltration, rather than a hostile takeover, but it doesn't mean he likes it.

"I don't plan on it; delivery day off." I ease the topic. "Oh, but we should talk to our patient at some point today."

"Yeah, I'll see if I can get close enough to touch him this time."

"No worries if you don't. We can try the 'we hate Jerry thing', and talk about the Bower people, and see where that takes us." Maybe he'll believe us, but I think the damage might already be done with him seeing us together.

Finishing up my cereal, I get up, and wipe out the bowl with a soapy cloth, and put it back on the table. Cole does the same.

A notepad and pencil rest on the counter for my picking. There's going to be too much information today, and I don't want to miss something.

Once Cole's finished, we leave the building. The sun is barely coming up. It's still dark out, but lighter than night. We start walking for our destination.

"How are you in just a sweater? It's cold." I shrug, figuring he doesn't really want an answer. It is a bit chilly, but I expect it'll warm to a more comfortable level soon. "I wish the weather would figure out what it's doing. If we're going to get snow again, then snow. If we're going to have spring, start keeping the temperature above zero."

"We're never safe from snow until after May long weekend." I remind him.

"Why do we live somewhere so cold?" He asks.

"Complacency?" I theorize. I wonder if the weather's the same wherever he lived in the UK before this. "People tend to stick around where they were born and raised. We have to live somewhere; why not somewhere familiar. There's pros and cons everywhere one can live. Yeah, it's cold here, but if we go further south, we'd have to deal with a lot more venomous creatures and disease carriers. Heat stroke might be more of a risk. We seemed to have a bit of a lull for attacks over the winter, could be because of the snow and cold. Spring and summer are coming, with the warm weather, there could be more attacks and movement; more people coming out from hibernation."

"Right. Should we be expecting more attacks? Have you seen things?" He tones *seen* differently than the rest of his sentence. He actually means, have I had any visions?

"No. I don't know. I haven't seen anything for the near future, but that doesn't mean something doesn't happen." I've had some visions, but I don't want to give too much away. What use are my visions, if I tell everyone everything and nothing happens as they do in the visions?

Lights are on in the market place; steady spots of light in the second floor. I can see a couple people walking around in various areas.

We are greeted by two men; I know their faces but not their names.

"Security detail?" Cole asks them.

"Henry thought it best to have security. He wanted you to have this." He gives me a walkie. "It's tuned to channel two. We're using it for the security channel. So that if anything happens, you will know about it immediately and with discretion. Then, if we have any questions about a situation, we can talk to you as it's happening."

I clip it to my pants, opposite of my other walkie talkie. "Great. Thank you. Is he upstairs?"

"Been there all night." He reveals.

"Okay, thanks. Have you been here all night?" I question.

"Yes."

How many hours would that be? "Is there a shift change? Do you have others to relieve you?" I don't want security getting burnt out. Mistakes happen when everyone is burnt out.

"Twelve hour rotations. There's four of us." He explains.

"I suppose you'd still want two people on at a time; at least. I'll put a job posting on the board for security. See if I can get you down to eight hour shifts." I write it down on the paper to do something about it later. Twelve hours seems like too long to work; especially when needing to be sharp for security. Eight was standard before. We should aim for that.

"We don't mind. Gives us something to do." That is one point.

"Yeah, but I don't want you burning out. It might seem fine right now, but once this place picks up you'll need to time to recuperate. Besides, right now, if one of you needs time off the others have to compensate. No one in security should be pulling a double shift." I reason.

"Speaking of compensation, Henry said you would let us know about that." One guard mentions.

"I don't know about compensation yet. We don't have much more than needs right now. Maybe, eventually we can get currency going, or points to spend at the market. But, right now, anything anyone does isn't compensated by more a thank you and a great job." I put my thumb up to reinstate the last bit.

"That's not fair." The one says.

He gets an elbow to the ribs by the other guard. "It's fine; for now. We can't expect special treatment. All the cogs in a clock need to work for the clock to work properly. Security is a need, so we do our part."

"We should get upstairs, and see what Henry's been up to." Cole moves me through an arm at my back. We ascend stairs. "He's fine." He whispers.

"Thanks." I whisper.

"Jaiden!" Henry makes a big show of welcoming me. A large shout of my name and arms thrown in the air. He waves his arms with an open armed point towards everything around him.

"Wow." The cubicles have been rearranged into long aisles with a space in the middle. Each cubicle and section has an order to it. "You've been busy."

"I kind of got it stuck in my head, and I had to work on it. I'm sorry if I overstepped my bounds." Henry apologizes.

I shake my head. I'll take the initiative over raising concerns that he was supposed to wait. "This looks great, so far. Show me what you've done."

Henry gives us a tour as he explains what he's done. "The whole floor is community use. I figured it was important that community items weren't hiding in a corner somewhere. We rearranged all the cubicles to make it easier for flow. Started arranging aisles by like items. We have our perishables here. Not necessarily food, but items people take to own, and that others might not want after someone's done with it. A larger space for building supplies, furniture, other large items. Yard work. Here is for smaller home items that could translate over to community use. Loads of room and sections for whatever we come across. Umm, I thought of a library type system for that section over there. Because there's some things like tools, that you might need for one job, and that's it. So if we did a library system, people could check each item in or out. They take it when they need it, and return it when they're done."

"That sounds perfect. Great idea." I say. That could work.

"Let's go upstairs." Henry instructs.

As we leave to go up the stairs, I think of a question. "So are you going to look after the library check in/out system, or do we need to find someone?"

"Best to find someone, so they can stay and monitor it." Henry says.

I jot a note down to put that job on the board. We'll likely need someone relatively soon.

Upstairs is dimly lit against the windows, but it still leaves most of the room dark. Henry turns on a flashlight and hands it to me. He does the same for Cole and himself.

"Workers must be on break, but it looks like they've gotten a fair ways. We'll start with this for the shops. I've made some cubicles twice their typical size, and some single size. I expect different merchants may require different spaces. I was hoping to get a few more of the generators for the market."

"Not just yet. In the rush of everything yesterday, there wasn't enough of a chance to make sure each place did actually get what they needed. If something more important needs electricity, but doesn't have a generator, I'd rather send one or two over there, before the market gets dibs on it. I didn't get a chance to see how many we got." I explain.

"Sure thing. It was just a thought." I smile and ignore his passive aggressive remark.

"Could you get me another list of people you've grabbed to work for you? It's fine, but I just need to keep track of who's doing what, and where for tracking."

"Yeah. Is that all?" His tone hardens. Henry doesn't seem to enjoy having to answer for accountability.

I take just a moment to think, but nothing comes immediately clear. "I think so."

"Well, then I should get back to work and find my workers. I'll have those lists to you by the end of the day." Henry says.

"Great. If you make it for just after supper, Dominique should be back, and ready to talk. It would be convenient timing for that meeting." I tell him.

"Sure thing, Boss." Cole extends his had to shake Henry's. Henry obliges. I extend my hand to shake as well, hoping not to make Cole's handshake a weird thing, but Henry ignores it. I continue the motion to sweep push my glasses a millimeter into place; don't be awkward.

We bid him and the two guards' farewell. The sun has risen to early morning light.

Cole and I walk half way back before I feel safe to comment. "Is it just me, or was he angry."

"A bit annoyed, yes. He thinks he can get away with things because you're a push over. Little girl, who has no business being in charge. But, it sounded like he would rather you in charge so he can take advantage of you, and get what he wants. He was very smug. Better to ask for forgiveness than to ask for permission type."

"I know the type." I've grown up around that type. It's nothing new. None of that information was anything new. I had already pegged him for it.

"Just keep it under wraps that you're only fifteen. Or, we might have instant mutiny." His warning isn't needed for me; not now. I make a mental note that Dominique needs to stop revealing personal information about me. I should talk to her about it.

"A child has no business being in charge." I half mock. Half of me is serious. Going by age alone, fifteen is a ridiculous age to be in charge. "A little girl." I exaggerate a scoff in displeasure.

"You carry yourself like you're older." He comments.

"I've had plenty of practice." Childish behaviour wasn't tolerated, even when I was a child. Take that away and people automatically assume you're a lot older than you are.

"So, should we go straight to the farm?" Cole asks as we near the hotel.

"I think so. I wasn't expecting to be done at the market so early; wasn't expecting Henry to have done all that work already. But, someone has to be up by now; unless they all decided to work through the night too." I dig the truck keys out of my pocket. I grabbed them up, so that I could reserve a vehicle. There didn't seem to be a need though, because only the previously assigned vehicles seem to be gone.

We get into the truck and Cole blasts on the heat. As we drive, he puts his hands in front of the heaters now and then, then more consistently once the heaters start putting out actual heat.

We get to the far gates and Cole gets out to push the doors open. He closes the gate once I get the truck inside and gets back inside.

"Do we know where they are?" Cole asks.

"Some are living off the farm at the houses; probably those over there. Sara and DeAngelo said they're in the house on the lot. But, I have no idea where that would be."

I drive until I come to, what appears to be, the farmhouse. There are two vehicles around. One parked on either side of the house.

I turn off the ignition and we exit. The air is colder now that we come out of a heated area. It's worse now than the walk this morning.

We walk towards the house.

"Are we sure they're awake?" Cole asks out loud just as I was wondering that myself. There's no sign of wakefulness.

"Jaiden! Cole!" Sara shouts as she runs over from a building nearby. She launches in and hugs me. I barely move my arms to hug her back, before she pulls away. "Good morning! I thought you were coming later."

"That was the plan, but Henry worked through the night and has the market already, basically, set up." I explain.

"And, how do we feel about that?" She looks back and forth from Cole to me.

 Cole answers her. "He seems like someone we might have to keep an eye on. Henry seems to only like Jaiden in charge because he thinks he can control her and get what he wants."

I try to spin some sort of positivity to the deal and his actions. "The market looks fine, and he's doing good things there. But, I'm making him sit down with Dominique and I, and we'll be going over rules. I'll make sure they are distributed and displayed to keep him accountable and honest. I know how to deal with his type." Plenty of practice.

Sara points her finger at me, and turns serious on a dime. "If you need back up, let me know."

"Thanks."

"Cole, DeAngelo's in the house. How about you go find him, and see if he needs a hand with anything?" Sara suggests.

"No, that's alright. I think I'll stick with you girls." He declines.

"If you want to go into the house; that's fine." I let him know.

"I've got it from here, Mr. Bodyguard." Sara rolls her eyes. She puts her hand to his cheek, and leaves it there for a few moments. Forcing a connection, so Cole can read her mind, but I feel left out of the conversation.

Cole finally relents. "Alright, I'll go help DeAngelo."

"So?" Sara loops her arm in mine. Her body uncomfortably close, making it awkward to try to walk. She leads me the way she had come from, but we continue outside; leading more towards the back of the farm. "How's things?"

"Hectic." I summarize. It's been a busy week.

"You look stressed." She observes.

"A bit stressed." I agree.

"Want to talk about it?" I shrug. "Don't give me that nonsense. Talk to me."

"Jusch-ahu-ugh." The gibberish allows for a moment to decide to talk a bit; but it all jumbles out. "I just- I'd prefer to be in the background. Dominique was supposed to be leading. She turned it into co-leading; which ultimately is fine anyway. There's no reason why she has to do it alone either; I suppose.

Logically, we'd work great as co-leaders based on our strengths and weaknesses. She's the people person and I'm not. But, it's- grating. I don't think a lot of the people like me, or respect me. And, she's gone every day. And, we discuss things at the end of the night, but it's not the same as if she were there the whole time. And, I'm just waiting for the time someone decides to mutiny and kill me to assume leadership." Instant regret has me back tracking. "I'm sorry. That's entirely too much information. It's not that bad, really."

"No. Obviously it's been on your mind. You probably don't feel like you have a bunch of people you can really talk to about things. Especially, with all those ears around." We walk in silence for a moment. She's right. Anything too polarizing or controversial needs to be muted. Let alone information I'd rather keep secret within a tiny circle. "Maybe you should ask Dominique to end the search for Rayleen. They're not having any luck finding her. No leads at all. No sign of her."

"I can't do that." It would likely mean we never find Rayleen alive, if they stopped now.

"Or, for her to stick around for a day, so you can show her everything and everyone. It's one thing to tell people that you're co-leading, but if all people ever see is you, then you're It." Sara's solution makes sense. "Most haven't even met her yet."

"Yeah. But, not yet. I have a plan. I hope it'll work." I specifically leave it vague because I don't have a plan, I had a vague vision.

"What is it?" Sara inquires.

"Can't say just yet." I say. Rayleen might die if we stop now.

"Alright. Have your secrets." Sara relents. We walk in silence. Rounding around the back, Sara leads me back towards the front. Showing me what we have in a voiceless tour. Only once we come upon some fenced in animals, does she start talking again. "Have you found a vet yet?"

"No, not yet." We don't even have anything close.

"Then I need John to come out. He knows how to take care of farm animals more than I do." Sara says. "Not much, but a bit more than I do. He might have some ideas."

"Sooner rather than later." I confirm. I see some fur through the holes in boxed homes. A couple chickens are out in the next enclosure over. "I'll talk to him tonight, and see what he says. Try to steal him away from Dominique for tomorrow." Maybe I should ask her to stay in tomorrow too. Get it all done at once that way. Or, I should stagger it, so people can still search.

"Think she'll give him up?" Sara smiles wickedly.

"I'll make a good case for it. She's an animal lover. We want these animals to survive, so that means giving up John for a day. She'll have to deal with it." I don't think I'll have trouble convincing her. If the animals die, that's less long term fresh food.

"Good luck with that."

"What animals are there?" I ask.

"Take your pick. There's a horse, three goats, two pigs, nine chickens, a rooster, a cow, and two sheep." Sara lists off.

"All alive?" I'm surprised there are so many. That's a bit of good luck, at least. A rooster with the chickens is the best part. That means we can have babies; more chickens and roosters eventually. Eventually enough for eating purposes, along with the eggs they'll produce.

"That's what's left. We already dragged off the dead bodies. But, most of the animals are emaciated. Found a woman down on the floor in the office. The door was locked, and it looked like she had collapsed; been that way for a while. But, she's probably why they're still alive. They were left to roam, their enclosures open, rather than trapped in their buildings. They might've run out of feed, so she was letting them out to graze on whatever they could. But, that kept them alive after she died. They all would have died if they had been trapped in their buildings. But, they also definitely had help getting through the coldest parts of winter."

"Good for them and for us. We just need to get those animals healthy again. Have you sexed them yet?" Sara raises an eye brow, stopping to give me a look. "Don't look at me like that. Have you figured out which ones are boys or girls?"

"No."

"We'll need to figure that out. Might put a priority on who gets treated, or who gets whatever animal feed we can find first."

"Vicious." Sara teases in mock horror.

"Survival priority. It would be best if we've got at least a boy and girl of each. We'll need to check for scars; just in case they've been neutered. Priority goes to the animals that can reproduce. The chickens and a rooster are great. That means you got one male. The chickens will lay eggs; some fertilized; some not. Eventually, we'll have enough chickens that we can start eating them too. I'll markdown that we need a strong light to check those eggs." I start marking it down on my list.

Sara asks, "Why?"

"To see which are fertilized or not." Sara still appears confused when I look up. "It was on a documentary I watched once. They look different when held up to a light, so you aren't cracking an egg open, and finding a chick inside."

"Good to know." Sara starts walking away. I look to where we are heading and spot a horse out beside another building. Even with the distance, I can see the outline of ribs.

"What kind of generators did you guys get? And, you got the solar panels right?" I ask.

"I know we got the solar panels. But, all I know is we have four generators. I have no idea about types, or how to hook them up."

"Okay." I make another note on my sheet. "When I find an electrician, I'll send them over here first. Maybe, see if we can find a bit more gas for you too. And, I've got those job posting and relocation requests on the board. Hopefully some people take the bait soon. Is there anything else you can think of that you need?"

"Umm, a lock for the gate; key lock. Door knobs and or dead bolts. Rekeyable ones; if possible. Oh, and there's seed. I don't know if anything will grow from them, but worth a try. Their things like oats, rye, wheat, flax. But it's food crop none the less. We'd have to figure out how to make wheat into flour; unless that's something you've already watched a documentary about."

"No." I answer. I assume there's maybe some drying out and grinding, but I'll have to figure that out later. Another note goes on my sheet. "I can take some to Marcus, and see if he can tell us anything about the viability. Can you get me samples?"

"Maybe?" Sara sounds unsure. "It's in a display case. It's all sealed in. I'm not sure how to get in there yet, especially without making a mess."

"You'll figure it out, I'm sure. Just make sure it doesn't get wet and moldy after it's removed, and before we can plant it."

"Right. Um. We started separating the tools." She starts.

I interrupt. "Yeah, I was thinking about that."

"Jaiden…" She warns against telling her any bad news.

"Well, after finding the stash at Canadian tire I don't think it necessary to move all the tools over from here. Sorry, if you've done a bunch of work on that."

"No, it's fine." She sounds a bit disgruntled. I know she has to be a bit annoyed at work hours lost.

"I was just thinking that a lot of the tools that you have here would be more farm specific. Or, specialized tools for black smithing or whatever. Or that, we would have already grabbed the updated version. If not, and if we can't find it at the Canadian Tire, Dominique said the construction store down the road looked like it was untouched."

"Hmm, so all that wood is just sitting there, and all that building material. We should go tell DeAngelo that." Sara veers off towards the house.

"Don't you want to finish the tour?" I ask.

"Oh, we can do that later." She brushes it off in a wave. "What did you call it? Survival priority."

I catch up to her, wondering if I've said something wrong; if I've made her upset. "Do you already have plans to build things?"

"Of course." She smiles largely.

We walk back to DeAngelo and Cole in a hanging silence. I can't help but to wonder if I've offended her. I think over to what I said. Maybe she's upset at the extra work. There are a few items she might have taken offense to.

"Good morning." I say when I see DeAngelo.

"Morning Jaiden. So, do we get to stay?" He asks.

"That was never up for question. I trusted you when you said we couldn't let this go, but I just wanted to see it for myself." I let him know.

My words lift all tension he has. His shoulders sink while his smile lifts. "It's great, isn't it?"

"Yeah, it's perfect."

"Good enough to make it the new base of operations?" His suggestion weighs on my mind.

"Maybe, eventually. But, not yet. Maybe, once we get to the point where we can connect these two places. Definitely outpost material, at least." I don't know if making this the new main base is the answer, but I can give myself time to think about it.

"Great! Focus everyone on the section in between, and it'll be done over the next week."

"It's not that simple." I admit.

"Jerry?" Cole asks me.

At times, I wonder if he can actually read my mind.

"What about Jerry?" Sara asks.

"We found out he has a history of taking over groups by force. He stole the hotel from another group. He wanted it and their supplies posts and they didn't give it to him, so he killed them and took it. I'm worried that he might try to do the same thing if I was elsewhere. Or, if we get too big. Or, if he finds out about this place before it's defensible." I say.

"So, we kill Jerry." Sara says. The suggestion is offered so much that I'm beginning to wonder if that's what I should do; sooner rather than later.

Cole beats me to an explanation. "No. Jaiden's infiltrating Jerry's company. Turning people's allegiances to her so that when we try to take over they won't retaliate."

"And, we can't just kill him because?" Sara asks.

"He's got people all over. Who knows what we could bring upon ourselves if we did anything rash. Part of what I'm doing is figuring out all of his outposts, protocols, all the people involved, where he gets his supplies, and more. Making it second nature for his employees to come to me. Making it that if anything happens to him, there's no question that they'll come to me to run things and we can absorb them. So that if he orders people to take us over, that they might turn on him instead. Or, at least warn us." I'm getting decent at running through this.

"Could you just stay at the farm to sleep, and go back to the hotel every day?" DeAngelo asks. "It doesn't seem safe for you."

"No. We've already had a few emergencies in the middle of the night. They'd know immediately if I wasn't there. We can make excuses for one time for me not being there, but once it starts being a regular occurrence, they're going to know something is up. And, again, I don't want Jerry to find this farm. It might be too tempting for him."

"We'll keep a bed here for you here. If it gets too dangerous, you'll move here; right?" DeAngelo says.

"Yes." I agree, unsure if I'll be able to keep to it.

"Have you had any visions of Rayleen alive?" DeAngelo asks suddenly.

I hesitate, then decide to tell a half truth. "Yeah, but it was a bit weird. The vision took place about five years into the future."

"You have visions that far into the future?" Cole asks.

"Yeah, but honestly the likelihood of a five year away vision happening, isn't great. Nothing would be allowed to change from what should've happened. Or, it would have to be something, like there was an outside event that caused it to happen. Like I can change anything over the next four, and a half years, as long as I'm at the right place, at the right time, and meet the right person, then the vision could still happen." I shake my head and throw my hands up briefly. "It's complicated."

"So, what are you doing five years from now?" Sara asks.

"I'm in Europe in castle ruins. We were trying to escape two groups fighting each other on dragons. Rayleen jumped into the moat. Dominique pushed me after I said not to jump into the moat, and then jumped in after us. And, Miles helped pull us out. I didn't see anyone else. I have no idea why we were there. But, I figure it'll be in about five years because Rayleen looked about ten or eleven."

"See, she'll be fine." Sara says.

"Well, yeah, maybe, maybe not. But, it requires whatever was supposed to happen at the point I had the vision to still happen. Maybe I let them keep searching, and because of that they find where she is. Or, maybe I told them to stop searching, and Darius comes to find out why, and Alexa leads us to her after Darius let's something slip. Or, maybe the breakfast guys get told Alexa wants Darius back, so they kidnap her, and bring her to Darius and Rayleen; then she kills him and brings Rayleen back.

That's the complication in all of this. I might have visions of the future, but the future can be changed because of my visions. Maybe Rayleen dies because I let them keep searching, when I was really supposed to stop them, and Rayleen dies when they come upon her, and they don't have the numbers to fight back, and they all die too. Or, maybe I stop the search, but wasn't supposed to, and we never see Rayleen again. Or, maybe I have a vision of us rescuing Rayleen, and I figure out where she is, so we go immediately, but she isn't there yet, and Darius finds out we were at that location so he never brings her there, so the search continues, or Darius kills her because of our clear intentions." I stop when I can feel myself rambling.

Everyone is stunned into silence. Unsure, of what to say about my rant. I should have stopped earlier.

Cole breaks the moment of silence with a joke. "Maybe it's a good thing I can't read your mind. I have a feeling it would come with a lot of headaches."

"Tension migraine syndrome. The emergency room doctor said I was the youngest case he'd ever seen." If I've got to be the best at something, it might as well for being the most stressed out person ever.

"Seriously?" Sara says.

"Yup."

"How?" She asks.

I shrug. It's self-explanatory. "When I get super stressed out, I get a migraine."

"I get it now why you'd be so stressed out; people are trying to kill you, and life's hard. But, why were you so stressed out before all this?" Cole pushes for further information.

"Life." I use to stall. "I didn't have a good home life. Comparatively, I actually don't get many migraines now. Life before was super stressful. But, no offense, let's not make this into therapy hour. I'd love to get back to figuring out what we need to get the farm up and running. Dominique found a construction store not far from here that has tools and wood, and stuff. Building materials." I segway into business needing discussing.

By later afternoon, Cole and I step through the door of our hotel. Speaking with my manager spends up time before the search team returns from their day out.

We catch up over supper before my exhaustion catches up with me in a series of yawns. I excuse myself to my room. Checking my phone one last time before bed.

My heart patters when I see a number one displayed next to the messages. Inside, James has responded to my message with a picture of his own.

James, aged with stress, holds a piece of paper he signed, 'Hi Jaiden'.

Now that I have confirmation James is who he claims to be, I paste in my prewritten message to him. Everything that I had figured out I needed to say to him, written, and ready for his appearance.

The letter updates him on our new location, what happened in Banff, and our revolution initiative, and progress thus far. Advising him Darius has, once again, kidnapped Rayleen, and asking him to connect me with his spy. I provide him my phone number, and request he contacts me, and provide his number for future contact.

I close the phone, and shut it down, placing it back in the window.

Dragging myself through changing and into bed. It doesn't take long to fall asleep.

"No." Dominique mouths to me. Tears stream.

Hand over my mouth, arms cage me. The sea of the mob sways me, threatening to surge me forward. Cole stakes me to my spot. Whispering, "They'll hang us too."

A hanging tree. Three bodies hang lifelessly from the limb. Sara. John. Rayleen.

A rope around Dominique's neck tightens, and the men lifting her disperse.

The mob looks on with satisfaction at their handy work.

I pull slightly against my binds; wishing to be able to do something. Knowing that my resistance is with myself, as my logic holds me back. You can't fight the mob.

I do anything, and I'll be next.

Hung for being a witch.

Hung for being werewolves.

Hung for being indigenous.

She kicks, and swings as the rope crushes her air pipe. Losing strength as the oxygen gets used up, and her body starves for air. Body twitching, and convulsing; I know the end is coming.

I should have known he'd be in charge of these types of people.

Chapter 35

"Why am I here?" I finally ask her.

Jaiden looks up from her fruit cocktail bowl. She ordered me here, but she hasn't said one word to me since we sat down. She finishes what's in her mouth, and then speaks. "I wanted to check in with you. See how you were doing? Thought you might've wanted different scenery for breakfast."

So, you brought me to Jerry's lounge; meters away from where Daniel was killed, and Rayleen was kidnapped? To talk about how I'm feeling about that. Fine job, Jaiden. "I'm fine."

Jaiden ignores me to look everywhere else. The lounge is busy. She looks like she's either looking for someone, or trying to ignore me. Why would she ask me here to talk with me, if she's not even going to pay attention to me?

"How's the search for Rayleen going?" She finally asks.

"Why don't you ask Nikki?" I huff. Jaiden finally settles her gaze on me.

"Different perspectives view events differently." She says.

"It's not. We haven't. You can't even call what we've been doing as searching." The fault of which lies with Jaiden. "You keep sending us on stupid errands. We're barely looking around. Look into a building through a window and move on. We barely every go inside. No houses. No real direction."

Jaiden doesn't react to my accusation. "When we were following James, we didn't look in buildings at all. He just took us around from town to town. Eventually we found her.”

“After James ran off, and did God knows what to find her.” I remind her.

“True, but that just got us to the jail. From there, we found out about Banff and found her. It worked out without looking inside every single building. At what were impossible odds. We’ll find her again. It’ll just take time, and a bit of luck.”

“Maybe.” I try to cut off the conversation by agreeing with her. I focus on finishing up my breakfast quickly. That way, I can leave whenever.

Jaiden finishes another spoon full of fruit before talking again. “Dominique says you’ll be going straight north, across the river this time. She said you’d get a big territory checked out. Maybe you’ll find Darius today.”

“Is that all were doing today?” I ask.

“Likely, yes. It’s always possible that you’ll end up running into something else, we haven’t really explored north of the river, but you’re main priority is finding Darius and Rayleen; as usual.”

I still don’t get the point of this. “I’m done.” My food is done with the one final bite. “Can I leave?”

I’m already moving when she responds. “Yes.” Whether she agreed to it or not, I’m leaving. Breakfast, this meeting, was useless. What was the point of all that. I look back at the conversation, and can’t find anything that was worthwhile.

I leave this hotel for the other one.

The truck is already at the front doors, packed up, and ready to go. Nikki opens her door. “Good, you’re back. We can get going.” An edge to her voice hints at her annoyance, but it has nothing on my own annoyance.

I place blame on Jaiden. “If you’re going to get mad, get mad at Jaiden. Whatever that was, breakfast, was absolutely useless.”

I climb into the back seat without another word. They let me sit on the outside this time. We drive a minute or so before we cross the bridge over the river.

There is a mixture of houses and stores in the area. John pulls into a parking lot and stops the truck. We get out.

Nikki instructs us to search. We spend hours making a big circle; stores, campground, store, mall, stores, garden, school, houses, school, houses, stores, apartments, houses, and back to stores.

My stomach growls in anger by the time we get back to familiar territory; around where we left the truck. It must be getting close to supper time. The sun is lowering. Our daylight will be gone sometime soon. The little bit of spring time warmth will disappear with it.

I spot the truck first, and the figure leaning against it. Sprinting to him, as he then does to me. He stops suddenly, so I stop with a lurch. Something is wrong.

Darius is here, but he looks alone. Where is Rayleen? My mind screams, but my mouth refuses to voice with Darius so close; a few feet away. Maybe he's here to take me to her.

"Did you love him?" Darius asks. His voice wavering in caution.

"I don't know." The wrong answer has him clenching his jaw. I should have said no. My heart clenches in fear.

"Do you still love me?" He asks quieter.

"Yes." I blurt. At this point I'm not sure whether I am or not, but I know it's what he wants to hear. It's what will get Rayleen back to me. I have to play him, so I can get her back safely.

Darius' straight lips curve into a smile.

"She misses you." Darius rewards my correct answer. A bit of relief swells inside me. He wouldn't say that if she were dead.

Misses. Present tense. It means she's alive currently.

"Where is she?" I ask softly. I don't want to pressure him or over step. I can't seem to breathe enough air. Small, quick breaths take over.

"Somewhere safe. She's waiting for you to join us." Darius holds his hand out for me to take.

My feet carry me towards him despite everything inside of me screaming to run.

I just want Rayleen back. I know what Jaiden meant. To do what has to be done. I'll go with Darius to get Rayleen; protect her. I'll turn into a vampire, and once I'm strong enough, I'll kill him and take her away.

"How about you bring Rayleen to us? We want to know she's safe." Nikki booms out from behind me. Her voice makes me jump. I stop and turn to look at her.

Stop! My mind screams at her. She's too close. She could ruin everything.

"She's not here." Sandra's voice is too close. When I turn to look, she's a few feet away; right beside Darius.

"Sandra." Darius looks and sounds genuinely surprised. I don't think he knew Sandra would be here. He meant to come alone; to come get me alone.

She's going to ruin everything.

People should just leave us alone. Darius would already be taking me to Rayleen, if it had just been the two of us.

"What? I brought back up. She has her back up, so you need yours." Sandra reasons to Darius.

"Did you kill her? Did you torture her?" Nikki questions behind me. She's getting closer too.

Darius answers the question, but not to Nikki to me; softly like a promise. "I wouldn't kill her or hurt her."

"No, but you wouldn't put an effort into keeping her properly safe around your goons." Nikki retaliates.

"Shale is guarding her." He reassures me.

That's good.

"I want to see Rayleen. Please take me to her." I beg him. Darius nods and smiles wickedly. Will Sandra let him?

"Of course." Darius steps forward.

Sandra's arm wraps around Darius' back. His mouth opens in a voiceless scream, and his face scrunches.

He stiffly turns and reaches towards Sandra, who backs away. A bladeless handle in her hand is pulled up to face level. She pinches the handle between two fingers to taunt Darius.

Her grin turns ecstatic as he drops to his hands and knees, then collapses to the ground. Blood seeps out a wound in his back; soaking his jacket.

Sandra goes to him. Her hand settles on his back. Metal rises up from multiple places throughout his torso and neck. She collects each piece in her hand, then melds them back to the hilt. A dagger reforms itself.

My heart thumps wildly. My stomach rolls with sick realization. She's killed him. "No! Please take me to Rayleen. I need her!" I beg her. Tears fall down just as I fall to my knees.

"She's already dead. I killed her. I'll show you." She cuts her hand with the newly formed blade, and shoves it over my eyes. Blood leeches into my eyes just like last time. Sandra lets me keep my thoughts and mind this time. It's just like watching a movie scene in my head.

It's dark, the kind of darkness eyes have adjusted to in the barest of light leaking from somewhere further away. Just enough to see, but not entirely clearly.

I'd still know the little girl anywhere. Her hair looks brown in the dark. She's dirty. Not in the same clothes she left in. Rayleen wears an oversized t-shirt. It's black with a crest over her heart. An angry bobcat, face and claws, over three letters WMS.

Her hands are tied in front of her. She sits with them between her crossed legs.

A hand pulls out Sandra's blade; my hands from this body I'm in. Drawing down, the blade buries into Rayleen's chest. Her dying scream chills my blood; gurgling sickens my soul.

The silence and still body kills me.

My own wail brings me back; on my knees in front of a grinning Sandra. Her pleasure is in my pain.

Darius, Daniel, and Rayleen are all dead.

Everyone I love is dead.

I might as well be dead. Is life worth living when all the people you love are dead?

Air rushes out of me as I'm knocked to the side. My right hand and knees scream in pain from the jolt with the ground.

Everything around me returns. Grunts from effort. Smacking as fists collide with bodies. Snarling creatures trying to intimidate. The cool bite of the cold air. Nikki's hand grasps at my waist.

I look back to where we just were. Nikki pushed me out of the way of a werewolf. Fear creeps in that I would have truly been dead if she hadn't tackled me.

No, I don't want to die.

She kicks him away from us, and gets herself up from the ground.

Sandra is gone. Her back up is attacking us.

I pull out my knife, and stab at the werewolf as Nikki tries to hold it off from us. The others are attacking each other.

It doesn't take long for the fights to be over. After deaths of two of them, the rest run off; uninterested in dying in confrontations. They run in different directions, so we can't pinpoint a base direction.

"Fuck. Where's Sandra?" Nikki yells to everyone.

"Gone." Connor says.

"Where?" She shouts. "John!"

There's no one left alive. I curse that. We could have gotten information out of them, if we had left them alive.

"She's gone. They're all gone. Sandra has to be covering their scents." John answers once he's transformed back into a person.

"It doesn't matter. Rayleen's dead." I whisper. In the aftermath, the devastation hits again. My chest feels run through.

"No, Darius said she's alive." Nikki argues.

"Sandra showed me her memories. I watched as I-, as Sandra killed her. Stabbed her with the same knife she killed-" I can't finish the sentence. Chocking up and crying out.

"She can't be. Sandra was lying. She has to be lying." Nikki looks behind her for the answer. "Connor?"

"I couldn't tell. Darius felt like he was telling the truth. But, Sandra might've killed Rayleen without his knowledge. He would be telling the truth as far as he knew. Sandra was blocking me. I couldn't read her." Connor looks from Nikki to Darius' body, then to me. "Blood magic visions can be memories or they can be faked."

"No. It was too real to be faked. She's dead." She's dead. Everyone I love is dead. Hot tears cool my cheeks as they fall.

I allow people to guide me back to the truck. Time goes in and out as we make it back to the hotel.

I leave the truck by myself.

"Hey Alexa." Pause. "What happened?" Pause. "Alexa? What happened?" The muted words float into my ears, but the words won't process.

Someone grabs my hand. I rip it away. I don't want to be touched right now.

"Rayleen's dead." I hear behind me. A hushed voice I wasn't supposed to hear. Those words, I hear clearly.

"Alexa?" Footsteps follow.

I want to be alone. Sprinting up to my room, I shut myself inside.

Collapsing at the base of the bed, I bury my face in my hands, and dissolve into timeless tears and pain.

A hand touches my shoulder. Jaiden is in front of me.

"GET OUT!" I screech.

"I need to know what exactly you saw. Sandra could be lying, but she might've shown you something that gives away their location." Jaiden speaks clearly and quickly. I resent that she can't take a moment to soften her voice. That she can't leave me be.

"Rayleen's dead." I choke out.

"If she is, then we can at least get her body back."

I shake my head. I don't want to see it again, but I'm not given a choice at her insistence. The memory stabs its way into my head.

Wanting nothing more than to get the very images she wants out of my brain. I go to tell her no, but something compels me to speak. Maybe she'll understand if I tell her.

"It was too dark. All I saw was her getting stabbed." I sob.

"I know it's hard. To have to remember things we would rather forget. But, there might be something in the details. One little clue about what you saw that could lead us to her. Flooring, doors, people, decorations, Rayleen herself."

Her clothes. They were different than the ones she was wearing when she was taken. "She was wearing a t-shirt with a bobcat. WMS."

"Like a school t-shirt?" Jaiden questions.

"I guess so; maybe."

At the confirmation, Jaiden bolts out of my room.

Left to myself again, intrusive images burn away freely.

Chapter 36

Wet cheeks cool when I step out of the truck. The crisp reminder has me in tears again. Shawn hugs me. I curl into his shoulder, until John trades off with him. I refuse to believe she could be dead. Alexa's certainty casts doubt and part of me knows Rayleen is gone now. I can feel it.

"Let's get inside. Warm up. Get some food. Explain what happened." John guides me inside. I expect to run into Jaiden, but she's gone. Maybe she went after Alexa.

We sit down. No one willing to get up to grab food. Questions come from those who've trickled in for supper early. Condolences start up the tears again and again; every time someone asks again.

Jaiden shouts suddenly when she returns. "Everyone! Grab weapons and flashlights. You need to go now! I think Rayleen might be at the Westpark Middle School."

"What?" I ask. People rush around to grab as she orders. I already have a blade, so I stay in place. "Explain."

"Sandra's blood vision showed Rayleen in a WMS school t-shirt. So I looked at schools in the area. Westpark Middle School fits the initials, and is in the direction that Darius headed off into with Rayleen." She hands John a map, and points to a circle on it.

"But, Sandra killed her." I tell her. Alexa saw it.

"I don't think she is. Not yet. And, blood magic can show things, memories or something made up. But it's easier to show a ninety nine percent truth and one percent lie, than to completely make up a scene;

especially when you want to convince a family member that their loved one is dead. Things would be off, details would be off if you make up too much.

Besides, big long hallways with lots of doors. Rectangular windows that lead to a big room, like a gymnasium." She connects what Alexa saw with what she saw in her vision. It would line up.

Connor adds to it. "Darius wouldn't come to collect Alexa, telling her she's alive, if Rayleen was already dead. He said Shale was watching her. He was telling the truth. Sandra wouldn't have enough time tailing Darius to have killed Rayleen without him knowing. So, she could be alive."

"Or at least she will be until Sandra gets back. With Darius dead, Sandra in charge, she's not going to keep her alive. She's not going to care what happens to her. That's why you need to leave now. Be prepared for guards and other victims. She's likely going to still be in the gym. Move quickly and don't hesitate. Every second counts." Jaiden continues, but with added urgency.

"Let's go!" I call to everyone left. Running to the truck with John and his keys, I yell, "Get in!" People climb inside in all manner of ways; filling the cab and the trunk. Other vehicles follow up behind us with others who left the room initially.

Jaiden comes to the truck door and opens it, but doesn't get inside. "Try to be quick, but stealthy. Don't hesitate or they will kill her before you can get to her."

"Aren't you coming?" I question.

"No. I'll get more heading out."

"Someone else can do that." I argue. She saw this happening, she should be there. She'll know exactly where Rayleen should be. I need her there to do whatever it is she does.

She lowers her voice. "I messed up last time. You have to go without me." What does she mean by that? "Go. I'll get you back up." She closes the door and rushes back inside the lobby.

"Let's go!" I order.

Chapter 37

Should I have gone with them?

The question has run through my mind since they left.

It only took a couple minutes to alert everyone. Security at the market took my message. They were going to gather more people and find Henry, and then go.

DeAngelo and the farm started heading out as soon as I started telling them what is happening.

I let Chief know there might be some injuries headed his way.

"Jaiden?" A voice calls over security's walkie talkie. It sounds like Henry.

"Here." I respond.

"Security told me what was happening. We're heading out now." He informs me. "I guess this means our chat is off today."

"Yeah, rain check for tomorrow evening." I tell him.

He doesn't say anything after that. I guess it's too much to say goodbye. Or acknowledge the new meeting date. If one doesn't happen, I bet his excuse will be that he didn't hear me say anything about tomorrow.

Should I have gone with them?

No. I screwed it up last time. What if I figured it out this way the last time too? Then, them going, the vision would happen, and I lead to Rayleen being killed.

Yes, because I might've been able to help. If the vision was going to happen as is, then I could interfere; somehow.

Yes, because if things weren't happening exactly like the vision then I'd know that too.

Yes, because then I wouldn't have to sit here not knowing if they are finding her or not.

I look through the windows, but I don't see anyone out there. If nothing was happening, they would return quickly.

I await a radio call. Dominique left too quickly without one. But, I managed to ensure a few radios went with the second round, and DeAngelo said they'd take theirs with them.

I tap my foot. My body is strung with anxiety. Maybe I should grab a vehicle and drive out there. But, by the time I manage that, maybe the whole thing would be over and I'd just waste the gas.

I need to make myself busy with something.

Finally, I set about putting out food for supper. People will be hungry when they come back. Nothing fancy. I set out the meat still covered in tinfoil from the earlier delivery. Cans of fruits and vegetables. Granola bars and cereal boxes. Everything is buffet style.

Cold pine needle tea sits. I wonder if people would rather it be warm after this. It might hold some comfort to them if it's warm. But, I don't know when they might be back. I can always warm it us when they return. If I do it now, it might be cold by the time they get back.

Should I talk to Alexa? Tell her what I figured out? Tell her to have hope for Rayleen? That she might return alive?

No. I don't want to get her hopes up. What if we don't find her, or we find her and she's dead, or they kill her then?

I organize papers. Stare at the board, while trying to think of improvements.

Chief knows that we might have people coming in tonight. A fight will be sure to cause some injuries. Maybe I should head over to the hospital.

Footsteps on the stairs peak my interest. There aren't many who stayed. The door opens and Alexa comes out. Her eyes are down and

I don't think she sees me peeking around the corner.

She ducks into the storage room. I hear glass clinking. She emerges with a bottle of rum.

I feel I should talk to her. It would be the right thing to do. And, she's here anyway. "Alexa?"

"What?" She turns around.

"I just—I don't know." I don't know if I should tell her once I see her face. Her eyes are puffy and red. She's been crying, likely, this whole time. If Rayleen is dead, and I tell her to have hope… It might make things worse.

"You done then? I just want to drink this." She holds out the full alcohol bottle, and gives it a little side to side shake.

It wouldn't be right not to tell her anything though. "A bunch of people went out to a school nearby; to look for Rayleen. We think that the shirt might've been a school shirt. And, we think she might be alive."

"That's enough Jaiden! She's dead!" Alexa sobs with confidence and runs off out the door. I hear the stomping on the stairs.

Well, I screwed that up. I shouldn't have said anything.

I throw my head back, then forward. Sighing exasperatedly.

I suck at this personal stuff.

I go back to the board and stare at it. Are there any jobs I could put up here? No. My mind blanks.

Another idea pops up to keep me busy. Rules. Concrete rules for how things are run around here. I can write some down, Dominique can write hers down, and we can get something agreed upon.

"What's with Alexa?" Kelly surprises me. I hadn't realized she was here. Though I guess the others left in a hurry.

"Sandra showed her a blood magic memory of her killing Rayleen." I tell her.

Kelly nods and mutters. "That's why she's bleeding."

"What?" I ask. I didn't notice her bleeding when they came in or when I talked to her; any of the times.

"She cuts herself." Kelly states as though it's nothing. She grabs a granola bar from the table. "She does it every time Rayleen is kidnapped." Kelly's attitude towards it makes sense now. It's become a normal thing at this point for Kelly to know this. She's desensitized to it.

It's Alexa's coping mechanism for her major stressors. Today, for obvious reasons, triggered the response. "Should we be worried?" She knows Alexa better than I do.

Her eyes narrow in offense. "I won't eat her. Miles would hate me."

"Not about that. I meant about the cutting." I quickly correct her assumption. I hadn't meant it that way.

Kelly shrugs. "It's not her first time."

Her cutting herself, then coming out here for alcohol. I would think she's moving on from one vice to another. But, I don't know her well enough to know whether suicide should be a concern. I ask Kelly outright. "Would she kill herself?"

Realization flashes in her eyes. "I don't think so. I don't know."

Cutting doesn't necessarily mean she will kill herself. Many people who cut themselves don't ever attempt suicide. "Okay, but, I guess it doesn't mean that we shouldn't be a little cautious. Like, if you start smelling a lot of blood or more fresh blood, we should go check on her. Today, was particularly rough."

"Yeah, yeah. I'll go back to my room and suicide watch her. Tell Miles to find me when he gets back; we need to talk." She looks beyond me. "Jaiden. There's people here."

We sent everyone after Rayleen. Could Sandra have been waiting for that? We're defenseless if she's come to attack us. I feel like a fool. I should have known it would be a trap.

A crowd files in through the doors. They don't attack on entering, but I am sure to be cautious. Ready to launch myself to the knives beside the meat.

But, they don't attack.

"Who are you?" I ask.

"Bower, we were told we'd be welcome." A deep voice responds from within the crowd.

I immediately relax tense muscles and we put down our makeshift weapons. The crowd parts and a shorter man walks from the center; he not much taller than me.

I walk over for a handshake; the first action in trying to repair the connection and do damage control. "From the Bower mall. Yes, I am so sorry about that. It's been a rough day. We had a run in with people who kidnapped one of us, but we got a clue to where she might be. And, for a moment, we thought you might've been the kidnappers here to attack while everyone else away."

"The little girl." He says.

"Rayleen. Yeah." They told him.

"You figured out where they took her?"

"A clue. The kidnappers showed us an image, and Rayleen was wearing a school t-shirt. There was a wild cat or bob cat in logo of the shirt and WMS letters. We think they might have her in one of the schools nearby." I tell them. Honesty is the best in this case; I believe. Give them a reason to trust us.

"West Park Middle School, just south west from here, mascot is a wildcat. It's not too far away; we could go help out." Bower offers. The extra people would be useful, if Sandra has large numbers.

"How would they know between us, and the kidnappers?" A man to his right asks.

"I could radio, and let them know you're coming." Bower nods. "Anyone listening?" I ask over the walkie talkie. I wait, but no one responds. "They might be in the school already."

"We should go anyway." Bower says.

"We're not getting killed because they don't know who's who." His second says.

"I can go with you, and I'll give you walkie talkies in case we get separated. Just tell them you came with Jaiden, and put me on over the walkie talkie if they need convincing." I turn behind me, and go to grab a couple extra walkie talkies from the counter. "Kelly watch Alexa."

Kelly leaves without any argument. I give the walkie talkies to Bower but he gives them to the other guy.

The Bower group has their own trucks. I'm directed to the passenger seat next to Bower. While most everyone else loads up into the backs of the trucks.

"Why did you stay, if everyone else went?" Bower asks me after we start moving.

"Everyone else didn't go at first. We figured it out, while only some of us were in the lobby. I stayed to tell some of the other allies, and send them along. There wasn't any vehicles left by then.

But also Alexa, the kidnapped girl's aunt, is depressed, and thinks Rayleen is dead because one of the kidnappers showed her a blood magic memory of her killing Rayleen. But we have reason to believe that was a lie, and that Rayleen is actually alive. Because Alexa's ex said she was.

Anyway, after I got others sent off, I was talking to Alexa and she doesn't quite seem right. She has a history of cutting herself. And, now I've got Kelly on suicide watch. So, that's why she had to stay just now."

We drive in all the right directions.

The sense of mistrust fades as we get closer, and I babble through the ride about the events.

Chapter 38

Rayleen is dead.

Just enough light to see, but not clearly. Rayleen's hair looks darker, she's dirtier, and wearing an angry bobcat crested black shirt.

Her hands are tied in front of her. She sits with them between her crossed legs. She looks up to me.

My hand pulls out Sandra's blade. Drawing down, blade buried into Rayleen's chest. Her dying scream chills my blood. The silent and still body kills me.

Darius is dead.

Sandra's arm wraps around Darius' back. His mouth opens, and his face scrunches as the blade is buried inside; as the metal explodes within his chest.

He reaches towards Sandra, who backs away. A bladeless handle in her hand.

Her grin turns wicked as he drops to his hands and knees, then collapses to the ground. Blood comes out the wound in his back.

Sandra puts her hand on his back to pull the metal out from where it's scattered. Metal rises up from multiple places throughout his torso, and neck. She collects each piece in hand, and then melds them back to the hilt.

Daniel is dead.

Darius' mouth snarls, and clamps down on Daniel's neck. A gargled gasp from Daniel is the last sound he'll ever make. My pain filled screech is short lived as his breath dies when a clump of tissue breaks way into Darius' mouth.

Warm blood squirts, and splatters over my front; some runs down my face. I can feel nothing else.

A bloody devilish grin as Darius lets Daniel's body fall to the ground. Darius spits out the chunk of meat.

A whimpered cry escapes me on impact. Jumpstarting a wave of desperate cries of pain. White hot pain encapsulates my chest.

Through the pain and tears I push myself off the door. Walking hands on the walls and door frame to stumble into the bathroom. My hands shake. I desire to let out my pain. I shed my jacket and pants; pulling my blade from it. My shoes come off. I turn on the flashlight on the counter.

Clambering into the tub, I sit on the edge with my feet inside. Goosebumps rise from the cold.

Rayleen is dead

One long slice along my left leg. I bite my hand to keep from crying out.

My hand pulls out Sandra's blade. Drawing down, blade buried into Rayleen's chest. Her dying scream chills my blood. The silence and her still body kills me. I killed her.

Darius is dead.

Another cut, on my right leg, digs deeper than usual. My eyes close as I throw my head back.

Sandra's hand on his back. Metal rises up from multiple places throughout his torso and neck. She collects each piece in hand, and then melds them back to the hilt.

Daniel is dead.

I hesitate for a moment as I cut in right under Rayleen's mark.

The pain isn't enough.

His mouth snarls and clamps down on Daniel's neck. A gargled gasp. Pain filled screech is short lived as his breath dies when a clump of tissue breaks way into Darius' mouth.

Warm blood squirts and splatters over my front; some runs down my face. I can feel nothing else.

A bloody devilish grin as Darius lets Daniel's body fall to the ground.

I can't take this. My hand drops the knife into the tub; I'll clean it up later.

It's not fair. Why would Sandra kill Rayleen? How could she kill a little girl? She's a monster.

I need a drink. Maybe it'll help.

I dab at the cuts with toilet paper. Laying the toilet paper over the cuts, I tape them on. I draw up my pants over the wounds. It stings and burns. I wipe away my tears and blow my nose.

I turn off my flashlight. Leaving my shoes in their place for this quick trip, I know I've seen alcohol in the kitchen storage in the lobby. I hope to go as unnoticed as possible.

Against the door to the lobby, I listen for noise, but it's terribly quiet. I open the door to no one. There is a minor relief that I won't have to deal with anyone.

Inside the room, I grab the first bottle I see. It hits against the others as I pull it out.

Fuck sharing. This one is mine now.

I walk towards the door when I hear Jaiden's small voice. "Alexa?"

"What?" I turn around.

"I just—I don't know."

"You done then?" I ask. I have no patience for her bullshit right now. "I just want to drink this."

"A bunch of people went out to a school nearby; to look for Rayleen. We think that the shirt might've been a school shirt. And, we think she might be alive."

"That's enough Jaiden! She's dead!" I declare. I wish she wouldn't do this. I run back to my room, brushing by Kelly, and close the door.

I saw Rayleen die with my own eyes, through Sandra's body.

Opening the bottle of rum, I gulp down as much as my lungs allow before they force me to breathe. I cough a bit to clear my throat of the drops inside.

More alcohol slides down my throat as soon as I can manage to drink it. Half the bottle is gone; just like that. Feelings whirl, untamed by the alcohol. I forgot about the lag between drink and feeling the buzz. It's not working fast enough.

Maybe I should just go to sleep. Then, I won't be able to feel anymore. Two little pills will let me sink in faster. I wash them down with rum.

I lie down for a while, and wait for the pills to work their magic. My neck gets uncomfortable, so I move it to another angle.

In a drowsy drunk haze, I recognize the feeling rising up from my stomach. The alcohol is hitting with a vengeance.

Oh, I don't feel good. I think I'm going to throw up, but sleep is pulling me in. I roll to my side. Recovery position. Lifesaving position. I can't recall what they call it. But, I know that if I throw up in my sleep, this way I won't choke on it.

If I stay still it'll help. My muscles feel disconnected with my brain. I don't think I could move myself to the bathroom if I tried.

The world turns out of focus, and swirls despite knowing I'm still. I close them, but my eyes keep swimming.

My chest aches as my heart races. My arm refuses to place upon my chest. My breath goes in and out in sync with my heart; never enough air making it through my shrinking throat. Mouth and throat dry out, and I'm sure I'm about to throw up.

But, my muscles loosen. I feel myself sinking in.

I don't feel right.

Chapter 39

We gather in together from a perimeter check. No one's had any issues; no people. Many of our own have joined us. Jaiden's likely sent everyone by now.

I'm starting to have my doubts. Surely, there would be more activity around if they were using this as a base. It's so close; someone should have noticed something by now.

"We go inside. Stealth. If you find Rayleen, don't hesitate to grab her." I order everyone with a hushed order.

The darkness veils all. Some proceed without aid, but I pull out a mini flashlight from my pocket. My human eyes are no help with this sort of darkness.

Spotlighting allows me to absorb things slowly in a dim haze.

Not many have flashlights with them. Most of the group seems to have the same issues with the dark.

We split off at every crossroad.

I creep along a long hall with what remains of the group. The wall dips in where two doors are. Rectangle windows reveal the inner workings of the gymnasium. People are inside.

I have to get inside there. Jaiden said Rayleen was in the gym.

"In here!" I declare as I open the door.

We charge inside, with me in the lead. I punch the closest guard to me, before they get the chance to react to our intrusion.

Their surprise wears off quickly. Miles plunges a knife into the heart of the guard I punched. He moves onto another, but that one fights back.

I scan the room with my flashlight.

People line the walls. They group in some places but not others. Three guards to watch over all these obvious prisoners.

Where are all the guards? There should be more.

"Rayleen?" I call her name a few times; each with more vigor than the last.

"Here." Her little voice twinkles.

I shine my light over in the direction of her voice. She shields her eyes from my light. Red hair gleams before I lower the beam to the floor. Shale kneels protectively beside her. He looks unsure of what to do.

Running to Rayleen, I scoop her up. A rushing wave of relief crashes into me at the same time. Tears boil over as my chest heats up with overwhelming joy.

"I've got you." I tell her. Hushing her tears and cries.

"Dominique." Miles says to get my attention. "Some others found more of Sandra's people; some of ours are dead."

"On our side?" He nods to confirm. I can't help but hope it's no one I know; though the same thought makes me feel awful the moment it's thought. "Are we still fighting?"

"No."

"Get everyone outside. Load up the injured people to go to the hospital." I command. "Take him with the other prisoners. He's one of the guards." I motion to Shale.

"Hey Miles." Shale says.

Miles responds with a quick, "hey." I wonder how they know each other, but not enough to ask in the current moment.

Rayleen has quietened, but I still feel her shaking. Her arms are wrapped tightly around my neck. I need to get her out of here.

I track back the way I came. We meet people along the way. Injured people are instructed to leave, while I get a few healthy runners to pass along a message to leave.

The very little light that had been left outside has faded over the time we've been inside. The moon does well enough to give a hint of things.

A small approaching crowd awaits us. In the middle of them out in front, is Jaiden. We meet somewhere in the middle.

"Jaiden? Bower." I'm just about to ask what's happening, but I recognize the man next to her as Bower from the Bower mall. Why are they there? "Alexa, come with you?"

"No, she stayed behind with Kelly." She looks at Rayleen and smiles sweetly. "But, I know she'll be super excited to know that you're alright. Let's get you back and cleaned up. We'll see if Alexa is awake when we get back."

I pull on her small hand a little to draw her attention up to me. "How about you hop in the truck; I'm going to talk to Jaiden for a moment."

"Hi, nice to see you again." I say to Bower. "So, what's going on?" I ask Jaiden. Are the Bower people here to help?

"Alexa might be super drunk, and not in the best state of mind." She quietens just a smidgen. "Kelly said that Alexa might be cutting again, she smelt blood, to deal with Rayleen's supposed death. Apparently, she does it regularly. And, right before Bower showed up, she came downstairs and grabbed a bottle of rum."

I pause. Her answer wasn't what I expected. It wasn't quite what I asked for. "And, you left her with Kelly, and came with the Bower group to help?"

"Yeah, they showed up. But it looks like we were a bit late."

"Missed the fun. Some of these people are going to need to go to the hospital. There was quite a few captives." I forgot to mention the dead people. But, before I can, someone else takes that chance to talk.

"Hospital?" Bower asks.

"We have some allies at the hospital." Jaiden explains to Bower first. "So how many do you think will need to go?"

"There had to be... fifty people they were keeping in there. Various health. There were a few battles, and some injuries that way. I've heard that a-some of our people might've died, but I have no idea who yet."

"I can't take that many people to the hospital. We need to separate people. Critically injured to the hospital. Those in need of food and rehydration to our hotel. Very minor injuries go with DeAngelo. We need to figure out who might've died."

"What about prisoners?" I ask.

"The market?" She asks, unsure until I agree. "Henry and security can guard them; keep them locked up; keep them safe. Until we can interview them, and figure out if they can be integrated."

"You would have them join you?" Bower asks.

"Contrary to what their movement would want you to believe, a lot of these people joined the attacking supernatural side because they weren't given a choice; or given no good choices. It was, join us or die. We're going to win, so join us or die. You show them that there is another way, and a good chance of survival, they flip." I snap my fingers for effect on the word flip. "I know good people who flipped the moment they were shown the better way could win."

"What's the better way?" Bower asks us.

Jaiden takes rein on this one. "One where we're all equal no matter what we are, and can live in peace; or at least relative peace." A horn honk interrupts her. I resist the urge to shush the truck making the noise. "You should get Rayleen back to Alexa; they've been apart long enough. Also, can you start to get everything set up at the hotel, and gather the medical supplies for minor injuries? I have a list in my room of all the empty rooms within the safety circle. We can start filling up the empty ones. If we need more food or water, contact Jules; they'll help. I'll deal here."

Honk.

"Yeah. Okay." I look between her and Bower. I don't want to just leave her here, but I don't think there's much choice. "You'll be at the hospital after that; I assume."

"Yeah. That would probably make the most sense. Chief will likely want to talk." She adds. "Then, probably the market after that."

"Okay. Stay safe." I hug her quickly.

"You too." Jaiden echoes in sentiment.

"What would you like us to do?" Bower asks as I leave.

Jaiden immediately starts responding. She's good under pressure, and such a control freak. I don't know why she thinks she sucks at this. She could handle it all on her own and be fine.

I get into the truck. Rayleen huddles in close as I take my seat. I wrap my arm around her. Her skin is chilled. I crank the heat on in hopes of thawing her before we get back.

It's a shorter trip back than it was getting to the school; at least in feeling. The truck goes slower over the same distance, but the anticipation made each second feel like a minute. Now, we have her and time has sped up.

I talk to fill the silence. Catching her up on some things while she's been gone. Like switching hotels and where to find Alexa and the farm.

John parks the truck. He moves to get out first. Rayleen launches herself out the moment after; running into John as she goes.

Before I can get myself out, Rayleen is around the corner of the hotel. Her excitement is catchy as a form of relief.

I leave her run. I don't expect she'll get lost.

Drunken Alexa may be a bit more emotional, but I'm sure it'll be fine. She's likely have cleaned up by now. Kelly would stop Rayleen if anything else happened; maybe.

I grab John's hand in mine, and lean against his arm as we walk.

Vehicle's drive by one after the other. I sigh. Out of one big event, and into another.

Reluctantly, leaving John's hand behind as soon as we get into the hotel, I go up the stairs to get the list from Jaiden's room.

She has all her papers still strewn about in a chaotic order. I find the room list after a couple scanning rounds through.

Back out, I pop by Alexa's room. It's quiet. I don't want to mess with their reunion. Alexa can get out of helping out, but I recruit

Kelly.

She answers the door with a hint of annoyance. "Hey. We got Rayleen back. But, there's a bunch of injured people. We'll need your help with them."

"Why not take them to the hospital?" Her annoyance tinges the question.

"We're getting minor injuries, and dehydration, and hunger. Major injuries are going to the hospital. Some are going to the farm. There were more people that we had anticipated." I explain.

She tilts her head in annoyance. "Fine. I'll pass out some food."

"Great." Kelly follows me down to the lobby.

The rush of people come in like waves at a pool. Rounds getting larger and larger as the time goes by, then stopping altogether at some point.

We pass out food and tea. Boiling whatever snow we can find when we run out of stock. Finding blankets to cover people.

I abandon Jaiden's list. Instead, fill up every room with people except for Jaiden's and Alexa's. Even giving up my own room, and moving into Jaiden's room. We can move people another day.

A blood chilling scream makes me drop bandages in shock. I catch eyes with John. He moves first; running down the hall. He enters Alexa's room first.

It's too dark for me to see.

The screaming continues.

Chapter 40

I adjust my position for the twentieth time in half as many minutes.

"What's going with you?" I look down the wall of chairs to Connor watching me fiddle. At his words, he wakes Cole. They wordlessly exchange a conversation, where Cole proceeds to pay me attention.

I still my bouncing foot. Conscious of each movement my body is making. I need to stop fidgeting; I'm making other people nervous. "I'm—just—I don't know; antsy."

"What do you mean? Is something wrong?" Cole sits up straighter with great attention. Cole looks thoughtfully to Connor, then concern creases his eyes when he looks over to me. I know what they're thinking; I've had a vision of something gone wrong. But, I haven't.

Whether it's the evenings events, or waiting in a hospital, or a combination of both; I can't tell. Maybe it's because these waiting room chairs are so uncomfortable. "No. Everything should be fine. Hospitals make me anxious."

"Then, why do you look like you're about ready for someone to pop out and shout boo." Connor asks.

"I don't know." They both look at me expecting more of an answer than that. I don't know exactly what to tell them. I'm not entirely sure of the answer myself. I go for a simple version of that. "Maybe it's just the day getting to me, or the waiting."

"Do you want to lie down?" Cole asks.

Without missing a beat I answer. "No, thanks."

"Go lay down." Connor insists. "Even if you don't sleep, just go lie down, and take a moment to relax. And, if you still want to argue, go grab Calli, and take her with you to cuddle."

As tempting as it sounds, I know the responsible thing to do, is to stay here, and wait for news on all our patients. Chief and that nurse took them all, and asked for us to stay here and out of the way. They would bring news when they got a chance.

No one appeared to have anything immediately life threatening. But, I suppose we might be working on the Wild West rules of injuries; that even a paper cut could become life threatening with the right set of circumstances.

"Jaiden!" Dominique shouts my name as she barges into the waiting room. My body jumpstarts with the sudden exclamation. Electricity zinging through every inch on me; prepared to do something at a moment's notice. What is she doing here?

I look at her for a moment caught in confusion and possibilities; turning sour as I see her solemn expression. Standing up, I greet her a couple steps away from my chair. Wet trails track down her cheeks.

She wraps her arms around me and squeezes tight. "What's wrong?" My mind immediately answers that someone has to be dead. I know it before she says it; Alexa. She killed herself. It's my fault. I shouldn't have left her alone. I shouldn't have pushed.

She pulls away, keeping her hands on my arms. "Alexa's dead. Rayleen won't stop screaming. She sounds like she's in pain."

"What happened!?!" Connor and Cole synchronize as they bound up from their chairs to settle around us.

Cole holds up his hand for Dominique to grab. Showing him what she's about to tell us. "Shit." He says as he takes his hand back.

"I don't know." Dominique takes a big breath and lets it out quickly. "Rayleen ran off to see Alexa. They didn't come back down, we we're so busy with everyone, and I just figured they were keeping to themselves or went to sleep. Then, Rayleen was screaming, and we went to check on her. They were in bed and Alexa wasn't breathing. And, Rayleen was screaming, but not like a mourning cry; like in horrible pain; like her whole body was on fire. And, she won't stop screaming. And, Alexa's dead; she has no pulse."

"You didn't check on Alexa when you got back?" There is as much accusation as there is question. I thought I had pressed that in enough, without needing to tell her specifically that she needed to make sure Alexa was mentally sound enough to receive Rayleen.

"No." She confirms what I had already figured.

She should have escorted Rayleen to Alexa. I told her Alexa was cutting and likely drunk. It would go with the point that someone should have gone with Rayleen. Or, caught up with her and Alexa to make sure it was all good. It may be on me too, for not making certain to actually tell her to do the obvious. "Did Kelly notice anything? Did she bleed out?"

"No. There wasn't any blood anywhere." So it wasn't the cutting or her getting stabbed.

"Do you think she killed herself?" I have to ask. With her cutting herself, and the timing of events, it would make sense.

"I don't know. We didn't really see anything there. We didn't really look. But probably, what else would it be?"

I have to make a lot of assumptions off her little words. Assuming that Alexa wasn't found hanging, or wrist slit in the tub. Assuming there wasn't obvious signs of suicide. That leads to the alcohol. Could she have died from consuming too much alcohol? "Was there vomit? Did she asphyxiate?"

"I don't know. I didn't see any." I need answers. Alexa is dead, and there is no immediate reason why. If she didn't bleed out, maybe she got so drunk she asphyxiated on vomit.

If not, there are any number of things that could have killed her, that could have many potential problems brought with it.

Problems which could also explain Rayleen's pain. Maybe there's poison or gas in the room, and prolonged exposure causes pain and death. It could be something contained to the room or it could threaten the whole hotel.

Maybe Sandra got in while we were gone, and did something. Or, she had someone slip in with the rush of strangers, and that person killed Alexa; somehow undetectable.

I walkie over to the hotel. "Can someone go to Alexa's room? See if you can find anything that might explain how she died. And, why Rayleen would be in pain. Check on Kelly."

I wait a moment for someone to reply. I start mentally counting to ten; enough time for someone to clear their hands, and unclip the walkie talkie from their belt. "Adam here. Give me a minute. I'll do it."

"Be careful. We don't know if it's something environmental or not." Could Rayleen have a toxin on her that could have done this? Was Alexa alive when Rayleen got in there, and touching Rayleen killed her?

Dominique touched her. I scan her over. She doesn't look like she's got anything wrong with her. Her eyes aren't abnormally dilated.

We wait anxiously for Adam's return. I walk to the door, taking a look for a doctor or nurse; for someone to ask questions to. There aren't any around who don't look busy. I don't want to pull away someone rushing from patient to patient.

"So, there's a knife and dried blood in the bath tub; not much though. Maybe a few drops. " Adam's voice cuts the silence.

I pace back into the waiting room. "She's a cutter. She was cutting to deal with things, but is there blood in the bed? Enough to bleed her out? Is the blade rusty?"

"No, not rusty." He pauses while assumedly going to check the bed. "Nothing in the bed."

I pick another theory. "Does it smell weird in her room? Like gas or something?"

"No."

"Maybe the alcohol was bad; poisoned?" I suggest.

"Smells normal."

"There has to be something to explain it." Unless it was natural. But, the timing would be off; more than coincidental. And, extremely unlikely for an assumedly healthy teenager. "Is there a suicide note?"

"No notes. Nothing looks odd. The room is lived in. No blood anywhere. Clothes on the floor. Bottle of rum. Sleeping pills. Garbage is empty." Adam stops listing off things from around the bedroom.

"Alright, thanks for looking." I switch to business. "How are things there?"

"Busy. But, we're running out of water and places to put these people." Adam admits.

"One moment." I switch channels. "DeAngelo? Sara?"

"Yup." DeAngelo answers.

"What do you have for open houses?" I ask.

"Four houses left, but if we bunk people up there's plenty of room for more." He says.

"Great. Mind if I send some your way?" I ask, though we both know he doesn't really get a choice. I'll be sending people there unless he brings up a huge issue.

"Sure thing."

"Thanks." I switch channels back. "Adam? Send one of ours with a truck full of people to DeAngelo. Send people who've already received medical attention and seem in the best health."

"Sounds good." He answers.

Just as I clip on walkie talkie back on, it goes off. "Bower here. Jaiden, some of the prisoners are in need of medical attention."

"Henry should have first aid kits in the community section, or do you need something that isn't in those? Did we run out already?" I stop myself before asking if people need to go to the hospital. I don't want to place the hospital in a position like that.

"Henry won't let us use supplies on the prisoners." Bower admits.

"Go get the first aid kits, and anything else you need to reasonably take care of the prisoners, and yourselves. If Henry has a problem with it, you tell him to call me." My security radio has been silent, but I wonder if I should call Henry on it. No, I'll let Bower deal with it for now, and check in after we have this situation resolved. I've already got a lot to deal with. I'm not going to search out fights on top of all this.

"Got it. Thanks." Bower cuts out.

"You think Alexa killed herself." Dominique asks roughly.

I sigh; back to this. "Maybe, it's possible, I don't know, but the timing would be more than coincidental for anything natural."

Chief enters the room. Dominique jumps up to great him. "I'm sorry. We were not able to resuscitate the woman you brought in. We put the little girl to sleep. We couldn't find anything wrong with her. She was uttering some strange words and screaming. Blood pressure up, heart racing. But, we couldn't find anything wrong with her. Is there perhaps something internal you are aware of? Or something from the environment which made her this way?"

"We don't know. We just rescued her from being kidnapped a couple hours ago. So, it could be anything with her. Did you figure out how Alexa died?" I ask.

"We have some clues, and could guess but we would need to perform a thorough autopsy with lab work drawn up." It goes without saying, that's not going to be possible with the world how it is right now.

"What about sleeping pills mixed with alcohol?" Connor asks. "We found both in her room."

"Yes, it's possible." Chief responds. I didn't know that combination could kill someone. I make note to research it later.

That brings another question. Did Alexa know this?

"What about Rayleen? Do you think that it could just be her reacting from finding Alexa dead?" Dominique asks.

"It's possible." Chief repeats.

"Could it be from her kidnapping? We could ask around, and see if something happened to her." Cole asks.

"Could she have come close to dying?" Chief asks.

I'm about to answer that she might have. My mind goes back to the blood memory. It's possible Sandra made up the whole scene based on a mostly innocent visit to Rayleen. It's also possible that Sandra scared or hurt Rayleen to make her scream; to make the blood memory appear more realistic.

It's also possible that things were overlooked in the rescue operation. Rayleen might've been so relieved to be rescued, that be forgot to mention a wound hidden beneath clothing.

However, Dominique speaks first. "I don't think so. She didn't look injured when we saved her. She didn't say anything. Why?"

"She had repeated the words 'wake up' a few times. Then, she said 'I'm dead'." Chief reveals.

"I'm dead. She said 'I'm dead'?" Dominique questions a bit distraught.

"Do you think Sandra messed with her head? Blood visions of dying?" I ask. It would make sense. Intense visions in your mind about dying could mess up anyone, especially a child. Sandra could have messed with Rayleen's mind to make her scream a scream she could repeat for the blood memory she showed Alexa.

"Anyone know anything about soul transfers?" John asks from the door way. I hadn't noticed him. Neither did Dominique, it seems. As soon as he talks, she rushes to him to grasp him tightly.

"No, that's not possible." Cole responds immediately.

"She said I'm dead. Alexa died next to her. Rayleen is a witch, and in serious pain; with no other explanation. Saying wake up and I'm dead; like the last thoughts on someone dying." John reasons. "Could she have accidentally preformed a soul transfer?"

My mind whirls. A soul transfer. That's something the Magic Council do to transfer knowledge through the ages. I assumed it needed a complicated spell or something. But, maybe not. You might only need a witch and a dying person under specific circumstances.

I'm which case; could Rayleen have done it accidentally and without knowledge of soul transfers?

"Shit, you really think she could have pulled Alexa's soul into her." Connor's face drops with disbelief. "It makes sense."

"No, she's a little girl. She can't do that." Cole argues.

"We don't know that. We don't know the process. Soul transfers are a well-kept open illegal secret. But, we do know cases have happened involving accidental transfers; especially with deaths of loved ones. They were just typically executed immediately afterwards for preforming illegal magic." Connor seems to convince Cole enough to relent.

"Illegal or not; I don't care. How do I fix her?" Chief asks.

"I don't know. Soul transfers are forbidden for everyone except the Magic Council Reps. They don't just let anyone know how to preform soul transfers or what happens. I don't even know if it's supposed to be painful or not." Cole tells him.

We need information and we need it now. It's an easy decision to reveal my two secrets. At least, to those in this room. "John, I need you to go back, fast. In my room, I have my cell phone tucked behind the curtain, on the window ledge. I need it immediately".

"Take mine." He pulls out his phone from his pants pocket.

I shake my head to decline. "I can't; I need mine. I have James' number on it. He'll only answer if it comes from my number."

John opens his mouth to say something, but Chief beats him. "Wait, you have phones that work?"

"Go, I'll explain." John leaves and I address all the waiting ears. Some need more information than others, so I decide to go over it all in a dump. "Yes. I was given a phone. There's a whole supernatural network that never went down. They had access to some better tech than humans, a different system, and have solar powered phones.

Honestly, they kind of suck for battery life, and it takes all day to get a good charge out of it, but it's better than nothing." Cole and Connor chuckle at this. I assume they know this bit, and can relate.

"I've been able to do research on it, find out what's happening in the world. And, more recently, I've been able to use it to get in contact with James; who is the Magic Council Rep for every magical person in the world.

They transfer souls of previous magic folk reps into the current one when they switch over. If anyone's going to have information on soul transfers, and whether or not Rayleen could have done one accidentally; it'll be him."

Chief opens his mouth to say something, but stops and closes it. He puts his hand up in a semi point, and shakes his head in a slight motion. "When you have the information, come find me. I have patients to attend to." Chief leaves so suddenly, I'm afraid of what his full reaction is to the news. If he's processing and fine, or upset; I don't know.

"When did you find James?" Dominique's voice roughens.

"Yesterday."

"You didn't tell me." I can't tell whether she's upset because I didn't tell her, or because I found James.

"I had to make sure it was him. I got confirmation this morning." Which means that we wouldn't't've had the chance to talk about it yet. "I was going to tell you tonight." I tell her, though I know it's not true. But, I hope it'll appease her.

"Who gave you a solar phone? Those things are expensive, and were impossible to find; even before this." Cole asks.

Connor continues. "Scalpers took them all as soon as people figured out this was coming. You basically had to promise a life of luxury in the apocalypse in order to get your hands on one."

"It was a gift, so I could keep in touch with some people." I'm vague on purpose, and they seem to realize it enough not to pry.

After an anxious wait, John returns with my phone. I take it from his out stretched hand, and then turn it on.

Finding James' messages, I press to call him. The phone trills to no response. Neither a disconnect or a message recording. I disconnect the call myself after it's been too long.

Typing up a message, I hope to get him that way. *Emergency! Call me! Alexa is dead. Rayleen might've accidentally preformed a soul transfer.*

I send the same message on SuperData. After, I go to the search. Accidental soul transfer.

Scrolling down the headlines, I search for any article that might help.

There are no official guides or pages shining light on it. The closest piece is the law revolving around soul transfers being illegal.

An article pulls up about a murdered woman whose husband transferred her soul into himself back in the 1950's. He was executed by the Council.

A small notation on a page stating that Magic Council Reps have been using soul transfers to transfer knowledge and longevity to the next in line for ages.

A blog wondering about the ethics behind such a tradition. Whoever becomes the magical peoples' rep ends up sacrificing the remainder of their life after their term. Questioning if this results in only certain types of personalities obtaining the role.

I scroll through more of the blog post, but nothing comes up pertaining to what I need.

My screen blackens in the middle of my scrolling. James' name comes up along with black and white buttons. I answer the call.

"Hello?" I answer.

"What happened?" James' voice sounds exasperated.

"Alexa's dead. Rayleen was with her when it happened, but no one else was. Rayleen started screaming in pain. Then she was saying 'wake up' and 'I'm dead'. The doctors have her knocked out now. But, we think she might've soul transferred Alexa into her." I sum things up slightly different from how I did in the message, but it's all the same point anyway.

Dominique comes up to the phone, and puts her ear close so she can hear. I put it on speaker phone for comfort.

After a long pause, James speaks lowly. "Do either of them have a crystal on them?"

I've seen one on Rayleen. A present from Alexa, from a while back. "Rayleen has a necklace with a crystal on it."

"Treat the pain and symptoms. Alexa's soul is battling with Rayleen's. When it's done, Rayleen will be dead and Alexa's soul will have control of Rayleen's body." James lays out like someone reading out how to treat the common cold; a no nonsense delivery.

"No. How do we stop that?" Dominique interjects.

James pauses deeply. Regret hangs on each second. I should have taken the call more privately. I don't want to make him regret keeping contact with me. "You can't. Children can't handle soul transfers. Just treat the pain and hope the body stays alive. You'll have a very confused Alexa to deal with in the morning."

"Is there a way to reverse it?" I ask, going out on a limb.

"No. I have to go."

"Thanks for the help." He hangs up before I can finish the sentence.

"James!" Dominique grabs the phone out of my hand. "He was useless." I take the phone back.

"Well, now we know it's likely she did a transfer. If all you need is a witch with a crystal, and someone dying." Dominique lurches and sprints out if the room. "Wait!" I shout.

Dominique springs down the hall to a room with purpose. I run after her, but she easily out paces me. John surpasses me in the race.

I can hear her scream from down the way. "Alexa! You fucking better listen to me. You're going to kill Rayleen if your soul takes over, and keeps fighting hers. Stop it. Let go, die, and let Rayleen live."

"Get her out of here!" A woman shouts as soon as John enters the room.

"No, she fucking killed herself! She doesn't get to take Rayleen too." Dominique's commotion brings more nurses and doctors to the room. They get ready to force her to leave.

"Dominique. This isn't helping. And, the doctors are telling us to get out of here, so let's go." John grabs onto her arm and turns her body. He pulls a little, hoping she will come with.

When she doesn't, I scramble for another approach before she's thrown out, but Chief is in the doorway, looking on the scene and looking for answers. "Sorry. My contact said that it is likely she did a soul transfer. He said to treat the pain and symptoms, and hope the body doesn't give out. She's upset because he also told us that children don't tend to survive soul transfers. So, the girl's aunt will likely end up taking over the body or killing it in the process."

Dominique rips her arm from John's grasp, turns abruptly and walks out. John follows after.

"We'll do what we can." Chief assures me.

I follow the pair back to the waiting room and sit across from Dominique and John. I watch for any sign she wants to talk.

After a long period of tense silence, Dominique asks, "What do we do now?"

"Wait and see." I answer when no one else dares.

"So, when Rayleen wakes up-" Dominique starts.

I finish. "She'll be Alexa."

About Jacey K Dew

Jacey is an author and mom who was raised in Leduc, Alberta by her adoptive family.

She took inspiration from familiar locations to set the scenes. Asking the question, what if supernatural beings took over?

Jacey started writing stories when she was sixteen and continues to have a passion for creating tales. Writing across genres in whichever story needs to be told next.

Jacey can be found at a multitude of social sites under the handle @jaceykdew and her website hub jaceykdew.ca

Her link page can quickly sort you to social sites, merchandise and book shop, blog, fan club, and a few retail stores her books are available at.

You can also sign up for her newsletter on the links page to receive the occasional email about on goings, book releases, bookish news, discounts and freebies.

jaceykdew.ca/about/links

Subscribe to SuperData to immerse yourself in the Three Souls Universe. Choose between free and paid levels to customize your reader experience. Free to access forums, emails, customizable profiles, freebies, discounts, behind the scenes information, and Ask the Author discussions. Or, choose a paid subscription to add physical mailed items.

jaceykdew.ca/superdata

Other Books by This Author

Vacation Romance

Skylar Bryson goes on the vacation of her lifetime. Tasting freedom and stepping out of her comfort zone while meeting interesting new people and gaining a different perspective. Will Skylar find more than adventure in Mexico? Once Skylar returns home her world is turned upside down. Will Skylar find her support system in her new companion, or should well enough have been left alone?

Coming of Age, Life Lessons Novella

Anna's parents had strict rules for life. Suddenly, at eighteen, her parent's deadly accident throws her life into turmoil. She has nothing more than her parent's rules to go by, but she soon learns that maybe her parent's beloved rules may be wrong for her.

Small Town Drama Novella

She never thought she'd have to return to the city in the crux of a mountain. When her mother falls ill, Kara is beckoned home and thrust into the world she left behind.